MW01295411

BE MY SAVING GRACE

Be My Saving Grace published by Rachel O'Rourke

Cover design by @WhatsaMattavich on Instagram

First Printing, 2023

Paperback ISBN: 9780975669402
eBook ISBN: 9780975669419

More great titles by Rachel O'Rourke can be found at
www.rachelorourke.com.au

Content Warning

By reading further, you, as the reader, are continuing with the understanding that not all possible triggers may have been mentioned. The author and any who contributed to this work cannot and will not be held accountable for a reader's actions, reactions, or state of mind after reading this book.

For further information, please scan the QR code for a list of possible content triggers.

Be My Saving Grace

Be My Saving Grace

RACHEL O'ROURKE

This book is dedicated to anyone who is struggling with a mental illness and/or past trauma. I wrote this story in the hopes that it could help others see that there is always a light within the darkness, sometimes we just haven't found it yet.

Acknowledgements

A big thank you to my wonderful husband who believed in my writing. Thank you to my small group of trusted friends who gave me honest feedback and support throughout the writing process, and most of all to a dear friend who shared her story about being hospitalised with Bipolar.

1. Tuesday

The screeching of his alarm assaults his eardrums, jolting his body awake and bringing him back to reality. He reaches out for his phone to shut the damn thing off, and fights the urge to throw it against the wall. That's the old him. The adolescent who would use fists and rage to solve problems. These days, his body doesn't have much room for anger. It's filled with this numbness that gets him through his day-to-day routine. He wakes, goes to work, helps those that he can, and then comes home to his one-bedroom apartment, with his frozen meals, his bed that only needs to be made on the right-hand side every morning because the left side is as empty as he is, and of course his cat, Socks.

Nickolas lies on his back, looking at the cracks in his ceiling with the water damage from when the apartment above him flooded. He takes three deep breaths. In. Out. Closing his eyes, he wills – no – begs his body to take him back to his dream, where he was happy, laughing, and feeling like himself again. To take him back to the one person he ever loved, when things were good. The soft jingle of Sock's bell distracts him from his thoughts and the tears lining his eyes. Gracefully, the cat jumps onto the bed, crawls alongside his body up to his neck, and nuzzles against his collarbone, purring good morning into his ear.

'Hey, gorgeous,' Nickolas mumbles. He scratches behind the cat's ear, kissing the orange fur on her head, and smiles softly. 'How'd you know I needed cuddles, hmm?'

Once again, ringing disturbs the silence of his lonely bedroom. Nickolas sits up and retrieves his phone. He rolls his eyes as he sees 'work' calling. He answers, using that polite tone of voice he uses only when he talks to anyone from work.

'Hello?'

'Nickolas, sorry, I know today is your day off, but, well, Jasmine came in this morning and hasn't been able to stop throwing up, so we're down a person. Do you think you can come in?'

Nickolas runs a hand down his face, his thumb and index finger pulling at his eyelids in the hopes that the pressure will wake him up enough to take on the day ahead, which looks nothing like the one he was originally planning. He coughs, clearing his voice, so he sounds sure of himself before he answers.

'Sure, no problem. I'll be there within the hour.'

'You're an angel, Nickolas.'

Nickolas scoffs. He thinks to himself how God must have a twisted sense of humour if angels can be put through hell.

'Now, Dot, no use telling lies when there's no one around to hear them.'

'One day I'll help you see your true value, Nykolai. One day you'll understand that you do good – and that says a lot about the person you are.'

'Yeah, yeah.' He plays off her compliment. 'I'll see you shortly.'

He hangs up. Although he doesn't believe a word Dot said, the tips of his ears feel hot. The red tinge that's taken over his body from hearing words of praise compared to the words of disgust and hate he is so used to hearing is still an adjustment for him. Nickolas clears the three missed calls; he was so deeply lost in the nightmare that it took more than one phone call to wake him. Socks is curled up on his pillow, taking advantage of the warmth it radiates, which has settled the cat back to sleep.

'What a life.' Nickolas shakes his head and gets up.

Luckily, he showered before going to bed last night, saving him time so he can get to work within the hour he promised. He turns the coffee machine on while he makes toast. Since his dream has left him unsettled, Nickolas doesn't want to risk eating a big meal with the queasiness in his stomach. He grabs a few muesli bars from the cupboard and chucks them in his backpack along with a yoghurt from the fridge, a frozen spaghetti and meatball meal, and a bottle of water. He figures if he gets hungry, he's sure Dot will have a plate of homemade cookies sitting in the break room that he can pick from throughout his shift. He fills up his travel mug with fresh coffee and sets it on the island with his keys and backpack. Grabbing a fresh uniform from his wardrobe, thankful that he did the laundry yesterday and didn't leave it for today, he dresses in black, knee-ripped jeans, a blue fitted t-shirt, and his Timberlands. Nickolas throws his uniform in his backpack and makes his way toward the door.

'Shit, almost forgot.'

He rushes back to the kitchen, grabs the cat treats and fills Socks's bowl, knowing that his cat will go to it after she's taken full advantage of the late morning sun.

Nickolas heads out, making sure his door is locked behind him, and takes the two flights of stairs down to the lobby. The building's rickety old elevator has trapped more people in it than it has delivered them to their floors.

He walks around the back of his apartment, where his Buick is parked. It's not much; it's barely worth anything if someone were to steal it to sell or strip it for parts, but it's enough to get him from A to B. In the South Side, that's all he needs. Nickolas jumps in and is surprised that the engine starts on the first try. He navigates his way through traffic as if he owns the road. He's made this journey hundreds, maybe even thousands, of times. He knows every route available that will get him to the psychiatric treatment centre where he works.

The car may run, but the heating shoots out more cold air than warm. The two back windows won't roll down, and the radio hasn't worked in over a year. But he loves it. It's his, bought with his own money that he worked for, that he earned.

The time on the dashboard clock says he's arrived within the hour, as he promised Dot. Nickolas scans his ID at the boom gate, so it lifts, allowing him to park around back. He takes his backpack and coffee, glad to see it's still hot, and walks towards the entrance.

The sun is shining down on Nickolas, trying to warm him from the outside in and fill that cold void that lives inside of him. Squinting, he walks towards the automatic doors that separate him from the world where the wind blows through his hair and onto his face, a world where the sky is blue, the leaves on the trees are green and the sounds of people talking, cars honking and children laughing can fill his ears. He leaves that world and steps into a different one, one designed to be monitored, controlled, and assessed. This world consists of bars on the windows, reducing the sunlight to a mere shadow on the wall. The air smells of disinfectant, and the only breeze is the recycled air coming through the ceiling ducts. In this world, the floors are blue, the walls are a light grey, and the ceiling is white. Nickolas has come to learn that two things can happen in this world: either the sick come to heal or they come to die. The decision is always up to them. It's the only power they are left with when they are admitted, and for most, it's a power their minds are too weak to handle.

Nickolas's eyes adjust from the golden sun to the fluorescent lights. Both are just as bright as each other, but his eyes are more comfortable with the one that's man-made. Nickolas heads to the front desk, ignoring the anxious family members sitting in the dark blue plastic chairs, picking away at their cuticles, or pacing the four-by-four room. He turns to look through the mesh gate that blocks off a corridor that separates the patients from the world. It's currently empty. He casts his eyes away from the hauntingly quiet corridor and looks at the reception desk in front of him. He taps on the glass, grabbing the attention of Darren behind the desk.

'Hey, Nickolas. I thought you had today off?' Darren's chipper voice comes through the glass.

So did I. But I hate letting Dot down, and she knows it. 'Well, since you're sitting at reception, you'd know that Jasmine went home sick.'

'I wonder why they call it morning sickness when it's more like a constant sickness.'

'Wouldn't know, man. Not my level of expertise.'

'Right, of course. Women, gross.'

Nickolas scratches his eyebrow. The brass knuckle tattooed on his left index finger reflects in the glass. He can't blame the guy for trying to strike up a conversation with him, but Nickolas believes there are two types of gays in this world. There are those like Darren, whose voice is a little too high, who acts like he's everybody's best friend, especially if they are women, and who looks as though he'd break if he did anything more than 'make love'. Then there are people like himself, a guy whose voice is rough enough to make everything sound like a threat, who hates socialising and doesn't even want to know the name of the guy whose hard dick is in his ass, fucking him rough without having to check-in mid-fuck to see if it's 'too much'. It's been so long since Nickolas has had a good pounding, or even given one, that he considers taking Darren up on that drink he's always trying to buy him. If he gets drunk enough, he could easily bend Darren over and be done with it. Suddenly the fog clears as he looks down at his colleague, and Nickolas realises he'd rather stick to his hand and anal beads than go down that path.

'Darren.'

'Yes, Nickolas?'

'Open the door.'

'Oh, right, duh.' Darren rolls his eyes and points at his head as he tilts it from side to side. 'Oops. I swear, sometimes I wonder if I should be in here with the patients.' Darren smiles at him.

Nickolas doesn't laugh, he doesn't even smile. This job and their patients aren't a laughing matter.

The buzzer goes off, indicating that the lock is disabled on the door that leads to the employee area. In his peripheral vision, Darren gives him a wave, but Nickolas pretends like he didn't see him. These patients are people. They have lives that need to be lived with family and friends who love them. Instead, they are being locked up, medicated, tested, and assessed like lab rats. Nickolas hates it here, but for some, it helps. For some, they are lucky enough to leave and live out the rest of their lives. Those patients are the success stories that get him through, knowing he has helped make a difference. He walks around the corner and makes his way towards the lockers to drop off his bag and change into his uniform. They used to be able to wear their own clothes from home, but the patients couldn't handle the constant change and had trouble differentiating between those visiting and those working, so in the end, uniforms were put in place. It's not so much the uniform itself that Nickolas hates; it's more the fact that it's purple. He feels like a giant eggplant, and the last thing he wants is to be sending those vibes to people, especially Darren, who isn't getting anywhere near his eggplant. Thankfully, he can still wear his Timberlands. The rules state that as long as there are no open toes or heels, any shoe is permitted.

He pulls his t-shirt off and throws the purple top over his head.

'I didn't know you had more tattoos.'

Nickolas pulls his top down.

'That's because you're not meant to know. In case you haven't noticed, Darren, this is a change room. My tattoos are on a part of my body no one sees unless I want them to.' He replies gruffly, already losing patience with this conversation.

'Alright, calm down. Don't have to bite my head off.' Darren holds his hands up in surrender.

'At least your knuckle ones make you look like a badass. I'm sure it comes in handy with some patients.'

Nickolas slams his locker door shut, hoping the loud bang is enough of a warning for Darren. He has considered getting his knuckle tattoos covered up. They're from his old life, one of hatred and violence. He doesn't want that seeping through while he works towards helping people heal. But they are also a reminder of the world he walked out on. A world that made him feel trapped and lost. He fought to survive. Not just physically, but mentally too. These tattoos are his form of battle scars, and he wears them with pride as he watches those around him fight battles tougher than any he has ever been dealt.

'Did you want something?' Nickolas sighs.

'Oh, right. Dorothy is looking for you. She's in room six.'

Nickolas nods and walks out, making sure to slip past Darren without any form of body contact. He walks down the corridor, stopping in the break room where he takes one last sip of his coffee before he leaves it on the table. He scans his key card at the end of the corridor. A door opens up to the fifteen patient rooms. At the next checkpoint, he scans his key card again and steps into the common room. His eyes roam the room quickly, making sure everything is running smoothly. A few patients are sitting in the room, while others are standing near the door to the dining area, anxiously waiting to be let in. A lot of these patients benefit from routine. For some, that can be as simple as eating, sleeping and socialising at set times during the day. This routine also includes scheduled appointments with their doctors and therapists. For others, it means sitting at the same seat at the same table for every meal. It means watching the same show on TV each day, never once missing an episode. Pleased with what he sees, Nickolas exits and makes his way toward room six, knocking before he lets himself in. It's a courtesy, but not one they always implement. These rooms are nothing but a place for each patient to sleep; Nickolas and all the other staff have the power to enter whenever they like. It keeps the patients on their toes, reminding them that there are always people around watching them, monitoring them.

Dorothy looks up as Nickolas enters the room. The bed has been stripped, and all remnants of the previous patient are now gone.

'Where's Sarah?' He questions.

'Her parents picked her up this morning.' Dorothy explains.

'Early release?'

'They saw the progress she was making and knew being away from family was hard on her, so they signed her out.'

Nickolas liked Sarah. Unfortunately, this patient was in a constant battle between the body and the mind. Sarah had been in and out of hospitals while suffering from an eating disorder, spent two years having her weight monitored, attended group therapy, and, at one stage, needed to be tube fed. It can be sad at times to see a patient he has bonded with leave, but not seeing them every day at work means they survived. They fought their demons and made it out.

'I'm proud of her. Hopefully, we don't see her back here.'

'She left you this.' He takes the cup of pudding from Dot's hand and smiles.

Over time, through the many conversations they shared, Nickolas learned that chocolate pudding was Sarah's favourite food; however, the fear of gaining weight steered her away from it. So, on nights while he was making the rounds, noticing that Sarah couldn't sleep, he'd knock at her door with a pudding cup for them both, not making a fuss when she refused to eat, though happy to have someone to talk to as Nickolas ate his own.

'Her favourite.' Nickolas smiles at the token Sarah left behind.

When patients couldn't sleep, protocol stated that they were to be sedated, a thrill that Brett, one of the other orderlies, enjoyed all too well. Nickolas, however, preferred to offer an ear rather than an injection. Eventually, over time, as Nickolas listened to Sarah's thoughts and fears, she began to push her limits by accepting the second pudding cup he would bring just for her, trying not to draw attention to her progress as she went from only tasting the dipped end of her spoon to eventually eating the entire cup.

'You got through to her like no other doctor or orderly ever could.'

Nickolas throws the pudding cup in the air and catches it. 'Just doing my job, Dot.'

'If I recall, your job doesn't stipulate sharing pudding during lights out.'

Nickolas thumbs his bottom lip, unaware she knew.

'Please. If I thought what you were doing was wrong, I would have put a stop to it long ago. Sure, it's not protocol, but sometimes we need to blur the lines to suit the needs of each individual. We follow a book of rules that don't always get through to some of these patients. You saw that. Not some doctor or a therapist, you.' Dot gives him a warm, motherly smile.

Nickolas coughs, pushing back any memories or emotions threatening to come to the surface.

'You probably saw a family waiting when you arrived – this room will be for their daughter, who they're admitting today.'

Nickolas nods, remembering the anxious parents pacing the waiting room.

'Anyway, as you know, Jasmine won't be in for the rest of the day, and Eric has called in sick, so I'm going to need you to work the night shift tonight also.'

'You're aware I'm scheduled to work the day shift tomorrow, right?'

'If all is quiet, take a nap in the break room. Sam will be working, as always, and Lydia can do most of the work. We just need the extra staff member on hand.'

'You know, if anyone else had asked, I would have told them to fu—' He stops himself from swearing. He can't, not in front of Dot. It just doesn't seem right.

'I know, honey. That's why I made sure to ask you and not have the others do it.'

Nickolas shakes his head as he leaves. In the common room, a couple of patients are painting near the window, some are playing ping pong while a few others are enjoying reruns of the Looney Tunes on the TV. He knows Brett must have chosen the channel since he recalls overhearing his colleague make a comment in the break room about Looney Tunes being a show fit for a bunch of looney patients. As if Nickolas has summoned the devil with his thoughts, Brett walks in from the dining room and makes his way over to the patients painting trees that they can see outside. Brett gives Nickolas a nod of recognition rather than an actual hello.

'Wow.' Brett's tone sounds more shocked than amazed. 'No wonder you're in here. If that's what you think a tree looks like, you must be crazy.'

Nickolas clenches his fists, pushing the anger down. Words are more powerful; that's what *she* had always told him. He walks up to Brett and decides to give this "using your words" thing a go, even if his fists are itching for blood.

'Brett. You think that's appropriate to say to our patients?'

Brett crosses his arms and looks towards Nickolas, standing tall to try and use it to intimidate him.

'You got a problem with how I do things around here, Nickolas?'

'These people, kids, they came here for help.'

'Some of them are long past help. Isn't that right, Hyde, or is it Jekyll?'

Brett uncrosses his arms and gives Ethan a pat on the back while chuckling at his inappropriate joke. The force from the pat pushes Ethan forward in his chair. Ethan is a patient who was diagnosed with DID, otherwise known as dissociative identity disorder or split personality disorder. Ethan is currently medicated to the point where the room would look like a spinning world of butterflies and rainbows. Ethan's head falls, his chin now resting against his chest.

As Brett takes a step towards Nickolas, his cocky smile drops along with his voice. 'You know, Nickolas. If you can't handle the way things are done around here, maybe you aren't cut out for this job. We're not here to be their friends and not everyone can be saved. You'd know that better than anyone.' The taller man pushes past and nudges Nickolas's shoulder as he walks away.

'Okay. Who's ready for lunch?' Brett calls out as he begins to usher people into the dining area. Nickolas pulls himself together and moves to help patients who need assistance to stand and walk towards a table to eat.

*

After lunch, Nickolas takes the patients who aren't involved in the group therapy session back to their rooms, while the others take a seat in the common room. The therapists believe the group sessions work better in an environment where the patients are all comfortable sharing with one another, leaving the offices strictly for one-on-one sessions. Besides its location, that's all Nickolas knows about what goes on in those sessions. His job as an orderly is to assist the patients. That means he delivers the medication that the therapists prescribe and the doctors administer. He watches over them to make sure they are comfortable and not causing harm to themselves or those around them, which also means during their scheduled shower times, and hourly checks during the night. He helps them from one room to another if their medication is making them drowsy or if they are too weak to support themselves, along with chaperoning them to the therapist's office when they have a one-on-one appointment. In no way does his job impact the treatment these patients are receiving, but to these patients, he is a familiar face – a person who can make it seem not so lonely in a world that has them cut off from everything and sometimes everyone. Some of these patients never have family visit them, only coming to collect them when treatment is complete. Others are lucky to have the regular weekly visit that is scheduled every Sunday afternoon between two and four.

He always works on Sunday. He likes to be there for the patients who aren't lucky enough to be graced with a visitor. Someone who checks in and reminds them that people care about their progress and treatment, or who asks them questions about their day-to-day lives to show they're interested. Sundays are when he feels as though he is helping the most. The days he sees some of the patients smile for the first time or talk outside of their therapy sessions. It's the day that Dot doesn't ask Nickolas to help with stripping the beds or handling the intake of a new patient because she knows the two hours of interaction Nickolas can share with the patients is helping him just as much as it's helping them.

The day is easy, calm. But a good day today could mean hell tomorrow. The mind is the most unpredictable part of the human body, and it has control over everything a person does and feels. Nickolas watches *Wheel of Fortune* with Ryder and

Cora, calling out the wrong answers even when he knows the right one. They get more entertainment from his guesses than they do from actually solving the puzzle and for a moment, as he laughs along with them both, he doesn't feel so numb inside.

He goes to everyone's room and strips the beds, replacing them with new sheets, and then returns the bin of dirty linen to the laundry room to be dealt with by the cleaning staff. He wheels out a trolley of books for those who wish to grab one to read or swap over the one they have finished.

After the dinner rush, Nickolas watches over the male patients while they have their allocated time in the communal showers. His eyes never wander. He looks past their naked forms and sees the patients for who they are: human beings. People in this world already prey on those most vulnerable. The stories he has heard from patients who have walked through these doors have made him sick to his stomach. This place is meant to be a safe space for them. A place to heal. When time is up, the patients change into fresh sweatpants, slippers, and a green t-shirt, and he escorts them to their rooms to settle in before lights out.

*

Nickolas is at the front desk when Darren walks through the corridor and stands at the threshold behind him.

'I'm done. I swear the afternoon shift feels like it drags on for-ev-er,' says Darren.

Nickolas rolls his eyes at the way his colleague drags out the word. He turns around and suddenly wishes he hadn't. Darren has changed out of his purple uniform and into white skinny-leg jeans and a floral pink-and-blue t-shirt.

The colour of the shirt hurts Nickolas's eyes, and with jeans that tight, someone needs to tell Darren he doesn't have any assets worth showing off.

Nickolas doesn't respond. He continues to check off the names in the binder against the cups of medication on the cart beside him, making sure each patient is accounted for.

'Jesus, Darren. That a woman's shirt?' Brett walks around the corner, looking relieved to be finished with his shift.

'No, Brett. It's called fashion. You should try it sometime,' Darren says, sing-song.

'No thanks. Don't need no queer sniffing around my ass.'

Nickolas claps the binder shut. 'Hey, fuckface. Even if you were begging for it, no guy would go anywhere near your ass or that pin-dick of yours. So why don't you scurry off home and jerk off while crying because your hand is the only action you'll be seeing anytime soon.'

Brett pushes past Darren toward Nickolas, both their chests out like two alphas ready to fight for their pack. Nickolas ignores the small laugh that escapes Darren's lips, assumedly at the way Brett opens his mouth with a comeback but fails to deliver. The automatic doors slide open, and Sam walks through to start his night shift.

'Everything alright here, boys?' Sam is like the wise old owl. The man's been working at the centre as long as Dot and has enough stories to make someone question the practice of medicine. Although the silver fox doesn't have his youth, he still has enough authority to make Nickolas and Brett step down and slowly walk away.

'Yeah. Brett here was just leaving.' Nickolas presses the button to release the lock on the door, allowing Brett to walk out and Sam to walk in.

Darren takes the door so it doesn't close behind Sam, and turns towards Nickolas. 'The day you two finally fight it out, I'm going to need a cold shower.'

Nickolas quickly scans the room to make sure no one is around and then gives Darren the finger as the smaller man exits.

Darren laughs.

Nickolas doesn't watch him leave, even though he knows Darren wants him to.

He waits for Sam to change and come back to the desk before he sets off with the medication. The patients have an hour left to relax in their rooms. As he's about to leave, the automatic doors open, and he raises his eyebrows as Lydia rushes in, quickly tying her hair up into a bun.

'I know, I know. I was studying, and then I fell asleep and if it wasn't for my mum calling me to remind me about our lunch date tomorrow, I would totally have slept through. But I'm here, and—' The strawberry blonde catches her breath. 'You're not Sam.'

'No shit. Was it the lack of grey hair that set you off, or the knuckle tattoos? I keep telling Sam it's never too late to get some ink.' Nickolas buzzes Lydia in. 'He and Dorothy are out back. If you hurry, I'll just say you were here and, in the bathroom, or some shit.'

'Thank you. I owe you.' Lydia dashes to the bathrooms to change.

'I saw that, Nykolai. Like I said, angel.'

Nickolas groans as Dot uses his birth name.

'Isn't it past your bedtime?' Nickolas teases.

'That it is. But I just wanted to make sure you were sorted for the night before I left.'

'Dot, this isn't my first night shift or my first triple.'

'I know. But today was meant to be your day off so—'

'JESSICA, NO! PLEASE! DON'T MAKE ME STAY HERE, PLEASE!'

Dot and Nickolas turn towards the automatic doors as a woman pushes through. She's a little older than him, and he can see that she's holding on tightly to the wrist of a kid who has seen better days. Nickolas takes in the way the kid's clothes are hanging off his body, which to anyone else may be mistaken for the wrong size, but Nickolas can spot the signs of a malnourished body the way a trained dog can sniff out drugs. The kid's eyes are dark around the outside, his cheekbones are slightly hollow, his waist narrow, and his pants are barely holding up.

'Finn. I promise everything will be okay.' Jessica tries to speak calmly.

'No. I'll go back on my meds. I'll, I'll— just please don't leave me here.'

Another guy comes running in with a bag, looking the same age as Nickolas, with slightly wavy brown hair; neither of them matches the deep, fiery red hair Finn has. If it wasn't for the heated commotion, Nickolas would have smiled at the way this guy's hair reminded him of Socks' ginger fur.

'JAKE! JAKE! You tell her. Tell her I'll get better. I'll be better,' Finn begs the guy standing beside him.

'Finn. It's okay. This is for your own good,' Jake reassures him.

Finn curls into himself. Nickolas can only assume he's trying to turn his body into dead weight, a tactic he is all too familiar with. Nickolas and Dorothy wait, without judgement, watching as Jake tries to bring Finn closer towards the front desk, while Jessica steps forward, moving away from the two men.

'Hi. Jessica Cunningham. I called earlier.'

Nickolas has no idea what she is talking about. To his right, Jake is whispering into Finn's ear. Finn's body relaxes, nodding along to what is being said to him as tears stream down his face.

'Jessica, yes. Sorry, we expected you earlier.' Dot takes some paperwork out and puts it on a clipboard before passing it through the gap at the bottom of the glass divider.

'I know, sorry. We had some...delays.'

'I understand. Is this your brother?'

'Yes.' Jessica looks over her shoulder. The woman is holding back tears, trying to stay strong while her brother breaks down in the middle of the room. The question is, are those tears for Finn or herself? It's never easy admitting a loved one, even if it's for their own safety. He would know.

Finn willingly walks towards the desk, his steps slow and calculated. Nickolas watches as Finn clasps his shaking hands together, and places them in front of him on the desk. Finn stands beside his sister, while Jake puts an arm around Finn's shoulder, giving it a gentle squeeze. Dot takes the paperwork back from Jessica and glances at it before passing it over to Nickolas.

'Do you know what medication he was prescribed?' Dot politely asks.

'Yes. But he hasn't been on them for the last six months.' Jessica retrieves a piece of paper from her handbag and slips it through the gap. Nickolas waits as Dot reads over the list, then passes it to him to attach to Finn's paperwork.

'It may all change. Tomorrow during his evaluation, the therapist and doctor will decide how they'd like to proceed.'

Nickolas assesses Finn's paperwork and reads over the diagnoses. Bipolar disorder. Checking Finn's date of birth, he confirms the kid is barely eighteen years old. Nickolas's heart drops at the thought of this poor kid, diagnosed with a mental disorder at seventeen. One that can make a person feel like everything they once knew about themselves is a lie.

'Finn Cunningham,' Dot addresses Finn directly.

Nickolas raises his head as Finn lifts his. Although Finn is looking toward Dot, his eyes still don't meet hers.

'As you are eighteen years of age, your family cannot admit you against your will.'

Finn's eyes connect with Dot's, hope flashing across his face until he sees that Jessica and Jake are still looking at him with sadness in their eyes.

'However, your sister here has acquired a certificate for an emergency admission, signed by the doctor who diagnosed you with bipolar disorder. This means that you'll—'

'Wait! Is that why you took me to the clinic today? Not to get my meds, but to get me analysed so you can lock me up?! Hand me over to someone else so I'm no longer your problem?!' Finn's sadness slips away as anger rapidly takes its place. Mood swings: a common trait with BP and one that is more prominent when unmedicated.

'Finn, listen to me—' Jessica tries to reason with her brother.

'All I've ever done is listen to you. But when have you ever listened to me? Listened to *my* needs.'

Nickolas presses the buzzer to open the door, preparing to step in if Finn's anger turns aggressive. He walks around the front desk as Finn makes a lunge at his sister and pushes Jessica up against the wall. The woman doesn't look scared, just shocked. Jake tries to talk Finn down, talk some reason into the fiery redhead, but it's useless. Nickolas gets behind Finn and grabs his arms. The sudden contact has Finn resisting, not wanting to be touched or pulled away from the threat he sees in Jessica. Locking Finn's arms behind his back,

Nickolas slowly walks Finn away, putting space between the brother and sister.

'Hey, calm down,' Nickolas warns him.

'Get off me. Don't touch me.'

'I don't want to hurt you. It's okay. I'm here to help.'

Nickolas keeps his voice calm, soft.

'Fuck off! You're lying. No one ever wants to help. You just want to get rid of me.' Finn's eyes meet Jessica's with his last statement.

'Nickolas, take him to room thirteen – it's ready,' Dorothy instructs.

'Wait, but that's—'

'I know. It's all we have available.'

The buzzer goes off, opening the door within the mesh fence. Nickolas takes a deep breath and begins to walk backwards. Nickolas tightens his grip as Finn drags his feet, desperate cries of protest escaping his mouth. It's a last-ditch effort to prevent the inevitable. As difficult as it is, Nickolas uses his strength to overpower Finn, continuing their path down the corridor towards the patient rooms. He thinks of other patients, having to overhear the struggle outside their doors. Generally, when a patient is this fired up and is resisting, an orderly would inject them with a sedative. Personally, Nickolas likes to keep that option as a last resort. Unfortunately, it doesn't always work that way.

'Get your fucking hands off me. That's all you assholes want to do, touch me. Let me go!'

Nickolas reaches the room and is thankful that the door is already open. He takes another deep breath in and presses his chest to Finn's back, using the grip on Finn's arms to lift him slightly off the floor and over the threshold. Nickolas makes a note of how easy Finn is to lift and, considering Finn is at least half a foot taller than him, it should not be that simple. The bed is in the middle of the room and Nickolas can see the restraints attached to the small metal frame. Dorothy must have set them up after Jessica had called through, not sure what state Finn would be arriving in.

'Finn. You need to calm down. I'd rather do this the easy way than the hard way and the only person that decides which way this goes is you.' Nickolas stays calm. Although the fight in Finn is frustrating, he knows tone is important, and getting himself worked up just as much as Finn will benefit no one.

'You're just like the rest of them. You don't want to help me.'

Finn throws his head back and knocks Nickolas in the nose. The force throws Nickolas off balance, but thankfully he doesn't feel any blood dripping down his mouth. All hope of calming Finn down with words is lost; force is now Nickolas's only option. He pushes forward, connecting Finn's legs to the side of the bed. With his right leg, he presses against the back of Finn's knees, causing them to naturally buckle forward. Finn's chest falls onto the mattress.

He pulls Finn's left arm above his head and straps his wrist into the leather restraint. Nickolas hates how quickly he can buckle the strap, a sign of how frequently he has had to use them in his time working here. Finn kicks out as Nickolas spins his body around, so he is lying on his back, no doubt hoping that those kicks will make contact. Nickolas quickly makes it around to the other side of the bed and grabs Finn's right wrist before he can try to unbuckle himself. Finn's body starts to convulse in the hope that the constant struggle and jolts will loosen his arm from Nickolas's grip. Nickolas pulls at Finn's right arm, grabs the restraint, and connects it within ten seconds of getting it around Finn's wrist.

Nickolas stands back to catch his breath, watching as Finn kicks around on the bed, pulling at the restraints. Nickolas closes his eyes for a moment, the sight of Finn lying on this bed, the same bed that—

No, he can't go there. Nickolas opens his eyes. He looks down at Finn, the fight slowly fading, tears once again appearing in the redhead's piercing forest green eyes.

'Please. Please don't leave me like this. I promise, I'll do anything you ask.'

'Finn, I'm sorry. They're for your own safety. Just rest and in the morning, things will be better.'

'Please—'

Nickolas can see Finn's eyes searching his body for some form of identification.

'Nickolas. M' name's Nickolas.'

'Nickolas.' Finn swallows. 'Please, just, loosen them a little. They're really tight.'

He has heard it all before. Promising to behave, to not do anything stupid or harmful. Requests to make the straps looser.

'Finn, it's only temporary. I'd rather not have to sedate you so please, try and rest.'

'Fuck you!'

Finn once again begins to pull and thrash around. Nickolas slowly slips out of the room, closing the door behind him, the automatic lock setting in place. He runs his hand down his face and covers his mouth, trying not to let what happened affect him. No matter how hard he tries, Nickolas somehow ends up leaving a small piece of himself with every patient he deals with. He knows he shouldn't, that connecting with them in any way can be dangerous, but mostly it's because he knows one day he'll end up with nothing left of himself to give. That thought scares Nickolas more than anything else. He walks away from the room, blocking out the cries of Finn's demands and protests, and makes his way back towards Dot.

His boss is still talking with Finn's family. Jake's arm is around his sister's shoulder and Jessica is leaning into the brotherly touch. She turns towards Nickolas as Dot buzzes the door open for him to walk back through. All eyes are on him as he makes his way towards the desk.

'Is he okay?' asks Jessica.

He can tell the sister's concern is sincere. This is a family that genuinely cares about the safety and wellbeing of their loved one.

'He seemed scared. For his own safety, I had to restrain him to the bed but that will only be for the night.'

Jessica covers her eyes with her trembling hands and tilts her head up to the ceiling.

'Hey. He'll understand. Once he is back on his meds, he'll understand why we had to do this,' Jake explains as he rubs his hand up and down Jessica's shoulder.

Jessica wipes her eyes and runs her fingers through her hair. 'I know.' She sniffs and wipes at her nose. 'When can we visit him?' she asks as she turns back towards Dorothy.

'Visiting hours are Sunday afternoon between two and four.'

'That's five days from now. No. No, he'll think we've abandoned him.'

'I'm sorry. Those are the rules.'

'Can we at least call? Find out how he's going?'

'Yes. You can speak to myself or Nickolas here. If we're available, we can give you a brief update, but anything Finn discusses with the doctor or therapist will of course be confidential, and up to him to discuss further with you.'

Nickolas doesn't miss the way Jake's eyes scan over his body, stopping at his knuckle tattoos and tough-guy exterior. He gets it. With the way he presents himself, he'd be wary of leaving someone he loves in the care of someone who looks like him too. This version of himself, who he is now, lets it slide. He reminds himself that whatever Jake does or says is a coping mechanism for the frustration he is feeling for his brother.

'Come on, Jess. Kate, Luke, and Liam are waiting,' Jake says, coaxing her to leave.

Jessica nods and allows herself to be pulled towards the automatic doors. The brunette stops in the middle of the entry and stares down the corridor that Nickolas took Finn through. Nickolas has seen the same look that's currently on Jessica's face many times before—the one that says they'd do anything for one last goodbye. Eventually, the siblings walk out, and suddenly Nickolas feels like the room is too quiet.

'Poor boy.' Dot sighs.

Nickolas draws his attention back towards Dot, noticing the sadness in her eyes.

'Doesn't matter how many times you see them like that, it never gets easier.' Nickolas says. He hopes it never does get easier. He never wants to become desensitised to this world.

'Hmm, I know. From what his sister explained, I fear he'll be here a little longer than the standard seventy-two hours.'

'Why d'you think that?'

Dot fidgets with some papers before picking her handbag back up and looking Nickolas in the eye. 'He ran away from home shortly after he was diagnosed. Police found him passed out in an alley behind some club in Boys Town after an anonymous phone call alerted them to his whereabouts. That was two days ago. The sister said Finn has no memory of what happened, and maybe that's true. But BP unmedicated...'

Dot doesn't have to continue. Nickolas knows. He has read up on the condition. He knows the signs: mood swings, hypersexuality, insomnia, suicidal thoughts—the list goes on. He hates to think what Finn was doing in Boys Town, or more so what was being done to Finn while in that state of mind. He hears the boy's words in his head, 'That's all you assholes want to do, touch me,' and 'I promise, I'll do anything you ask'.

He's brought back to reality when the buzzer alerts him to the door being unlocked. Dot holds it open so Nickolas can walk back through, allowing her to head out for the night.

'Shit, it's almost lights out,' says Nickolas.

'It's okay. Lydia came by and took the med cart. It's under control,' Dot explains.

Sam walks out of the corridor, a cup of coffee in hand with a few cookies, no doubt homemade by Dot. Sam steps in, ready to take his place behind the desk for the remainder of the night, just like he has done for the past fifteen years.

'You better hurry home, Cinderella. Don't want your carriage turning into a pumpkin,' Sam teases.

Dorothy blushes at Sam's joke. The hour is nowhere near midnight, but the underlying message is clearly not lost on his boss. 'Oh, Sam.' Dot waves him off and turns towards the doors to exit.

Nickolas takes a look at the monitors behind the desk and his eyes find the door to room thirteen. Of course, he can't see or hear anything, but he can't help but wonder if Finn has settled down or if he is still begging to be let go.

Sam groans as he takes a seat, turning on the small radio beside the phones to make the place seem less lonely.

'You settled for the night old man?' Nickolas asks.

'You watch it. This old man still has some fight left in him.'

Nickolas chuckles. 'Whatever you say, Sammy.'

'How many times have I told you? Sammy is the name of a prepubescent boy. My hair is turning grey and my balls dropped long ago.'

'No shit, they're hanging so low on the floor I could use them to mop the place up.'

Sam laughs.

'Anyway. I'm going to make the rounds before lights out. Maybe close my eyes for a few.' He explains.

'You got the day shift again tomorrow?'

'Yeah. Today was meant to be my day off but Jasmine and Eric called in sick.'

'They organised a replacement for her yet? The girl is due in a few months.'

'Beats me, man. I just work here.'

He pats Sam on the shoulder and goes back through to the corridor towards the break room to see if he can find Lydia. He tries not to think of Finn lying in a gutter in Boys Town. Of what Finn must have endured to end up there, and with no memory. Nickolas has visited that side of town once or twice. He remembers the copious amounts of drugs, guys tweaked out of their minds while getting fucked in any dark corner available to them. Men as old as Sam hitting on guys as young as Finn, if not younger. He never walked away with more than a blowjob, happy to get the fuck out of there and ride his dildo back home, instead of bending over for any of the creeps in those places.

He finds Lydia making a cup of coffee, the med cart empty with the checklist sitting on the top.

'Hey. How'd it go?' Nickolas nods toward the cart.

'Good. No issues.'

'Good. Sam's out front so just drop that off with him, then you can keep studying for a bit if you need.'

'Thanks. This upcoming test is stressing me out.'

'How long you got left?'

'Five months. Then I'll be back here, and instead of you bossing me around, I'll be the boss of you.'

Nickolas scoffs. 'You wish. Maybe the boss of Dorothy, but I don't listen to a thing the therapists say besides what drugs to hand out. And even that is already organised for me.'

'You ever thought of doing more? You know, work your way up to becoming a nurse or EMT.'

'Nah.' Nickolas grabs a bottle of water from the fridge and unscrews the cap. 'I don't want to be responsible for these patients, I just want to make sure they are getting looked after. You know.'

'She'd be proud of you.' Lydia gives a small smile and leaves.

Nickolas brings his hand up to his heart. He closes his eyes, takes a small breath in through his nose, and releases it out through his mouth. *Would she be proud?*

Glancing at the time on his watch, he sees there are ten minutes left before lights out. He walks out of the break room and opens the door to the ward, checking to make sure each patient's door is locked for the night before he reaches door thirteen. He looks in through the small glass window and notices the way Finn is curled into himself, slightly shivering. Nickolas unlocks the door, concerned when Finn doesn't make a move from the noise of the door opening.

'Hey, man. I'm just going to pull some blankets up for you. Can get a bit of a draft in here at night,' Nickolas explains.

He assumes Finn is ignoring him as his eyes stay locked onto the wall. Nickolas pulls the blankets at the end of the bed up and over Finn's body. A soft whimper leaves Finn's lips, and Nickolas crouches down. Hoping to make himself look less threatening, he brings himself to Finn's level.

'Finn. You okay? Are you in any pain?'

'Please take these off. Please, Nickolas.'

Nickolas wants to reach his hand out and touch Finn, just a gentle hand on his arm to let him know it's going to be okay. But he doesn't. He knows he shouldn't. So instead, he offers him words of encouragement.

'Try and get some sleep, Finn. In the morning, I'll take them off, okay?'

Finn pulls his wrists down, trying to cover his eyes with his hands, but the chain doesn't reach that far. The quick force sends a loud clanging sound into the once-quiet room, echoing against the walls.

'Just go. I'm used to people lying to me about wanting to help. Figures you'd be no different.'

Nickolas bows his head. The lights suddenly go out in the room, the glow from the moon and the shine from the corridor lights being the only things keeping Finn from complete darkness. Nickolas slowly stands up and leaves, making sure the door is locked behind him.

He runs his hands down his face and heads back to the break room. The couch is calling his name. Nickolas hopes he can take a quick power nap before the routine check-ins are due. He sits down, Lydia's head already in her books, the walkie on the table beside her in case Sam needs to make contact. A sigh of exhaustion escapes his lips as his head lays back against the cushions. He closes his eyes, waiting for sleep to take over his body, but he's too wired. His mind is consumed by

Finn's words. He doesn't understand why Finn's comment is affecting him so much, especially when he's had worse things said to him. But a part of Nickolas wants Finn to trust him. To know he is here to help him and to make sure he leaves this place as the best version of himself. He wills his body to shut out all thoughts of Finn and tells himself that there is always tomorrow. Bridges were never built overnight.

2. Wednesday

Nickolas wonders how anyone can be laughing this early in the morning. As his body starts to wake, he groans from the kink in his neck from sleeping at a weird angle. He regrets the decision to use the couch as a makeshift bed, but he needed the rest.

'Fuck. Keep it down assholes,' Nickolas grumbles.

'Morning to you too, Nickolas,' says Eric, using the last of the coffee to make himself a cup, though Nickolas finds it thoughtful that Eric has already started the process of making a fresh pot.

He sits up, rests his elbows on his knees and runs his fingers through his hair, gently pulling at it to wake himself up quicker.

'Rough night?' Eric asks.

'If it was, no one told me.'

'Shit. Lucky you. Been a while since I got to sleep through a whole night shift.'

'I wasn't meant to. Lydia was supposed to wake me up to check—'

'I know, I know. But you looked so peaceful and it's not like I haven't done the hourly checks before.' Lydia cuts in, acting way too chipper for six a.m.

'Not the point,' Nickolas grumbles.

'Okay, so next time I need to walk down the corridor and see that every patient is asleep, I should wake you after you worked a double, soon to be a triple. Is that right?'

Lydia's sass reminds Nickolas of *her*. He can't decide if he likes the reminder or not.

'You said all the patients?' Nickolas clarifies.

'Mhm.'

'No issues in room thirteen?'

Lydia purses her lips and tilts her head a little, acting as though the question requires the strawberry blond to remember what had happened weeks prior. 'Hmm, nothing out of the ordinary. Why?'

'Nothing, nothing. Just...new patient.'

Eric walks out, ready to start the morning, while Lydia goes to the locker room to retrieve her bag. Nickolas stands up, groaning as he stretches out his body, craving a hot shower to help loosen his muscles. Instead, he settles for hot black coffee, the muesli bar that he packed in his bag the day before, and two cookies that were left over from Dot's baking. Nickolas takes a sip of his coffee and winces as it burns his tongue and his throat, before warming his stomach. He reads the roster on the wall, pleased to see Dot is working the morning shift along with himself and Eric. Sky, Hayley, and James are scheduled for the afternoon shift.

'Heard you were out like a light last night?' Sam chuckles, walking into the breakroom, placing his coffee cup into the sink and giving it a rinse.

'I was surprised myself. My body generally wakes up automatically on the hour when I work nights.'

'Ah, don't sweat it. The night was thankfully uneventful. Lydia got her studying done and then kept me company for most of it.'

Nickolas smiles. It's so small that if Sam hadn't been looking directly at him, the older man would have missed it.

'Jasmine is in this morning. She has settled out front with a bucket and some plain crackers, just in case.' Sam explains.

'Fuck. I don't know how women do it. Pregnancy seems like nine months of hell.'

'Maybe so, but it just shows how much stronger women are compared to us mere men.'

Nickolas raises his coffee cup in cheers and then takes a sip, cursing himself for burning his mouth once again.

'Dot's here so I'm heading home.' Lydia announces, walking back into the room. 'Got to get some sleep before I come back in tonight.' Lydia picks up her books that are piled on the table and slips them into her bag before heading out.

'Hey,' Nickolas calls out.

Lydia turns towards him before leaving the break room.

'Thanks for last night. You did good.'

'I know.' Lydia smiles and turns around to leave, radiating confidence.

'She is going to make a damn good therapist,' Sam comments.

'She'll give me a run for my money, that's for sure.' Nickolas puts his cup in the sink. He knows he's had enough coffee to help him function. At least for the time being.

'Morning, gentleman. Raspberry and white chocolate muffins. Help yourself.' Dot places a tray of baked goods in the centre of the table before turning back towards Sam, placing her hands on her hips to show some authority, but Nickolas smiles, thinking how it reminds him of the look a grandmother would give if he were to walk through the house all dirty and muddy after playing outside. At least that's what he thinks it would look like. He doesn't have any references to base it off.

'Go home. Jasmine is here and your shift ended ten minutes ago,' Dot demands.

'Yes, ma'am.' Sam picks up a muffin and gives Dot a wink as he takes a bite and leaves the room.

'You two really should just hook up and be done with it,' says Nickolas.

'Hook up?' Dot still has her hands on her hips. Nickolas can feel the power that pose possesses. 'Back in my day the chase and the romance were the best forms of foreplay. Once you met someone, that was it. None of this hit it and walk away nonsense.'

Nickolas chuckles. 'It's "hit it and quit it", Dot.'

His boss swats her hand in the air like what she said still meant the same thing. 'I'm glad you got some sleep. When I left yesterday you looked exhausted.'

'I was fine until...' Nickolas cuts himself off.

Dot nods in understanding. 'Have you checked on him this morning?'

'No.' Nickolas looks down at his feet. A sudden feeling of guilt settles inside of him. He feels as though he's abandoned Finn by dumping him in his room after he was admitted. 'I was about to, though. Eric is getting the dining area ready for breakfast, so I'll go open up the patient rooms.'

He looks at his watch. Wake up isn't for another hour, but it doesn't feel right to leave Finn any longer.

'I'll help with wake up; you check on Finn. A familiar face is probably what he needs right now to help him adjust,' says Dot.

Nickolas goes to take a piss and then reapplies his deodorant before making his way back to the break room. After Dot puts her food away, they both make their way towards the corridor of patient rooms. Dot heads towards the common room to see if Eric needs help, giving the patients the extra minutes of sleep, rather than waking them before the designated time. Nickolas, however, walks straight to door thirteen. He puts his key card against the door to unlock it, gently pushing it open so as not to startle the patient. Nickolas's eyes focus on Finn, whose body is in the exact position he was left in the night before. The restraints allow the patients to roll onto their side or back, but Finn's still lying with his back toward the door, his legs curled into his chest with the blanket Nickolas had placed on him draped over his torso and legs.

'Finn?' Nickolas whispers. 'Hey man, it's time for breakfast. Think you can get up and come eat some food?' Nickolas makes his way around the bed, so he is within Finn's eyesight.

Finn is awake. The dark circles around his eyes are worse than how they looked the night before and it's evident from the dried tear stains on his cheeks that he spent the night crying.

Nickolas slowly kneels in front of Finn. 'Morning. Did you get much sleep?' He asks a question that he already knows the answer to.

'How about we slowly take these restraints off, hmm? I think I heard that today they were serving pancakes in the dining area.'

Moving slowly, not wanting to startle Finn, Nickolas reaches for the left restraint and begins to unbuckle the clasp.

'Fuck,' Nickolas whispers.

He accidentally breaks his own rule about not swearing in front of patients as he pulls the leather away from Finn's wrist, shocked by the damage to his skin – blisters and a few tears that have crusted over with dried blood. It's obvious Finn spent the night pulling at the cuffs. As Nickolas brings Finn's left arm down to his side, Finn doesn't move, his body acting as a puppet and Nickolas, the puppeteer. Leaning over, he unbuckles Finn's right wrist and inspects the damage. He's relieved to see there is no blood, just some bruising and blisters.

'Finn, can you sit up for me? I need to get you to the infirmary so your wrists can be cleaned and bandaged, okay?'

Finn isn't responding. Nickolas moves the bedding away from Finn's body when the sudden smell of urine hits his nostrils. Nickolas closes his eyes and sighs. One of the many reasons he hates restraining patients is stripping them of their dignity when they wet the bed because they're not able to get themselves up and use the toilet inside their room.

'I'm sorry,' Finn mumbles, his cheeks flaring.

'Hey, no, Finn, it's fine. This is my fault. Not yours.' He takes his time so that Finn listens to every word and hopefully believes him. 'I'm sorry. I should have checked on you during the night, made sure you were okay, asked if you needed the bathroom. The other orderly that did the rounds, she wasn't aware of your...situation.'

Finn still doesn't meet Nickolas's eyes.

'How 'bout we get you cleaned up? You can use the showers while everyone is eating, we'll get your wrists looked at and then get some food afterwards.'

It's small, but Nickolas smiles at the slight nod Finn gives him.

Nickolas snakes his arm under Finn's neck and helps him sit up. He puts a clean pair of sweatpants, a green t-shirt, and facility-issued slippers into a shower bag for Finn.

'Okay. Let's slowly get you standing. You can hold onto me if you need,' says Nickolas.

'I'm not an invalid.' There is a little more attitude in Finn's voice, and Nickolas can't help but huff out a small laugh. Attitude means personality and a personality means Finn hasn't slipped into a depressive state of mind, like Nickolas was concerned about. Slowly, Finn stands on his own and shuffles his feet, adjusting as he puts weight on his legs. Nickolas keeps a small distance, allowing Finn to feel as though he isn't being coddled, but keeping close in case he suddenly needs the support. He stands beside Finn. Even though he is the orderly and Finn is the patient, he wants him to feel as though they are equals. Standing in front of him might give Finn the sense of being a prisoner, and standing behind him might make him feel as though he is being watched. Nickolas wants him to feel safe. Safe with him.

Finn stops a few feet before the doorway. 'Is...is anyone else out there?' He looks down and Nickolas follows his line of sight, to a wet patch on the front of his denim jeans.

Nickolas opens the door and sticks his head out into the corridor. It seems empty enough, as quiet as a psychiatric treatment centre can be first thing in the morning. He sees Dot about to step out of the common room in preparation to wake everyone up and raises his hand, signalling for her to wait before unlocking each room.

Pushing the door fully open, Nickolas turns back around and gives Finn a warm smile. 'C'mon. Everyone else is still sleeping, so no one will see you.' Nickolas presses his back against the door to hold it open. Finn's shoulder brushes against his chest as he steps through.

Standing in the corridor, Finn does a sweep of the area, 'This looks nothing like the other place I was sent to.' Nickolas takes note of the sadness in his voice.

'Showers are this way.' He leads Finn back towards the entrance of the patient corridor but turns to the right rather than towards the mesh fence and door that they came through the night before. Nickolas scans his key card to unlock a door, walking Finn into a room that has three office doors to the left and three doors with a small square window with a shutter blind. Finn's body trembles. Nickolas wonders if the air against his wet clothes is the cause or if it's from seeing the doors to the solitary rooms in front of them. They continue toward a doorway to the right which opens up to another corridor. They enter, a sign saying *Male Showers* is on a wall to their left with another advertising *Female Showers* further down.

'You're lucky, man. You got the whole place to yourself. Means you don't have to worry about the hot water running out.' Nickolas's joke has Finn smiling for a second before closing himself off again. But one second is still a moment that Nickolas was able to get Finn out of his own head. He places the clean clothes on the bench where he sits down and waits.

'Ahh, are you going to—' Finn stops mid-question.

'Sorry. I know having some guy watch you shower isn't ideal, but I'm just here to make sure nothing happens to you. I promise I'll stay seated on my bench, but I can't leave you alone in the room.'

'I get it. It's fine. Not like I'm not used to guys watching me.'

Nickolas cracks his knuckles, his body begging to fight these guys Finn speaks of. It's unnerving for Nickolas to feel this sense of protective behaviour towards a patient. Thankfully oblivious to Nickolas's rampant thoughts, Finn kicks his shoes off, bare feet now touching the tiled floor before removing his t-shirt, pulling it from the back of the neck and over his head. As Finn unzips his jeans, Nickolas looks down at his own hands, studying his tattoos.

Once the water is running, Nickolas looks up and the first thing his eyes zone in on are the dark bruises on Finn's back. Some of them are starting to turn a slight green colour, on their way to healing, while the rest are still a deep shade of purple. As water droplets trickle down Finn's body, the bruises that make Nickolas's stomach drop are the ones that almost look like handprints on either side of his patients' hips.

'Are the bruises still there?' asks Finn.

Nickolas coughs. 'What? Oh, ah, yeah.' He coughs again. 'Sorry, I didn't mean to stare.' He looks down at his shoes, bites his lip and wills his mouth to keep shut and for his mind to let it go. But he's never had the willpower to just 'let things go'. 'What happened?'

Silence.

Nickolas figures Finn is going to ignore his question. It's not like the guy has to tell him – he's just the orderly after all, not a therapist or doctor. It's none of his fucking business. But a part of Nickolas feels like it should be his business. He has this urgency to know Finn's story more than any other patient he's worked with in the past. Maybe even more than – no. No, no one could ever mean more than her. But maybe, on some level, Finn's recovery is just as important to Nickolas as hers was...maybe.

'Don't know. Woke up with them, with no memory of how I got 'em.' Finn's voice sounds detached, almost like it's been rehearsed. Sometimes if a person says something enough times, they can begin to believe it.

The water turns off.

Nickolas is used to having to tell the patients that their time is up, so he looks up to see why he can't hear the sound of running water and is met with the most beautiful dick he has ever seen – even compared to porn – staring him in the face. It causes Nickolas's brain to go offline for a moment as he saves the image to memory.

'Like what you see?' Finn's voice is low, filled with pride and lust.

Nickolas stands up. He's close enough to radiate his own body heat onto Finn's dripping skin, however, he still stands with enough space between them to keep his uniform dry. A cocky smile appears on Finn's face, as though the redhead assumes he has won.

He takes great joy from Finn's stunned expression as he shoves a scratchy towel towards his wet chest. 'Dry off. Get dressed. Those wounds need attending to.'

Nickolas walks away and stands near the door. He doesn't watch Finn get dressed. Instead, he curses his body for responding to the proposition.

Was Finn hoping to use his body in exchange for something?

Is that what Finn has been subjected to for the last six months?

'It's fine. I'm dressed so, you can look now.'

He turns back around and Finn shuffles towards him, eyes on the floor while carrying the soiled clothes in the laundry bag. Finn pushes past and stands in the corridor, waiting for Nickolas to follow. The guy's behaviour is giving Nickolas whiplash, but he understands. He doesn't question it or judge. It's typical behaviour for an unmedicated bipolar patient.

The infirmary is right next to the shower block, and Nickolas scans his key card to unlock the door, then holds it open for Finn. The walls are painted a soft yellow colour, probably because someone somewhere said it was soothing. Cabinets with locks on them are hanging on the walls, three beds are to the right with white curtains between each, and a chair is situated in the middle of the room. A woman looks up from a computer as Nickolas walks in behind Finn.

'Nickolas, hey. What's going on?'

He stands at Finn's side. 'This is Finn. He came in last night and we just need you to attend to some blisters before they get infected.'

'Sure.' The woman's attention is directed to the patient. 'Finn, I'm Dr Winslow, but everyone just calls me Lexi. Do you mind taking a seat for me?'

Nickolas can leave Finn alone in here, but he doesn't want to. After what just happened, leaving right now would make it look as though he's upset with Finn's behaviour. Maybe even angry. He can't let Finn think that. Not only would it not be the case, but he needs Finn to know that he is on his side, no matter what Finn says or does. Nothing is going to push Nickolas away. He gives Finn a reassuring smile to let him know Dr Winslow can be trusted. Finn takes a seat, eyes on the floor to avoid eye contact with everyone in the room.

'Okay. Let's have a look, shall we?' says Lexi.

Lexi has only been working here for a year, but Nickolas enjoys the doctor's bedside manner more than the asshole that held the position before her. He watches as Lexi announces that she's about to touch Finn's wrist before doing so. At his nod of approval, the doctor carefully inspects the wounds. The shower washed away the dry blood, exposing gashes that now don't seem so deep.

'I'm going to put some antibacterial cream on these, which should also help soothe the blisters. I'll wrap them up and you'll be good to go.'

Lexi gives Finn a warm smile, but the guy keeps his eyes on the ground. The doctor turns towards Nickolas, trying to gauge if there are any other concerns he wants her to look over. Nickolas knows she can't help with Finn's bruises, but he wants to make sure every part of his patient is taken care of. However, those injuries happened before Finn was admitted and therefore is none of their business, so he keeps it that way. Gaining trust is the only thing these patients have left that allows them to feel as though they are still able to make their own decisions, and Nickolas wants Finn to be able to trust him.

With some gauze around Finn's wrists, Lexi wheels her stool away, allowing Finn to stand and exit.

'Ready for those pancakes?' Nickolas claps his hands and rubs them together to emphasise his excitement.

At the mention of food, Finn looks up for the first time since the showers and gives a small half-smile. They walk side by side back towards the patient rooms, neither of them saying anything, but as they get closer to the common room, Finn begins to slow his step.

'Hey, it's okay,' Nickolas says reassuringly. 'The dining area is just through here.'

Finn crosses his arms to hide his wrists under his armpits. Although there are only blisters underneath the bandages, he understands that to anyone else in that room, it would look like self-harm.

Nickolas opens the door with his key card and the silence of the corridor vanishes, replaced with the commotion of the patients in the common room. He holds the door open for Finn, who slowly takes a step inside. Finn freezes in place, taking in his new surroundings. They continue to walk in together. Nickolas doesn't know if Finn does it on purpose or if his subconscious has him gravitating towards something familiar – or someone – but Finn's shoulder brushes up against his own as they keep in step, heading towards the dining area.

'Hey, Nickolas. You all good?'

He spots Eric in the craft corner – today it's clay – and gives him a small nod to let his colleague know he's alright. Scanning his key card to open the door to the dining area, he once again holds the door open for Finn to step in first. As he pulls it closed behind him, he watches Finn's shoulders relax at the silence that follows.

'Take a seat wherever. I'll get us some food,' Nickolas instructs as he steps out back, making sure Finn is still in his eyesight, even though there is nothing in the room that could put the guy in harm's way.

'Yo, Aiden.' Nickolas leans against the doorframe waiting for their cook to respond, wanting to stay in Finn's presence. Aiden comes out with a hairnet on his light brown hair, drying his hands off with a towel.

'Nickolas, hey.'

He gives Aiden a nod hello. 'Hey, man, you got any pancakes left? Maybe some juice or fruit.'

'Sure. Just for you?'

'Nah, me and a patient. Missed breakfast due to a trip to the infirmary.'

Aiden nods in understanding. 'I'll bring it out to you.'

Nickolas heads back to the table Finn has chosen and takes a seat across from him. They sit in silence, Finn's head bowed, arms resting under the table. It only takes a few minutes for Aiden to come out with two plastic trays, each with a plastic cup of fruit salad, two banana pancakes with syrup, and an orange juice box. Plastic utensils are placed on the side, with a napkin.

'Thanks, man,' says Nickolas.

'Just call out if you want more.'

Nickolas picks up his knife and fork and digs in. Sneaking glances, he sees Finn pick up the fork and poke around at the food.

'Real five-star food you got in this place,' Finn jokes.

Nickolas plays along. 'Sorry, the chef at the Ritz was busy, but I promise Aiden is the next best thing.'

Finn tears pieces of his pancake apart but doesn't take a bite. Its similar behaviour presented by patients suffering from eating disorders. They think if they play around with the food, then the orderlies will believe they ate something. Guess again. Nickolas has seen it all before.

'You can eat it warm or you can eat it cold. Either way, you aren't leaving that seat till you eat something,' explains Nickolas.

'What are you going to do, strap me down and force-feed me?' Finn bites back.

'If I have to.'

Finn looks up, anger simmering in his eyes, but only a little.

'But I don't want to have to do that, Finn.'

'Well, what if I don't want to eat?'

'Unfortunately, what you want is not something you get a say in, at least not for a while. This place is more about what you need. And right now, based on the way your clothes were falling off your body last night, I'd say what you need is food.'

Finn glares at him.

'Look man, you can hate me all you want. But even if you don't believe it, everything I'm doing is to help you.'

Finn stabs a piece of pancake onto the fork and eats it.

He smiles. 'Told you they're good.'

Nickolas keeps eating, happy to sit in silence if that's what Finn wants. He moves onto his fruit salad, pleased to see Finn doing the same. Considering how much of his meal Nickolas ate before Finn had started, he's surprised to see they are now equal with what's left on their plates.

'So, what's the plan?' Finn questions.

Nickolas takes a bite of a strawberry, cocking an eyebrow at Finn's question. 'The plan?'

'Yeah. You going to pump me full of drugs, sit me down with a shrink and then send me on my merry way?'

Nickolas is concerned. 'Why? Is that what they did at your last place?'

Finn doesn't answer him.

'No, man. At least, I don't think so. My guess is the doctor will re-evaluate your medication, probably adjust your dosage since you've been off 'em for so long. The therapist will sit with you, see how you're going, maybe ask why you went off your meds, and then go from there.'

Finn stops eating. 'You guess?'

'I'm not a doctor. I'm an orderly. You know, monitor the patients, take you to where you need to be. Clean the rooms.'

'Wouldn't need to clean them if you hadn't restrained me.'

Nickolas stops eating. Finn is still looking at him, unwilling to break eye contact.

'Once again, I'm sorry.' He emphasises the apology to prove how much he means it. 'But it's my job to make sure you and everyone else are safe,'

Green eyes stare back at his own blue one, until Finn breaks eye contact and forks a piece of watermelon into his mouth.

'So, not a doctor,' Finn clarifies.

'Correct. Not a doctor. Just been here long enough to know how the process works.'

Nickolas stands up, his food now finished and walks over to the cart to discard of his utensils and place his dirty tray on the pile to be cleaned. He opens the juice box, popping the straw through the little hole in the top, and sucks the contents down in one go. He catches Finn studying every move he makes.

'You done?' asks Nickolas.

'What? Oh, um, sure.' Finn stumbles over his words.

Nickolas walks back to the table and takes Finn's tray. He picks up the untouched juice and offers it to Finn, who shakes his head, and Nickolas shrugs as if to say, 'Your loss.' He makes sure all the utensils are accounted for as he puts the tray back on the cart.

Nickolas looks at the time on his watch. 'Come on. Time for your first appointment.'

It's not lost on Nickolas how the mention of doctors and medication makes Finn curl into himself. Every little step he takes to help bring Finn out of his shell is lost the minute he's reminded of where he is. Just like before, Finn gravitates towards him as he holds the door open for him to step through. Nickolas tries to make small talk as they walk towards the therapists' rooms.

'So, the common room is used in the morning until lunch. The space is then allocated for group therapy, and those not involved go back to their rooms.' Nickolas scans his key card and opens the door that leads them into the corridor. 'Group goes for an hour. Then those patients go back to their rooms also. Anyone who has one-on-one appointments generally has them scheduled for the morning. Sometimes it can be after group, but that depends on the patient. If you have to attend both, then you'd have a morning session and then group in the afternoon rather than two sessions back-to-back.'

Nickolas is simply talking to fill the silence, but it seems to be calming Finn down. He can tell by the way his shoulders drop and his head rises, their surroundings no longer drawing fear from Finn.

'Dinner is served at five. At six everyone gets an hour in the common room before breaking off for showers. Back in your room before eight, lights out at nine.' Nickolas stops outside one of the rooms they saw this morning on their way to the showers and turns to face Finn. He knocks on the door and a woman with black hair in a bun, wearing black-rimmed glasses, and looking as though she is in her mid-thirties, steps out and smiles at Finn.

'Finn Cunningham?' The woman asks.

'Yes,' Nickolas answers. It's his job, even if Finn can answer for himself. Orderlies have to confirm that the therapists are about to sit with the correct patient. Finn turns to Nickolas, eyes pleading to not be made to go inside.

He gives Finn a small smile of encouragement. 'Go on, I'll be back to take you to your room once you're done with Dr Hale.'

Finn looks down at his feet as he walks into the office and Dr Hale closes the door behind them.

Nickolas exhales, and runs a hand down his face as he makes his way towards the back rooms. His lungs feel as though he's been holding his breath underwater. He's only three hours into his shift but after working a double yesterday, he's surprised he's still functioning. He walks past room thirteen, now Finn's room, and steps inside. Dot has stripped the bedding and is sponging down the rubber mattress with warm, soapy water.

'There you are. Haven't seen you all morning,' Dot comments.

'I just dropped Finn off at his evaluation.'

'Ahh.' Dot gives him a nod, rinsing out the sponge and giving the mattress one more wipe down for good measure.

'Here, let me help you.' Nickolas steps forward.

'Nonsense. I'm done now. I came in looking for you and noticed what happened.'

'It was my fault.'

Dot stands up, dropping the sponge in the bucket and putting her hands on her hips.

'How was Mr Cunningham having an accident your fault?'

'Lydia didn't know he was restrained, so during the night checks she didn't think to ask if he needed the bathroom. If I hadn't slept through the night, it wouldn't have happened.'

'I see.' His boss picks up the towel and dries the mattress, so it's ready for new sheets.

'That's it? That's all you're going to say?'

Dot holds out a new sheet. 'Take this end, will you? Help me put it over the other corner.'

Nickolas takes the sheet and covers the top half of the mattress, tucking it in.

'That's all I have to say because I can already see on your face that you feel guilty about it. It was a mistake. You learned from it and, yes, although that would have been uncomfortable for Mr Cunningham, unfortunately, worse has happened to some of these patients from mistakes being made.' Dot immediately looks up, regret evident on his boss's face. 'Oh, Nykolai, I didn't mean—'

Nickolas's legs give out from under him, thankful the bed is there to land on. He leans forward, pressing his palms into his eyes as tears fall down his cheeks. The warmth of Dot's body presses up against him, her arm wrapping around his shoulders, coddling him like a little scared boy. He doesn't fight it. Sometimes he still feels like that little kid that grew up in fear.

'You know what happened wasn't your fault.' Dot speaks softly.

Nodding slowly, he drags his palms across his eyes, wiping the tears away as he does so. 'This room, being in here...it still haunts me. I'm surprised that I was even able to get Finn through that door last night.'

'It gets easier. This place is full of ghosts. It's probably one of the only things that make working here so difficult.'

'I don't know how you've done it for all these years.'

'The same way you've been doing it for almost two years. You do it for them.'

He turns to face Dot.

'This isn't your standard job,' Dot continues. 'People don't grow up saying they want to take care of the mentally ill. Something happens in their lives that makes them take a job like this. That's why finding the right person to work here, who wants to help and not just wants to take home a pay cheque, that's the challenge.'

Dot begins to rub circles into Nickolas's back. He thinks about pulling away but it's soothing, like a mother's touch.

'The number of times I've wanted to fire Brett...God, that man infuriates me. But I have no grounds to stand on that would justify his termination, at least nothing solid. And if I did, I'd be left to find a replacement and I still haven't found one for Jasmine yet.'

Dot removes her hand from his back and places it on his knee, giving a gentle squeeze to get his attention.

'You, Nykolai, you are the right person for this job. You are compassionate, caring, sensitive to the patient's needs and their situation. But you're also tough. Not just physically, but mentally as well. It can be hard not to take the job home with you, and you know how to separate the two. Most of the time.'

He huffs out a chuckle.

Dot stands. 'Let's go. Few more rooms you need to look in on. I'll go see how Eric is going. Once you've done that, go have a break.'

'I told Finn I'd get him when his evaluation is finished.'

'That's fine. You'll be done before he is.'

Dot picks up the bucket of water and follows Nickolas out of the room. He collects the laundry bin and continues to change the bedding in the remaining rooms.

It's ten a.m. when he gets to the breakroom. He makes a beeline for the coffee, thanking whatever God is out there that someone made a fresh pot. He sniffs his mug as he brings it up to his mouth, the smell melting whatever tension he was holding on to. Caffeine may be known to increase anxious behaviour, but for Nickolas, it has always calmed his nerves. His eyes land on Dot's homemade muffins and he eagerly picks one up and shoves a third of it into his mouth.

'Easy there. Don't need you choking on the food.' Jasmine walks in, rubbing a hand over her stomach as she makes her way toward the sink to refill her bottle with water.

He chews his food and swallows before answering. 'Hey. How you feeling?'

'Better. Thanks for covering for me yesterday. You must be exhausted. Can understand why you're inhaling the muffin.'

'It's fine. Lucky for you, I don't have a life outside of this building, so I was free to work.'

'What a waste. Look at you. You should have guys lining up down the street begging to take you out.'

'Not interested.'

'Nickolas.'

He rolls his eyes. The way Jasmine says his name is so condescending, he hates it. He goes to defend himself because, for some reason, the way he has chosen to live his life needs defending, but the faint ring of the phone going off saves him as Jasmine waddles out of the room to answer it.

Five more hours till he can go home, take a long hot shower, and curl up on the couch. By then, Socks will seek out his attention, demanding he fill up her food bowl, empty her litter tray, and then if she feels like it, she'll accept his love and affection. He glances at his phone. No messages or calls, of course. He has no one in his life he keeps in contact with, making sure never to give out his number to any random guys because he doesn't need them thinking their hook-up is more than that. But he still checks as if he's expecting to see something pop up on his screen.

He finishes his coffee, grabs another muffin, and then makes his way to the front desk to look over some paperwork. As he gets closer, the phone rings again. He hears Jasmine answer in that sweet phone voice reserved specifically for calls. Nickolas is looking for the group therapy schedule, seeing if any of the patient names have changed, when Jasmine taps him on the arm to grab his attention.

'It's for you. A Jessica Cunningham.'

Fuck. Dot told Jessica to call for an update, but he'd completely forgotten that his name was included in that comment.

'Ah, can you patch it through to the phone in the break room?'

'Sure.'

Nickolas isn't used to dealing with family members. That's not his job. He doesn't give updates or bad news, hell, he doesn't even give good news. But Dot is helping Eric and he's the one who has been monitoring Finn, which means he's probably the best person for Jessica to speak with. He takes a seat at the table, the flashing red light on line two blinks at him like a warning light as he picks up the phone to accept Jessica's call.

He coughs, clears his throat, and hits the flashing light. 'Hello.'

'Nickolas?'

'Yeah.'

'It's Jessica, Jessica Cunningham. Finn Cunningham's sister.'

'I remember.'

'I was just wanting to know how he went last night. If he's okay.'

Is Finn okay? He could lie and then have Finn explain everything that happened when they visit in four days, or he can be honest and have a screaming Cunningham going off at him. If

Jessica is anything like Finn, he figures she could get heated when pissed off.

'He, ah, he had a rough night. Although he wasn't agitated throughout the night, when I checked on Finn this morning to collect him for breakfast, I noticed he hadn't slept much and had urinated the bed.'

'Oh, Finn.' There is sorrow in Jessica's voice.

He wants to tell Finn's sister it was due to neglect on his part, but he moves on. 'I unclasped his restraints and it was obvious that he had been pulling at them throughout the night. His wrists were bruised and blistered with a few tears in his skin.'

Jessica is silent.

'I took him to the showers to get cleaned up, and then to the infirmary. His wounds were attended to, and the doctor confirmed that they were minor once assessed. He ate and is currently in his evaluation.'

He can hear soft breathing. He waits over a minute for a response.

'Hello?'

Jessica sniffs. 'I'm here'—another sniff—'sorry. I'm here.'

This is another reason why Nickolas doesn't talk to the family members. He doesn't know how to handle them when they get emotional. Doesn't know what to say or do. Maybe it's because no one has ever been there for him when he's needed someone to lean on. Someone to tell him everything will be okay.

'Is he on his meds?' asks Jessica.

'Not yet. I'm sure after his evaluation, the doctor will decide what the best cocktail will be to start him on.' He looks around the room. His break is over, and he doesn't know what else he can offer Finn's sister. 'I, ah, have to get back.'

'Right. Of course. Sorry.'

He goes to hang up when he hears something come through the phone. He puts it back to his ear. 'What?'

'I said, thank you.'

'Just...doing my job.'

He puts the phone back on the receiver and hangs up. A warm tingling runs through his body. He isn't sure what it is, or why it's happening, but he shakes it off as he heads to the bathroom to take a piss before heading back out into the patient corridor to make his way back to Finn.

He rounds the corner, just as Dr Hale's office door opens. Nickolas's eyes peak over Dr Hale's shoulder so he can see Finn. The guy looks frustrated. At who, Nickolas isn't sure, but the Finn that stepped inside that office is not the one that is stepping out.

'I'll see you tomorrow, Finn,' the doctor states.

When Finn ignores Dr Hale's comment, the doctor turns towards him.

'Nickolas?'

He turns and looks at the therapist, giving her his full attention.

'I have put Finn's name on the group therapy list, please make sure he is there in today's session. I've emailed Dr Winslow a list of the medications I'd like to start him on. Make sure he takes them this evening when the med cart makes its rounds.'

'Yes ma'am. I'm not working tonight but I'll make sure to leave a note for whoever is.'

Dr Hale gives him a nod and then closes the office door.

They begin walking down the corridor toward the common room.

'Fucking bitch.' Finn mumbles.

Nickolas raises his eyebrows at Finn's comment. 'Looks like I don't need to ask how that went.'

'They're all the same. Treating us like we're just another name in the system. They think an hour of conversation is all they need to figure us out.'

'I guess that's why she added you to group. More time to help assess rather than just the one-on-one sessions.'

'Right, because opening up in front of a group of crazies is going to help.'

Nickolas stops walking and Finn instantly notices.

'I understand you're angry and frustrated. But don't take your shit out on everyone else in here. Some of these people personally admit themselves because they want to get help. Others know they need the support. Either way, they can't control what's going on just as much as you can't.' He takes a step closer. 'You're not ready to accept your diagnosis, fine. You can keep that bed warm for as long as it takes. But if I hear you speak that way again, calling the other patients that, then we're going to have a problem.' He sets off towards the door to the common room and waits. Finn is still standing where he left him, head slightly bowed. 'Cunningham,' Nickolas calls out to him, grabbing his attention.

Finn is a foot away before he starts on an apology. 'I didn't—'

'I know.' He brushes Finn off. 'C'mon, there are some people I want you to meet.' Nickolas unlocks the door, opens it, and waits for Finn to walk through. He locks the door behind them and heads towards the TV, where three people similar in age to Finn are seated.

'What's everyone watching today?' Nickolas asks the small group.

Three heads turn towards him and smile like it's Christmas morning.

'Nothing as good as what's in front of me,' says Cora, who winks up at him.

He blushes, but it's more from embarrassment than from the fact that Cora is hitting on him. 'You know the way to my heart, don't you Cora?'

'I do what I can. Helps that I have others helping me out.' Cora taps her index finger to her temple.

He gives the young girl a soft smile.

'Who's your friend?' Ryder asks, looking past him.

'Oh, guys, this is Finn. I thought maybe you could show him what's what.'

Finn leans into Nickolas and whispers into his ear. 'Really? Treating me like the new kid at school that needs to make friends.'

He gives Finn a genuine smile, ignoring the smartass comment. 'You want to act like a kid, I'll treat you like a kid.'

Finn turns back to the group and takes a seat in one of the spare chairs.

'Hey, I'm Ryder. This is Cora and Alex.' They all raise a hand and smile.

'Uh, Finn.'

'Whatcha in for, Finn?'

'Cora. You can't just ask him that?' Alex smacks Cora's arm with the back of her hand.

Finn scratches the back of his neck. Nickolas stands to the side, aware that he's hovering around them, curious to see how Finn interacts with everyone.

'I'll go first.' Cora sits up straight, almost acting proud for sharing. 'Cora. Seventeen years old. Auditory hallucinations.'

Finn frowns.

'It means I hear voices. That's how I'm so good at hitting on Nickolas here.'

'Okay, okay,' says Nickolas, 'moving on.'

It's all fun and games, but he still has to be cautious. Patients can get emotionally attached to their doctors, nurses, or, in Nickolas's case, orderlies. He hears stories all the time of patients being taken advantage of because they're vulnerable and seek out affection from those treating or caring for them while in a facility. It's easy for rumours to spread and what is as simple as being friendly can suddenly be seen as something more.

'Fine, I'll go next. I'm Alex. Sixteen. Pica, and you're cute.'

Nickolas widens his eyes at Alex's comment.

'Ha, um, thanks but, I bat for the other team,' Finn casually replies.

Nickolas's eyebrows shoot up, reaching the top of his hairline, surprised at how carefree Finn is about announcing his sexuality to a group of strangers. He sneaks a glance at Finn, and Finn is looking towards him. Nickolas gives his attention back to the group.

'Why are the cute ones always gay?' Alex pouts, picking up the pillow and hugging it to her chest.

'Probably because men are shallow and looks are the only thing we have to work with,' Finn explains.

The group breaks out laughing but Nickolas can see Finn is serious. What they took as a joke seemed to be the redhead's way of speaking the truth from past experiences. His concern for what happened to Finn grows each time he opens up.

Finn quickly chuckles, perhaps as a way to make himself fit in and hide behind the laughter.

'Damn, cute and funny. Yep, you're totally gay.'

Finn shrugs in agreement. 'Um, pica?' He cocks a ginger eyebrow in question.

'Oh. It means I like to eat non-nutritive objects. You know, like, paperclips, cotton balls. Oh, I once swallowed a USB.'

Nickolas thumbs his bottom lip, noticing how Finn doesn't know how to respond. The redhead is out of his element which is oddly entertaining for Nickolas.

'Anyway. I'm Ryder. Twenty-one, and bulimia has ruled my life for the last five years.'

'You've been here for five years?' asks Finn.

'In and out. If not here, then other places. Some specific to the disease, others a little more forceful. Doesn't matter the treatment, I just can't seem to fight the battle in my head.'

Nickolas gives Ryder a small smile who, at the moment, is looking closer to the side of healthy. Ryder's face is still a little hollow, wrists appear fragile, but his condition was worse when he was admitted three months ago.

'So, your turn,' says Cora, tapping her knees like a drum roll.

'Finn. I'm eighteen, and they think I have bipolar disorder.'

Nickolas coughs.

Finn sighs and rolls his eyes. 'I *have* bipolar disorder.' Finn turns and looks up at him. 'Happy now?'

'You want to get out of here, don't you? You just took one step closer to the door.'

Finn's shoulders deflate, bringing his attention back to the group. All eyes are on the new kid, all without a hint of judgment, disgust, or confusion.

'Been avoiding your meds, I'm guessing.' Ryder's tone is soft, almost understanding as to why Finn would have chosen not to take them.

Finn nods and then turns to the TV. Nickolas scans the common room and notices Dot walking back in. His boss points to Eric and then thumbs over her shoulder to indicate it's his colleague's turn to go on break.

'Actually, Eric, before you go.' Dot makes her way over to the group where Nickolas is standing, Eric making his way towards them.

'Ryder, it's time for your appointment with Dr Hale. Eric here will take you.'

Ryder stands up. Nickolas reaches out to help, knowing how fragile the guy is. Ryder wobbles a little, but steadies, then releases Nickolas's arm to take Eric's and walks out of the room.

'Nickolas, would you please go to the craft corner?' Dot instructs.

'Sure.' He gives Finn a small nod of encouragement before making his way to the few patients who are enjoying getting their hands dirty. Although a part of him wants to be able to shield Finn from the many inappropriate questions Cora will send his patient's way, Finn seems the type to only answer what he feels comfortable sharing. If Cora oversteps, he is sure Finn will put her in her place.

Time passes quickly. Finn laughs once or twice, and the sound sends warmth through Nickolas's body. It sounds natural.

Is this the first time Finn has allowed himself to let go and laugh?

*

Eric walks back in from his lunch break with Ryder alongside him. Dot announces it's time for lunch. His boss begins to assist the few patients who are standing by the door patiently, wanting to make sure they get the same seat they have been sitting in for every meal, while Eric helps Ryder walk in behind them.

Nickolas pulls out the wet wipes they have on a shelf in the craft corner to clean everyone's hands before allowing them to make their way into the dining area. He keeps cleaning up, wanting to make sure the area has nothing on the floor that could be a hazard. When he sees a pair of slippered feet standing not too far from him, he looks up to see green eyes looking back at him, with a mop of unkempt red hair.

'You coming to eat with us?' asks Finn.

Nickolas straightens up, a small smirk on his face. 'Already got my one free meal for the day, Cunningham.'

'And you shared it with boring old me?'

'I never pass up the opportunity for Aiden's banana pancakes. You had nothing to do with it.'

Finn chuckles. Nickolas likes the way Finn's face lights up when he's happy. 'Guess you'll have to starve then.'

'Nah. Dorothy made some muffins that I ate on my break. I'll just grab a pizza or something when I finish my shift at three.'

'Oh.' Finn's face drops a little.

'I'll be back tomorrow in the afternoon.'

'Cool. Um, I better go get some food.'

Finn wanders off towards the dining area. Nickolas hangs back for a minute or two before joining Eric and Dot in monitoring the patients. He suddenly has the urge to stay rather than go home, where he can get out of these purple clothes that are starting to smell a little ripe, have a hot shower and get into his comfy bed.

*

Lunch goes well. Nickolas only looks over to the table that has Finn, Alex, Cora, and Ryder a total of four times in the hour they have allocated to eat. As everyone begins to return their trays, Dot does a utensil count, making sure no one has pocketed an item or broken any pieces off, while Nickolas steps out to the common room and begins setting up the chairs in a circle for group therapy. Today's session has seven, eight including the therapist. The remaining patients will be escorted back to their rooms. Once finished, Nickolas stands at the door to the dining room, reminding those who have group to take a seat, while the ones not involved make their way to the exit, awaiting Dot and Eric to escort them out.

Finn is the last to leave the dining area. The six patients are sitting in their chairs, patiently waiting for the therapist to arrive, with a seat still empty for Finn.

'Be honest. I'm not going to have to sing kumbaya or some shit like that am I?' Finn asks.

Nickolas thumbs his nose, trying to hide his smile, but a chuckle escapes his lips in defiance. 'I promise, no singing. But

I'm never around for the sessions so, in terms of what comes up, I have no idea.'

Finn rocks back and forth on his heels. 'Great.'

'Not much of a sharer?'

'Actually, us Cunninghams are probably known for sharing a little too much. I mean, three boys living in the one bedroom, you kinda learn to block things out if you know what I mean.'

Nickolas openly chuckles and he doesn't mind that Finn sees it because the smile it brings to the redhead's face is worth it. 'Look, if you don't feel like sharing today, there is always tomorrow. But maybe don't knock it till you've tried it.'

He gives Finn a small push towards the group, guiding him to an empty chair, and then makes his way to the door. Dr Hale steps through, giving Nickolas a nod as he helps the last patient waiting to be taken back to their room.

Eric is asked to stand outside the common room door while group goes ahead, just in case Dr Hale needs assistance with a patient. With the remaining patients in their rooms, Nickolas makes his way to the break room to grab himself a drink. He was so caught up with the lunch rush and preparing for group that he hadn't noticed that his other colleagues had started the afternoon shift. Nickolas walks into the break room, Sky casually enjoying one of Dot's wonderful muffins.

'Hey, Sky,' he greets her.

'Hey. Have you tried one of these? *Mmm*, so good.' Sky answers, taking another bite.

'I think three is my limit.'

His colleague rolls her eyes and then shoves the last of the muffin into her mouth.

'Can you do me a favour?' Nickolas asks.

'Sure. What's up?'

'When I leave this afternoon, can you keep an eye on Finn Cunningham? He's in room thirteen and he starts his new medication tonight. Last night was rough for him, so...'

'Sure. No problems. And before I leave, I'll ask Lydia to keep an eye on him during the night.'

'Thanks.'

He leaves it at that. Just a concerned orderly caring about the wellbeing of their patient. Nothing more. It has nothing to do with the fact that Nickolas wants to be the one keeping an eye on Finn. It will be Finn's second night in this place and the beginning of a new cocktail of medications. Medications that Finn has been avoiding for the last six months. Nickolas tells himself he's allowed to be concerned.

*

When the clock strikes three, group is finishing up and Nickolas, Dot, and Eric are ready to head home for the day. Nickolas stands at the staff area door and he spots Finn walking out of the common room. The freckled face looks up and automatically locks eyes with him before making his way over.

'Going home?' asks Finn.

'Yeah, my bed is calling for me.'

Finn slowly nods his head.

'You...you okay?'

'Oh, you know...tired.'

Nickolas doesn't push. It's not his place to know that part of Finn's recovery. What he does know is Finn isn't lying when he says he's tired. Last night wasn't easy and the first day is always exhausting because it's an information overload.

'So, ahh. Guess I'll see you tomorrow?' Finn questions.

'Yep. I'm working another double, hence the need for sleep.' Nickolas offers more information than necessary to help settle Finn's nerves.

Nodding slowly, Finn looks back down to his feet before turning to leave. Finn lightly brushes a shoulder against Nickolas's as he passes by. It's small, gentle, a simple touch that Finn probably needs. Human contact can go a long way for someone's mental health during their treatment. Nickolas waits for

Finn to enter room thirteen before he walks back to his locker to retrieve his belongings and head home.

*

The mid-afternoon sun hits Nickolas's face as he stands outside the automatic doors, taking in a breath of fresh air for the first time in over 24 hours. Jumping into his car, he throws his backpack on the passenger seat and drives home on auto-pilot. He parks in the allocated spot behind his apartment, then steps out and makes his way around the front.

The sounds of his keys jingling in the door brings Socks out to greet him. His cat rubs her face against him, purring as she walks in a figure eight around his legs.

'Hey, girl. Did you miss me or are you just hungry?'

He bends down and picks Socks up, holding her against his chest as he walks to his little kitchen to dump his backpack and keys. His cat rubs her face against his neck, and he smiles at the affection. 'Yeah, missed you too.'

Nickolas puts Socks back on the ground near her bowl and fills it with food, leaving his cat to eat as he empties the litter box. He grabs a beer from the fridge, takes note of the lack of food inside, and plonks himself down on the couch. He chugs half the beer before his feet are up on his coffee table. He feels on edge, not sexually, but as though his body is itching to move. It's the adrenaline fading after working three shifts back-to-back. He leans his head against the back of the couch, taking another swig of his beer.

The soft jingle of a bell rings in his ears as delicate paws land on his lap.

'Oomph.'

Socks kneads at his legs before curling up against his stomach.

'Sure, make yourself comfortable. Not like I wanted to take a shower or get out of my work clothes or nothin'.'

He runs his fingers through Socks's fur. The afternoon sun shining through his window causes the colour of his cat's fur to glow. It mimics a certain ginger whose hair lights up the gloominess of the patient corridor and the darkness that room thirteen brings to Nickolas's life. His mind begins to wander. Is Finn okay? Will Finn *be* okay? Will Finn handle showering with the other patients or will the extra bodies cause him to panic?

He doesn't understand why he is so fixated on Finn, more so than any other patient he has had since working there. Sure, Finn is attractive. If he had met him at a club or down the street, Nickolas would probably make a move. But that's not what has him wanting to go back and sit with Finn, have a conversation even. It's not the reason why Nickolas wants to make sure Finn gets the best treatment available so the redhead can walk out feeling like everything might end up being okay. Whatever it is that's calling out to him, Nickolas knows he needs to be careful.

3. Thursday

'No, no, no, no, no. Please! Wake up! Please, no. Don't leave me, please. HELP!'

Nickolas sits up in bed. His eyes fly open like a deer in headlights. Sweat drips down his forehead, as he wills his body to take in lungfuls of air. He's stuck in that feeling of fear and hopelessness. As his heart begins to slow down to a normal pace, he runs his hands down his face, willing his mind to forget the images that haunt his nightmares.

He jumps at the shock of Socks leaping onto the bed and landing on his legs. 'Jesus Christ. You know, if I die, no one will be around to take care of you.'

The cat stretches out her back and begins to walk closer towards him to receive her morning cuddles. He's thankful that Socks came to his aid. They say misery loves company and they're not wrong. Nickolas chooses to enjoy the company of a furry four-legged friend over someone who will bitch and moan if he forgets to grab milk on the way home or complain because he is working too much and therefore doesn't have enough time to go out and socialise as a couple. He's happy just the way things are, or so he keeps telling himself.

He lays back against his headboard and closes his eyes. His mind wants him to return to the moment before he woke up, putting him smack bang in the middle of the nightmare. Nickolas quickly opens his eyes before he sees the blood again. He hasn't had any nightmares for a while, but most likely due to the time he has been spending in room thirteen, they've returned. Like an old friend reminding him that although they have been away, they will always come back to say hello. He picks up his phone and looks at the time. It's only six a.m. Considering he has the night shift tonight, he should try to get more sleep.

Lying back down, Nickolas rolls onto his side and pulls Socks against his chest. Soft purrs begin to match his breathing. In through the nose, out through the mouth. The cat's soft vibrations mixed with her body heat give him a sense of calm. Nickolas closes his eyes and takes his mind elsewhere. He visualises himself on a beach, the warm sun beating down on him, creating the serenity of a peaceful summer's day. He takes a few steps on the sand, his toes going from the hot softness to a cooler mud-type texture from the water washing up against the sandbank. The waves come in slowly, a soft blanket of water washing over his feet before it's swept back into the ocean. Nickolas's body begins to relax, preparing to go back to sleep now that his mind is at ease.

He is still on the beach feeling calm and at peace when he suddenly feels a warm hand slip into his own, giving it a reassuring squeeze. Nickolas looks down at his hand, making sure he hasn't imagined the touch. He can see his fingers intertwined with another hand. H-A-T-E separated with someone else's fingers between each letter of his tattooed knuckles. Nickolas's eyes slowly make their way up the hand within his. Small freckles litter the skin that's as white as his, and he wants to count every single one of them. The loose-fitted shirt has a few buttons undone at the top, allowing the ocean breeze to blow the collar open a little further, and Nickolas realises he is holding the hand of a man. He's surprised, he was expecting someone else to be beside him – hoping it was someone else. The warmth from their hand grounds Nickolas. It anchors him to the sand, preventing him from jumping into the ocean and allowing it to sweep his body under the waves, away from the world and the responsibilities that are waiting for him back on land. Finding the courage, his eyes wander up the man's chest and neck till he is met with a warm smile, kind green eyes and soft red hair.

'Finn?' Nickolas asks.

'Hey, Nick.' Finn's voice is soft, smiling brightly as he says Nickolas's name, and it takes his breath away.

'What are you—?'

'I don't know, man, it's your dream.'

'This doesn't mean...I'd never...You're my patient, Finn.'

Finn squeezes his hand again. 'It's okay. Friends can hold hands too, you know.'

Nickolas is still hesitant. It's a dream and yet his subconscious is screaming at him to step back. To set boundaries. But his heart feels like it's beating for the first time in months. 'I wasn't expecting you to be here.'

'Me neither. I mean, we only just met, so I must have made a great first impression.'

'Are you always this cocky?'

'Maybe. Maybe you're just imagining me like this.'

Finn pulls Nickolas's hand slightly and leads him down the shoreline as the sun beats down on them.

'So, who were you hoping you'd see?' asks Finn.

'No one,' Nickolas lies.

'Didn't seem that way when you looked up and saw my face smiling back at you.'

'If this is my dream then why are you getting on my nerves?'

Finn laughs. 'Fine. You want me to tell you why I think you're dreaming of me?'

'Enlighten me.'

'I think we can help each other.'

Nickolas stops walking, turning to face Finn head-on.

Why am I still holding Finn's hand? I have the power to let go, don't I?

Nickolas ignores that thought and focuses on Finn's comment. 'Help each other how?'

'You're hurting, Nick. And a part of you is holding onto that pain to punish yourself.'

Nickolas finally lets go of Finn's hand, but it's so he can cross his arms over his chest.

Why did his subconscious choose Finn to tell him this?

'And me?' Finn begins to explain. 'Well, I'm hurting too. In more ways than I'm ready to admit. In ways that I can't bring myself to share with my family. But maybe a friend – someone who won't judge me or try to fix me with medication and therapy – is all I need to help move on from it all.'

'So, you're saying we can help one another...what, heal?'

'Something like that.' Finn shrugs.

Nickolas thumbs his bottom lip.

'Think about it. But I better get going.'

'Go where? This is my dream.'

'Exactly. Which means you must be ready to leave.'

Nickolas checks if the beach is still behind him, trying to determine if he's still asleep. But as he turns back towards Finn, the redhead is gone, and the ocean is slowly beginning to fade. Nickolas turns his head left and right in the hopes that he can see where Finn walked off to. The sun has vanished, and Nickolas stands in darkness with a heavy weight appearing on his head.

Nickolas wakes up to Socks lying across his face, her fur covering his eyes. He lifts his cat off and brings the ginger furball down to his chest as he slowly opens his eyes, adjusting to the late morning light seeping in through the curtains. He strokes Socks's fur, trying to make sense of his dream.

Why Finn? Sure, Nickolas cares for him, but he cares about all his patients. About their health and wellbeing. It's not like he has spoken to the guy long enough to know if anything dream Finn said was true. *Is Finn hurting?* Nickolas understands that BP can twist a person's mind and cause them pain in ways others don't understand, but the bruises...Finn can't remember what happened when the cops found him passed out. Could that be what dream Finn was referring to? Is that how he's hurting?

Socks jumps off his chest and leaves the bedroom as he sits up and leans over to retrieve his phone. 10.13 a.m. He slept for another four hours, yet the dream felt like it lasted two minutes. Nickolas's new position has his bladder screaming in protest. He groans as he stands up, not sure if he will even make it to the bathroom in time to relieve himself. Nonetheless, he holds it in until he gets to the toilet, the pressure of his bladder vanishes as the sound of a waterfall in his bathroom hits his ears.

Nickolas washes his hands and chucks on sweatpants. He stumbles out to the kitchen to make himself some food. He sits down on his couch, munching on a bowl of cereal and turns the TV on to distract his mind.

At a quarter to eleven, he figures he should probably start getting ready for work. Although he showered last night, having another will help him fully wake up from his restless night of dreams. He gets in under the spray, the hot water running down his back, soaking his hair as it flattens against his forehead. Water droplets land on his eyelashes. He brings his right hand up to his heart and traces the tattoo on his left pec muscle. Whenever he feels on edge, tracing the tattoo always seems to calm his pounding heart and racing mind. He washes quickly, not having time to dawdle since he's due back at the ward for a twelve p.m. start.

The cold air hits him as he exits the shower, goosebumps litter his skin as he runs the towel over his body to dry off. He finds a clean uniform set in his drawer, and throws it on the bed as he gets dressed in dark blue jeans, a black t-shirt and his denim jacket. He takes the uniform into the kitchen to pack into his backpack and rummages around in search of food. He finds the last frozen meal in the freezer, a tin of BBQ Pringles, and a muesli bar. He makes a note to do grocery shopping tomorrow since he'll have time before his night shift.

Nickolas is one of the few employees who doesn't mind working doubles. Everyone else has families to go home to or partners to spend time with. He doesn't mind taking on the extra work so they don't have to miss out. Sometimes he wonders if he will ever be in the position where he can say, 'Sorry, I can't work that day, I've got a date.' He shakes his head and reminds himself that he needs to actually stop working if he wants to find someone to date him. So, really, no, that day won't be coming around any time soon.

Remembering to leave food out for Socks, he fills the cat's bowl and then bends down to give her a quick scratch behind her ears and a kiss on the head.

Today's car ride seems quicker than the ones before. He doesn't speed, he gets stopped at a few traffic lights, and yet suddenly he is scanning his ID to open the boom gate to park his car. Clouds are rolling in, making the outside feel just as gloomy as inside the centre.

He walks in, the front desk occupied by Brett and Jasmine, who are talking. Nickolas tries hard not to roll his eyes, not ready to face any of the bullshit Brett will no doubt throw his way.

Jasmine looks up, doing her job as a receptionist to greet everyone who walks through the automatic doors. 'Hey, Nickolas.'

'Hey, Jasmine. Feeling better today?'

'Like a whole new person. I guess finally being in the third trimester has fixed the nausea.'

The side door buzzes, indicating it's open for Nickolas to walk through. Jasmine has one of those friendly faces that calms anyone who walks through the door. She knows how to read people, which is why Nickolas loves working with her. Jasmine can tell when he wants to keep his head down and get the job done, or when he's happy to stand around for a minute or two and chat. The receptionist also knows that Nickolas can only tolerate so much of Brett, so he's thankful that Jasmine is rushing him through, getting him away from the arrogant shit-head as quickly as possible. Nickolas steps through the door and heads straight to the lockers. Considering he was ready to punch Brett in the face on Tuesday, he just needs to avoid him for the next three hours before Brett heads home for the day. Shouldn't be too difficult.

Darren is in the locker room when Nickolas walks in and makes his way to his locker.

'Who pissed in your Cheerios this morning?' Darren asks.

'No one. Just had a shit sleep.'

'You know, the best way to sleep is with a warm body beside you.'

Nickolas holds his middle finger up and aims it over his shoulder in Darren's direction.

'Just saying, offer is on the table.'

Nickolas takes his jacket off and hangs it in his locker. He pulls his shirt over his head and throws it in his bag before replacing it with his purple cotton shirt. He kicks off his shoes and unbuttons his jeans. Nickolas pulls them off from the ankles and slips into his purple cotton pants. Yep, he looks like a walking fucking eggplant.

In the break room, he puts his food in the freezer and notices a plate of blueberry muffins sitting on the table. He takes one, eating it quickly so he can make his way toward the common room. Unfortunately, he isn't quick enough, as he's still chewing the muffin when Brett enters the break room.

Brett looks towards Nickolas, huffing in his direction. 'I thought gay guys treated their bodies like temples or some shit.'

Nickolas bites his tongue.

'Met the new patient today. Looks like just another kid that used his mental illness as an excuse to become an addict,' comments Brett.

'What?' Nickolas doesn't care that he spits crumbs onto the floor. The only new male patient they have is Finn, which means Brett's comment is aimed at his patient.

'I heard him talking to the chick who would rather eat her fork than her food about taking drugs as payment or some shit like that. I don't know. Because I didn't recognise him, he piqued my interest, but then I got bored and tuned out.'

Nothing about that sentence is comforting, especially not Brett taking an interest in Finn. He walks out of the break room and makes his way towards the common room.

Inside, Hayley and Darren are interacting with some of the patients. Sky and Dot are in the dining area, getting it ready for lunch, but Nickolas's eyes roam the room until they land on the bright red hair connected to porcelain skin that's dotted with freckles. Finn. Nickolas slowly makes his way over to his patient, curious as to why Finn is curled in on himself while sitting alone looking out the window.

'Didn't feel like sitting with your friends today?' Nickolas takes the empty chair across from Finn, whose wrists are still bandaged, and he makes a mental note to ensure they have been cleaned and rebandaged this morning.

'Watching TV for a couple of hours and sharing our feelings in a forced group therapy session doesn't make them my friends.' Finn's words have no heat in them. They are coming out slow, monotone. Almost as though Finn is daydreaming.

'Fair enough. But they sure can help the time go quickly around here. Beats watching the clouds move in the sky.' He follows Finn's line of sight, the window offering a view of the shifting black clouds

'Whatever.' Finn brings his legs closer to his chest and hisses a little, the motion seems to cause Finn discomfort.

'You okay? You hurt somewhere?'

'It's the meds. It's always the fucking meds.'

Nickolas opens his mouth to speak but Dot interrupts the room. 'You can now make your way into the dining area for lunch.'

Nickolas turns back to Finn, who hasn't moved a muscle. 'Come on, time to eat.'

'Not hungry.'

'Well, you got to eat, man. Let's go.' He stands, but Finn doesn't budge. The room is almost empty. Nickolas looks over to Dot, who is giving him a look to see if he needs assistance, but he waves his boss off. Dot walks into the dining area, leaving himself and Finn alone in the room.

Nickolas steps in front of Finn and squats down so they are at the same height. 'I get starting medication for bipolar isn't a walk in the park, but I don't want this to be any harder for you than it already is. So, I'd rather you walk in that room and take a few mouthfuls of food so no one comes back to me and instructs me to force-feed you.'

Nickolas stands back up, looks down at Finn and holds his hand out to help him rise from the chair. Finn rolls his eyes before accepting Nickolas's hand. He tries to ignore the warm electricity that shoots up his spine from the touch. It feels exactly like his dream, Finn's hand in his, giving each other strength and warmth. He gives Finn's arm a slight pull to help lift him off the chair, catching the way Finn tries to mask his pain as the redhead stands on shaky legs.

'You good to walk?'

'...'m fine.'

Considering Finn's persistence at being fine, he doesn't let go of Nickolas's hand. They take their time shuffling towards the door to the dining area. Nickolas finds the closest seat for Finn to sit in while he goes to collect a tray of food.

'What's on the menu today, Aiden?' asks Nickolas.

'Chicken and corn soup. Bread roll and chocolate pudding,' Aiden replies happily.

'Perfect,' says Nickolas.

Aiden nods toward Finn. 'He okay?'

Nickolas didn't have to turn around to see who Aiden was referring to. 'Medication side effects. Hopefully, the food will help.'

He takes the tray back over to Finn, whose eyes are on the table as the soup is placed in front of him.

'Even if you just eat the broth, it will help.' Nickolas explains.

Finn carefully picks up the plastic spoon, swirling the soup around in bowl.

'You going to count how many spoonfuls I take?'

'If I have to. But I'm going to put some trust in you while I go over to talk to Dorothy. So don't let me down.'

Nickolas steps away and finds Dot guarding the entry, watching over everyone in the room.

'He doing okay?' Dot keeps her voice low. It's never easy for patients to overhear the orderlies talking about them, even when it's their job to discuss how the patients are progressing.

'From what I can tell. This morning would have been the second dose of his medication, but it's obviously affecting him.'

'Six months being off them, it would be a shock to his system. Like starting at square one.'

Nickolas glances over at Finn, pleased to see his patient take a mouthful of soup, chicken and corn included.

'No issues during the night?' asks Nickolas.

'From what I heard, everything went smoothly. Apparently, Cora was up singing, said she had to sing goodnight to the voices in order for them to allow her to sleep. But nothing too concerning.'

Dot gives Nickolas a quick side glance.

He smiles softly at his boss and makes his way back over to Finn. The spoon is now resting on the tray.

'Not bad. You even found room for the chocolate pudding,' says Nickolas.

'If there is one thing I've learnt growing up with five siblings, you always eat the dessert first.'

'Five, wow. Looks like we both come from families that couldn't keep it in their pants.'

'Or didn't believe in birth control.'

Nickolas laughs.

'Touché. It *is* the South Side. Money would rather be spent on booze than condoms.'

Finn lets out a small chuckle.

People are already packing up, the other orderlies checking over the cutlery as patient's hand their trays in, stopping at the door to the common room for Dot to assess before letting them through.

'God, I really don't feel like more fucking therapy today,' Finn explains.

'You had a session this morning?'

'Yep. The best way to wake up in the morning is to replace your coffee with medication and a one-on-one with a shrink.'

'Ya just got to sit there. The therapist can mark your name off a list to show you're following your regimen.'

'For today maybe. If I want to get out of this joint, participation is expected.'

'Then do it.' Nickolas takes a seat in front of Finn and waits for those green eyes to look up from the table. 'Look, Finn. No one is judging you in there except yourself. So, whatever is holding you back, just remember that you'll never see any of these people ever again and all they want to do is help you so you can leave.'

'How is group therapy meant to help? We're all in here for different reasons.'

'True. But when you had your evaluation, they obviously thought you could somehow benefit from it. Maybe it'll help with socialisation, trust, hearing how others cope when they leave.'

Finn scoffs. 'If they coped so well, they wouldn't be back here.'

'Exactly. Do you want to follow in their footsteps?'

Finn looks up.

'Didn't think so. Just...give it a go, Finn. Everyone here wants you to be able to leave and live your life.'

Once again Finn and Nickolas are left sitting alone in an empty room. Nickolas stands, making his way to the exit and waits for Finn to follow him. The chairs are laid out, waiting for those in group to take a seat. Some have gone to take toilet breaks before the session begins while Darren, Hayley and Sky have begun to take those not participating back to their rooms.

He watches Finn stand and walk towards him, reaching out to grab his elbow once they meet. 'I want to get better. I just fucking hate that this is my life now.'

Nickolas helps Finn walk towards the chairs. 'Won't be like this forever. Once you find the perfect cocktail to help manage your bipolar, you can actually live a pretty boring life, just like the rest of us.'

Finn gives him a scowl.

Brett opens the door to the bathroom after one of the patients has finished and calls out to the group. 'Anyone else? If you piss your pants, you can stay in them till shower time.'

Finn leans into Nickolas. 'He's kidding, right?'

'I wish. Thankfully he finishes at three, but if he was working the afternoon shift, I wouldn't put it past him to stick to his word.'

'Jesus.'

Finn takes a seat, movements less stiff, a sign that the joint pain is starting to subside. He gives Finn a soft smile, making quick eye contact with others in the group to make sure they are also comfortable before walking out towards the patient corridor. He holds the door open for Dr Hale, who is walking towards him. Nickolas smiles at the doctor's request for Brett to leave the room before taking a seat to begin the session. As the door closes behind Nickolas, he catches green eyes watching him leave as he passes Hayley, who is on door duty.

*

Nickolas makes his way towards the infirmary, walking like a man on a mission as he ignores those that he passes. He knocks on the door and is pleased to see Lexi isn't with a patient.

'Nickolas, hey,'

'Hey. Ah, can I ask you something about a patient's medications?'

'Sure.' Lexi points to the chair Finn sat in only yesterday. Nickolas accepts, thinking over how much Finn's behaviour has already changed since sitting in this chair.

'Finn, Finn Cunningham. Bipolar disorder.' He watches Lexi type the name into the computer. 'Just want to know what side effects he may experience from his medication,'

'Is he showing any signs?'

'It looked like joint pain when I saw him before lunch. He seemed to be cringing when he moved, but I'm not sure of the medications he has been prescribed.'

Lexi looks back to the computer, types a few things in and clicks the mouse a couple of times. 'Looks like they have started him on quetiapine as his antipsychotic. Dosage isn't as high as if they had him on lithium, but my guess is it's because he's been unmedicated for six months, so they want to build his tolerance back up. Ah, they have him on sertraline as his antidepressant, olanzapine for his mood stabiliser and B12 for energy.'

Nickolas has no idea what the drugs are, but he does understand their usage when it comes to treating bipolar. 'Okay. And side effects?'

'The list is endless. But I suppose the most common are dizziness, weakness, vomiting, joint pain, loss of appetite, and tremors. You have agitation, insomnia, or sleepiness. Would you like me to keep going?' Lexi turns back to Nickolas with a smile.

'No, no. It's okay. Just handy to know what to look out for, you know.'

'Wanting to know so you can help is a lot more than others would do. Let me know if he shows any signs. Some will pass once his body has adjusted, but if they don't, I'll speak to his therapist, and she may suggest adjusting the dosage or the drug itself.'

'Yeah, okay. Oh, and did anyone bring him in to get his bandages changed today?'

'No. Not yet.'

'Right. I'll bring him by after his shower.' He stands up, making his way to the exit when Lexi calls out to him. He turns back around, but doesn't step into the room.

'How are you doing? Sleeping okay?'

'Better. Had another nightmare last night. Just when I think I'm moving past them, they come rushing back like the plague.' He scratches the back of his neck, feeling vulnerable being so honest with his feelings.

'It's to be expected. During the day, your mind is busy, it doesn't have the time to be reminded of things. But once you close your eyes; actually stop, your mind has time to go back and think over everything. Triggers, memories. Hence the saying, "mind of its own".'

Nickolas scuffs his shoe on the floor and looks down at the invisible rock he pretends to kick.

'I can prescribe you something if you need help sleeping. But sometimes the easiest way to calm the mind is to let go of what you're holding onto.'

He sniffs, thumbing at his nose. 'Thanks, Doc. I better get back out there.'

He makes his way back down the patient corridor, heading to the break room to grab a drink. He walks past Ethan's room, taking a peek inside to make sure everything is okay, when he stops in his tracks. Nickolas generally leaves the patients to enjoy their time alone in their room, especially since Ethan doesn't participate in group therapy and it seems all the alters are currently at bay. But the sight of bruises around Ethan's arm catches Nickolas's attention. They're almost high enough that the sleeve from the green shirt could cover them, but when Ethan stretches out to pick up a book, the sleeve rise just enough for Nickolas to see them. If there is one thing he can spot, it's a bruise trying to be hidden from others.

He gently knocks on the door, making sure to get Ethan's attention before stepping into the room. 'Hey. Thought I'd check in, make sure everything is going okay.'

'Hey. All's good. Currently have everyone asleep so I have the whole room to myself.' Ethan's humour is a coping mechanism that he uses to help accept his condition. Nickolas admires the way Ethan can act as though sharing his body with four other personalities that can take over at the drop of a hat is as normal as shaking someone's hand.

'I was never big on having roommates. I prefer to live on my own too, ya know.' He takes another step closer and crouches down, not wanting to look dominating as he asks his next question. 'Hey man, how'd you get that bruise on your arm?'

Ethan looks down and pulls at the left sleeve, no doubt trying to cover what has already been seen. 'Oh, I'm not sure. Woke up after one of my alters took over and suddenly had it.'

'You sure? I mean, I didn't notice it on Tuesday and since then, you've been yourself.'

'I'm pretty sure.'

Nickolas stands up, not wanting to push the subject. If he has learnt anything from his experience working here, it's that trust comes from being patient and showing that he cares.

'Okay. Well, just know that you can talk to me if you want. If—if someone did that, then we should know, so it doesn't happen again,' Nickolas casually states.

Ethan nods in understanding, and that's all Nickolas needs. He'll keep an eye out when he sees Ethan around the other patients, though he hopes Ethan will talk to him before anything goes too far.

*

Nickolas unlocks the door to the employee area, making his way towards the break room for a much-needed cup of coffee while most of the patients are in group. He walks in and sees that Dot is already there, pulling a water bottle from the fridge.

'Great muffins today, Dot.' Nickolas can't pour the coffee quick enough, tempted to forgo the mug and tip it straight down his throat.

'Help yourself to more. Less for me to tempt myself with.' Dot smiles while patting her stomach.

'I thought that's the benefit of getting old. You can just let yourself go and not care how you look.'

'Sure. If by "getting old" you mean dying at fifty-five of a heart attack. If anything, you need to watch what you eat more as you get older than when you're younger.'

'That's some real Benjamin Button crap right there.'

Dot laughs. 'Jessica called today. I just got off the phone with her.'

Nickolas takes a sip from his cup, keeping his eyes on Dot.

'Wasn't much I could share besides letting her know Finn is on his medication and slowly adjusting to it.'

He brings his cup down and looks at the black liquid. 'I introduced him to some other patients. Hopefully, it might help him feel a little less alone.'

'I noticed.' Dot's words make Nickolas look up, a small smile on her face. 'Just remember, he is one out of fifteen patients we have here. They all need your help – some more than others, I know. But just make sure you're helping for the right reasons.'

'And what might those be.' His words have a little more venom in them than he would like to admit, especially when talking to Dot.

'Just don't get too attached. Finn needs to help himself and if he knows you'll come to his aid whenever he cries for it, he won't learn to stand on his own.' Dot gives his bicep a gentle squeeze and then walks out of the room.

He hates to admit it, but Dot is right. If Finn had screamed to be excused from group, Nickolas would have escorted his patient out without a second thought. But he'd then sit Finn down and try to help him process why leaving seemed necessary and hope that, come tomorrow, he could convince Finn to try again. Maybe what Dot said is true, but Nickolas would do the same for any of these patients. At least that's what he tells himself as he makes his way back out into the patient corridor.

*

Nickolas steps out of room ten after helping a patient breathe through a panic attack. As he leaves, he keeps the door open knowing if he closes the patient off from everyone, it won't help the situation. He steps into the corridor, accidentally bumping into Brett.

'Watch it. I know taking it up the ass makes it hard to walk, but can you at least try not to knock anyone over while you're at it?' chides Brett.

'Sorry. I have a habit of just walking through dog shit when I see it in front of me.' Nickolas gives a polite smile, motioning his hand in front of him, giving way for Brett to continue walking while Nickolas stands by and waits.

'Whatever, homo. I'm done for the day.' Brett puts his key card to the door to open the entry to the back rooms, and Nickolas can't help but give Brett the finger as the scumbag walks through the door. As the common room door opens, Nickolas quickly puts his arm down beside him as he catches Finn eyeing him off with a cocked eyebrow and a questioning look. He doesn't move as the patients make their way out and back into their rooms. Finn slowly walks towards him.

'Look, I know I was a bit of a dick before, but I don't think I deserved a 'fuck you' behind my back,' says Finn.

'Ha, ha. That wasn't aimed at you.'

'Really? Because I don't see anyone else in the corridor, and I'm pretty sure I'm not *that* drugged up.'

'Brett just left.'

'Ah. "Stay in your own piss" guy?'

'Among other things.'

'Then he deserves it.' Finn looks down, scuffing slippered feet against the floor.

The other patients are now moving close around them.

'Thanks. For pushing me or whatever,' says Finn.

'Just doing my job. Did it help?' asks Nickolas.

'I mean, I didn't share if that's what you're asking. But listening is just as good.'

Nickolas nods. 'It's a start.'

Darren walks by and Nickolas feels hungry eyes checking him out. Unfortunately, Finn also notices the unwanted attention from his colleague.

'Guess I better let you get back to it,' says Finn.

His patient walks into room thirteen and closes the door. Nickolas could easily walk in there to explain what just happened with Darren, but he doesn't.

*

Nickolas, Dot and Darren start collecting everyone from their rooms right before five p.m., asking them to make their way towards the dining area for dinner. Nickolas knocks on Finn's door, waiting a few seconds before entering as he does with every patient. He steps in. The room is empty. His heart begins to race as panic sets in. He calms the second a body walks out of the bathroom attached to the room. Finn is wiping wet hands on grey sweatpants to dry them, surprised to see him in the room.

'Sorry. I knocked but you mustn't have heard me.' He takes a deep breath to calm himself down before continuing. 'Uh, anyway, it's dinner time.' He points a thumb over his shoulder to the door. He waits for Finn to exit before walking out behind him.

'Finn!' Cora calls out.

Cora and Alex each take one of Finn's arms and link it with their own, chatting along with the redhead as they head towards the common room and into the dining area.

Why does he suddenly feel jealous? He shakes it off as he takes Ryder's arm to help walk the patient to the dining area.

Nickolas looks around, pleased to see that all the patients are settled. They're all eating, talking amongst themselves or minding their own business. The smell of the chicken pasta bake is making Nickolas salivate. He glances at Finn a few times, noticing only half of his meal has been eaten and catches the soft smile on Finn's face from talking with Cora, Alex and Ryder. Ryder's plate shows all the pasta eaten with a pile of cheese to the side, most likely scraped off to lessen the intake of calories. He looks back at Finn whose face is suddenly pale, the smile is gone, and before Nickolas can go over and ask if Finn is okay, he's leaning over the side of the table, puking dinner onto the dining room floor.

The room goes silent. A few patients groan in disgust, but most are just curious. Nickolas acts fast, grabbing a bucket from the kitchen area and bringing it to Finn's side. He crouches down beside his patient, making sure to avoid the vomit on the floor as he places the bucket in Finn's arms, then rubs circles over his back.

'Hey, it's okay. Let it out. I got you.'

Darren is beside him, cleaning up the mess on the floor. Dot is asking for everyone to get back to their food while Nickolas attends to Finn. How anyone could keep eating after seeing what their food looks like coming back up, he has no idea, but he knows Finn would prefer not to have the attention of everyone in the room. Finn stops vomiting for a moment. A few tears have dried on his pale cheeks from the lack of oxygen getting into his lungs, causing his green eyes to water.

'Come on, let's get you to your room,' says Nickolas.

On shaky legs, Finn stands up. Nickolas holds Finn close to his side, supporting his weight while holding the bucket to his chest. Dot holds the door open for them and then scurries ahead to unlock the common room door. The soft nod from his boss is all the permission he needs to take care of Finn and not worry about the other patients, knowing Dot and Darren will handle it. Finn's room isn't too far down the corridor and thankfully, the door is still open.

Nickolas carefully sits Finn on the bed just as the redhead hurls into the bucket. At this stage, it's more liquid than substance, but Nickolas can hear the strain as Finn heaves into the bucket. Nickolas walks into the bathroom to grab some paper towel and wets it under the sink with cold water. He brings it back to Finn and dabs it across his sweaty forehead.

Finn looks weak, so Nickolas grabs the bucket before it slips from Finn's fingers.

Finn lays down on his side, green eyes closing from exhaustion. 'Fuck, I hate this.'

'I know.'

'No, you don't. You have no idea what it's like.'

Finn's voice breaks and the sound of it tears Nickolas apart. He pulls the blankets over Finn's body, noticing how he's trembling. He takes the bucket to the bathroom, empties it into the toilet and rinses it out before bringing it back to Finn's side.

'You know, you'd think having a job like this would involve cleaning a lot of vomit. But honestly, it's been a while for me,' Nickolas states.

'Gee, thanks. I'm honoured.'

'No better way to get to know someone than to clean their vomit.'

'I don't know. Wiping someone's ass seems pretty friendly to me.'

Nickolas chuckles, thumbing his nose.

A soft smile appears on Finn's face, though it's still pale, which is saying something since Finn is usually as pale as a vampire. Finn's eyes look softer than before, a sign that the vomiting may be subsiding.

'Well, it's still early days. Never say never,' says Nickolas.

Finn groans and turns into the pillow. Nickolas suspects from embarrassment more so than pain.

He reaches out, moving a strand of Finn's matted hair and looks into cloudy green eyes. 'Try to rest. I'll come back to see you when it's time for a shower.' Nickolas doesn't remove his hand from Finn's forehead. His fingers gently stroke the wavy red hair.

Finn looks up at him, eye contact never breaking. 'Okay,' Finn whispers.

Nickolas leaves, not turning back because one look at Finn will make him want to stay at his bedside until he's fallen asleep. He looks at the time on his watch. It's 6.28 p.m., and showers are scheduled for seven. He makes his way to the front desk. Bypassing Jasmine, he grabs the patient folder and adds notes to Finn's file for the therapist to look over tomorrow. Knowing it's a side effect, the doctor may consider swapping Finn's medication after having such a strong reaction.

Dot catches him coming out of the employee door and sends him off to eat. He protests, saying he can wait, knowing that it's almost seven o'clock, but his boss assures him that Darren can handle the patients.

'What about Finn?' Nickolas asks.

'Go eat, then you can help Finn once everyone else is back in their rooms. The poor boy could use the rest.'

He nods, the door closing behind him as he makes his way back towards the break room. He grabs his frozen meal, chucks it in the microwave, and watches his food spin as the minutes count down. Nickolas scoffs the food down. He still has time before his break is over, but he uses it to make his way towards the dining area, the need to help Finn at the forefront of his mind.

Aiden is putting the last of the dishes away as Nickolas walks through the kitchen doors.

'Hey, man. Dinner was good tonight,' says Nickolas.

'Hope so. When I saw that guy puke, I panicked that I had undercooked the chicken,' Aiden explains.

'Nah, it's all good. His medication isn't agreeing with him.'

Aiden gives Nickolas a nod.

'I was hoping you might have something that could help settle his stomach. Maybe some plain crackers or ginger ale,' Nickolas asks.

'I'm pretty sure I do. Give me a second.'

Nickolas waits by the door as Aiden heads out back. He comes back into view a few minutes later and hands Nickolas a couple of packets of crackers.

'Thanks, Aiden.'

'No problems. Hope he's feeling better.'

'Me too.'

Nickolas heads back to Finn's room, the corridor feeling eerie. Gently opening the door in case Finn is asleep, he pokes his head inside and is pleased to see Finn's eyes are closed, his breathing shallow and even. He leans against the wall opposite Finn's bed and slides down, using it to support himself as he brings his knees up to his chest. He sits, rests, and waits for Finn to wake.

Nickolas thinks back to how he got here. A kid from the South Side with tattoos on his knuckles, designed to scare those around him, or perhaps more so to help protect him in some way. He took drugs as a way to cover the pain caused by his father and drank alcohol to spark the fire inside himself when he needed the strength to fight back. He had hurt people because he was afraid or because he was told to. And now, his main focus in life is to help people who probably feel just as scared as he once did. He has more blood on his hands than he would like to admit, some of it justifiable, but most belonged to innocent people who found themselves in the wrong place at the wrong time. Will the guilt of his past ever go away? Maybe he doesn't want it to. If his subconscious can manifest Finn within his dreams, telling Nickolas how he is holding onto the pain of his past, of his mistakes, of what happened in this exact room, as a way to keep punishing himself, then deep down that must be what Nickolas is doing without even realising it. He takes in a deep breath. Does he deserve to no longer feel all this guilt? Has he paid his dues?

'Anyone ever tell you it's creepy to watch someone sleep?'

Nickolas shakes his head, focusing on Finn's groggy words and pushing his thoughts into the back of his mind.

'No. But that's mostly because I sneak out before they catch me.'

'Typical.' Finn groans as he tries to move.

'How you feeling?'

'Like I ran a marathon that I didn't prepare for.'

'Think you can stand?'

'Why?'

'Hot shower might help your muscles. And you kinda smell like sour cheese.'

Finn and Nickolas both laugh.

Nickolas pushes himself up off the wall to stand, making his way over towards Finn. 'Come on, tough guy.' He snakes his hand under Finn's armpit, pulling gently until Finn is sitting. He lets go, giving his patient a moment to adjust while he goes to retrieve the fresh clothes left by one of the day shift orderlies.

He bends down to wrap his arm around Finn's waist and helps him stand from the bed.

It's a little past eight o'clock. This is the hour the patients get before lights out. The privacy Finn will have in the showers will hopefully be refreshing after having everyone watch what happened in the dining room. They step into the room, the air still humid from the multiple showers that were running not too long ago.

'You right to undress yourself?' Nickolas slowly lets go, not wanting to step away too quickly in case Finn needs to hang onto him.

'If you want to take my clothes off, all you got to do is ask.'

Nickolas freezes, Finn's words catching him off guard.

'Sorry. I—I know you're trying to help. I just hate feeling so...'

'Vulnerable?'

'...something like that.'

Finn begins to undress. Nickolas keeps his distance but is ready in case Finn loses his balance. As Finn takes his boxers off, Nickolas keeps his head held high and makes sure his eyes stay level with his patient's head. Finn shuffles forward and turns on the shower. Nickolas takes a seat on the bench, once again putting Finn's clean clothes to the side and the dirty ones in the bag.

'Can I take these off?' Finn calls out.

Nickolas looks up, his eyes landing on Finn's torso. He notices for the first time a tattoo on Finn's ribcage, what looks to be a phoenix rising from ashes. Nickolas scans down the small trail of peach fuzz going from Finn's navel to pubic bone and swallows. He knows where that hair leads because Finn shoved it in his face only yesterday. Nickolas has Finn's gorgeous dick and trimmed ginger pubes burnt into his mind. He forces himself to look back up at Finn's face, red hair almost a dark brown under the spray. Water droplets drip down golden eyelashes and under any other circumstances, Nickolas would jump up and join Finn in a heartbeat. Instead, he pulls himself together and sees his patient holding up bandaged wrists, now wet from the water.

'Oh, yeah. We were meant to get them changed earlier. You can—you can take them off.' Scratching the back of his neck he looks down at his shoes. 'Pull yourself together, Nickolas,' he whispers to himself. 'The, ah, the bruises are almost gone.' Nickolas calls out.

'Forgot I had them since I don't see them.'

Nickolas thinks that's a lie, but that's for Finn to live with, not him.

'Fuck.' Finn places a hand on the tiled wall.

Nickolas stands up. 'You okay?'

'Ye—yeah. Feelin' a little dizzy though.'

He picks up Finn's towel. 'Come on. Let's get you back to your room.'

Nickolas makes his way forward as Finn turns off the water. He holds out the towel for his patient to take, only for Finn to place a hand on his shoulder for support.

'Fuck, I feel like I have the world's worst hangover but didn't even get to enjoy the drinking,' says Finn.

'We better get some water into you. Besides, you're due for your medication.'

With the towel wrapped around Finn's waist, Nickolas helps him walk back towards the bench. Finn sits down to dry himself off, only standing when needing to put boxers and sweatpants on. Once fully dressed, Nickolas stands by Finn's side, offering support as they walk out.

Nickolas knocks on the door to the infirmary and is surprised when he doesn't see Lexi sitting at the desk. It takes him a moment to remember that Dr Murphy is their night shift doctor.

'Can I help you?' says Dr Murphy.

'I need the blisters on his wrists to be examined.' Nickolas says and guides Finn to the chair, who is now hanging onto him like life-support.

'Patient's name?'

'Finn. Finn Cunningham,' Nickolas clarifies.

Dr Murphy types Finn's name into the computer before assisting in any way. If Lexi were here, she'd make sure Finn's needs were met first, then deal with the paperwork. Nickolas bites his tongue as he waits.

'Nickolas...' His name falls from Finn's lips.

He crouches down beside Finn, a gentle hand on his patient's knee. 'I'm here, hey.'

Finn opens his eyes, squinting from the bright light in the room. ''m gonna be sick.'

Nickolas snatches a tray close by and shoves it under Finn in record time. The tray isn't big enough, causing the excess vomit to land on the floor and on Nickolas's shoes.

'Are you kidding me?' Dr Murphy spins around on his chair, repulsed at the sight.

''m sorry.' It's barely a mumble, but Nickolas makes out Finn's apology.

'Why the hell is he vomiting everywhere?'

'Gee, maybe because of the medication you lot have him on,' Nickolas bites back. 'You're the doctor. Maybe if you hadn't spent the last five minutes reading his damn file and just done what I asked, I could have taken him back to his room to rest and possibly prevent him from throwing up all over your damn floor.' Nickolas wants to throw in a few profanities, but he can tell Dr Murphy is the type who would happily report his ass for language used towards a superior. Instead, he stands beside Finn, whose head has lolled to the side and is resting against Nickolas's rib cage, as Dr Murphy takes Finn's wrists and gives them a quick examination before letting go.

'They're fine. I'll put some cream on them again, but leave them out to air rather than wrap them – they'll heal quicker.' The curtness in his voice makes Nickolas ball his hand into a fist.

'You want to maybe help him with the vomiting and dizziness too?'

The doctor doesn't even look up to address Nickolas's question, focused on slapping the cream onto Finn's wrists and getting them out of the room.

'All part of the adjustment. He has to ride it out, but if it doesn't ease up, then we'll consider changing his medications.'

'Awesome. Swap one side effect for another. Great help.' Nickolas gives the doctor the okay symbol with his hand to replace the middle finger he'd rather shove in Dr Murphy's face.

'Here. Take care of this.' Nickolas shoves the vomit-filled tray into the doctor's hands so he can help Finn stand. Side by side, they walk back to Finn's room. It must look as though Nickolas is carrying his drunk friend, and in another life, maybe that could have been them. But in this life, Finn is suffering, and the medication that is supposed to make things easier is taking a toll on his body.

'Come on Finn, we're almost there,' he encourages.

'Spin-ning.'

'I know. Just a little further.'

Nickolas opens Finn's door and uses the last of his strength to get him sitting on the bed. A paper cup with pills and a small cup of water sits on the floor. Lydia must have dropped them off while Finn was in the shower. He suspects Dot filled Lydia in on where he was before going home for the night.

'Finn, try and sit up for me for a few more minutes, okay?' says Nickolas, before he goes to the bathroom, wets some paper towel under the tap, and walks back to wipe the vomit still on the corner of Finn's mouth. Once it's gone, he grabs the water and pills, bringing them up to Finn's mouth while keeping his hand on his shoulder to steady him.

'Okay, now I need you to take these and have some water. It'll help,' Nickolas explains.

Finn thankfully obliges. Nickolas has no idea if another dose of medication will help or make it worse, but at least Finn has the pills in his system. As Finn sips his water, the lights in the room go out. It must be nine o'clock. Nickolas is left standing in front of Finn, using the light from the corridor shining through the window in the door to help him see his surroundings. He takes the cup of water away from Finn and leaves what's left of it on the floor beside the bed.

'Lights out. Time for you to rest.' Nickolas gently manoeuvres Finn to lay down, green eyes already closing. As Finn's head hits the pillow, Nickolas crouches by his patient's side, gently rubbing Finn's arm to soothe him.

'Try and get some rest. I'll check on you in an hour.'

Nickolas doesn't move straight away. The calmness of the dark room and the soft shallow breaths coming from Finn drifting off to sleep bring a sense of comfort to Nickolas. His eyes scan over Finn's body, his hands reaching for the blanket at the end of the bed to place over the fragile boy. Nickolas heads for the door and slips out.

Letting out a deep breath, Nickolas walks straight to the door to the break room so he can get a drink and have a moment to himself.

'There you are!' says Lydia, the booming voice almost hurts his eardrums.

'Fuck! What do you want?' Nickolas scolds.

'Nothing. I just haven't seen you.'

'You've been here for an hour. You have all night with me, so I think you'll survive.'

'Whoa! Alright, grumpy cat. No need to jump on the defence.'

Nickolas grabs a fresh cup and fills it with the steaming hot coffee. 'Shit, sorry. Just, long day.' He takes a seat at the table with Lydia and reaches for the last muffin.

'Dorothy told me you were helping that new patient. Finn, is it?'

He nods his head as he swallows the sweet fluffy goodness of Dot's baking. 'His medication has a list of side effects a mile long, and that's only for one drug. He's on three, plus the vitamins.'

'How'd you find that out?'

'Asked Lexi.'

He takes another bite of the muffin, ignoring the look on Lydia's face. Okay, so maybe he has never looked into what medications a patient has been prescribed. He decides to move on and not overthink it. He finishes his food and, not wanting to be scrutinised by Lydia any further, picks up his coffee and walks to the front to greet Sam. He rubs his neck to relieve some of the tension.

'Hey old man, how's it all looking?' Nickolas asks.

'Quiet. Which is generally good. But you never know in a place like this,' says Sam.

'Night's still young.'

'Don't I know it.'

Nickolas takes a sip of his coffee and grabs Finn's file. He makes additional notes about the dizziness and continued vomiting so the therapist and doctor can look over it when they see Finn tomorrow and puts the file back.

'Why do you smell like sour milk?' Sam looks Nickolas over, eyes zeroing in on the white marks on Nickolas's shoes.

'Shit. Forgot to clean them. Sorry, man.'

'You mind doing that, then? Not even a mouse would like the smell of that.'

'Whatever. Hey, did Dot leave any notes for me?'

'No, no note. She said something about checking on room thirteen for you in the morning though.'

Nickolas nods and leaves. He makes sure to always leave a spare change of clothes and shoes in his locker in case bodily fluids land somewhere on him. Thankfully it's not something that happens frequently. No vomit landed on his clothes; he's still a nice shade of purple with no white stains. Jesus, the jokes Darren would make if that ever happened. He unlaces his Timberlands and shoves them in his locker, pulling out the old pair of Converse he keeps in there. He'll clean his shoes when he gets home, before his shift tomorrow night. His body sags, the cry for sleep calling to him. He glances at his watch: it's been forty-five minutes since lights out, long enough that he can go check on the patients and, of course, check on Finn.

Making his way back out to the corridor, he passes the break room as Lydia makes her way out, almost colliding with one another.

'Oh, hey. Wasn't sure where you were so I was going to do the rounds,' Lydia explains.

'It's fine. Keep studying. I'll do this one,'

Lydia smiles at him and spins on her toes, heading back to the pile of books. He heads out into the quiet corridor and starts at the closest room. Completing the hourly room inspections is simple: quickly look in each window and make sure patients are sleeping or lying down. The main focus is to ensure no one is agitated or doing something they aren't supposed to. That's why he sometimes checks before that hourly mark; it allows him to catch patients off guard that may be keeping track of the time.

He makes it to the end of the first row of rooms, nothing concerning grabbing his attention. Crossing the corridor, he makes his way down, inspecting the remaining rooms, pleased to see that it might be an easy night for them all. When he gets to Finn's room, he walks past it to look in on rooms fourteen and fifteen first. Satisfied with what he sees, he makes his way back to room thirteen and, unlike the rest, he unlocks the door, quietly walking inside as he closes the door behind him.

'Been an hour already?' Finn's voice breaks through the silence.

'Close enough. Wasn't sure if you were asleep or not.'

'Were you planning on watching me sleep some more? That's a little too Edward Cullen for my taste.'

'Who?'

Finn chuckles.

Nickolas makes his way over to the bed, crouching down so he is eye to eye with Finn who is lying on his side. 'How you feeling?'

'Dizziness has stopped and no more vomiting, so that's something.'

Nickolas can hear the hesitance in Finn's voice. 'But?'

Finn pulls one hand out from under his armpit, trying to hold it straight in front of himself only for it to tremble mid-air. 'The tremors have kicked in.'

The concentration on Finn's face, no doubt trying to focus enough to stop the tremors, saddens Nickolas. He reaches out, placing his left hand under Finn's, their palms touching, while his right hand rests on top. He holds their hands in mid-air, Finn's still trembling between his, while gently rubbing his thumb on top of Finn's hand.

'It's okay,' Nickolas whispers.

Finn's face softens, and his eyes no longer show frustration at not having control over his body.

Nickolas brings Finn's hand down to the bed and doesn't let go.

'There was a reason I stopped taking my meds, Nickolas.'

Nickolas waits. He knows from experience that things are always easier to say in the dark, a way to hide the shame, fear and guilt.

'I don't like how they stop me from feeling and yet make me feel too much at the same time,' explains Finn. 'They make me numb; all my emotions are gone, and I'm just this shell of a person. I have no control over my body, like—like someone else is pulling the strings. The tremors keep me awake when all I want to do is sleep, and when I tell my brain to make them stop, they just get worse.'

Finn sounds exhausted. Nickolas gives Finn's hand a gentle squeeze. A cloud moves across the night sky, allowing moonlight to shine into the dark room and illuminate Finn's face. A soft smile appears on the redhead's face. Nickolas likes to see Finn smile. It makes Finn's eyes sparkle a little and Nickolas can tell that a true smile from Finn would light up his whole face and everyone else in the room. Finn squeezes his hand in return. As the clouds once again cover the moon, Nickolas's eyes adjust to the darkness. He pulls his hands away, raising his left hand to push Finn's fringe off his face before gently combing his fingers through his red hair. Nickolas's hand trails down to the back of Finn's head, holding it in place as their eyes lock onto one another.

'It gets better. I'm not saying it's going to be easy, but you have people here to support you through it. Your family...none of us want you to have to suffer. And what's happening right now will pass.'

'What if I can't wait that long?'

'You're stronger than you think, Finn. These side effects, they don't last forever. Your body adjusts to the medications, you balance out, and you can go on living your life. Having bipolar doesn't define who you are.' He slowly pulls his hand away, letting his words sink in. 'If you feel hungry, I was able to get some dry crackers for you. You were asleep when I brought them in, so I've left them on the floor near the cup of water.' Nickolas points to them on the floor, hoping Finn can make them out with the little light they have to work with. 'Tomorrow is a new day. Get some sleep.'

'Wait.'

Nickolas hasn't even had a chance to stand up before Finn calls out to him.

'Will you...can you please stay here? Till I fall asleep?'

Nickolas shouldn't. Lydia might wonder what's taking him so long and come looking for him. But he can't say no to Finn, not when this boy before him sounds so small, so desperate. Nickolas sits on his ass and turns, so his back is up against the wall. They are no longer facing one another, but from where Finn is lying, he'll be able to see Nickolas's knees pulled up to his chest, that he's there, waiting, just like Finn asked.

Nickolas doesn't speak. He sits and listens to Finn softly breathing in and out, so he can pinpoint the moment his patient has fallen asleep. He traces the tattoos on his knuckles, running his fingers over the scars that litter his hands. The memories come back to him, reminding him of what caused each one to appear and mark their claim on his skin. As he sits in the dark, alone with his thoughts, it dawns on Nickolas that the panic he always feels when he's had to spend any amount of time in this room is simply gone. He's somehow found the courage to disconnect this room from the tragedy that took place in it, his mind now claiming it as the room that belongs to Finn. Nickolas wants this room to feel like a safe space for his patient. A place for Finn to take comfort in when everything outside of the room becomes too much to handle.

Despite the nightmare Nickolas had woken up from only this morning, when he walks past this room, he no longer goes cold with fear. No flashbacks invade his mind as he walks over the threshold. No, instead he opens the door with the hope of seeing Finn better than he was the day before. He looks forward to the conversations they may have, even if it's as small as discussing how Finn is feeling.

Could his dream be right? Could he and Finn help one another heal? Dream Finn wasn't wrong. Nickolas has been holding onto the pain to punish himself, but if he lets go of that feeling, of the guilt and regret, then he has nothing left, and he isn't ready to do that. But he is ready to let go of this room, and as he releases a deep breath, allowing a small piece of that weight to unclench itself from around his heart, he hears Finn let out a quiet snore. With the knowledge that Finn is sound asleep and safe, Nickolas quietly slips out and joins Lydia for the remainder of the night.

4. Friday

By seven o'clock the next morning, Nickolas is back home accepting purrs of love from Socks. He throws his keys and bag onto the kitchen countertop, careful not to trip over Socks, who's weaving in between his legs as he walks away from the front door.

'Okay, okay. C'mere, gorgeous.' He lifts up his cat, smiling as the furball rubs her head in the crook of his neck, purring louder now that he is giving her attention. He never saw himself owning an animal, let alone a cat. He figured if he was ever going to get a pet, he'd end up with a Staffordshire Bull Terrier or a German Shepherd. But the day Nickolas went to the pound, he had to walk past the cats in their cages to get to the dogs further in the back, and the minute his eyes landed on the little body curled into itself, head sleeping against the cage door, ginger fur all tussled with her adorable little black paws, Nickolas fell in love. He figured that with his hours, a cat would be easier to take care of since they are more self-sufficient than a dog.

They opened the cage for him, and he carefully placed his hand near a tiny black nose so she could sniff it and decide how to proceed. He moved slowly, cautious of the cat's hesitancy towards a stranger coming close. The last thing Nickolas wanted was to walk away with a scratched-up hand and have it stinging all day while he worked.

'She was dropped off a few days ago,' said the shelter volunteer. 'Someone found her in a box in an alley. She seems to be okay, and based on her size, I'd say she's only a few months old.'

The kitten didn't seem happy about being interrupted from her sleep, but was curious about his hand. The cat stretched its neck out, not wanting to uncurl herself from the warm position in the corner. Sniffing his hand, the ginger fur ball was soon rubbing her face against his fingertips. Nickolas smiled, his heart warm after being cold and empty for so long. 'I'll take her.'

He slowly reached forward with his left hand and gently picked up the kitten, holding her in his arms and bringing her close to his chest. He went to the pound searching for a pet to compensate for the loss in his life, which is not always the smartest choice when committing to the responsibility of an animal. However, as the kitten snuggled her head into the crease of his elbow, Nickolas knew he was making the right decision.

Now, five months later, Socks – named purely for the black paws that contrast against her ginger fur – is the only lady in Nickolas's life, and Socks uses that to her full advantage.

'What do you think? Should we catch up on some sleep or should I get all the errands done first and then sleep before work tonight? Hmm.'

Socks leaps out of his arms, landing gracefully on the kitchen countertop near his bag, and paws at his keys.

'You're right, should probably go grocery shopping before we starve to death, and you're forced to eat me.'

Socks jumps off the countertop and makes her way towards the food bowl.

'Well, I guess that settles it.'

He fills the bowl with some biscuits and then heads to his bedroom to retrieve his basket of dirty laundry. His apartment came with a washer and dryer that took up half the space in the bathroom, but he preferred it over the communal laundry rooms most apartments have in the basement. He puts on a load of dark purple tops and pants, then grabs his Timberlands from his backpack and places them on top of the washer to remind himself to clean Finn's vomit off them before his shift tonight.

Nickolas makes his way back towards the kitchen, does a scan of his cupboards and fridge while making a list in his head of the things he'll need, then picks his keys back up to leave.

'If I'm not back within an hour, call for help. You know the neighbour will come banging if you meow loud enough.' He bends down and scratches behind Socks's ears before leaving the apartment.

The supermarket is only walking distance away, but since he'll need more than just the essentials, he takes his car. Nickolas jumps back in behind the steering wheel and just like before, his body drives on autopilot, knowing where to go without even having to think about it. He slows down as he comes to a red light. While he waits for it to turn green, he wonders if this life he's living could even be called *living*, or if he is merely a character in someone else's story. It's a strange thought, but how could Nickolas think differently when he looks at what his life has become. His existence is so routine that it's almost robotic. He works fourteen days straight before he gets only two days off. His life consists of work and then going home to sleep. He eats, visits the grocery store, and then heads back to work to do it all over again. If he has the time or the energy, he might make a trip to the gym, but nothing else has a place in his life. The light turns green and he accelerates, a burst of adrenaline taking over his body while still being mindful of the speed limit.

Nickolas's mind goes back to questioning his existence and he decides he must be delusional from lack of sleep. Every day he is met with unpredictability when it comes to his job. He never knows who will be admitted or who will be released. Who's going to relapse or the conversations he'll need to have with the patients he's been entrusted with. He lives a life of predictable habits and unpredictable workdays, but nothing could have prepared him for an eighteen-year-old redhead, a patient nonetheless, to be the first person to come along, settle down in Nickolas's predictable routine and begin to break down the walls he's spent years building up.

So no, his life may revolve around structure, but that doesn't mean he isn't living. To be alive means to feel. To live and breathe, experiencing the joy, pain, love, and sadness of this world. As Nickolas pulls into the car park, he wonders when the joy and love will come back into his life, balancing out the pain and sadness he feels most of the time. He pushes the door open, locking it behind him as he tries to think back to a time in his life when he felt those 'happy' emotions...nothing comes to mind.

*

As he walks the aisles with his basket, picking up foods he can eat on the run like muesli bars, chips, yoghurts, and pop tarts, his mind can't seem to break away from work – or more specifically, Finn. Finn's name alone puts a small smile on Nickolas's face. People meet in the most bizarre ways every day. They could bump into one another on the street and spill coffee down their shirt. They could meet online, through work, or a friend. Either way, nothing but friendship is what Nickolas can offer Finn, at least while he is a patient.

Fuck.

He stops. His hand frozen mid-air as he goes to reach for the box of Froot Loops. Does he want more than a friendship with Finn? Is that what is happening? Nickolas slowly retrieves the box and places it in his basket. Finn is attractive, there is no denying that. With hair that shines like a sun ray, green eyes that look like the ocean after a storm, and freckles that make Nickolas want to play connect the dots on Finn's skin.

'What the fuck?' Nickolas mumbles to himself as those thoughts cross his mind.

Nickolas has never thought of a guy like this. He runs a hand down his face as he makes his way to the frozen food section. He's the type to get what he wants from a guy and then walk away, never going back for round two because he doesn't want the guy to get the impression that it means anything more than a quick fuck. But with Finn, it's different. He craves something more. He wants to talk to Finn, listen to anything and everything the guy has to say. Finn makes him laugh and the redhead has a cute puppy dog look that makes Nickolas want to say yes to anything Finn asks. Fuck! What is happening? He grabs his usual meals, the ones he knows taste like food and not cardboard once heated up. He considers shoving his head in the freezer for a few minutes as it might help clear his mind.

Finn is a patient. And no matter what, Nickolas would never act on his feelings because the last thing he would ever want to do is be accused of taking advantage of Finn while in a vulnerable state of mind. He slams the freezer door shut. Feelings? Did his mind just go there? No, no he doesn't do feelings. But, then again, isn't that what he had been hoping for back in the car park? Joy. Love. Those are emotions, feelings. Both of which seem like something he may get to have one day...with Finn.

He grabs some fresh meat in case he one day decides to cook and storms back towards the front of the store, ready to check out and head back home. What if Finn doesn't want more? What if Finn doesn't want *him*? Finn is spending all day, every day, in a psychiatric treatment centre with fourteen other patients and nine different orderlies. Anyone in that situation would latch onto the first person who treated them like a human being when stuck in a place like that. And maybe that's all it is. Finn mentioned that this isn't the first time he has been committed. Perhaps Nickolas is just the first person outside of Finn's family to show kindness and because of that, Finn wants to stay by his side, talk to him and be comforted by him while Finn's body goes through the adjustments of being medicated. Or, maybe whatever it is Nickolas is feeling, perhaps Finn is feeling it too.

He takes everything out of the basket and chucks it onto the conveyor belt.

'How are you this morning?' a voice behind the counter asks.

'Fine,' Nickolas grumbles without looking up at the cashier, dropping the empty basket on the floor to be collected by the store clerks.

'You know, if you ever want someone to cook for you, I'd be more than happy to.'

Nickolas freezes. He looks towards the guy talking to him, seeing his face for the first time. The cashier is young, a little smaller than Nickolas, and to his surprise, a freckled redhead. He assesses the guy's red hair and instantly decides it's not the right shade and the cashier's face has way too many freckles. Nickolas curses himself as his mind automatically compares this guy to Finn. He looks at the name tag. Byron. Who the fuck names their kid Byron?

'What makes you think I can't cook?' Nickolas bites back.

'Sorry. I mean, I just thought with all the frozen meals that—' Byron stumbles on his words.

'Maybe I don't have the time to cook. Ever think about that?'

'You're right. Sorry. I never should have assumed—'

'Maybe next time you'll just do your fucking job instead of hitting on your customers.'

The kid turns pale, eyes casting back down to Nickolas's items while scanning them and placing them in a paper bag. Truth is, Nickolas can cook. He took over the responsibility when he was still living at home, knowing it was the only way any of his siblings would get to eat, and stealing food to cook was cheaper than takeout. Nickolas could find the time to cook if he wanted to, but cooking for one is more depressing than a frozen meal, at least that's how he tries to justify it. He hands over the cash, picks up his three paper bags, and makes his way to the car.

Driving back to his apartment, Nickolas replays his interaction with Brice, no Brian, fuck, whatever his name was, and figures he probably overstepped. The guy took him by surprise and Nickolas wasn't in the mood to be hit on. Maybe that's half the problem – it's been a while since he's had anything shoved up his ass, so his bitchy side is starting to show. He's probably due for a visit to Boys Town, but working night shifts has made that a challenge. His collection of dildos will have to do.

He isn't surprised to return home and find Socks curled up on the couch, licking herself clean as the sun shines in the front window.

'Such a lady. Hope you don't spread your legs like that for just any guy.'

Socks stops licking and holds her leg in the air, head tilting towards him. He chuckles at how cute she looks.

Nickolas packs away all his food and puts a few items in his backpack for work, so he doesn't have to do it later. The washing is finished. He grabs his uniforms and shoves them all in the dryer and then picks up his vomit-covered shoes to clean in the sink. He grabs a bowl and mixes some warm water with white vinegar and soap – a trick Dot taught him on his first shift. He dabs a cloth into the bowl and cleans away the creamy white vomit. He hopes Finn is feeling better today. He'll only get to see the redhead when he goes around with the med cart before lights out and even though it's only going to be a short visit, Nickolas can't deny that he's looking forward to it.

He puts his shoes in front of the window to dry and makes his way to the bathroom. He steps in the shower, always preferring to wash off the smell of the treatment centre before he heads to bed. He grabs his shampoo and scrubs it into his scalp. His mind wanders to what Finn could be doing at the moment, perhaps hanging out with Ryder and Cora. Was Finn able to get up and eat breakfast this morning or did Dot have to bring food to his room? Maybe Finn is in session with Dr Hale. As he considers how Finn's day could be going, his imagination turns to a different memory of Finn – the one in the shower. The one of the redhead lathering his body in soap and standing in front of Nickolas with confidence as Finn displayed his beautiful nine-inch dick in front of his face.

Nickolas's dick twitches. His hands roam over his body as he scrubs his skin, the sensation making his semi turn into a full-blown hard-on. He accidentally knocks his dick as he soaps up his thighs, a groan leaving his lips as the pleasure shoots up his spine. It's been a few days since he has had a release, the build-up evident in how sensitive he is to the touch. Grabbing his dick in his right hand, Nickolas lets out another sigh as the pressure makes his body scream for more. He leans his left hand on the wall, needing the support as he slowly strokes himself from tip to base.

Keeping his mind blank, Nickolas closes his eyes and enjoys the sensation. His breathing hitches as his thumb teases his slit, the water washing away his precum before he can spread it around his tip. The water falling on his body suddenly becomes soft kisses ghosting across his skin. Each drop like a tender moment between lovers. The darkness in his mind vanishes as it paints a picture of luscious pink lips attached to beautiful milky white skin. A moan echoes in the bathroom as he gets closer to the edge of his orgasm—

'Fuck—'

He twists his wrist, changing his pace from slow, to fast, to slow again, wanting to be teased as he earns his release. Nickolas clenches his ass cheeks as he feels his orgasm building. His balls begin to tighten, his dick throbs, and as he bites his bottom lip, green eyes and shiny red hair pop into his mind, displaying a smirk and a half-cocked eyebrow as Nickolas paints his hand with cum.

His eyes shoot open as he gasps for air. He's still coming, three thick strings of cum have made it onto the shower curtain while the rest drips down to the base of the bathtub. He doesn't know if his struggle to breathe is from the intense orgasm or the fact that he just saw Finn's face as he came. He wants to bask in the afterglow, but the guilt is eating away at him and destroying the relaxed feeling he normally gets after jerking off. He shakes his head, trying to think of anything else besides Finn. Grabbing the soap, he cleans himself off as quickly as possible, the hot water beginning to turn cold, a form of punishment. He cleans down the shower curtain and then gets out, drying off his hair and body before making his way into the bedroom.

Socks is on his bed, not caring about the sudden sounds of drawers opening and a deodorant can spraying in the air. Pulling up a fresh pair of boxers, Nickolas throws his towel onto the floor and climbs into bed. He grabs his phone from the bedside table and sets his alarm for five p.m. If he falls asleep now, he'll get at least seven hours, but as he sets his phone back down, frustration keeps his eyes from closing.

He runs his hands down his face. 'What the fuck, Nickolas?' He brings his hands back to his sides and releases a deep breath. Finn is not just some guy he can picture when he needs to get himself off. Finn is his patient. If he had bumped into Finn at the grocery store or in a club, then he'd one hundred percent rub his dick raw picturing those lips and hands doing anything and everything to him. But that's not how they met.

They met with Finn screaming to go home. With the guy begging not to be touched or used. Nickolas rolls to his side, disturbing Socks as he shifts on the mattress. His ginger furball decides to move closer to him, probably to steal his body heat. As Socks positions herself against his stomach, curling into a ball and purring from the new comfortable position on the bed, Nickolas can't help but run his fingers through her fur in the hopes that it will settle his mind.

It's not like Finn knows Nickolas thought of him while jerking off. Maybe Finn would find it flattering. Or maybe he would find it completely creepy and demand that Nickolas be taken off his services. It was an accident. Yep, that's how Nickolas decides to process what happened. Finn had been on his mind and because the redhead was the last person he had been thinking of, it was only natural for the guy to pop into his head. Completely justifiable, right? Nickolas buries his face into his pillow. Yeah. He is fucked.

*

'Alright, alright.'

His hand stretches out to shut off the annoying alarm. With the room now silent, Nickolas rolls over, groaning. He feels like he overslept due to the deep sleep, surprised that he didn't wake before his alarm. Nickolas rubs his hands over his face a few times to wake himself up. He can't help but laugh as Socks walks across his head and stretches out over his forehead, deciding it's a comfortable enough place to fall back asleep.

'You right? You know, as much as I'd love lounging around, this life of luxury you live costs money, so one of us will have to go to work.'

Socks doesn't move.

'Yeah. Figured it was me.'

He lifts the cat up. Socks lets out a small meow at being moved and is not too thrilled to be placed onto the cold side of the bed.

Nickolas stands up, shuffles to the kitchen, and grabs a bowl, milk, and his box of Froot Loops. He tries to ignore the aches and pains in his body. For an almost twenty-two-year-old, he sure feels like he's thirty-five these days.

He takes his bowl to the couch, turns on the TV, and sits back while he watches a rerun of *Friends*. It's the one with the cheesecake and Nickolas finds himself laughing along with the audience. During the commercial break, he makes a toasted cheese sandwich, thankful it's ready before the show comes back on.

Nickolas makes his way into the bathroom to retrieve his laundry. He takes out his uniforms to fold, making sure to keep one to the side for his shift this evening. He picks up his shoes by the window where he's pleased to see the stain and smell of sour cheese is gone, and places the uniform in his backpack with his shoes beside it.

He walks back into the bathroom to finish getting ready. Nickolas puts a little more effort into his hair, styling it with gel so it sits nicely and doesn't lay flat on his head. He brushes his teeth, splashes cold water on his face, and sprays on some more deodorant for good measure. He grabs whatever is lying on the floor that's still clean enough to wear and chucks it on. Timberlands on his feet and backpack in hand, he leaves food and water for Socks and makes his way to the door.

'Okay, no parties while I'm gone, Socks. I'm trusting you. You can have a friend or two over, but clean up afterwards – and no boys.'

He stops in front of his front door with his hand on the door handle.

'Listen to me. I'm talking to my cat like a child. Fuck, I need to get laid. This is not healthy.'

He shakes his head and walks out, making sure the door is locked behind him.

*

He walks toward the centre, the streets busier than usual. Everyone must be taking advantage of it being a Friday night, going out for drinks, or a meal. Hitting the clubs in the hopes of hooking up. The psychiatric centre isn't directly in the heart of the city, but it's close enough to still have a crowd of people hanging around, depending on the night. Nickolas steps inside and sees Sam already behind the desk, but before he can ask, Sam answers the question for him.

'Jasmine had an ultrasound booked, I offered to start a little earlier for her so she could make the appointment.'

The buzzer goes off as Sam unlocks the door for him to step through. Nickolas makes his way to the lockers, following the chatter coming from the others who are changing so they can go home.

Nickolas walks to his locker as Brett continues his story.

'I swear, I was this close to sedating him. One minute I'm standing outside the room, minding my own business, and the next I hear Dr Hale yelling for him to calm down.'

'What happened?' Eric asks. Nickolas hates how his colleague is always interested in patient gossip.

'No idea. I ran in and the kid had knocked over his chair, yelling something about being judged for his actions. I had to pin him against the wall to calm him down. He was surprisingly strong for a faggot.'

Nickolas slams his door closed, the echo of the bang drawing everyone's attention to his presence in the room.

'The fuck you just say?'

'Hey, Nickolas. Didn't know you were in here.' Brett's smile is proof enough that he's lying.

Everyone cowardly goes back to their lockers. No one cares that Nickolas is gay, or if patients are. Brett on the other hand is begging to have his teeth knocked out from using such language.

'I was just telling everyone here about that twink that just checked in. Finn, is it? Fucker has a few skeletons in his closet that caused a few screws in his head to come loose if you ask me.'

Brett turns to Eric, a cocky smile on the asshole's face, elbowing Eric to try and get him to laugh at the inappropriate joke. Brett's ego gives Nickolas the chance to lunge across the locker room, grab him by the shirt, and push the asshole into the lockers. The force knocks the wind out of Brett's lungs, the height difference not at all intimidating Nickolas as he looks up into shocked eyes, hate and rage evident in his own.

'Careful there, Nickolas. If I didn't know any better, I'd say it looks like you've gotten a little attached to this kid. Wouldn't want rumours like that spreading around now, would we?'

It's been a while since his knuckles felt flesh against them and Brett would make a great candidate.

Nickolas grips Brett's shirt tighter, bringing his face close enough so that their noses are almost touching. 'I have so many reasons to happily beat your ass to the point of you needing a straw to eat. But so help me, if I ever hear words leaving your mouth that disrespect a patient, no matter their sexuality, then I'll make sure to break more than just your jaw.'

'Hey, Nickolas, break it up, man.' Eric gently puts a hand on Nickolas's shoulder, hoping it will bring him out of his rage.

Nickolas regretfully releases Brett. He steps back, not taking his eyes off the asshole, and makes his way back to his locker on the other side of the room.

'Whatever. I got better things to do than spend more time than I have to in this shit hole,' says Brett before he grabs his bag and leaves.

Nickolas continues to get undressed. Deep down a part of him wants to warn Brett about going near Finn, but he hates to admit that what his colleague said is true. The last thing he needs is rumours to go around about him and a patient, and after three days, the only orderlies that have been on Finn's service have been himself or Dot. Lydia never questioned where he spent his extra time when he would go on his nightly checks and Dot understands that Finn trusts having Nickolas around compared to the other orderlies. He would never take advantage of a patient's trust, but if Brett ever suspected anything, he would make Finn's time in here very uncomfortable.

Nickolas is working another double – night shift, then the day shift. He normally wouldn't mind, but Brett's scheduled to work the day shift with him, and he's dreading having to spend eight hours with the prick. He's going to have to be cautious in front of Brett with how he behaves around Finn. It's the only way to keep his patient safe. Nickolas pulls his top off over his head, ignoring the looks coming from Eric and Hayley as he grabs his uniform and throws his purple shirt over his tank top. The room has emptied by the time he is changing his pants. Lydia walks in as he's closing his locker door.

'Why did Hayley just tell me to avoid you like the plague? Does she not know that if she feeds the beast treats, then you calm down and relax?'

Nickolas gives Lydia the finger but chuckles nonetheless. 'Treats aren't necessary; just had another run-in with fuckface.'

'Ahhh, Brett. Working night shifts means I hardly see his mug, but I've heard all the stories.'

'Count yourself lucky.'

'Well, if you do need treats, looks like Dorothy made some carrot cake.'

'I have no idea how she finds the time to bake for us every day, but the day she doesn't bring anything in, we better get her checked out by the doctor.'

Lydia giggles. It takes Nickolas a second to smile because although it sounds like a joke, he means it. If Dot was to stop baking, then something would have to be seriously wrong.

Nickolas makes his way back out to the front desk, grabbing the medication folder so he can prepare the med cart.

'We in for a long night, Sam?' asks Nickolas.

'Friday night. Never know what trouble people can get themselves into,' says Sam.

'Well, we're at capacity. One of the perks of being a small facility.'

'Less chance of the patients being ignored, more chance of being the first to get shut down when the funding runs low.' Sam gives Nickolas a knowing look as he gets back to his paperwork. Everyone's medications are in order and he has forty-five minutes before lights out, so he makes his way towards the exit. Sam buzzes him through each gate as Nickolas pushes the cart in front of him. He knocks on the doors of every patient who requires medication, handing them a paper cup of pills that sit on top of a number that matches the room they're allocated in, as well as a paper cup of water. He makes small talk with the patients he knows are comfortable with it and then moves on after ensuring that they have swallowed every pill.

He knocks on Cora's door, the interruption has the young girl looking up from a book, and when their eyes meet, a small smile appears on Cora's face.

'Gotcha party favours here. Ten bucks a pop. Interested?' Nickolas jokes.

'Always.' Cora laughs, taking the cup and downing the pills before Nickolas can hand over a cup of water. 'You seen Finn yet?'

Cora's question catches him by surprise. 'Nope. Shift just started. Got to make the rounds.'

'He didn't do too great in group today. Been in his room ever since.'

Nickolas freezes for a second as he makes a note on his chart, quickly shaking it off so he can continue writing. It's not his place to ask what happened. Group is private, it's for the patients only. That's why the orderlies wait outside. But that doesn't mean every part of him isn't screaming to find out what happened.

'He needs someone like you, you know,' said Cora.

Nickolas turns towards Cora, his eyebrows raised high at the young girl's comment. 'I'm just an orderly, Cora. What he needs is the help this place can give him.'

'You and I both know that's a load of shit. This place does what it can, but you, Dorothy, Hayley, and James – you guys make the difference around here. You guys actually treat us like human beings and not lab rats.'

Nickolas closes the folder and makes his way towards the door.

'He needs someone he can open up to, someone he can trust. And from the way he was acting today, all anxious without you being around...my guess is you're the only one he feels that way with.'

Not wanting to ignore Cora, Nickolas gives her a nod and leaves the room. He knows that if he had replied, he would have said something he shouldn't and he can't let that happen. He makes five more stops before he lands at the last room: number thirteen. He has twenty minutes left before lights out and he's planning to spend every second of them making sure Finn is okay. He knocks on the door and waits a few seconds before entering. Nickolas is somewhat relieved when he sees Finn on the bed, but it's the position that tells Nickolas that something isn't right. Finn's legs are pulled into his chest, arms wrapped around them to keep them in place.

Nickolas's soft, deep tone breaks the silence of the room. 'Hey, man. Long time no see.'

Finn looks up and tries to smile.

'Got your meds. Feeling any better today?' Nickolas holds out the cup.

Finn's hand trembles as he lets go of his legs and reaches out to take the cup from Nickolas. He accepts the cup of water with his other hand, and a spark of electricity shoots up Nickolas's spine as his fingers brush against Finn's. Green eyes widen. Nickolas coughs to try and break the moment and takes a step back to his cart so he can write notes in his folder.

Finn swallows the pills before answering Nickolas. 'Vomiting stopped. But the tremors have been on and off all day. Give me some milk and chocolate syrup and I'm sure my hand will be able to shake you up a chocolate milkshake.'

It's a terrible joke, but Nickolas laughs. He looks up and can see Finn is pleased to have made him smile. Joking at his patient's expense seems to lighten the mood for Finn, so Nickolas plays along. 'I'm more of a thickshake kind of guy. Think you got enough power in those hands to whip in some ice cream?'

Finn puts both hands out in front, trying to hold them steady, though it looks as though a puppeteer is pulling on each hand, making them wobble from left to right. 'I'm sure I can make it work. I'm generally pretty good when it comes to using my hands.'

The smile falls from Finn's face once the words leave his mouth. Finn's arms wrap back around his body, gripping on tight. Nickolas suspects it's in hopes that it will steady his hands. Slowly, Nickolas steps forward, taking a seat at the end of the bed, though he waits to make sure Finn is comfortable with him being in his personal space. 'How was today?' Nickolas asks.

Finn rests his chin on his knee, soft eyes looking at Nickolas. 'Who told you?'

'Told me what?'

Finn scoffs. 'Please. Don't act like you don't all talk about us in your break room, gossiping about what crazy thing someone did today.'

'Finn. I started work fifty minutes ago. I got changed and began doing the rounds with the med cart. I can assure you if anyone is gossiping, I didn't take part in it.'

'Nothing was written in my file that you came across?'

'I don't read them. I write about incidents that happen on my watch or reactions to medications but anything else is not my place to read.'

'Huh.' Finn seems to relax.

'I mean...' Nickolas hesitates.

Finn lifts his head from his knee.

'Brett may have been running his big fucking mouth in the locker room. But I was pretty quick to shut him up.'

'Coming to my rescue are ya, Nick?'

Nickolas blushes at the way Finn abbreviates his name.

'Nah. I'll just take any excuse to punch that prick.'

'His face does look like it was meant for a beat down.'

'The words that come out of his mouth don't help his case either.'

Nickolas looks at his watch and sees it's almost nine p.m.

'I better head back. Get some sleep okay. It'll help.'

'I'll try.'

He gives Finn a reassuring smile and makes his way to the cart to leave.

'Hey, Nickolas.'

'Yeah?'

'Thanks. No one has ever defended my honour before. I'm generally the one having to throw a punch or two.'

Nickolas wants to explain that it wasn't just the comment about Finn that made him go after Brett. He considers explaining that he didn't even get to punch the guy, just threaten him a little, not wanting Finn to get the wrong idea. However, hearing that he is the first to defend Finn, it makes Nickolas feel proud. He gives Finn a nod and walks out, locking the door behind him.

Back in the break room, he watches Lydia go through the files of each patient as he makes a cup of coffee, the first of many he will no doubt be having over the next twenty hours.

'What's that about?' Nickolas nods towards the paperwork.

'Visitors' Day is on Sunday. Making notes about anything we need to inform the families about. Not many of our patients at the moment are minors so shouldn't take too long.'

Visitors' Day. It's one of the best and worst days for the patients. It gives them a chance to finally see loved ones and a conversation about anything besides their treatment, but it's also a reminder that they're stuck in this place. It must be hard to watch loved ones leave to live their lives outside of these four walls while the patients stay behind and continue being told what to eat, when to sleep, and what they are allowed to do each day.

'Well, if you're good, I'm going to see how Sam's going,' says Nickolas.

'Sure. Want me to do the first check?' Lydia asks.

'Nah, I got it. Besides, I'm going to probably need to sleep later since I'm working a double. You can do it then.'

'Works for me.'

He grabs two plates, a knife and cuts a slice of carrot cake for himself and one for Sam to enjoy out front, balancing both plates in one hand so he can carry his coffee in the other.

'Alright old man. Dot wants to kill us through sweets, so figured we might as well do it together.' He hands a plate over to Sam, taking a seat for himself against the corner of the desk.

'That woman knows the way to a man's heart,' says Sam.

'Would be nice coming home to something like this every night, that's for sure.' Nickolas lets out a groan of delight as he shoves the cake in his mouth for a second bite.

'I'm sure it would be nice just to come home to somebody, baked goods or not.'

Nickolas shoves the last piece of cake into his mouth, glaring at Sam as he chews the deliciously moist cake. 'What are you getting at, old man?'

'I'm just saying, maybe it's time you find someone to settle down with?'

'What the fuck? I'm twenty-one. This ain't the 1950s where you need to be married with kids by the time you reach the legal age of drinking.'

Sam chuckles. 'True. But I'm not saying you need to get married. I'm just saying you should go out looking for someone you'd like to actually have a conversation with, a meal. Not just...you know.' Sam waves a hand instead of saying the word.

Nickolas knows what Sam's hinting at. Playing with the crumbs on his plate, he figures if there is anyone he could ever talk to about this stuff, Sam would be that person. 'I've, ah, I've maybe been thinking the same thing recently. Kind of. Man, I don't fucking know.' He puts his plate on the desk and rubs his hands down his face. 'I've spent so long avoiding a relationship because I couldn't risk having one. And now, now it's like I wouldn't even know where to begin if I wanted one.'

Sam knows about Dominic, Nickolas's homophobic, abusive father, who is rotting away in prison on a life sentence while Nickolas picks up the pieces of what little life he has left.

'Start with a drink. A conversation. You don't have to spill your life story to them straight away. Just, start with a friendship,' says Sam.

Nickolas nods. 'I kinda...I kinda met someone already that I want to do those things with. Ya know, talk. Be their friend; if that's all I can be with them. But...it's complicated.'

'How so?'

'It's the way we met that makes things complicated.'

'He's not a prostitute, is he?'

'You really think I need to pay for sex?'

'I'm not saying you did. I'm just asking if that's what he does.'

'No. He's not a hooker.'

'So, what's the problem?'

He could say it. He could open his mouth to Sam right now and explain that it's a patient. But then he risks his job – not just getting taken off Finn's services, but possibly getting fired, never getting hired anywhere else, and finding himself unemployed. He can't do that.

'Never mind. It's pointless. Doubt this guy feels the same way.' Nickolas explains as he scratches his left eyebrow, hoping Sam takes the hint and doesn't push any further.

'Kid, I've known you now for, what, four years? More? In that time, not once have you ever been interested in anything more than a...a hookup? Is that what you kids call it?'

Nickolas smirks and gives Sam a nod.

'The best things in life aren't meant to be easy. They're messy and complicated. That's what makes them worth fighting for. Whatever the issue is with this guy, if you want something to come from it, even if it is only a friendship, then you need to do whatever it takes to make it work.'

Sam's right. Finn won't always be his patient; at least he hopes not. He wants more than anything for Finn to balance, get released and then, well, then this issue won't be an issue.

Nickolas looks up at the clock on the wall and sees it's time to check on the patients. He collects their plates and his now-cold coffee.

'Thanks, Sam. I'll think about it.'

'Don't think too long, kid. If this guy has been able to grab your attention, then I'd say he's the type to be snatched up fast.'

He makes his way back down the corridor, dropping the dishes off into the sink and heading back out without saying a word to Lydia. His key card opens the door to the patient corridor and off he goes, inspecting each room one by one, peeking into the windows to make sure the patients are asleep and safe. Like he has done since Finn arrived, he leaves room thirteen till last, and as he looks in, he can see Finn is still sitting up on the bed in the same position Nickolas left him in, looking out towards the moon shining through the small window.

Nickolas knocks, and when Finn's head turns towards the door, he unlocks it and lets himself in.

'Can't sleep?' Nickolas asks Finn, standing at the threshold.

'One of the many side effects. First, all I wanted to do was sleep; now it feels like I've had coffee injected into my veins.'

'Do you feel like you're slipping into mania?' It's a blunt question, but it's his job.

'Not that kind of awake. My mind isn't racing. I do want to go to sleep; I just...I can't.'

'Something on your mind?' Sam's words play in Nickolas's head: *Talk to him. Be his friend.*

'Is this what my life will always be like?' Finn's question is quiet, scared almost. 'Will I forever be testing out new drugs until they find one that works, only to realise after I've gone out and done a bunch of stupid shit that my body's built an intolerance and I got to start all over again? Hmm?'

'Maybe. Maybe not. Some people can last years before needing adjustments.'

Finn lets go of his leg and scratches the back of his neck. Nickolas notices Finn's hand is still trembling.

'Do you want me to give you something to help you sleep?'

'Rather not. The last thing I want is more drugs pumped into my body.'

'I'll come back in an hour to check on you. Why don't you lay down, maybe that will help you sleep.'

Nickolas turns back around. He closes the door behind him, heads back to the break room with his mind focused on making a fresh cup of coffee, since he didn't get to finish his last, and not on Finn.

*

At a quarter past eleven, Nickolas walks by all the rooms while he does his routine inspection. As he approaches room thirteen, panic sets in as he sees Finn pacing back and forth against the wall. Not bothering to knock, Nickolas lets himself into the room, making sure the door is closed behind him.

'Finn, you okay?' Nickolas keeps his voice calm, level.

'You know, it's bad enough that I have no control over my body when it comes to the vomiting and the shakes, but now my dick?'

Nickolas's eyebrows shoot up as he tries to understand what Finn is talking about.

'My body couldn't sleep, so I thought, hey, maybe if I rub one out it'll help me rest. But no. The medications took that away from me too. My dick is as soft as a fucking noodle, Nick.'

'It's only temporary, Finn. All of it is.' He explains calmly, though he could imagine how frustrating it would be. 'You said it yourself; the vomiting has stopped. I'm sure this one will pass too.'

He takes a step closer as Finn's pacing picks up speed.

'Finn.' Saying his name does nothing to settle Finn's frustration.

'Finn. If you don't calm down and get back on the bed, I'm going to have to sedate you or restrain you.'

'NO!' Finn stops. The mention of restraints has Finn panicked, his green eyes wide and filled with fear.

'I don't want to do either of those things, but it's protocol if I find a patient struggling to rest and stay calm.'

Finn walks towards the bed, body trembling, head shaking 'no', cautious of Nickolas's movements. 'No. No restraints. Please, Nick.'

He sits at the end of the bed. He wants to reach out and touch Finn, help calm the guy down and try to take away the fear in those green eyes. 'Finn. Look at me. Hey, what's going on?'

Finn won't make eye contact. His body is trembling excessively, to the point of it no longer being a side effect of the medications. Finn's body is reacting to fear, terror even. Nickolas reaches out and takes Finn's hand, hoping that he won't pull away from the touch. As his fingers entwine with Finn's, Nickolas gives a gentle squeeze, hoping it will bring Finn back into the present.

'I—I remembered.' Finn's voice is barely a whisper.

Nickolas isn't sure what Finn's talking about, but he waits.

'In group today. We were discussing things we have done to try and mask our disorders. How we coped without the help of medication.'

Nickolas knows he shouldn't be hearing this, especially if it has to do with other patients. But if Finn wants to share his story, then Nickolas is ready to listen.

'Someone mentioned something they did, and it's like hearing their story opened up the flood gates and everything that happened when I was away came rushing back. And, and I panicked... I panicked because I was remembering these things that I didn't want to remember. And before, well, before I could act like everything was okay, but it wasn't. It isn't.'

'Is that why you couldn't calm down? Why you kicked the chair?' Nickolas asks.

'Brett?'

'Brett.'

'That asshole really has a big mouth, doesn't he?'

'One day I'll shut it up.'

Finn offers a small smile, but his green eyes still read pain and sadness as he looks down at their fingers that are still entwined.

'I was working at the Glory Hole.' Finn begins to share. 'I started with just bartending, but the money was in dancing. Then dancing turned into party favours in exchange for lap dances and suddenly I was using drugs to self-medicate rather than taking whatever the doctors wanted to put me on that made me feel like a walking zombie.'

Nickolas gives Finn's hand a gentle squeeze, not wanting to speak and risk saying something that will cause Finn to stop sharing.

'I needed a place to stay. Six months away from home, I couldn't afford a hotel and I didn't have any friends I could crash with. So, I found my only option was if I went home with someone.'

Nickolas cringes inside as he pieces together what Finn is telling him.

'One night this guy said he had a hotel; he was out of town for work and offered me $400 to stay with him for the weekend. He looked decent enough and I really could have used the money, so I said yes.' Finn takes a shaky in and out. 'We get to his room, had a drink, and then I ah...' Finn takes a moment. 'I woke up, face down on the mattress, naked with my arms and legs tied to each corner of the bed.'

Nickolas feels like he's going to be sick. A tear rolls down Finn's face. Nickolas wants to hold Finn in his arms and whisper how sorry he is. He wants to search the city for this asshole and make him pay. But all Nickolas can do right now is stay strong for Finn.

'I tried to get free but every time I pulled at them, they just got tighter. I begged him to let me go, to stop.' Finn continues. 'I remember the pain and my voice breaking from how much I was screaming. Eventually, I must have blacked out or...spaced out. The next thing I remember is the cops finding me in the alley. I don't know how I got there from the hotel, but when asked about my bruises, I said I didn't know because at the time I honestly couldn't remember...until today.'

Finn's tears land on their joined hands.

'So please, Nickolas. Please don't restrain me. I can't— I can't feel like that again. I can't go back there.' Finn's voice breaks. 'I think, part of me remembered even if I couldn't remember...the night I arrived here, and you had to...my subconscious knew, and I panicked. I fought so hard to get free. But now—I can't...' Finn mumbles through his heart wrenching sobs.

Nickolas cups Finn's face, 'Finn. Please look at me.'

It takes a moment but eventually, Finn's beautiful green eyes reach Nickolas's.

'I promise. You'll never be restrained again, okay? I'm so sorry that I did that to you. Took you back to that moment. If I had known, I'd...I promise that you never have to be scared about that happening again.'

Finn nods in understanding.

Nickolas waits for Finn to feel comfortable enough to continue speaking.

'I wish...' Finn takes a breath. 'I wish the mania could make me forget, you know? Like it could put a blanket over everything I did so I don't have to deal with it once the fog clears.'

Nickolas rubs his thumb over Finn's hand. He hopes it's calming in some way. If he could, he'd bring Finn into his arms, offer him a hug to show how much he cares.

'Did you report the guy?' Nickolas asks.

'What's thc point? I had the guy's first name, but no idea if it was real, and once they knew I was working at the Glory Hole, where witnesses had seen me taking drugs, the cops would have turned around and pinned the blame on me.'

Nickolas hates how accurate that statement is.

'I mean, maybe they're right. Maybe I am to blame. If I had just stayed home, taken my damn pills, then it never would have happened.'

'Are you fucking serious? Finn. None of that was your fault. You hear me? You went there of your own free will. But what he did to you...you never agreed to any of that.' Nickolas's heightened emotions cause him to swear, but he doesn't care, and Finn doesn't seem bothered by it either.

As Nickolas reluctantly removes his hands from Finn's face, the latter wipes away fallen tears. Neither make a move to let go of the other's hands.

'Trembling's stopped.' Finn sounds surprised.

'I can't imagine how you must be feeling right now,' Nickolas offers. 'It's one thing to live through what happened, but it's another for the memories to suddenly come flooding back to you, taking you to a place your mind is trying to protect you from.'

'Sounds like you're speaking from experience.'

'We all have our demons. It took me a long time to get rid of mine, but some are still haunting me.'

This time, Finn is the one to squeeze Nickolas's hand, giving Nickolas his strength.

'Why is it that one conversation with you has been easier for me than any of the conversations I've had with the therapist?' Finn asks, eyes searching for something as they look back into Nickolas's. Searching for an answer perhaps, or a reason.

'It's the tattoos. They lull you into a false sense of security.'

'Right. Because "Hate You" with the image of brass knuckles on your index finger screams safety.' Finn laughs as Nickolas gives shrugs. 'What's with the tattoos anyway?'

'What? You don't like them?'

'Did I say that?'

In that moment, as he hears the playfulness in Finn's voice, Nickolas realises they still have their fingers entwined. As much as he should, Nickolas doesn't want to be the first to let go.

'Short version,' Nickolas offers, 'it was kind of a rite of passage within my family. We all got knuckle tatts to try and set an image.'

'Hmm, boy scout playing angry teen?'

'More like closeted gay son playing South Side thug.'

Nickolas doesn't miss the way Finn's body language changes as he admits to being gay. Up until this point, the playfulness they have been sharing, the touches, it could have been put down to Nickolas doing his job, being a kind, friendly orderly to his patients. But now, now he has given Finn a reason to analyse every touch they share, search for a deeper meaning behind every question asked and answer given.

'It was meant to be kind of a 'fuck you' to my dad.' Says Nickolas, bringing the conversation back to his tattoos. 'I don't know, maybe having 'hate you' inked into my skin was more a reflection of how I saw myself than how I felt about him.'

Finn isn't the first patient he has sat with at night, talking to them to help settle their minds so they can sleep. But he hopes Finn knows this is different. Nickolas never opens up about his life to patients, never touches them. Not unless they need his assistance. And although all they are doing right now is holding hands, to some, that can be more intimate than a kiss.

Finn's door suddenly opens, the bubble bursts and their hands regretfully let go. Nickolas turns towards the door to see Lydia standing at the threshold looking unsure of what's happening within the room.

'Sorry I—it was time to do another round and I hadn't seen you so I wasn't sure if—'

'It's fine. Sorry. I lost track of time. Finn was just having some difficulty with his medication.' It isn't a complete lie, but it seems to be enough.

'I've checked the other rooms,' says Lydia, 'so it's fine if you want to—'

'No, I was just leaving.' He wasn't, but he knew he had to. Nickolas can feel Finn's eyes on him as he stands up from the bed and makes his way towards the door. 'If you're still awake when Lydia does the next round, she can give you something to help you sleep.'

Finn sags at the mention of Lydia doing the next check. But what his colleague just saw could be taken the wrong way, so Nickolas needs to step back. At least for tonight.

'Thanks. I'm sure I'll be fine,' Finn explains.

With a quick nod, Nickolas follows Lydia out of the room and locks it behind him. No one says a word until they're in the back rooms.

'Everything okay?'

Nickolas knows that's not the question Lydia wants to ask, but he answers it nonetheless. 'Yeah. Like I said, just some side effects. I'll go write them up now.'

'You sure you want me to do the next check?'

'Wouldn't have said it if I didn't want you to. Besides, I'm going to try and get some sleep.' It's past midnight. Day shift starts at six o'clock and he could use a few hours of rest before then. He ignores the look on Lydia's face as he makes his way to the front desk. Sam is doing a crossword while the radio plays softly in the background. They don't acknowledge one another as Nickolas picks up Finn's file and makes a note about Finn's tremors temporarily stopping, the inability to sleep, decreased sex drive, or, more accurately, erectile dysfunction. Lastly, in bold red letters, he makes a note stating under no circumstance should Finn be restrained due to past trauma. He signs his name beside the note so the other orderlies can come to him if they decide to question it.

He puts the file away and heads back to the break room to lie on the couch. Thankful that Lydia has returned to studying, Nickolas turns so his back is to the room with his face buried in the cushions. He closes his eyes, pushing out the image of

Finn lying in an alley, or feeling helpless and scared in some room, and replaces it with Finn's smile and the way Nickolas's body felt alive when their hands touched. As sleep takes over his body, he knows that he can no longer fight it. He wants Finn in his life. Whether it be as friends or more, all Nickolas knows is he can't imagine a day where Finn isn't in it.

5. Saturday

'Hey, it's time to get up.'

Nickolas can feel soft tapping on his bare shoulder. He groans, wanting to ignore the disturbance, but the soft kisses being pressed from his shoulder blade to his neck are waking up other parts of his body.

'If you don't wake up now, you'll be late for work.'

'I quit,' Nickolas mumbles.

'No, you don't.'

'Fine. I don't. But I'd rather stay in bed with you.'

'Trust me, there is nothing I'd prefer than spending all day in bed with you, naked, sleeping, fucking...But it's time to get up.'

Nickolas feels the tapping on his shoulder again.

'Hey, wake up.'

The tapping becomes more of a nudge, causing an agitated groan to escape his lips.

'Nickolas, wake up,' Lydia demands.

Nickolas wakes from his dream to find Lydia hovering over the couch, a hand on his shoulder shaking him awake. Nickolas pinches the bridge of his nose, his mind foggy from his dream of lying in bed and being woken up by Finn.

'Sorry. I figured you might want to be awake before Brett and Hayley arrive,' explains Lydia.

'Thanks.' Nickolas coughs. 'What time is it?'

'Just after five. Enough time to grab some coffee, freshen up.'

Nickolas is surprised he slept a solid five hours. He never used to sleep for long periods when he napped during night shift. His body clock always knew he needed to keep waking up so he could check on the patients. He was thankful that not only did Lydia allow him to rest, but that he could trust her to handle any situation that may arise while he did so.

'Everything okay overnight?' Nickolas asks.

'I let you keep sleeping, didn't I?'

'Doesn't mean there wasn't an issue.'

'Everything was fine. Finn had fallen asleep by the time I did the midnight check.'

Sitting up, Nickolas brushes off Lydia's comment like it's no big deal, secretly relieved to hear that Finn didn't need to be sedated. He walks over to the coffee machine. Making a fresh pot, he leans against the kitchen counter with his arms crossed over his chest while he waits for it to brew.

'Sure you want to leave the life of a night shift orderly and become a therapist?' He asks.

'And keep covering for you while you sleep?' Her lips purse. 'No thanks. I'm looking forward to my nine-to-five job thank you very much.'

Lydia's sass makes him laugh. She knows the hours he puts in – a lot more than any of the other orderlies – and for that, Lydia never questions if he needs to close his eyes for a few hours at night. He'll miss working with Lydia, but he's proud to see one of his colleagues striving for something more. The coffee machine beeps and Nickolas pours himself a cup, grabbing a Pop-Tart he'd brought from home and placed in the cupboard last night before his shift started.

'Breakfast of champions I see,' Lydia comments.

'Used to be coffee and a cigarette,' Nickolas says before taking a sip of his coffee.

'You smoked?'

'Like a chimney.'

'Why'd you quit?'

'When I started working here, it wasn't that easy taking a smoke break. Found myself going longer and longer before I was able to get away and light up. Eventually, I just stopped altogether.'

'Good for you.'

Nickolas can't help but throw Lydia a sarcastic look of thanks, biting into his strawberry Pop-Tart and allowing the mix of sugar and caffeine to wake him up. He walks out to see how Sam went during the night; his Pop-Tart is finished before he makes it to the front desk.

'You awake old man?' Nickolas asks.

'More than you were from what I saw.'

'Anything happen while I was out?'

'Nothing. Real easy night.'

'Good, let's keep it that way.' He gives Sam a pat on the back and walks towards the lockers. He splashes water onto his face to wake himself up, pleased to see the bags under his eyes have faded. He reapplies his spray deodorant and closes his locker door as he hears Brett and Hayley making their way to the locker room.

'Here we go,' he mumbles to himself, and turns towards the entry.

Brett holds his hands up in surrender. 'Whoa, tough guy. I come in peace. It's too early in the morning to throw a punch.'

'I don't care what time it is. Keep your mouth shut and we're good.' Nickolas leaves. The less time he needs to spend with Brett, the better.

Wake-up time for the patients isn't for another hour. He heads back to the break room, sits down with another cup of coffee, and scrolls through his phone. Lydia has already left for the day, so he enjoys the few moments of peace before the other two join him.

'Hey, Nickolas, any coffee left?' Hayley asks while walking into the room.

'Should be.' He doesn't take his eyes off the phone, randomly checking local news or his Netflix app for new releases.

'How'd it go in the Arkham Asylum last night?' Brett adds to the conversation.

'Man, what's your fucking problem?' demands Nickolas.

'What?'

'Do you enjoy being a blatant asshole or do you generally have no human decency left in that pea-sized brain of yours?'

'I'm just calling it as I see it. The sooner you realise that everyone in this place has their screws loose, the quicker you'll learn that not everybody can be saved.'

'If that's how you feel, why don't you quit? Save all of us from having to put up with your bullshit.'

'You know I would. But I think I'd just miss your ugly mug too much. Plus, the benefits are great.'

Nickolas wants to punch that smug look right off Brett's face. His hands ball into fists. The pressure of his nails digging into his palms cause his knuckles to crack. He still has nine more hours of working with this douchebag. He stands up, pushing his chair against the floor, pleased to see his sudden movement has caught Brett off guard.

'Just go get the dining area ready. I'm sure Aiden has arrived by now and could use the extra help,' Nickolas instructs.

Brett scoffs. 'Who put you in charge?'

'How about you do as I fucking say and mind your own business.'

Technically Brett has been working at the ward longer, which would give him seniority. But since Nickolas is working a double, that means he gets to continue his position as first in charge until Dot starts her shift this afternoon. Nickolas plans to use that power to his full advantage.

'Hayley, you can get the med cart ready,' Nickolas orders.

Neither of them makes any sign of moving.

He raises his eyebrows in question. 'Why are you both still in front of me?'

Hayley moves out first. Brett slowly follows, their eyes locked on one another. Brett's reluctance to accept Nickolas's orders is clear. Once the room is cleared out, he stands in the silence and lets out a breath. Today is not going to be easy.

Thirty minutes later, Hayley returns with the med cart. Nickolas follows her out to the patient corridor so they can deliver the medication to the patients together. After opening the first half of the rooms and administering medication to those who require it, Nickolas instructs Hayley to go into the common room to watch over the patients waiting for the dining area to be open for breakfast. He keeps going with the remaining rooms, unlocking each one, waking those who are still sleeping while greeting good morning to the ones already awake.

He gets to Finn's room and enters without knocking. Nickolas isn't sure why he decides to let himself in unannounced, but when he sees Finn sitting up in bed, he feels a sense of disappointment, secretly hoping he could have gently woken the redhead himself.

'Hey, thought you'd still be sleeping.' Nickolas takes a few steps away from the door so he can't be seen from the corridor.

'Didn't sleep much. I kind of made it look like I was sleeping when Lydia did the checks.'

'Finn.' Concern is evident in Nickolas's voice.

'I'm fine. I just–I wasn't ready to sleep yet and I–I didn't want to be sedated.'

Once again, fear appears on Finn's face. Those green eyes unable to hide the truth.

'If you sedate me then I can't wake up and sometimes, the things I dream...I need to be able to wake up.'

Nickolas knows a thing or two about nightmares and there is nothing worse than feeling paralysed by the fear of what your mind is forcing you to relive. He gently nods. Nickolas makes his way deeper into the room, grabbing the last cup of medication and water before passing them over to Finn. He swallows both and passes the cups back to Nickolas.

'Well, when you're ready, make your way to the common room. Breakfast is in fifteen minutes,' Nickolas explains.

He turns around to leave, but his body is begging him to stay. He wants to hug Finn good morning, run his fingers through messy red bed hair and make sure Finn's feeling okay. He pushes it all down. Out of all the days, today is the one day Nickolas needs to keep those feelings at bay, knowing Brett's eyes will be following his every move.

Nickolas steps out into the corridor and makes his way towards the backrooms. He walks to the reception desk and returns the med cart for Dr Winslow to collect later. Jasmine's sitting at the desk, already speaking to someone on the phone. Why people are already calling at a quarter to eight in the morning, who fucking knows. He gives Jasmine a small wave and then makes his way back to the common room.

The minute he walks into the room, Nickolas searches for Finn, who is already casting his beautiful green eyes towards the door, as though waiting for him. Nickolas is drawn towards him, like when two magnets are forced to separate and they naturally pull at one another to reconnect, needing to be close. As much as it pains Nickolas, he casts his eyes towards the other side of the room and makes his way over to some of the patients chatting in the corner.

He doesn't have to look at Finn to know those eyes are sprouting confusion. Nickolas swallows the lump in his throat and chats with Ethan, pleased to see the bruises have faded and no others have appeared.

'Alright. Time to eat. Let's go, up we get. We don't have all day,' Brett instructs.

Nickolas locks eyes on Brett, whose obnoxious voice continues barking orders at the patients. If Brett thinks being in a room full of people will stop Nickolas from biting his head off, then the fuck-knuckle for brains has severely underestimated him. Nickolas helps Ethan up, walks him to a seat, and decides to stay in the dining area to avoid being alone with Finn.

As the patients line up to collect their breakfast from a selection of toast or cereal, Nickolas catches Finn's eyes on him as he follows the other patients through the cue. He feels hot under Finn's stare. He tries to look anywhere in the room but at Finn, and his eyes land on Brett, noticing how his colleague's gaze shifts from Finn to Nickolas. A small smirk appears on Brett's face as he leans over to whisper something to Hayley.

'Fuck.' Nickolas scratches his eyebrow. This isn't good.

The patients are sitting down, happily enjoying their meal when Nickolas goes up to grab some food for himself. He sits down with his back to Finn. Unable to enjoy the taste of his food, he shoves it down quickly, needing this all to be over so he can distract himself with the other patients back in the common room.

Taking his tray over to the cart, he puts his dirty dishes in the tubs and his utensils in the bucket. He stands beside the cart, waiting for each patient to slowly walk up as they return their dirty dishes, keeping count of the utensils they return to make sure they are all accounted for. Nickolas is so wrapped up in analysing everyone's tray and counting in his head that he forgets to keep his distance from Finn. He is suddenly faced with the tall redhead, crowding his space and preventing him from being able to walk away.

'Thought we could have eaten together,' says Finn.

Nickolas takes Finn's utensils, so he can place the tray down on the cart. 'You seemed okay to be sitting with your friends.'

'Again, not my friends.'

'Well, it's more than what some people have in here. Thought I'd keep Ethan company.'

'You didn't even speak to him.'

'And how would you know that?' Nickolas cocks his eyebrow, a spark of pride warming his chest as Finn's words confirm how closely he was watching.

'Everything okay over here?' Brett's words cut through the tension, though none of it is making either of them uncomfortable.

Still, Finn takes a step back as Brett crowds their space and Nickolas makes himself look busy as he takes the cart so he can wheel it into the kitchen.

'Peachy. Why don't you start getting everyone back in the common room, Brett. I got this.'

Nickolas leaves before Brett can answer back, hoping Finn takes the hint to get the hell out of there. He pushes through the kitchen doors, letting them swing closed so he is away from prying eyes. He rests his hands on the sink and takes a deep breath. Whatever it is about Finn, it's intoxicating. He can feel his skin itch when he isn't around the green-eyed beauty – the same feeling an addict gets when they haven't had a hit. Whatever Finn wants from him, Nickolas would gladly give it, and that's what's so dangerous. It scares him to suddenly have these feelings towards someone, feelings he has never experienced before in his life. It frightens him even more that he's willing to risk everything he has worked towards for a person he has only just met.

He doesn't know Finn, not really. He knows his name and his age. He knows about his struggles with bipolar disorder, but besides that, who is Finn Cunningham? Nickolas rubs his hands down his face, applying enough pressure to drag his skin down, and feel a slight burn as he pulls at it. Finn's health comes before anything else. Nothing can ever happen. No matter how deeply his body is craving it.

Walking out into the common room, Nickolas sees Finn chatting with Ryder and Cora. Hayley is setting up the craft activity for the day, which looks to be some fabric shapes and glue. The activities have to be safe for the patients, but sometimes Nickolas questions if the system knows how old their patients actually are.

Brett is hanging around the bathroom, and Alex is nowhere in sight, which explains Brett's location. Due to Alex's condition, bathroom breaks need to be monitored in case she decides to eat a roll of toilet paper or find a loose screw and swallow it. Nickolas makes his way over to where a few patients are playing a card game and sits down beside them. He doesn't join in on the game, merely gives some words of encouragement or congratulations when someone wins. Mostly, Nickolas sits there so he can still hear what Finn is saying, making it feel as though it's a conversation he is sitting down and taking part in.

'So, the guy thought giving us five bucks to guard a truck full of Amazon deliveries was a smart thing to do in the South Side. Wrong. My siblings and I cleaned that thing out in a matter of minutes. Once we opened everything, we sold most of it and only kept a few things for ourselves.'

Ryder and Cora laugh at Finn's story and Nickolas can't help but chuckle to himself as he pictures exactly how that would have played out. He's all too familiar with the ways of hustling to survive in the South Side. The sound of laughter that erupts from Finn after the redhead finishes telling the story has become Nickolas's favourite sound.

'That's crazy. How old were you?' Cora asks.

'Like, fifteen. But that's nothing. Been doing crazy shit to help my family get by since I could talk,' Finn explains.

There is a brief moment of silence before Cora speaks up. 'How are the tremors?'

'I thought they had stopped. Then at breakfast, I don't know. They just, started up again.'

Nickolas wants to turn around. He wants to take Finn's hand again and hold it tight in his own until the tremors stop.

'Alright, here's your little Frankenstein. Looks like she didn't eat any nuts or bolts.' Brett ushers Alex back to the group.

'Seriously?' says Finn with a deadpan look on his face.

'Oh, I'm sorry. Did I hurt your feelings there? I got to say, did you get committed for the right disorder? Because from here it looks like you have Parkinson's disease, not bipolar.'

Nickolas balls his hands into fists. His knuckles are turning white and all he can see is red.

'Want me to get you some maracas so you can play us some music while you shake them about?' says Brett.

He stands up, ready to go all South Side on Brett's ass, but the rage dies the minute he sees Finn already standing, crowding Brett's personal space with nothing but hatred in those precious green eyes.

'The fuck you just say to me?' yells Finn.

'Hey, walk away,' Nickolas instructs, placing his hand on Finn's chest.

Finn ignores him. Nickolas knows that a fight between Finn and Brett would end in Finn's favour. Everyone from the South Side knows how to hold their own. They have to if they want to survive. There is nothing that he'd like to see more than Brett getting knocked out, but this place would look at Finn's outburst of anger as a setback from recovery and Brett isn't worth that.

'Brett. Go take over the craft corner,' orders Nickolas.

Brett's eyes are still locked onto Finn's, a smart-ass smirk plastered on his face.

'GO!' Nickolas yells.

Slowly, Brett steps back, eventually turning around and walking over to Hayley. Nickolas's hand is still on Finn's chest, preventing the redhead from attacking Brett. Nickolas lets out a sigh and then notices the time on the clock above the door.

'Hayley!' Nickolas calls out.

Without any hesitation, Hayley hurries towards him.

'Take Finn to his appointment with Dr Hale. When you get back, Ethan can be taken to his appointment with Dr Lance.'

Finn looks at Nickolas, shocked. He pulls away from Nickolas's touch, like it's suddenly burning, and storms off towards the exit before Hayley can even ask Finn to follow. Nickolas stands there, watching the door to the common room close behind Finn. His heart sinks, knowing that he's the cause of some of Finn's anger and pain.

'Thought you would have taken Gingersnap to his appointment,' says Brett.

'Someone has to stick around here and make sure you don't torture the patients.' Nickolas says loudly. He regrets saying it in an area where all the patients can hear him. He isn't thinking clearly, and he knows it's because of Finn.

*

Once Hayley returns from taking Ethan to his appointment, Nickolas leaves the common room under Brett and Hayley's care so he can attend to the patients' rooms. He grabs the dirty linen bin from the laundry room and heads back to change the bedding in all fifteen rooms. Once finished, Nickolas collects the cart full of fresh clothing to be distributed to each patient.

Normally, Nickolas hates doing these tasks. He prefers to spend time interacting with the patients, but today he needed to get out of that room. He needed the quiet. The repetition of stripping beds, dropping off clothes, and making his way from one room to another soothes him. As he returns the now empty cart, the door to Dr Hale's office opens and Nickolas feels a magnet pull as he sets eyes on his redhead.

His? Shit. No. *The* redhead. Finn is in no way and will probably never be his.

'Ah, Nickolas. Perfect timing,' says Dr Hale. 'Finn's session finished a few minutes early today, so I figured no one would be here to escort him back. Lucky for Finn, you were walking past.'

The way Finn is avoiding Nickolas's eyes makes him feel like he isn't so lucky.

'No problem. Would you like me to collect Ryder for his session?' Nickolas asks.

'Yes, thank you.'

Dr Hale closes the door, leaving Finn and Nickolas to stand there in silence. He begins to walk back to the common room, pleased to see Finn is at least walking beside him.

'Good session?' asks Nickolas.

'Like you care,' Finn spits back.

'I wouldn't have asked if I didn't.'

'Whatever.'

Nickolas feels whiplashed. The door to Finn's room is on his right, and without thinking, he grabs Finn's wrist and drags him inside, closing the door behind them.

'Look,' Nickolas begins. 'I'm sorry if you had a rough session, but I don't think taking it out on me is going to help.'

'Oh, so now you want to talk to me?' Finn argues back.

'What?'

'Look, I get it. If you don't want to talk to me after what I told you last night, that's fine. Just don't pretend that you care. I don't need that, especially from you.'

Finn looks down and Nickolas can't help but gravitate towards him, crowding Finn against the wall with his body.

'Hey, that's—that's not it.' Nickolas drops all heat from his voice, hoping Finn can hear the sincerity in it. He cautiously brushes his fingers against Finn's hand. When there is no sign of the redhead pulling away, Nickolas gently wraps his hand around Finn's wrist, noticing the quickened pulse beating against his fingertips.

'I'm sorry that I've had to keep my distance today. But don't ever think your past, your struggles, could ever make me think any less of you.'

Finn's head slowly rises, green eyes meeting Nickolas's. Even with the height difference, he can see in Finn's body language that the redhead feels small in comparison to him.

'Then why are you avoiding me?' There is an ache in Finn's voice.

'To protect you.'

There is a softness in Finn's eyes before it quickly changes to confusion.

'Brett is a sadistic, power-hungry asshole that would happily make your life a nightmare if he knew that you were more than just a patient.'

Green eyes widen enough for Nickolas to see the gears turning in Finn's head. Nickolas immediately releases his grip; his hand is cold the minute Finn's warmth disappears. Stepping back, Nickolas looks down, no longer able to meet Finn's eyes.

'That's not what I— what I was meant to say was— I didn't mean...' Nickolas begins to panic.

'Nick.'

'We should go. We've been gone long enough, and Ryder is due for his appointment.' Nickolas turns back around and opens Finn's door. He holds it open for the redhead, who stops in front of him, the privacy of the room gone.

'Nick, what you said—'

'Don't. Just...just forget it, okay?'

Finn gives him a small nod and then walks out of the room. Nickolas is relieved to see Finn has walked ahead and is now waiting to be let into the common room. As his key card unlocks the door, Finn steps forward and brushes an arm against Nickolas before walking over to Cora, Alex, and Ryder. He breathes out, trying to steady himself. He stands at the door for a couple more seconds before calling out for Ryder.

Ryder walks towards Nickolas, stronger than yesterday. The door closes and they make their walk back to where Nickolas just returned from.

'You alright, man?' asks Ryder.

'What? Yeah, why?' It takes Nickolas longer than it should have to give his reply.

'You're just a little pale. I mean, more than usual. You could pass as Casper's relative at this point.'

Nickolas chuckles. 'Shut up! Probably low blood sugar or something. It's my lunch break soon, so that'll help.'

They reach Dr Hale's office. Nickolas quickly raps at the door and passes Ryder on so he can head back. He stops at the bathroom, needing to relieve his bladder and give himself a moment to process what happened before he returns to the common room.

Upon his entry, Nickolas gives the room a quick scan, taking note of where everyone is. If his heart skips a beat when he locks eyes with Finn, well, that's for Nickolas to know and no one else.

Time moves quickly. Nickolas asks Hayley to continue taking patients to their appointments while he keeps an eye on Brett. He's surprised to see Brett getting involved with the patients at the craft corner and not just harassing them about their art-work. Nickolas loses track of time until Dot, Darren, and James step into the room, ready to start the afternoon shift. James walks towards the dining area, most likely instructed by Dot to get it ready for lunch while the others fan out. He spots his boss walking towards him.

'No bloodshed I see, that's always a good sign,' says Dot.

'Trust me, it was hard to resist,' Nickolas replies.

'You want to grab some lunch? You've been here the longest, the others can wait.'

Feeling like he is being watched, he gives a quick scan of the room and is surprised to see that it's not Finn's eyes on him, but Brett's.

'Thanks, that'd be good,' says Nickolas.

Dot smiles. 'I made a sponge cake with homemade jam and fresh cream. Make sure to have some.'

'What did you bring for everyone else to eat?'

A slight blush appears on Dot's cheeks as she playfully hits his arm.

Nickolas laughs. It's these kinds of moments that he shares with Dot that make him wish he had longer with his mother, who left when he was young. Not wanting to dwell on it, he decides to leave and feed his mind with food instead of thoughts.

The silence of the break room is both a relief and a curse. He has never done well with silence, growing up in a house full of chaos on the noisy streets of Canaryville, where he learned to sleep to the sounds of screeching car tyres, backfiring motors and gunshots. Nonetheless, he boils some water for his instant noodles and sits on the couch to enjoy his meal in peace. Of course, that doesn't last long.

'You were gone for a while this morning? Took another nap, did ya?' Brett questions.

Nickolas closes his eyes and counts to three, hoping that when he opens them, Brett will be gone, and it was simply a hallucination from the lack of food in his system.

One. Two. Three.

Fuck, guess not.

'Working. Something you struggle to do sometimes,' explains Nickolas.

'Right. Didn't know that involves long walks with patients.'

Nickolas keeps eating to make it look as though he isn't fazed by the comment. He waits for Brett to retrieve a water bottle out of the fridge and take a sip before answering.

'Patient needed the bathroom.' He makes sure not to call Finn by his name.

'And he couldn't just use the one in the common room when he came back?'

'Not sure why someone's bathroom activities are of any interest to you, but the patient was bustin' and I, for one, didn't feel like cleaning up piss because I made the guy wait.'

Brett nods, slowly walking back towards the door. 'See that's where you and I are different. If it was me, I would have made the guy clean up his own piss.' Brett winks at him and walks out.

Once again, Nickolas closes his eyes and counts to three, trying to clear his mind so he can go back to enjoying his food. He opens his eyes, pleased to see he is alone, and brings a forkful of noodles to his mouth.

'Oh, Nickolas. There you are,' Jasmine chimes in.

'Jesus Christ.' He whispers it under his breath, not wanting Jasmine to take offence.

'There's a Jessica on the phone asking to speak to you.'

Finn's sister. Nickolas puts his food on the table and makes his way to the front desk, reaching it quicker than Jasmine, as she slowly waddles behind him. He clears his throat before picking up the phone.

'Nickolas speaking.'

'Nickolas! Jessica. Cunningham. How's Finn? Is he okay? God, I hate that we can't visit him.' Jessica mumbles a few more things before there is a break long enough for Nickolas to answer all the questions.

'Finn's adjusting. The medications seem to be working but, like everything, the side effects are wearing him down. He's not giving up though. He's strong.'

He hears a sniffle on the other end and Nickolas can tell Finn's sister is holding back tears.

'He is,' Jessica agrees.

It's not his place to ask, but he has to know, for Finn. 'Are you planning on visiting him tomorrow?'

'Yes! Of course. Two o'clock, right?'

'Right. Two till four. I'm sure he'll love it.'

'Thank you. Compared to the last place...just, thank you for caring about my brother's wellbeing.'

A lump forms in his throat. It's Jessica's words that once again remind Nickolas that Finn is his patient, and people are trusting him to take care of Finn.

'Just doing my job.' Nickolas feels a little awkward. He coughs, wanting to go back to his food before his break is over and he has to step back into the noise.

'Guess I'll see you tomorrow,' Nickolas adds.

'See you tomorrow,' says Jessica.

He hangs up as Jasmine returns to the reception desk.

'Sorry. Took me forever to walk back, and then I realised I might as well make a toilet stop while I'm up.'

'It's all good. If that's everything, I'm going to go finish my lunch.'

'Sure, go. That's all I needed you for.'

As Nickolas walks to the break room, he decides that he isn't going to tell Finn about the phone call. Visitors have made promises before and the last thing he needs is to give Finn hope about family visiting, only to be disappointed if they decide not to show.

When he returns to work, the patients are in the middle of eating lunch. Dot sends Brett and Hayley off to have their break, giving Nickolas a moment to feel like he can breathe again. His eyes search for Finn the minute he knows Brett can't see him, and smiles when his eyes catch Finn smiling back at him. Nickolas gives Finn a small nod, breaking eye contact so his patient can continue to eat.

He walks over to Dot, making sure he speaks softly enough that Finn can't hear what he says.

'Finn's sister called again. Don't think I've ever had some-one inquire about their family as much as she does. It's nice to see.'

'Hmm, yes. I spoke to her yesterday too,' says Dot.

'You don't seem too happy about it.'

'Well, I mean, it's nice to know Finn has family looking out for him, but he needs to be able to do this on his own. If his sister is constantly babying him, scrutinising him to make sure he is following his routine and medication regime, I just...' Dot lets out a sigh and turns so Nickolas has his boss's full attention. 'I just fear he might end up back here.'

Nickolas frowns.

'What?'

'I'm not saying he will, I'm saying...I don't know. I may be wrong. I hope I'm wrong. It's not my place to step. It's just a feeling I have. Something I've seen many times before.'

Nickolas is shaking his head before Dot has finished speak-ing. 'He's stronger than that. I know it. He doesn't want his disorder to define who he is, and the only way for that to be the case is to make sure he doesn't end up back here.'

Dot gives Nickolas a nod and turns to face the patients sitting in the room. His boss walks over to the collection cart and starts taking stock of the dirty dishes and utensils as the patients bring their trays up.

Nickolas takes his place by the door, standing in a way that lets him watch the patients head back into the common room while keeping an eye on those remaining in the dining area.

James gives Nickolas a nod while walking past him and goes into the common room to set up for the group session. Nickolas acts as though he hasn't noticed the way Finn is lingering back, waiting for everyone to clear out. With the dining area empty and Dot returning the dishes to the kitchen area, it gives them a moment alone, away from prying ears as Finn stands before him.

'I'm sorry for the way I acted earlier. You know, after my session,' says Finn.

He smiles. 'It's fine. You had every right to be upset.'

'Still. I shouldn't have treated you that way. Not after everything you've done.'

Nickolas cocks an eyebrow.

'It's been a long time since someone has actually...cared about how I'm doing. My family, sure they care. But I don't know, it feels more like they want me to get better so it's one less thing to worry about.'

For a brief moment, Nickolas worries that what Dot was saying about Jessica may have some truth behind it. He wants to pull Finn into his arms, hug the redhead tight and reassure him that people do care about him, even if it turns out that Nickolas may be the only one.

'I, ah, I told Dr Hale that I remembered about...what happened.'

'That's great, Finn. That's really great.'

'She is going to help me process it, but she said bringing it up in group might help.'

'Whenever you're ready.'

Dot returns from the kitchen and both of their heads turn towards the noise of the door swinging open.

'I better get out there. Get to my seat before group starts.'

'Good luck.'

Finn walks into the common room as Dot slowly steps towards him.

'Everything okay?' asks Dot.

'Yep. All good.'

Dorothy keeps walking and Nickolas follows.

James has the chairs set up. The patients that know they have a group session are already sitting, waiting, while the others are standing by the door.

'James, can you please start escorting the remaining patients back to their rooms?' Dot instructs.

James begins to usher the patients out one by one.

'Nickolas, you can stand at the door today. I'll ask the others to help get this place looking good for the visitors tomorrow,' informs Dot.

There are two patients left by the time Dr Hale comes in to begin the group session. James and Dot walk them back to their room while Nickolas closes the door behind him and stands guard in case any of the patients need assistance. He only has an hour left of his shift, and although standing outside a door, as if he is a bouncer at a nightclub, is probably the slowest way to kill time, it is also the only thing he wants to do.

Standing guard, so to speak, allows him to be close to Finn. He can't hear what's being said behind the door, but a part of him settles knowing that, if Finn needed help, Nickolas would be the one called to assist.

He isn't sure how much time passes before he hears raised voices coming from behind the door.

'Boo-fucking-hoo. Don't play the victim when you put yourself in a situation for that to happen.'

'Sasha, you need to calm down.' Dr Hale instructs.

'No! I'm sick of all these people feeling sorry for themselves because of what happened to them when they were the ones stupid enough to leave themselves vulnerable to be taken advantage of.'

Nickolas goes to open the door but stops. He hasn't been called in to help yet and, from what he can hear, no one is at risk of getting hurt. It's purely heightened emotions during a group discussion.

'Leave myself vulnerable? How the fuck is being drugged my fault?'

Shit. That's Finn talking, defending himself.

'You're telling me you didn't already have something else in your system before you went back to that guy's hotel?'

Nickolas grips the door handle a little harder and for the first time in his career, he has a desire to hear what's being said behind that door.

'So, what if I did? I still knew what I was doing. What I wanted.' Finn yells. 'But being shackled to a bed and raped was not what I had in mind when I agreed to go back to that guy's room.'

Nickolas's heart feels heavy as he hears Finn's voice break when saying the word 'rape'. It pains him that he can't go in there and comfort Finn.

'Whatever. You think I wanted to grow up in a house where I was raped daily? No drugs were involved. No shady shit. Just me and the one person who was meant to protect me in life.'

'Sasha, that's enough. This is a safe space and not a chance for you to attack Finn for opening up about his trauma while manic.' Dr Hale orders.

After that, Nickolas can't hear what's being said behind the door. He slowly releases his grip on the door handle, his knuckles ache from clenching it so hard, but eventually he spins around so he's facing the corridor.

It's almost time for Nickolas to go home for the day when a sudden breeze sends a shiver up Nickolas's spine. He turns to see Dr Hale holding the door open, allowing the patients to walk out and make their way back to their rooms.

'Everything go okay?'

He doesn't generally ask, but he wants to let Dr Hale know that he's aware of the heated argument that took place not too long ago.

'Nothing I couldn't handle. Thank you, though.'

Finn walks towards him, hands in the pockets of his grey sweatpants and a sullen look on his face.

'Finn. You did well today. Progress.' Dr Hale sounds proud. 'I know Sasha didn't make it seem that way, but everyone in this room is dealing with their own struggles. Sometimes taking it out on others is easier than trying to face their fears.'

The words resonate with Nickolas. Finn simply gives Dr Hale a nod and a half-smile before walking past them both, returning to room thirteen. Her mind already elsewhere, Dr Hale walks towards the offices, reading over notes as the clip-clop of heels echoes throughout the corridor. It's three o'clock. Nickolas is ready to go home to shower, eat and sleep, thankful that he has the afternoon shift tomorrow. However, a part of him isn't ready to leave, not yet, not before he checks on Finn.

Making his way to room thirteen, he's surprised to see Finn has left the door open. Nickolas takes it as a sign that Finn was hoping he would stop by, sure that had the redhead wanted to be left alone, the door would be closed.

'I, ah, thought I'd say goodbye before heading home,' says Nickolas.

He sees Finn sitting on the bed with his back against the wall, legs stretched out before him. Finn is looking at him, tracking his every movement. It's the first time Nickolas has enjoyed a person following his every move.

'Will I see you tomorrow?' Finn asks.

'Course. I got the afternoon shift.'

'Do you ever get a day off?' There's a smile in Finn's voice.

'I get two days off after working fourteen days straight.'

'Jesus. When do you have time to do anything?'

'It's shift work. I'm not always working doubles but, I mean, everyone else kinda has a family or something, so I offer to work more to help out. Give them a chance to spend time with their loved ones.'

'Don't you have anyone you want to spend time with, Nick?' There is sadness in Finn's voice, along with a touch of curiosity.

'No one in my life worth sharing my time with, besides my cat. She's probably the only one that can tolerate me anyway.'

Finn doesn't seem to buy it.

Nickolas scuffs his foot on the floor, no longer wanting the attention to be on him.

'Maybe we can change that...' suggests Finn.

He looks up. There is kindness in Finn's eyes. Nickolas opens his mouth only to close it, not sure how to respond.

'I'll see you tomorrow, Nick.'

Nickolas is thankful Finn ends their conversation; not sure he would have been able to form a sentence coherent enough to get him out of there.

'Yeah, ah...' He coughs. 'See you tomorrow, Finn.'

He walks back out, closing Finn's door and making a dash to the locker rooms to grab his belongings. His cheeks are warm, and he wouldn't be surprised if they are the same shade as his uniform. Waving goodbye to everyone as he makes his way to the front, his brain is working on autopilot after Finn's words have caused a short circuit.

In his car heading back home, Nickolas plays every conversation in his mind. He analyses every touch, every look, every smile. Surely, he isn't imagining things, is he? The way Finn looked at him today, the soft words of kindness before he left. Maybe Finn is beginning to see Nickolas as something more. It's a hopeful thought and it scares Nickolas more than if it were true. Hope has never been kind to Nickolas. It's always something he has desperately held on to, only to be pulled away from it and knocked down even further.

Nickolas curses and grips the steering wheel tight. This wouldn't be an issue if he had kept his mouth shut and simply accepted Finn being angry at him. Now, the best thing to do is act as though he never said those words. If he admits to himself that Finn is more to him than just a patient, then he'll also have to deal with the disappointment if Finn doesn't reciprocate those feelings. But if Finn does feel the same, then he's stuck between wanting to be with him and having to be professional. A balance that would be impossible to maintain.

There is a reason doctors and surgeons are not allowed to treat family members. It's because their feelings cloud their judgment. Nickolas is no doctor, and just because he stitched himself up once or twice back when he was a kid doesn't make him a surgeon either. But he knows a thing or two about feelings getting in the way of rationality. How one's judgment can blur, causing people to get hurt because of it. He could never forgive himself if something happened to Finn because he let his feelings get in the way of his treatment.

He parks his car in the empty car space behind his apartment. He exhales, turns the engine off and sits there for a minute or two, his palms pressed into his eyes. The logical side of his brain battles with his emotional side, causing Nickolas to think of the one person he wishes he could talk to about what's going on. And as that person comes into his mind, everything else stops, and tears fall from his eyes.

6. Sunday

Sweat drips down Nickolas's back. His tank top sticks to his skin and at this point, he wonders why he even bothered wearing one.

One-one-four.

Jab-jab-hook.

Right foot forward, a slight bend at the knees. Nickolas hunches into himself as he covers his face with his fists.

One-one-four.

Jab-jab-hook.

Music is blaring in his ears. A playlist he made to keep the blood flowing, the anger present, and the adrenalin pumping.

Eminem's song *Venom* always stops Nickolas from overthinking and getting stuck in his head with his self-destructive thoughts. The angry lyrics and his fists hitting the leather are the only things he wants to be able to feel as his skin burns from the pounding he's been giving the bag for the last thirty minutes. Nickolas woke up earlier than he would have liked after working a double, his mind was racing as if he'd snorted a line of coke. He was restless. The pent-up energy inside him needed to be released. He used to subdue the itch by going off to collect debts for his father, allowing his fists to get dirty in the process. But that isn't him anymore.

There was only one place that was going to help him with the pent-up energy, so he changed his clothes, packed a bag, and made his way to the hole-in-the-wall gym not far from his apartment. The equipment is basic, the lighting is dim, and all Nickolas needs are the few weights they offer and the punching bag, currently held together with duct tape and hanging from the roof, to keep him satisfied.

One-one-four.

Jab-jab-hook.

With each punch, he tries to push everything out of his body. All the noise that's keeping him awake.

South Side trash – punch.

Abusive father – punch.

Homophobic colleague – punch.

The need to protect Finn – punch.

Rapist pigs of this fucked up world – punch, punch, punch.

He finally stops. He wraps his arms around the bag, hugging it tightly as he tries to take in enough air to stop the burning in his lungs. He squeezes his eyes shut, fighting back the memories that are trying to break free from the cage he's locked them away in. It isn't enough. His body is aching. He can barely move his arms. But everything is still so loud.

'Hey man, you done yet or what?' a voice breaks through the music in Nickolas's headphones.

He rests his forehead against the bag. His heart rate is finally starting to settle.

'Yo, if you're lonely, rent a whore. Some of us want to use the bag to work out,' the same voice adds.

Nickolas turns around. 'What the fuck you say to me?' Some blonde-haired wannabe punk who's a foot taller than Nickolas, but has no muscle, is staring him down. One punch, and Nickolas knows he could take the guy.

'What, you deaf now too?' The blonde puffs out a scrawny looking chest, thinking it will intimidate him.

'Bitch, does it look like I'm fuckin' done? No. So why don't you walk over and lift something that has a number higher than your IQ and when I walk away, then you'll know I'm fucking done.'

Whether it's the way Nickolas's eyebrows shoot up, the way his chest puffs out, or his knuckle tattoos, it seems to be enough for the blonde to take his advice and walk over to the other side of the gym. Either way, Nickolas was done with the bag, he just didn't want to give that smug asshole the satisfaction of thinking he had given it up because of some tough-guy attitude.

Nickolas picks up his backpack from the corner of the room, takes out the small towel and soaks up the sweat dripping from his hair, down his face, and around his neck. The songs on his playlist have come to an end. He removes his knock-off AirPods and reaches for his water bottle. He takes a few mouthfuls before throwing his bottle back into the bag. Nickolas peels his tank top off his body and reaches down to grab the spare shirt he brought with him to change into.

'Nice ink,' a deep voice comments.

Nickolas tenses. He turns around to see who's talking to him, quickly pulling the shirt over his chest as his eyes land on some juicehead that no doubt doesn't have a dick anymore after being on steroids for so long. He decides to ignore the comment and continues to pack up.

'Any meaning behind them?' the juicehead continues.

'If there was, probably would be something personal, right? So why would I go telling a stranger about them?' Nickolas bites back.

'Okay. So how 'bout I buy you a drink and that way I'm no longer a stranger?'

He thumbs his bottom lip and checks the guy out.

A smirk appears on the juicehead's face.

'Thanks, but no thanks,' says Nickolas.

'Shame. Would have been fun.'

The juicehead gives Nickolas a wink, walks back to the corner and begins to jump rope. Nickolas makes a dash for his car before anyone else decides they can try and have a conversation with him. He unlocks the door, gets behind the wheel, and throws his bag onto the passenger seat. He is fucked. Honest to God fucked and not in the way he could have been had he said yes to that guy. Finn has dug his way under his skin and no matter what he does, he can't shake him. Everything comes back to Finn.

His dreams are flooded with silky red locks and eyes that particular shade of green after a storm has cleared and the sun is breaking through the clouds to shine upon the water. He dreams of playing connect the dots with freckles that litter pale skin, and although he never actually sees a face, when he wakes up, he knows all of it is pointing him to one person. Finn. While he ate his cereal that morning, a rerun of Annie was playing on the TV, and Nickolas couldn't change the channel quick enough as he saw the fiery redhead talking back to the owner of the orphanage. After he'd changed the channel and his eyes focused on a random documentary about sharks, Nickolas couldn't help but think of the fire in Finn's heart, similar to that in Annie herself. It was at that point that he decided he needed to get out of the house and punch something to distract himself.

Getting back home from the gym, he glances at his watch as he makes his way around the front of his apartment building. Nickolas still has two hours to kill before he's due at work and no fucking clue what to do. He makes his way into his apartment and heads straight for the shower. Socks doesn't even look up from the windowsill, too busy basking in the rays of sunshine to say hello.

Resting his phone on the bathroom countertop, Nickolas figures that if he plays some music, there'll be less of a chance that his mind will wander to places it shouldn't while his body is wet and naked. He puts his music on shuffle, turns the water on, and sets the temperature more on the colder side. Nickolas hisses as the cool water mixes with his body heat, and he shudders as his body temperature adjusts and possibly begins to go into shock.

For the first few minutes, Nickolas simply stands under the showerhead, closes his eyes, and feels the water run down his body. Finally, his brain is quiet. He rolls his neck, hoping it will loosen the kinks, and for the first time in a long time, he feels relaxed.

'Reow.'

Nickolas jumps as an orange blur lands on the shower curtain, legs stretched out like a starfish.

'For fuck's sake.' His hands are curled into fists, held up in front of his body, automatically in fight mode from the sudden fright.

'Meow.'

Nickolas pulls the curtain to the side so he can poke his head out. Water drips onto the tiles as he tilts his head towards Socks, who seems to be enjoying the climb up his shower curtain.

'Glad to see you're enjoying yourself. You going to pay for the new curtain or shall I just enjoy these claw marks as new decor?'

He pulls the curtain shut and decides he should finish cleaning himself and get out. Socks is meowing again, but he can no longer see a shadow hanging beside him. Looking up, he's surprised to find the furball balancing on the curtain rod, looking down at Nickolas as the water falls onto his face.

'If you jump, you get wet. And we all know how well that turned out last time.'

He chuckles at the memory as he rinses the soap off his body. He turns the water off and is thankful Socks decided to simply watch him from above.

Grabbing the towel, Nickolas dries himself and then wraps it around his waist. He steps out and makes his way towards the mirror, swipes away the condensation so his reflection is looking back at him. The music is suddenly muffled. Curious as to why, he looks down at his phone and laughs at Socks, who has decided to jump down and sit directly on it.

'I know. I've been working a fair bit lately, haven't I?'

Nickolas scratches behind Socks's ears and smiles at the way his cat instantly begins to purr from his touch. He marvels at the contrast between his ghost-white skin against the sunset colour fur. Nickolas's mind is taken back to his hand stroking Finn's beautiful red hair when he was sick. Even his cat reminds him of Finn. He is doomed.

'Guess I had a thing for redheads without even realising it, hey.'

Socks meows back at Nickolas, jumps down and swishes back into the living room. He leans on the countertop and stares into his reflection in the mirror. He looks torn. The internal battle between his feelings for Finn and the professionalism he needs to uphold is taking a toll on him, tearing him apart from the inside out. Nickolas hasn't felt like this since he decided to admit to himself that he was gay. Once he came to that realisation, no longer able to lie to himself, it was easier to lie to his family, since telling them the truth would be the same as signing his death warrant.

He takes a deep breath, holds it, and releases it along with every fear and worry he is holding within. He knows what he has to do. There's no denying it now. Looking at his reflection, Nickolas stands up straight.

'I fucking like you, Finn Cunningham. And when you get released, because *you will* get released, that's when something more can come from all this.'

The minute the words leave his mouth, his shoulders relax, his eyes look deeper in colour, and the weight on his shoulders vanishes enough to make him feel like he's standing a few inches taller. He smiles at himself. This is what's best. Instead of trying to push those feelings down and pretend they don't exist, instead of saying it can never happen, he's just going to tell himself that one day it can. The noise in his head is suddenly gone, and this time it won't be coming back.

*

The sun is out, shining brightly overhead as he walks into work. As soon as he steps inside, the natural light is replaced with the glare of fluorescent lights, giving the illusion that the sun is always shining, even if it were pouring rain outside. He doesn't allow the way his job resembles working in a cage to dampen his day. No. Today is different. Today he's filled with optimism.

'Hold on. Stop,' Jasmine instructs.

Nickolas does as asked.

'What's going on? What's— what's this foreign thing on your face? Is that...is that a smile?'

'Jesus.' He wants to give Jasmine the finger but figures an eyeroll and a scratch of his eyebrow is enough for her to know he's not amused by the joke.

'Did you get laid? I swear that's the only thing that can explain this.'

Of-fucking-course that is the moment Darren walks in since they are working the same shift today.

'Who got laid?' Darren asks.

'Nickolas,' Jasmine offers.

Darren does an over-exaggerated gasp, and this time Nickolas does decide to give his colleagues the finger.

'No one got laid. I went to the gym, had a good boxing session and now I'm here to work, okay?'

'Ahh, that explains it. You got to hit something,' says Jasmine.

'Whatever.' Nickolas barely gets the words out in between his chuckles as Jasmine laughs along with him. This feels nice. He's always gotten along with Jasmine and, well, Darren he can handle when the guy isn't being so *Darren*. But it just feels different today, and he knows Finn is the reason for that.

Nickolas quickly changes into his uniform, then grabs the few snacks he brought with him and throws them into the cupboard in the break room. Dot's in the room, and Nickolas is always happy to share a shift with his boss.

'Ready for today?' Dot hands Nickolas a chocolate cookie with white chocolate chips.

He automatically takes a bite before answering with a nod.

'Good,' says Dot. 'I'm worried Ryder's family may not visit today, and according to the notes in his file, his last two sessions haven't been that promising. So, he may need the support.'

Like every Sunday, Nickolas dedicates his shift to spending time with the patients who don't get a visitor. For those two hours, he does whatever he can to make them feel like they haven't been forgotten.

'I'll send Brett, Eric, and Hayley on break while everyone has lunch. Hopefully one of them is already in the dining area setting up.' Dot explains.

'Who knows with those three? The less time I'm around Brett the better, that's all I care about,' says Nickolas.

'Yes, I know. Why do you think I try to plan it like that?' Dot gives Nickolas a knowing look.

'Well, what can I say, there is always at least one workplace asshole. Brett takes the mantle.'

Darren walks into the break room, places food in the fridge and together, all three of them make their way to the common room. Dot unlocks the door and holds it open for he and Darren to walk through. A hand reaches out and gently takes his arm, holding him back from following Darren into the room.

'I know it's hard, but try not to walk up to Finn the minute you step inside,' suggests Dot.

Nickolas blushes, looking at his shoes like a kid who has been caught with his hand in the cookie jar.

'I have eyes and ears, Nickolas. You know I don't believe any gossip, since it's generally created through boredom, but I know what I see.'

'There's nothing—'

'I know. That's not what I was getting at. You're good at your job and I know you'd never do anything unethical. But just be aware that not everyone knows you the way I do. Rumours can be dangerous and hard to prove false, okay?'

Nickolas gives Dot a nod of understanding as she releases his arm. He scans the room quickly to get a sense of where everyone is. His heart begins to race as he notices the one person in the room who can brighten up his day. Finn is playing a card game with Cora and Alex, and Nickolas is not at all surprised to find Finn looking up at him from behind playing cards.

Has Finn been watching the door, waiting for me to walk through?

The thought alone warms Nickolas from within and he hopes his body isn't as flushed as he feels. The redhead is smiling bright, and Nickolas notices a small tremor in Finn's hands while he holds the playing cards. Nickolas takes it all in. Finn's looking well, rested, and has gained some weight, making him look healthy compared to the version of Finn that walked through those doors five days ago. Nickolas gives the redhead a quick nod, before casting his eyes away and walking towards some patients on the opposite side of the room.

Although he'd like to walk straight up to Finn and spend the day talking to the redhead, after their conversation yesterday, it's safer for them to keep their distance. Brett is on shift, but now, after Dot's little reminder, Nickolas may have to be concerned about his other colleagues too. As Nickolas sits, he looks over at Finn one more time, who, while smiling, gives him a small nod in return. A nod. It's so simple. A universal sign that everyone would understand, and yet, between himself and Finn, it says everything they can't speak out loud in a room full of people.

Distracting himself with a game of Scrabble, Nickolas is surprised to hear Dot call out that it's lunchtime, the last thirty minutes going quicker than he had expected. Nickolas offers to pack the game up so that the patients he was playing with can make their way into the dining area.

'You going to grab some food?'

Nickolas is already smiling at the sound of that voice before he sees the person it's connected to. Nickolas squints a little as he looks up, the ceiling lights reflecting in his eyes as it casts a glow behind Finn's head, like he's an angel from above.

'Figured I'd get something at dinner. I made sure to eat before coming in,' Nickolas explains.

'Ah, lunch for one. Sounds riveting,' says Finn.

'I wasn't alone.'

The smile falls from Finn's face.

Nickolas slowly stands up. 'I enjoyed a lovely bowl of cereal while Socks sat beside me, grooming herself.'

Finn catches on to what Nickolas just said and breaks out laughing.

Nickolas loves that sound. He wants to hear it every day. Finn's laugh is infectious, and he finds himself joining in on the joke.

'I'm sorry. I shouldn't laugh, but Socks? I'm hoping that's your cat because otherwise, you may have some kinks that I'm not down with.'

Nickolas continues to laugh while swallowing the lump in his throat. He tries not to overreact to the comment about kinks because that leads to thoughts about maybe one day, he and Finn getting to explore something sexual together. Hopefully.

'Yes. Socks is my cat,' Nickolas clarifies. 'She has black paws that make it look like she's wearing socks, so I figured the name was perfect for her.'

'That's adorable. But also makes it sound like you're a six-year-old naming your first pet.'

'Well, she is my first pet. So, I guess I'm making up for lost time.'

The laughter dies down and Finn's soft eyes stare back at him.

'I never had any pets either,' says Finn. 'Unless you count the strays my brother would bring home, which we had to save before he tortured them.'

'The fuck?' *What is it about Finn that has Nickolas saying things he shouldn't?*

'Long story. No harm came to any animal, but for a minute there he was showing signs of becoming a serial killer.'

Once again Nickolas and Finn are the only ones left standing in the room.

'You better get some food,' he tells Finn.

He stays back. Dot and Darren watch over everyone while he packs away the activities. They only have thirty minutes after lunch before visitors will be allowed to enter, so he wants to make sure the space is clean, the chairs are properly set up and games are close by for those that may need a distraction. The room is big enough to hold all fifteen patients and a maximum of two visitors per patient. Sometimes, the patients who don't receive a warm hug with a bright smile request to go back to their room to be alone. Nickolas tries to convince them to stay. The solitude of their room would only make things worse, but he understands how hard it would be for them to sit and be surrounded by something they don't get to enjoy themselves.

Nickolas stands in the middle of the room, hands on his hips as he looks around. Everything seems in order, so he joins the others in the dining area. He immediately seeks out Finn. He can't help it. His body automatically needs to know Finn's whereabouts when he sets foot into a room, not feeling settled until he knows where to find the green-eyed beauty. Watching Finn eat and chat with the others, Nickolas spots Ryder a few seats down, playing with his food and placing the smallest amounts onto a fork before slowly bringing it up to his thin lips. Nickolas can see the fight between body and mind playing out in front of him as Ryder opens wide and takes a bite of the food. Nickolas keeps his eyes on Ryder as he makes his way towards Dot.

'Did Ryder's notes happen to mention a lack of appetite?' asks Nickolas.

Dot scans the room to find Ryder before answering Nickolas's question. His boss lets out a sad sigh. 'His weigh-ins have been showing signs of weight loss again. He isn't being as open in his sessions or group. He says he isn't purging, but perhaps he has stopped eating instead.'

'Yesterday, I took him to his session with Dr Hale, and he had the strength to walk on his own. I considered it a sign of improvement,' says Nickolas.

'Unfortunately, it seems he was putting on a front. Acting like he is getting better when, really, he isn't.'

'Shit. I'll keep an eye on him.'

Nickolas floats around the tables, seeing how everyone else is doing as he makes his way over towards Ethan, who he's surprised to see eating alone.

'Hey man, can I sit with you?' Nickolas asks.

A small nod of Ethan's head is all Nickolas needs to take a seat.

'How you been?' asks Nickolas

'Fine. Why?' says Ethan.

'No reason. Just checking in. It's kinda part of my job but don't tell anyone, okay?'

The smile is small, but not as much as Nickolas would have liked to have seen from Ethan. He goes for small talk. Simple questions to get yes-or-no answers about the food or the crafts. Asking whether Ethan wants to play a game with him later or if he needs a new book to read. Ethan doesn't give him much, but it's all Nickolas needs to know that he's at least tried and is available to talk to if Ethan needs to. He stands up, pushes his chair back into the table, and gives Ethan a pat on the back as he tells him to enjoy the food.

A small whimper falls from Ethan's lips. Nickolas's hand is still resting on Ethan's back between the shoulder blade and spine. Nickolas knows he didn't put too much pressure when he gave a pat goodbye, but by that whimper, it is evident that Ethan is in pain. Nickolas doesn't move his hand away; instead, he kneels so he is level with Ethan.

'It's fine. Really.' Ethan quickly explains. 'I slipped on the soap in the shower and my back bumped into the wall a little too hard and—'

Nickolas delicately moves his hand and pulls Ethan's shirt back just enough so he can peek down the collar and catch sight of the beginnings of a dark grey bruise.

Nickolas keeps his tone calm. 'Ethan. If this happened last night, then why does the colouring of the bruise look fresh?' Nickolas waits. 'Why don't we get out of here? Talk someplace private,' Nickolas suggests.

'N-no, that's okay. I still have some food left to eat, and—'

'You can bring it with you.' This time, Nickolas's voice doesn't give Ethan the chance to say no. He stands, waiting for Ethan to follow, before they walk out of the room together, taking a seat furthest away from the dining area door. Dot is watching him with a confused look, but he gives his boss a reassuring nod to let Dot know he will explain later.

'Ethan.' Nickolas's voice is low, his tone even and calm, as if he were talking to a child. 'What happened?'

'Please don't ask me that,' Ethan begs.

'How come?'

'Because if I tell you, then this—this is nothing compared to what will happen to me.'

'So someone is doing this to you?'

Ethan nods but doesn't offer up any further information.

'If I don't know who, then how can I stop it from happening again?'

Ethan looks at the tray of food and gives Nickolas nothing else, shutting down momentarily, and for a second, Nickolas is concerned he has pushed to the point where one of Ethan's alters may have taken over to shield Ethan from having to continue an uncomfortable conversation.

Noise begins to make its way into the common room as the patients trickle back in. Nickolas decides to drop it and vows to keep an eye on Ethan. 'I'm here to help. We all are. I'm going to keep an eye out, so you don't feel like you have to be the one to tell me. But if you decide to share the name with me, I'm here.'

Nickolas takes Ethan's tray, knowing full well that he has finished eating, and was merely hoping to use it as an excuse to get out of talking.

'That is not a face I like to see when coming back from a conversation with a patient.' Dot has been waiting for him, needing to know what has him so concerned.

'Trust me, it's not one I like either.' He rubs his face, keeping his back to the patients so no one can read his lips or overhear their conversation. 'Someone is hurting Ethan.'

'Hurting how?'

'Physically. A few days ago, I noticed a bruise on his arm. He claimed it happened from something one of his alters must have done. But today he has one on his back. It's like he's been pushed hard into something. Whoever it is, he's too scared to give a name.'

'Oh my.'

Nickolas is thinking more around the lines of 'fuck', but sure, 'oh my' works too.

The other three walk back into the room, their lunch breaks over.

'Right. Okay. We'll keep an eye out. I want you to examine him for bruises each day. Hopefully, if the person catches on that we are watching and monitoring, they may stop,' says Dot.

'Speaking from experience, if they know we are watching Ethan, they'll just find a way to hurt him without leaving a mark,' explains Nickolas.

Dorothy's sympathetic eyes land on Nickolas's. Dot gently runs a hand up and down his arm, knowing how close to home this is for him.

'I know,' says Dot. 'But for now, we just need to help him the best we can with the information he has given us and get ready for the visitors.' Dot squeezes Nickolas's arm before walking back into the common room. His boss walks towards each orderly, giving them instructions for the next few hours.

Nickolas already knows the plan. He and Dot will stay in the room to monitor the patients, while Darren and Hayley will remain at the front desk to help escort the visitors into the room as they arrive. Dot will send Brett and Eric to clean the patient's rooms, as they wouldn't have been tended to this morning, making sure they have clean clothes, toilet paper, paper towels, and fresh sheets. With the way Brett and Eric work, that should keep them busy until the end of their shift.

The orderlies and patients disperse. Nickolas wonders over to Finn.

'Feels like everyone is on edge. Waiting to hear if they have won the lottery or something,' Finn comments.

'For some, a visit from family does feel like that. We never let the patients know if family has mentioned if they'd be coming to see them in case something changes and that excitement turns into disappointment,' Nickolas explains.

'That happen often?'

'Unfortunately, yes. It can do a lot of harm to a patient's recovery.'

'Well, I doubt anyone is coming to see me. My sister is working three jobs to help support my siblings, and my eldest brother is off at college. Honestly, it's probably been easier for them since I've been in here.'

'Finn?' says a woman's voice.

Finn's head shoots up at the sound of Jessica's voice. Nickolas notices the single tear that falls from Finn's cheek as the redhead stands up, suddenly looking a few years younger as he falls into Jessica's embrace.

Nickolas turns and sees Finn's brother slowly walking towards them, no doubt taking his time so Finn can have a moment with Jessica. Finn's shoulders are shaking, possibly from tears of relief after keeping up a tough exterior for so long, a shield to avoid disappointment, had no one shown.

'I'll leave you guys alone,' says Nickolas.

He takes a seat with Ryder, aware that the twenty-one-year-old may need most of his attention today. Nickolas tells himself that it's not because Ryder is the patient sitting closest to Finn, allowing him to keep Finn within earshot so he can overhear his conversations. Nickolas knows he shouldn't listen. Finn deserves privacy while being reunited with family. But since the redhead's arrival, Nickolas has been ignoring his brain when it's been telling him what is ethically the right thing to do, so why would he suddenly start now?

More visitors make their way into the room while Jessica tells Finn stories about some people named Kate, Luke, and Liam, which Nickolas assumes are Finn's siblings.

'You look good. Are you good?' Jessica asks.

'I'm good, Jess. The ahh, the side effects are slowly wearing off, but I feel clear,' says Finn.

'That's so great, Finn.'

'Mum?' asks Ryder

Nickolas is brought back to what's happening around him when Ryder turns towards a woman walking up to them. If he heard correctly, Ryder called this woman mum, and honestly, Nickolas could not be more relieved that Ryder has someone here for support.

'Hey, honey.' The woman leans in for a hug.

Ryder stays seated, too shocked and possibly weak to stand. Nickolas decides he should move and let them have some time together.

Most of the patients have someone here for them, except three. It's only been thirty minutes, so there is still time for visitors to arrive. Cora is sitting by the window, and he makes his way towards her, pleased that he is still in earshot of Finn.

'Have you made any friends in here?' asks Jessica.

'I mean. I don't know if I'd call them friends but, I have a few people I like to talk to. Some more than others,' says Finn.

'Do they have bipolar too?'

'Ah, no. No, it's just me from what I can tell.'

Cora picks up a deck of cards, shuffles them and then deals out seven cards each, offering a pile to Nickolas without even asking him if he wants to play.

'Do you have any sevens?' Cora asks.

Nickolas laughs as he realises Cora's game of choice. Go Fish.

'I'm ah, I'm glad you guys came to visit. I wasn't sure if you would,' says Finn.

Nickolas's heart breaks hearing the sad tone in Finn's voice.

'Of course we would. We would have come sooner if we were allowed but the rules on visiting here are bullshit,' says Jessica.

'Ha, yeah. It kinda works though, with establishing a routine for us.'

Nickolas is so proud when he hears those words. It means Finn understands the system and accepts it as part of the treatment.

'I call every day. Nickolas gives me an update on how you're doing. So don't think for a minute we wouldn't prefer to have you home.'

'Wait, you talk to Nickolas?'

'Yes, sometimes Dorothy but mostly Nickolas. Why?'

'No reason, I just, he never said anything.'

'I don't think the orderlies are meant to tell you what goes on around here, Finn. Plus, he doesn't seem like the talkative type.'

Ouch. But Nickolas can't deny that it's kind of true. If he doesn't have to talk to someone or doesn't want to, then the look Nickolas gives will say it all. Considering the only time Jessica and Jake met Nickolas was the night Finn was committed, it probably wasn't the best first impression.

'Do you have any queens?' asks Cora.

Reluctantly, Nickolas hands over the queen of hearts in his hand.

'He's actually been really helpful. I don't think I would have adjusted so quickly without him,' explains Finn.

'Really?' says Jessica.

What's that supposed to mean? It is his job to take care of the patients in this place.

'What's that supposed to mean?'

Sounds like Finn feels the same way. It makes Nickolas smile.

'Nothin', it's just...considering the stories you told us about the last place you were in and, I mean, the guy has "hate you" tattooed on his knuckles. It's just a surprise they would even let someone like that work here,' says Jake.

'You don't know him like I do, okay? Hell, half the guys I've met looked decent, and they turned out to be low-life scum,' explains Finn.

'Do you have any twos?' asks Nickolas.

Cora hands over a card while Nickolas does a fist pump in the air, earning a laugh from Cora and, if he's not mistaken, a laugh from Finn too.

'What's so funny?' Jessica asks.

'Nothing. It's nothing.'

Smooth, Finn. Nice cover. Nickolas feels himself blushing at the thought of Finn glancing in his direction, when the red-head should be concentrating on Jessica and Jake.

There is an hour left for visitors and Cora is still playing Go Fish with Nickolas.

'You doing okay?' Nickolas asks Cora.

'I had a feeling no one was coming this week. It's my sister's birthday and when it comes to deciding who gets priority, the golden child always wins.'

'I'm sorry. I'm sure it's hard on everyone in your family, but it's not fair that they hold something you have no control over against you.'

'I know that, now. Maybe not a year or two ago, but now I'm in this place for me, not for them.'

These are the moments that make Nickolas love his job and remind him why he does it.

'So, can I come home soon?' Finn asks.

Nickolas's ears perk up. There has been no talk or mention of Finn's release. There is a pause in the conversation, which makes Nickolas nervous.

'What? What's with the looks?' says Finn.

'Do you have any nines?' asks Cora.

'Finn. Your therapist called us yesterday. She thinks...she thinks it might be best if you stay a little longer,' says Jessica.

'A little longer? What? Wh-why?' says Finn.

'Nickolas? Any nines?' Cora asks again.

'Huh? Oh, sorry, ah, Go Fish.' Nickolas looks down at his cards, hoping Cora will believe he is studying them, trying to decide on what card to ask for next.

'She didn't say why, just that she believed it would benefit you more. Maybe once the side effects pass, she'll feel more comfortable sending you home,' explains Jessica.

'The side effects? Jessica, you know they can sometimes take months to fucking pass. And what if the therapist decides to make an adjustment? Are you saying I'll have to extend my time even longer?' Finn's voice is rising.

Nickolas scans the room. No one's concerned about the loud voice in the corner, but it puts him on edge.

'I'm not sure, sweet face. It's just what she recommends,' says Jessica.

'God, don't call me that. I'm not a kid anymore,' exclaims Finn.

'Fine, *Finn*. But maybe this is the best place for you at the moment. If they do need to adjust your meds, at least you'll have the right support here, people watching you.'

'I knew it! I fucking knew it. You're glad I'm locked up. You're relieved that I'm out of your way, just one less problem you need to deal with.'

'That's not what I said.'

'But it's what you meant.'

'Finn, Jessica didn't mean that,' Jake chimes in.

'Shut up, Jake. What would you know? You go off to college and suddenly it all falls on me. I had to step up and make the extra money since you were no longer there to help.' Finn's voice begins to shake.

Other visitors are beginning to cast their eyes towards Finn.

'I'm not smart like you, Jake. I brought in money by sucking guys off in an alley while they called me their little slut,' explains Finn.

Cora looks at Nickolas, no longer focused on the game as Finn's words are no longer able to be ignored.

'Wait, what?' questions Jessica.

'Oh, now you want to act all worried? You didn't seem to ask any questions when I handed the money over to you, Jess. I was seventeen. No job was going to pay me that kind of cash, and you know it. You just chose to ignore it.'

There's a moment of silence before Finn speaks again. 'You...you think I'm Cassandra, don't you?'

'Of course not,' says Jessica.

'Bullshit! That's why you got me locked up. Because you thought I was going to act like her and drive Liam across state lines. Or steal all our money and host a fuckin' rave at the house. You just wanted me gone so you can pretend everything is peachy fucking keen.'

'Finn, you need to calm down,' Jake chimes in.

'Don't tell me what to do! I'm so fucking sick of everyone telling me what to do when they have no idea what I'm going through.'

The room is so quiet you could hear a pin drop. Nickolas quickly makes eye contact with Dot, letting his boss know he'll handle it. Dot walks around the room to settle the visitors; Darren and Hayley follow Dot's lead and the small murmur of voices slowly beginning to pick back up.

Nickolas gives an apologetic smile to Cora, who happily waves him off. Cora gets it. He turns around, his eyes landing on Finn, who is now standing up. Jessica and Jake are still in their chairs, a look of panic on their faces.

'Are you ever going to let me leave? Hmm? Or am I going to live out the rest of my life medicated and locked up?' Finn directs the question towards Jessica and Jake.

'Finn, Finn look at me.' Nickolas calmly speaks, easing his way closer towards his patient, not wanting to startle Finn by suddenly being in his face.

'Nickolas!' Finn is crowding him, frantic. 'Nickolas, you said I have people wanting me to get better, right? That I have people waiting. Well. Guess you were wrong.'

'We want you to get better, Finn,' says Jessica.

'Do you? Because this shit, it never ends. My meds will always need adjusting. Whether it's after one year or five. You going to keep watch? Make sure I don't do any crazy shit? How 'bout if I'm having a bad day and disagree with you, you going to accuse me of being off my meds?'

'Hey, Finn. How 'bout we go for a walk, hmm?' Nickolas hopes his words will distract Finn as the redhead begins to step towards Jessica.

'Fuck you, Jessica!' Finn is now towering over the seated woman. 'You should have left me in that alley to die!'

Nickolas steps forward and wraps Finn in his arms, his chest flush with his patient's back as his arms lock in front of Finn.

'Finn, it's okay. Everything is okay. I need you to listen to my voice and try to calm down. Can you do that?' Nickolas keeps his voice calm.

Finn's breathing is ragged. He tries to break free, anger fuelling his body, wanting to fight with anyone and everyone.

'I got you, Finn. You don't have to fight. No one is going to hurt you. I made you a promise, remember? But I need you to calm down so I can keep that promise.' Nickolas keeps his voice low so only Finn can hear him. No one else needs to know what he is saying, it's not about any of them, it's about Finn. It's about what Finn needs to stay calm, to feel grounded. It takes a minute or two, but he feels it, the moment Finn relaxes and slumps in his arms. Under different circumstances, it would almost be kind of nice, but nothing about this is nice. Finn's family was meant to come here and offer encouragement. To wish Finn well and stay positive. Instead, they made Finn believe that his worst fears were coming true.

'I think you two need to leave.' Nickolas addresses Jessica and Jake, still holding Finn in his arms.

'It's not four o'clock yet,' says Jessica.

'Wait, what? No, we get to say when we leave,' says Jake.

'Actually, Jake, you don't. See, based on Finn's current state, it's my job to decide what's best for him and right now that's neither of you. Our patients don't always get visitors and your behaviour right now has not only disturbed their visit, but you're also causing more harm to Finn by being here. So yeah, it's time for you to go home.'

Nickolas releases his grip on Finn, repositioning his patient so he's holding him against his side rather than from behind.

People are looking. Finn's eyes stay on the ground, no doubt avoiding their stares and the shame he must be feeling over his outburst. Nickolas opens the door to the corridor, cursing under his breath as he steps out of the common room and sees who's before him.

'Well, lookie here. Finally got to give Cunningham that sedative, hey?' asks Brett.

'Go home, Brett.'

'Damn. I always get to miss out on all the fun.'

'This isn't fun you sadistic prick. This is someone's life. It's not a joke. It's not something you can control and poke fun at.' Nickolas pushes past Brett.

'Nick...' Finn sounds weak.

'We're almost there, Finn, it's okay.' Nickolas pulls Finn against his side a little tighter.

'It's also not our job to get handsy with the patients. Even if this one is used to giving it away to anyone that asks,' Brett calls out.

Nickolas stops outside room thirteen. If it weren't for Finn slumped in his arms, he'd use Brett as a punching bag with the leftover energy from his gym session this morning.

'You have no fucking clue what you're talking about. I suggest you go home while you can still walk out of here,' says Nickolas, as he opens Finn's door.

Nickolas makes his way towards the bed. He lowers Finn down onto the mattress, watching as he curls into a ball the minute his head hits the pillow. Nickolas crouches down. He sees the tear stains on Finn's face, unaware that he had been silently crying as they made their way back to the room.

'Please don't hate me.' In the silence of the room, Finn's whispered words are deafening.

Nickolas runs his fingers through red hair, brushing it off Finn's face so he can see those green eyes. 'Why would I hate you? You did nothing wrong back there.'

'Because of what I said...about what I did.' Finn's hair is soft under Nickolas's fingers. It's everything he ever dreamed it would feel like, if only he was able to enjoy the sensation under better circumstances.

'Finn, I could never hate you. Did I like hearing what you had to do? Of course not. But I also know that you did it to survive. To help your family. I know that you never would have put yourself through that if you thought there was another way.'

Finn's eyes close, relaxing into his touch. Nickolas continues to run his fingers through Finn's hair, gently massaging his scalp as he does so, amazed at how calming the action is, not only for Finn but also for himself.

He isn't sure how much time has passed before he tells Finn, 'I'll be back, okay?'

'What?' Finn sits up, his relaxed state replaced with panic.

'Don't worry. I'll be coming back. I have to go check in with Dorothy to make sure they don't need my help.'

Finn nods.

Nickolas steps out of the room, looking back at Finn through the window in the door to find him still sitting up on the mattress, head hanging low. He walks back to the common room, pleased to hear the voices of the patients and their families have picked back up, echoing throughout the room. Dot is sitting with Cora, who seems to be the only patient that didn't get a visitor this week. He makes his way towards his boss, but Dot stands before he reaches them.

'Not here.' Dot signals for Nickolas to follow, walking towards the dining area where they'll have more privacy.

Once inside, the door still open so they can see the patients, Nickolas speaks first. 'Did they leave?'

'Eventually. Finn's brother didn't seem too thrilled to be told what to do,' comments Dot.

'He also has no problem working his brother up into a state of panic while he's adjusting to his bipolar medication.'

They both take a moment, Dot well aware that Nickolas needs to cool himself down.

'Did anyone say anything?' asks Nickolas.

'Yes, unfortunately. I'm sure none of the patients will say anything to Finn, but everyone likes to gossip. Most of those visitors will walk out happy to have a story to tell that doesn't involve their own family,' explains Dot.

'God, Finn is going to hate himself even more once he realises he was practically yelling his business to a room full of strangers.'

'That's what we're here for, to help channel that hate towards something or someone that actually deserves it. I'm sure his sessions will focus on it also. We just need to make sure he doesn't spiral.'

'Do you need my help in here?'

'No. Go and make sure Finn is okay. Darren and I can handle everyone. Just come back when it's time for dinner.'

Nickolas nods and makes his way back to Finn.

He finds him lying back down on the bed, curled into a ball, with the blanket covering him from the waist down. Closing the door behind him, Nickolas takes his place on the floor beside the bed, happy to sit there until Finn needs him.

An hour passes. The corridor gets noisy as the families hustle out, making their way to the exit.

Finn's sweet voice, laced with sadness, suddenly fills the room. 'I'm never going to leave this place.'

Nickolas turns his head, making eye contact with Finn as he speaks.

'Of course you are, Finn.'

'No, Nick, I'm not. Leaving this place means having something to fight for. Something that will give me the strength to want to get better so I can get released. What do I have, my family? I was always just a shadow in that house.'

'Shadows don't have family that visits them, who take time out of their day to catch the L into the city and see how treatment is going. That makes you a person, not a shadow.'

'Jessica always said how great it was that she didn't have to worry about me. How easier it was for her knowing that she could rely on me and Jake to help out with my younger siblings. Eventually, she just stopped checking in. Stopped noticing when things weren't right. When *I* wasn't right.'

Nickolas makes a mental note to bite off Jessica's head the next time they speak. Going off at Jake today doesn't seem enough after hearing Finn's struggles.

'My mother also has bipolar,' Finn explains.

'Is that...is that who Cassandra is?'

'Mhm.' It's the first time Finn makes eye contact with him. 'She refused to take her medication. She'd come home manic, and we'd have the best time. She was our mum again, even though we were aware it wasn't really her, you know? It was almost enough to make us forget the horrible things she had done. Then the depression would set in, and we'd be left to pick up the pieces, up until the point where she'd run off again.'

'Life in the South Side. We were all dealt situations that made us grow up faster than we should have. It's not right, and it's sure as fuck not fair, but how we choose to move forward is what makes us or breaks us.'

A few fresh tears fall down Finn's face. 'I think I'm at my breaking point, Nick.'

Nickolas scoots closer towards the bed. Finn's hands are curled together, but Nickolas reaches out and lays his hands on top of them.

'Then let me help piece you back together.' Nickolas whispers the words – a secret promise shared between them both. He leans his forehead against Finn's, giving his tender, freckled hands a gentle squeeze of strength. 'I know right now it feels like the sky is falling and your mind is telling you to stand there, to take the hits, to let the sky drop down on you because you think you deserve it, but that's today. Tomorrow, you could wake up and decide to take that step to the side, so the sky falls beside you. We can't let what we feel today decide how we should feel for the rest of our lives.'

Finn slips his hand out from under Nickolas's so it can lay on top, squeezing Nickolas's hand tight. He catches sight of a fresh tear slowly trickling down Finn's face.

'From now on, don't get better for them. Fuck them. Get better for you,' says Nickolas. 'You have so much life to live, Finn, and I can promise you, it doesn't have to be anything like it was. It can be so much better if you allow it.'

It happens so quickly. Soft wet lips press against Nickolas's. The electricity from the kiss has him shocked, freezing him in place. When his brain comes back online, Nickolas pulls away and removes his hands from Finn's touch.

'Finn...we can't.' He looks down, not able to face Finn. It hurts to be the one to burst the bubble they had created for themselves within the space of the room.

'...I thought...' Finn's voice breaks.

'I know. But we can't.'

'You don't want me?'

Nickolas's insides are screaming. Of course he wants Finn. He wants Finn so badly that breaking apart from that kiss is the hardest thing he has ever had to do. He wants Finn in a way he has never wanted anyone before. He wants to wake up to Finn and make the redhead breakfast in bed. He wants to hold Finn's hand as they walk down the street to buy groceries. He wants lazy Sundays on the couch with Socks curled up between them, and nights tangled in each other arms as they drift off to sleep together.

'No, that's not...you're my patient,' Nickolas explains.

'It's not like you're my doctor.'

'It doesn't matter. It's still not right. I wouldn't feel right.'

Finn rolls over, facing the wall, and surprisingly that hurts more than if Finn had gotten angry and yelled at him.

Nickolas lets out a sigh. This is his fault. He got too close. He led Finn on, leaving him more confused and unwanted than Finn already felt.

'How 'bout I go get us some food? Hmm. We can eat in here, away from everyone else,' Nickolas suggests.

Finn doesn't answer.

Nickolas knows he won't be able to get Finn to willingly eat in the dining area, and after today, he figures a meal away from prying eyes is the least he can do. Finn just needs some time.

'I'll be back. I promise.' He stands, wanting to reach out and give Finn a reassuring touch, but he doesn't. He shouldn't. He can't.

The common room is empty; all the patients are happily sitting in the dining area, with Dot and Darren keeping watch. Nickolas makes eye contact with Dot. She gives him a nod, a sad smile, and looks back towards the patients as Nickolas grabs a tray with enough food on it for himself and Finn to eat.

'Hey, Aiden. Do you have any of those chocolate pudding cups out back?' Nickolas asks.

'I'm pretty sure I got a few left.'

'Can I grab two?'

'Sure, I'll go get 'em.'

Nickolas patiently waits. He looks down at the food on offer for tonight. Roast chicken with veggies, a side of gravy, and a slice of chocolate cake. Seems like a decent enough meal to try to get Finn to eat. Two plates of everything barely fits on the tray, but he makes it work.

'Sorry, I thought I had them in the main fridge, but they were in the back of the one we use for storage,' Aiden explains while passing over the dessert.

Nickolas grabs the pudding cups and puts them on the tray, one on top of the other to save space. 'All good. Didn't mind waiting. Thanks, man.'

As he leaves the room, he gives Dot another nod to say thanks. Nickolas balances the tray against the wall and his waist so he can scan his key card and unlock the door. He uses his foot to hold the door open as he grabs the tray with both his hands and makes his way towards room thirteen. Nickolas leans the tray against his side one more time so he can open Finn's door after unlocking it. He loses his balance a little as his foot pulls the door open, causing the tray to wobble in his hands. He stands like a statue while holding his breath in the hopes that nothing falls and crashes to the floor.

'Fuck, that was close.' He chuckles as he realises how stupid he would have looked if people had been around to see him. He pulls the door open wide enough with his foot to rest his hip against it, slipping inside the room with the gap he made.

'I don't care if you're not hungry man. It was like a juggling act getting this food in here without dropping it, so that alone means you need to eat at least half.'

Nickolas looks up from the tray in his hands and he drops everything to the floor.

Blood.

So much blood.

Finn's body is lying on the mattress, lifeless, face more pale than usual.

'No, no, no. Not again. Please, God, no.' Nickolas runs to the bed. The prong from the restraints attached to Finn's bed is bloody. The puncture wounds on either side of Finn's wrists look deep, skin torn from Finn trying to pull the prong against tender flesh. The cuts are harsh, pulsing with blood.

Nickolas pulls his shirt off and tears it apart. He applies pressure to each wrist, his shirt damp beneath his hands as the blood seeps through.

'HELP! SOMEBODY HELP! DOROTHY! DARREN!' He screams so loud he can feel his throat tearing.

He prays someone hears him. He knows he can't take the pressure off Finn's wrists. Blood is still pouring out from the wounds.

The door clicks open. Nickolas hates to take his attention off of Finn, but he needs to make sure whoever is at the door knows what needs to be done.

Dot's gasp sets Nickolas off. 'Oh my—I'll get Dr Winslow.'

'Hurry! I don't think he has much time.' Nickolas's voice is weak, but he gets the words out.

Dot runs out.

Nickolas casts his eyes back towards Finn. 'Please Finn, please don't leave me.' His face is wet from tears. His arms are hurting from the pressure he is putting on Finn's wrists, but all he can do is force himself to tighten his grip because Finn's life depends on it.

'Stay with me, Finn. Come on. You can fight this. Stay with me. Please'

7. Monday

The only way Nickolas is able to track the time since Finn was admitted to the infirmary is through the change in staff members. He has been sitting beside Finn's bed, a blanket wrapped around his shoulders, as he watches the monitors beep, a sign that Finn's heart is still beating while he lies unconscious, as pale as the white sheets.

He's holding Finn's hand. No one questions or comments on his behaviour; they just give him a sad smile when they walk in to get an update before they leave the room and head back to the other patients. Nickolas knows he should be resting, but he can't. The darkness that takes over his mind when he closes his eyes is consumed with red, and not the red of Finn's hair; no, this is an angry red. A deep maroon red that leaves a smell in the air strong enough to seep into Nickolas's nostrils and remain there for hours to come.

Blood.

Blood on his hands. Blood on his clothes. Blood on the mattress, dripping down onto the floor and pooling around his shoes.

Nickolas forces his eyes open whenever the memories start to come back, his breathing ragged and his hand gripping Finn's tight, scared of letting go. With every beep of the machine, what happened the day before flashes in his mind on an endless loop.

Beep—

The door flies open.

Beep—

Lexi rushes in with a gurney.

Beep—

Dot takes one of Finn's wrists from Nickolas's grasp.

Beep—

Lexi is talking to him, but all Nickolas hears is white noise.

Beep—

'Nickolas.'

Beep—

'Nickolas!'

Beep—

'Nickolas! I need you to let go.'

Beep—

'It's okay. We've got him.'

Beep—

He felt hands on his arms pulling him away from Finn. He watched in slow motion as Lexi and Dot transferred Finn's body to the gurney.

Beep—

Finn's body being wheeled out of the room.

Beep—

Once again, he was left standing in room thirteen, where Nickolas had now lost the only two people he had ever cared about.

'Hey, you okay?' Lexi asks.

Nickolas is brought back to reality. 'Sorry. I zoned out.'

'When was the last time you ate? Or slept for that matter?' Lexi is standing in front of him, arms crossed and looking at him as a concerned friend more than a doctor.

'Ahhh. I was—we were about to eat when—'

Lexi's shoulders sag, realising what he is implying. It's coming up to at least nineteen hours since Nickolas has eaten, more since he has slept.

'I'll get Dot to bring you something to eat. But you really should be resting. You're not even rostered on right now.'

'I'm not leaving.' His voice is firm. Lexi didn't even suggest that Nickolas should leave, but he wants it to be known that he isn't going to abandon Finn. Nickolas isn't going anywhere until Finn wakes up, and even then, he will only leave if Finn asks.

'He's going to make it, Nickolas. We gave him a blood transfusion which should help him recover quicker. Once his body regenerates enough blood, he'll wake. And when he does, it's because you saved him.'

Nickolas looks down at Finn's hand in his, unable to make eye contact with Lexi. He listens to the beeping, and his eyes avoid the bandages on Finn's wrists. There's a needle in Finn's right hand to help with fluids, and where the transfusion took place. The heart rate monitor is attached to Finn's right index finger, allowing Nickolas to hear the comforting beeps of Finn's heart. A tube is poking out from under the blankets, running along the side of the bed where a catheter has been inserted, and it scares Nickolas how peaceful Finn looks right now, knowing he was so close to losing him.

Lexi continues to work, acting as though Nickolas is invisible. He appreciates being ignored because that's all he wants to feel. Invisible. He doesn't want anyone to look at him or talk to him, he just wants the panic, fear, and guilt running through his body to vanish, and the only way that is going to happen is for Finn to wake up.

At some point, Dot takes a seat beside him. 'I hate seeing that look on your face. I feel like it only just disappeared and now it's back again.' Dot has a bottle of water in one hand and a tray in the other.

Nickolas looks at the sandwich, the bowl of fruit salad, and a lemon tart sitting on the tray before him. His stomach grumbles, but he can't bring himself to eat, the thought alone making him nauseous.

'I know you don't feel like it, but I also know you're going to want to help Finn when he wakes up,' Dot offers. 'You're no good to him if you pass out because you haven't eaten or kept hydrated.'

Nickolas takes the bottle of water from Dot and takes a sip before going back for another and chugging the whole bottle down in one breath. He gasps as he pulls the bottle away from his lips.

'Thanks. Guess I needed it.' Nickolas pants.

Dot nods, passing the food to him.

He slowly picks at it, not wanting to make himself sick by eating too quickly.

'You know what I'm going to ask you, right?' says Dot.

Nickolas nods, taking his hand away from Finn's and placing it in his lap. This is the last thing he wants to do, but he appreciates the fact that Dot waited to do so.

'So, how did this happen?' Dot questions.

Nickolas thinks back, playing every little detail in his head. He keeps his head down and his voice low as he begins to replay what happened. 'Once I returned Finn to his room after his family had visited, he was showing signs of dropping into a state of depression. He was scared – worried that I would view him differently after learning about his past.' Nickolas hates how his words describe Finn like a subject and not a person. It reminds him of all those medical TV shows where the characters speak as though it is just another day at work, ignoring the fact that they had only moments ago killed a person on the operating table.

'Why would he be concerned about that?' asks Dot.

Because there is something more building between us than just a friendship.

'I'm not sure. It could've been shame. Embarrassment. Either way, I made sure to let him know that I would never judge anything he did to survive.' Nickolas takes a moment, biting his lower lip before continuing. 'I left to check in with you. When I returned, he hadn't moved from his place on the mattress. We discussed his fears of never being able to leave this place. His family and then—'

And then Finn kissed me, and my world felt whole and broken all at the same time. I wanted so badly for it to keep going but I knew that anything that happened while Finn was in this state of mind would be wrong, and I'd end up feeling like all the other guys that took advantage of him. All those men Finn gave himself to as a way of saying 'thank you for taking care of me'.

'Then?' Dot gently pushes for Nickolas to proceed.

'Then I went to get him food, thinking it may be a good distraction and when I returned, that's when...that's when I saw...'

Dot places a hand on Nickolas's shoulder. He uses the back of his hand to wipe at his nose before making eye contact with Dot.

'You did everything right. You had already left the room once at this point, so leaving for a second time wouldn't have seemed like something you needed to be concerned about doing,' says Dot.

Except he kissed me and I rejected him. I rejected him the same way his family and this whole fucked up world have been rejecting him. I was the cause of all this.

'I should have taken the restraints off his bed.' Nickolas looks up, his eyes locking with Dot's.

'Nykolai. For the last six days, Finn hasn't shown any signs of self-harm. None of us could have foreseen this. He has been restless, has had trouble sleeping, and that is why the restraints have not been removed from his room.'

'Sure as shit doesn't feel that way. It was my job to—'

'It was all our job.'

Nickolas scoffs, knowing full well what a load of shit that is.

'You weren't hired to be Finn's keeper. He was brought here to be taken care of by the multiple staff we have on rotation. Not just you. Unfortunately, these things happen. Doesn't matter how much we try to protect everyone under our watch, if they want to, they find a way.'

Finn starts to stir. Dot stands up to retrieve Dr Winslow while Nickolas reaches out and slowly places his hand on top of Finn's, not wanting the touch to startle or cause a panic.

'Nick...'

Hearing his name fall from Finn's lips constricts his chest. 'Hey, Finn. I'm here. I'm right here.' Nickolas stands, so he's towering over Finn. He gently runs his fingers through Finn's red hair, waiting for him to open his eyes, to see the life inside of them shining back at him.

Footsteps approach and Nickolas regretfully pulls away. He stays beside the bed, his hands in his pockets, waiting for the moment he can reach out and touch Finn again. Dr Hale, Lexi, and Dot walk into the room. Dot stands beside Nickolas while Dr Hale and Lexi circle the bed.

With a small torch in hand, Lexi pulls Finn's left eyelid open, shining the torch back and forth. 'Finn, can you hear me?' Lexi opens Finn's right eyelid and does the same.

Nickolas wants to pull the torch out of Lexi's hand and shine the damn thing in *her* face.

Finn squirms away, the light no doubt irritating. 'I took a sharp object to my wrists. I'm not deaf.'

Lexi turns the torch off, the doctor's eyes casting up at him before turning toward Dr Hale.

'Well, safe to say we don't have to ask if you know what happened,' says Dr Hale, opening a folder to take notes.

Finn's eyes are now open, head turned to the side, avoiding eye contact with everyone in the room.

'Finn, I'd like to discuss what happened, to try and understand what brought on the feelings that led to you wanting to harm yourself,' says Dr Hale.

Nickolas looks from Dr Hale to Finn, then back to the doctor again when there is no response.

'I've spoken to your sister—' Dr Hale explains.

'WHAT!?' Although his cloudy green eyes look as though they're trying to shoot laser beams out of them and burn a hole through Dr Hale, Nickolas sighs in relief at seeing Finn's eyes light up in general.

'It's protocol to call an emergency contact when a patient harms themselves. Once you and I have spoken, I'll be able to update your sister, but she was deeply concerned and upset to hear what happened.'

Guilt flashes across Finn's face. Nickolas takes his hand out of his pocket and places it on Finn's shoulder. The motion gets Finn's attention. He turns towards Nickolas, eyes wide, as though Finn didn't even realise he was standing there. He gives Finn a soft smile with a small squeeze of encouragement before Dr Hale interrupts their silent exchange.

'Unfortunately, until we have a discussion, I won't be able to release you back into your room and I'll have to—'

'No! No, it's—we can talk,' says Finn.

'Okay. Dorothy, Nickolas. I'm sure you both have other patients to attend to.'

'I'm off the clock,' explains Nickolas.

Dr Hale looks at him with a tilted head. 'Well, you're not a family member, so I'm still going to have to ask you to leave.'

Dot and Lexi have already stepped aside, beginning to make their way towards the exit. Nickolas begins to follow, stopping behind Dr Hale, who is writing a few more notes. He makes eye contact with Finn, and those soft green eyes give him a small sense of peace. He can see on Finn's face that he doesn't want him to leave, and after the events that took place following their kiss, it's a relief to know he hasn't lost what had been building between them. Nickolas gives Finn a small nod, miming, 'I'll come back'. A smile appears on Finn's face, and he nods. Nickolas averts his attention back to Dr Hale, taking it as his cue to leave.

Outside the infirmary doors Dot stands, holding out a fresh uniform, a towel, boxers that they use for the patients, and some soap.

'Clean up. Take a break. He is probably going to be in there for a while, so come to the break room and eat,' Dot instructs, giving no room for discussion.

He takes everything from Dot's hands, who has already begun to walk away before he has the chance to say thank you. Nickolas makes his way towards the locker room to use the shower, aware of the staff continuing their work around him. A few patients do a double-take, noticing someone walking down the corridor who isn't dressed like them or in all purple. Nickolas suddenly remembers that he's still only wearing a black tank top, his work pants, and the blanket draped over his shoulders. He avoids their stares and keeps moving forward.

*

He turns the hot water tap, barely adding cold water. Steam fills the shower room and opens up his lungs. The bathroom is small, mainly there in case they need to wash vomit off themselves or a quick rinse after working a double shift. Or in this case, blood. The water at Nickolas's feet turns red as it washes away the dried blood still encrusted on his hands. The evidence of what happened staining his skin as he sat with Finn, too afraid to leave his side long enough to wash the blood off his body. He takes the soap and scrubs at his hands till they're raw. The hot water mixed with his frantic rubbing makes his white skin bright red.

His mind wanders. Red blood on the mattress, on the floor. A lifeless redhead in his mind flashes to black hair to red, back to black. The bloodied restraints replaced by bloodied utensils. Nickolas's knees buckle from under him, and he crashes to the base of the shower. Tears mix with the water streaming from above as he pulls his legs to his chest and rests his head between his knees, no longer able to keep it all together.

All the emotions he was holding in as he sat beside Finn, trying to be strong, come flooding back so quickly.

Happiness – for finally finding someone he could see a future with.

Alive – the second Finn's lips touched him.

Scared – of losing Finn when Nickolas told him they couldn't.

Regret – for leaving Finn so vulnerable.

Fear – when he found Finn's lifeless body on the mattress, thinking he had once again lost someone he cared for.

But most of all, guilt – that Finn never would have tried to kill himself if Nickolas hadn't turned away.

Those emotions hit him over and over again, reminding Nickolas that everyone he's cared about always ends up getting hurt because of him. If he had never gotten close to Finn, then he wouldn't be lying in a bed right now, wrists bandaged, taking a questionnaire to find out if he is still suicidal or safe to be left alone. He should stay away. Let Finn continue with treatment alone. He could work night shifts until Finn gets released. It would work. But the mere thought of it has Nickolas's insides screaming. He wakes up happy to start his day, looking forward to seeing the smile on Finn's face when the redhead sees him walk into the room. It's enough to make everything else feel inadequate in comparison. Nothing and no one have ever given Nickolas that feeling before just from a smile, and he isn't ready to give it up.

He knows he is being selfish if he continues to work beside Finn after what happened between them. He knows Finn's health and wellbeing come before his own. He's spent the last twenty-one years of his life putting everyone's needs and wants before himself, so what's a little more? If it's what Finn wants, he will do it, in a heartbeat. The now cold water is refreshing as it streams down his red and puffy face, however, the rest of his body begins to tremble as the adrenaline fades, adding to the chill of the water.

On shaky legs, Nickolas pulls himself up, his hands pressed to the wall for support as he turns the taps off. He stands there for a moment and takes one final deep breath in and out. He tells himself that even if she isn't alive, at least Finn still is.

He exits the shower and dries himself off, all while avoiding his reflection in the mirror. He gets dressed and makes his way back out towards the break room, knowing he needs to eat before he passes out.

There is a plate of food on the table. Nickolas looks around wondering if it belongs to anyone or if he is now hallucinating from the lack of food.

'It's for you. Dorothy dropped it off and asked me to tell you in case you didn't pick up on her hint.' Hayley is on the couch eating an apple while scrolling through her phone.

Nickolas gives Hayley a small thanks before sitting down and slowly eating the food, enjoying the silence, thankful that she finds the updates on social media more interesting than talking to him.

'Are you working today?' Hayley's voice eventually cuts through the crunching of his food.

Guess Hayley caught up on her social media.

He doesn't look Hayley's way when he answers. 'Got the afternoon shift.' At this point, every orderly would be aware of what happened, and no doubt aware of where Nickolas has been since the incident yesterday afternoon.

'Maybe you should take today off,' Hayley suggests.

'I'm fine,'

'I know. But that's not why I said it.' Hayley waits a moment. 'Brett is also working the afternoon shift.'

Nickolas drops his fork and looks up.

'Fuck. That's the last thing I need to be dealing with today.' He rubs his hands over his face and glances at the clock on the wall. It's half past eleven, which means the asshole will most likely be arriving soon. Protocol states that a staff email is to be sent to inform them of any incident that took place while others weren't working. It helps avoid any comments or questions being asked in front of the patients. Though that has never stopped Brett before.

Nickolas stands up, puts his rubbish in the bin, and makes his way back to the infirmary. He doesn't bother knocking as he walks in, noticing Dr Hale and Dr Winslow are in a discussion while Finn lays in bed, staring up at the ceiling.

'Change his medication from quetiapine to lithium,'

instructs Dr Hale. 'From what I gathered, his dosage of quetiapine and sertraline were too low, causing him to go into a depressive state quickly after seeing his family. Up his olanzapine to help stabilise his moods and increase his sertraline, it should help prevent depression and panic attacks. And keep up with the B12s.'

Nickolas can't help but overhear the conversation, jumping in as soon as Dr Hale is finished explaining the treatment plan for Finn. 'Wait. You're saying his medication did this?'

Both doctors turn towards Nickolas, unaware he had entered the room.

Dr Hale lets out a small sigh. 'I believe so. We can never be too sure with patients that suffer from bipolar disorder. We started him on a low dosage as he'd gone six months unmedicated, aware that it would need increasing at some point. I'm hoping with this new cocktail it will help Finn adjust better.'

Dr Hale walks towards the door, not bothering to stick around for any further questions. Standing there frozen,

Nickolas processes the information. Does this mean his behaviour after the kiss wasn't the last straw that pushed Finn to his breaking point? If so, what else does that mean for them? If the dosage of mood stabilisers were low, causing the risk of Finn to slip into a state of depression, then maybe whatever they were building wasn't real. Maybe it was just Finn looking for a good time away from the monotony of his new routine.

Lexi places a hand on his arm, speaking softly so Finn doesn't overhear. 'He's been asking for you.'

Nickolas breaks out of his thoughts. He looks at Lexi, his mind processing the words but unable to respond.

'I'll give you two a moment.' Lexi leaves the infirmary, and as the door closes, it's once again only him and Finn. Nickolas makes his way towards the bed. From the angle of the curtain divider, Finn wouldn't have been able to see him when he entered the room. But if Finn is in tune with the sound of his voice the way Nickolas is with Finn's, then Finn would have known of his presence the minute he spoke to Dr Hale. Nickolas cautiously makes his way towards Finn, his footsteps echoing in the room, causing a head of floppy red hair to turn towards the sound and lay green eyes upon him.

'Hey.' Finn's voice is soft, but Nickolas is so pleased to be hearing it again.

'Hey.' He takes a seat in the chair next the bed, keeping his hands to himself while his eyes wander to Finn's wrists, wrapped in freshly changed bandages.

'They want to keep me here for another night before I can go back to my room and start joining the others again.'

'That's good. That's...that's a good sign.'

'Yeah...once they adjust my meds again, I'm sure I'll be having a blast as I shake and vomit alone in my room, where I'll either sleep the day away or pace like a lion stuck in a cage.'

Finn is trying to make light of the situation, but Nickolas knows Finn is scared; he can see it in the same green eyes

Nickolas sees in his dreams. He gives Finn a soft, reassuring smile before breaking eye contact and looking down at his hands clasped tightly in his lap.

'I'm sorry.' The brokenness in Finn's voice pulls at his heart.

Nickolas leans forward, still keeping his hands to himself no matter how desperately he wants to touch Finn at that moment. 'What do you have to be sorry for? You did nothing wrong, Finn.'

'I'm sorry that I did it. That you—you had to find me like that.' Finn is on the verge of tears, trying to take deep breaths in to steady the quiver in his voice. 'I swear, I didn't want to die.' Finn's voice breaks. 'It was just...at that moment I suddenly felt...I felt like nothing was ever going to get better. That I'll forever just be this burden that no one will want in their life. My family...you.'

'Finn—'

'I'm sorry about the kiss. If I could take it back, I would. Just...I just don't want things to be weird between us now because of me and my fucked up mind.'

'Don't.'

'Don't what?'

Nickolas looks down, not able to meet Finn's eyes. 'Don't take it back.' He hears a small intake of breath before having the courage to look back at Finn. 'I thought that...I thought what happened might have been because I...' Nickolas rubs the back of his neck.

'You thought I did this because you pushed me away...' Finn's words make Nickolas's guilt feel like a bucket of cold water has been thrown over him.

Nickolas doesn't deny it.

'Dr Winslow said you've been by my side since they wheeled me in here.'

Nickolas nods.

'Was that out of guilt?'

'What?'

'Did you stay by my side all night because you felt guilty or because you wanted to be here for me?'

Nickolas wants to say both, but no matter what had led Finn to end up in the infirmary, fighting to survive, he would have been here fighting alongside Finn. 'Because I wanted to.' He doesn't break eye contact.

'If I wasn't in this place, and I had kissed you, then wh—'

'Then I would have kissed you back. And I wouldn't have let you go.' The weight that lifts from Nickolas as he finally admits how he feels is only short-lived. 'But that doesn't change what I said, Finn. You're still my patient. Nothing can happen between us.'

Silence falls between them. They both break eye contact, giving each other a moment to collect themselves. He hopes that Finn understands that he isn't saying never, just, not now.

'I'm sorry I put you through that.' Finn breaks the silence. 'The guilt. The worry. I can't imagine what that must have felt like.'

'I didn't think I'd ever feel like that again,' says Nickolas.

Finn's head tilts, but he doesn't push for answers. 'I know that it was the medication, and I know that I didn't want to die. But I also know that a part of me felt alone and like this never-ending cycle of either feeling everything or feeling nothing was the life I had ahead of me. I just felt...tired. I know it was stupid and, fuck, if it wasn't for you, then...' Finn wipes the tears away before they threaten to fall.

Nickolas reaches forward, his hand stopping mid-air as he goes for Finn's hand and instead decides to place it on Finn's arm, right above the bandages.

'God. Jessica is never going to let me out of her sight ever again.'

Nickolas chuckles. 'Maybe. But at least it shows she cares.' He gives Finn's arm a gentle squeeze. 'She does care, Finn.

Even Jake.' Nickolas takes a moment so his words can sinks in. 'My point is, the fact that they worry about you taking your meds, or hurting yourself, or running away, shows that they care about what happens to you because they care about you. However, they do need to learn their place and not overstep.'

They both laugh a little, enjoying the bubble that they have comfortably set back up between them.

'So, are you just my orderly or can I at least call you my friend?' The question has Finn looking hopeful.

'I think we can work with friends. I don't sit by just anyone's bedside or visit their room for late-night chats.' Nickolas smirks.

They chuckle between themselves, not to cover any awkward moment but because they finally feel relaxed around each other, like the way it was before. Enjoying the moment between themselves, they miss the sound of the door opening.

'They always say laughter is the best form of medicine.' Dot is at the end of Finn's bed, a warm motherly smile on his boss's face. 'I hate to interrupt, but Nykolai, your shift started thirty minutes ago.'

'Nykolai?' Finn cocks an eyebrow.

Nickolas glares at Dot, who gives him a knowing smile; that was no slip of the tongue.

'Nobody calls me that.'

'Wait. You're telling me that you know my full name, my medical condition, and I don't even know your real name?'

'Nickolas is my real name, it's just...ya know, the version everyone can pronounce correctly.'

'I feel the trust has broken a little here, *Nykolai*.' Finn acts disheartened by crossing his arms and huffing.

Well fuck. Hearing his birth name fall from Finn's lips sends blood straight to his dick, and for a moment he has to wait before standing.

'As much as I'm sure Finn would prefer the company, I do need to pull you away,' says Dot.

'It's fine, Dorothy. He was starting to get boring anyway.'

Nickolas, now able to stand, rises to his feet and gives Finn the finger. 'You know, you keep up the attitude and maybe I'll just leave you alone for the rest of the night.'

'Is that a promise?'

Nickolas laughs. 'Get some rest, Finn.'

He makes his way to the door while Dot follows close behind him. The hurt, guilt, and worry that has been hanging over his head is now gone. A smile spreads across his face. Everything that has been building between them wasn't just a result of Finn's medication. It's real. They are real, and although nothing can come of it right now, he still has a friendship with Finn, and that's more than he could've hoped for.

Dot closes the door behind them and stops Nickolas in his tracks. 'I'm not sending you out there with the other patients.'

'What? You just said—'

'I know what I said. I also know how it would look if you got paid to spend a whole day beside a patient's bed talking.' Dot lets out a breath before continuing. 'Brett has made a few unsavoury comments and for the sake of everyone, I'm making sure to keep you two separated for as long as I can manage.'

Nickolas clenches his fist by his side. 'What's he said?'

'Not the point. For now, I'm going to get you to clean out the patients' rooms, give them fresh clothing, and then when group starts, you can go back and sit with Finn, so you and Brett don't cross paths. I made sure no one did those jobs this morning because I had a feeling I'd need to pass them off to you.'

'You, Hayley, and Darren go home at three, Dot. I'll have to see the guy at some point because no way could he and Sky handle everything before lights out.'

'Let me worry about that, but until then, you have a job to do, so shoo.' Dot's hands make a shooing motion, like how a parent ushers their kids away from ruining a surprise or a present hidden in a room. Is that what Finn is? A present? A gift sent to him that's caused him to open up from the shell he was living in? A part of him wonders if Finn feels the same.

Nickolas makes his way to the laundry room, fetching the bin for the dirty linen, and heads towards the patients' rooms while they enjoy their lunch. He works quickly. Usually, he takes his time, knowing that if he's tasked himself with these jobs, then it's because he wants to enjoy the time alone and to give himself a break. But the quicker he finishes, the quicker he can get back to Finn. He returns the bin, then grabs the cart with fresh clothes for each patient, which is labelled with their room number. He finishes as lunch begins to wrap up and everyone who isn't involved in the group session starts to make their way back to their rooms.

He makes a stop at the break room, fetching himself a bottle of water and a couple of peanut butter and chocolate chip cookies that Dot had brought in that day. Food in hand, he makes his way to return the cart, then heads into the infirmary to sit with Finn. Nickolas finds him sitting up in bed with an empty tray of food, and colour back in that beautifully freckled face. Well, enough colour to make his pale skin not look transparent.

'I hope you're ready. Your taste buds are about to have their world rocked.' Nickolas holds the cookies in his hand towards Finn.

'Oh, um, hi. Who are you?' asks Finn.

Nickolas stops dead in his tracks. 'What?'

'I was waiting for my friend Nickolas but, sorry, I've never seen you before. What's your name?'

He can see the smile Finn is holding back, no longer able to keep up with the joke. 'You're a fucking dick.' Nickolas laughs along with Finn, taking a seat in the chair that's now rightfully known as his while biting into one of the cookies. 'You don't get a cookie now.'

'Oh, come on, Nykolai. I was only joking.'

'I swear I'm going to kill Dot,' Nickolas mumbles the words with a mouth full of delicious peanut butter and chocolatey goodness.

'If I promise not to call you by your real name, then can I have a cookie?'

'Nickolas is my real name. It's like a nickname.'

'Hey, whatever you say. I for one feel much more at ease knowing who exactly is taking care of me.'

'Eat your fuckin' cookie and shut up.' He shoves the baked goods towards Finn, who accepts it like a kid receiving a gift from Santa.

Finn takes a bite and moans, 'Holy fuck who made these? It's like Christmas in my mouth.'

'Told you your taste buds were about to be rocked.' Nickolas takes another bite, trying to ignore the sounds escaping Finn's mouth.

Another moan falls from Finn's lips. 'The things I would do for anything that has peanut butter and chocolate mixed together.'

'Dot's amazing at baking. Each day she brings something different to share with us. Have to work twice as hard at the gym if I want to enjoy it all.'

'Trust me, a little extra junk in the trunk and hips to hold onto is a guy's wet dream.'

Everything feels so easy. The conversation isn't awkward, the teasing is fun, and the banter back and forth has Nickolas feeling as though he and Finn have known each other for years.

Nickolas swallows, tilting his head and cocking an eyebrow. 'You sayin' I'm a catcher?'

'Please, with an ass like that, it would be a crime for you to be a top.'

A slight blush spreads across Nickolas's face. Has Finn been checking out his ass this whole time? He makes a mental note to do a few extra squats when he goes to the gym next.

Nickolas takes another bite of his cookie, swallowing before he responds. 'It's been a while since I've...bottomed.'

'So, you're verse?'

'Kinda. I mean. I prefer to bottom, but I—' Nickolas thumbs his nose, feeling extremely vulnerable. He isn't sure how the conversion turned to preferences in the bedroom, but he isn't about to shy away from it like he would with others. As much as he hates talking about his sex life, opening up about it to Finn seems normal, comfortable even.

'The way I grew up, I was taught never to trust anyone, and since bottoming left me feeling vulnerable, it called for a lot of fucking trust.' Nickolas keeps his head low, unable to make eye contact. 'That's why I mostly top. Trust isn't easy to form when you're having one night stands so...'

'So, you've never been in a relationship?'

Nickolas scoffs, then looks up and continues to eat, his silence being his answer.

'What? You too cool for a relationship?'

'Bit hard to have a relationship with someone when my life was at risk if my dad found out I was gay.'

'Oh. Shit. I didn't—'

'It's whatever. Story for another day maybe. Besides, I had responsibilities that took priority over having a fuckin' relationship.' Nickolas opens the bottle of water and drinks half of it just so it gives him a distraction.

Finn holds the half-eaten cookie in his hand and Nickolas looks between Finn and the cookie as his stomach grumbles. Wordlessly, Finn holds the cookie out to Nickolas, offering it to him like it will make all his troubles disappear. Without even thinking, he leans forward and takes the cookie between his teeth, eating it directly from Finn's hand while watching the redhead's eyes widen and pupils dilate.

'Now I know what all those people meant when they said feeding someone can be erotic.'

Nickolas gives Finn the finger as he laughs around the cookie, trying not to choke on it. This time Nickolas hears the door open. He turns around and sees Dot walking towards him. He looks down at his watch. 'Jesus, that went quick.'

'I'm afraid so,' agrees Dot. 'Group is about to finish. Think you're going to be able to work the rest of your shift without having to make a report to HR?'

'Can't promise anything,' Nickolas jokes, kind of.

'Well, I've left some paperwork you can file for me, but Hayley and Brett won't be able to manage dinner alone, so you'll have to show your face.'

Nickolas nods.

'James will handle the med cart and obviously you'll inform Lydia that Finn will be staying the night in the infirmary where Dr Murphy will watch over him.'

'Like that doesn't sound creepy,' Finn adds.

Nickolas turns towards Finn, lost in the discussion with Dot and forgetting for a moment that Finn was in the room with them.

'If you actually get some sleep like you're supposed to, then you won't even know he's here,' Nickolas explains.

'Right, 'cause that's any better. Some dude just hovering over me while I sleep.'

'Nah, Dr Murphy has an addiction to online poker. He plays during his night shifts, thinking no one will notice, so he'll be too distracted to watch your freckled face sleep.'

'I'll have you know, the lack of sun from being cooped up in here has decreased my freckles immensely.'

'Sure thing, tough guy. Let me get a permanent marker so I can play connect the dots.'

Nickolas can sense Dot is watching the exchange between him and Finn. This is the first time he has felt so open and carefree in a long time. No staff member or patient has ever seen him act this way, at least not since *she* died. He wishes Dot would leave. It feels as though his boss is intruding on something special, causing the hairs on the back of Nickolas's neck to stand like he needs to protect what is his. The conversation between him and Finn is harmless. It's pure banter back and forth, the type of behaviour exhibited between friends. However, he is still Finn's orderly and is meant to act somewhat professional. Dot allows Nickolas to bend the rules, knowing that he is still doing right by the patient when he does. He just has to remember not to bend the rules so far back that they snap.

Dot coughs.

'Right. Sorry. I better go,' says Nickolas.

'It's fine. Not like I'll be going anywhere,' says Finn.

He leaves, noticing that Dot hasn't followed. As soon as he exits the door, he stops, leaving it ajar just enough to hear any conversations that may be taking place without him.

'I'm glad you're feeling better, Finn. It's never easy seeing a patient go through something like that.'

'Thank you. I'm glad to still be here.'

There's a pause, and for a moment Nickolas thinks perhaps Dot has finished talking to Finn.

'Nickolas isn't like anyone else that works here.'

The words put Nickolas on alert, concerned where this conversation may be going.

'He actually cares about the patients. He doesn't just work here; he makes an effort with each and every one of them. He wants them to smile and not feel so trapped, so to speak.'

'I've ah, kind of noticed that.'

'I'm saying this because he has gone through just as much as some of the patients that are here.'

Nickolas panics. For a moment he fears Dot is going to tell Finn what happened.

'I understand it can be tough being in here, sometimes lonely. But please don't take advantage of his kindness.'

'I...I wouldn't. I appreciate how thoughtful he is, his help, his...his friendship.'

'I can see how well you have progressed since being here, even with this setback. Whether that has to do with you, or with Nickolas's persistent desire to help those that walk through these doors, just be aware every one of these patients needs him as much as I can see you need him. Remember that.'

He's heard enough. Nickolas scurries off, hoping to get some distance between him and the infirmary before Dot exits and sees he was eavesdropping.

*

Nickolas has been sitting at reception for the last two hours, filing the paperwork Dot had left for him while casually talking to Jasmine. What would have taken half the time to complete has doubled due to his mind replaying what he overhead between Finn and Dot. He analyses and dissects every single word, trying to make sense of the conversation. Does Dot suspect something is going on between him and Finn? Something more than friendship? Is she accusing Finn of taking up all of his time, to the point where he can't attend to the other patients? What does Dot think? That it is all a ploy to get Nickolas's attention? Nothing she said was negative, and what Dot did have to say about Nickolas made him feel somewhat proud, but that doesn't mean he shouldn't be concerned.

He looks at the time, noticing dinner is about to begin. He stands up, ready to make his way towards the dining area to assist, praying that he doesn't punch Brett in the face while doing so. Jasmine answers the phone, so he turns to leave.

However, the sound of fingers clicking catches his attention. He spins around, watching Jasmine point to him and then the phone while still talking to whoever is on the other end.

'Yes, if you just hold on for a moment, I'll be able to find someone for you to speak with.' Jasmine puts the call on hold and turns back towards Nickolas. 'It's Jessica Cunningham. She said she is still waiting on an update about her brother, Finn.'

Nickolas closes his eyes and takes a deep breath and slowly exhales. He doesn't want to have this discussion out in the open, so he asks Jasmine to send it to the phone in the break room where he knows he'll be alone. Brett and Hayley can wait.

Once in the break room, he sits down, picks up the phone and connects the call. 'Jessica? Hey, it's Nickolas.'

'Oh my god, Nickolas. Is Finn okay? I've been pulling my hair out all day. No one is telling me anything, the fucking therapist said she'd get back to me hours ago and the last I he-heard...' Jessica's voice breaks, her small sobs coming through the receiver.

'I'm sorry you haven't been updated, but I can promise you he is okay. He's awake. Eating, smiling, laughing. He'll be allowed back into his room tomorrow.'

'Oh, thank god.'

Nickolas can still hear her soft sobs.

'I should be there with him. He shouldn't be alone right now. He...he needs me.'

'He needed you when you came to visit.' Nickolas knows the comment is completely out of line, but what if Finn hadn't woken up?

'What?' The sorrow that was in Jessica's voice moments ago is gone.

'Finn felt alone. He felt like no one wanted him, that no one actually cared what happened to him. He had spent almost a week waiting to see his family and the minute you came to visit, you tore him down.'

'Are you saying it's my fault he tried to kill himself?'

'No. It was his medication that caused that. But your actions didn't fuckin' help.' Nickolas is angry now. He's had enough. 'God, I am so sick of you people playing the victim card when you aren't the ones living every single day in this place. You all act like you should be getting a fuckin' medal because you have a family member committed in a psych facility and it's so hard for you to be dealing with that. Well, how the hell do you think he feels? You'd know if you actually took the time to ask him, and not just ask for the sake of it, but actually ask and act on it.'

'Excuse me. What gives you the right—'

'It's my job to make sure every single one of these patients gets the best care and support so they can walk out of here and live their life. That's my right. If something or someone is preventing them from bettering themselves, then I'm going to say something because at the end of the day, I don't give a shit about you. You're not my patient. Finn is.'

The silence on the other end is so rewarding that Nickolas holds it, waiting for Jessica to be the first to break it.

'I don't know what you think you know about me and my family, but you've known Finn for a week, if that. I've been raising him, along with my four other siblings, since I was fourteen.'

'Congratulations. But while you were doing that, Finn was feeling neglected. He was trying to get by so you had one less person to worry about. Then he got diagnosed, so imagine how that made him feel. We're South Side. We all have shit to deal with. But don't go acting all high and mighty for doing a good thing, because if you really cared, you'd be doing it without wanting the credit. Finn needs people in his corner right now, and unless you're willing to do that for him, you need to back the fuck up and let him get the help he deserves.'

He can tell Jessica wants to jump in, but he doesn't allow it. 'You wanna know the first thing Finn did when he was told we notified you about his attempt? He panicked. He panicked because he knew you'd forever latch onto him like a child that can't take care of himself, and he knew that you had more important things to worry about than him. Even as he lays in bed, healing from self-inflicted wounds, he is more worried about you and how you'd react than he is about himself.'

Nickolas lets Jessica stew in those thoughts only for a minute before deciding he has had enough. 'As much as I'd love to stay and chat, I have fifteen patients waiting for me, your brother included. I've updated you on how he is going, and you can call every day as you have for further updates. But just know, the next time you visit, maybe you should think about what Finn needs from you before you come and see him.' He hangs up. If Jessica wants to report him, so be it. He has a clean record; one complaint isn't going to do jack shit when he knows he is in the right.

He storms out, making his way to the dining area to help with what's left of dinner. Nickolas steps into the room, anger still bubbling inside of him from his confrontation with Jessica as he grabs a tray for Finn.

'Well, well, well. Look who has decided to show his face and do some work,' Brett comments, loud enough for some of the patients to hear.

Nickolas clenches his teeth. He tells himself to ignore Brett and not to bite.

'Dorothy said you were around, but I haven't seen you all day and your shift started five hours ago,' Brett continues to push.

Who is Nickolas kidding? In no universe could he ever allow this asshole to believe he has one upped him. 'Unlike you, Brett, I actually make sure things get done around here. Now, do I have to babysit you while the patients eat, or can I grab a tray and take it to the infirmary for a patient?'

'Oh, that's right. Heard about Finn's little attempt. Hey, you better get back to him in case he did it right and finished himself off this time.'

Nickolas doesn't even think. He swings his right arm back, putting all his force into a punch that connects with Brett's left cheek. The impact knocks Brett to the floor. Hayley and the patients all stop what they're doing as they turn towards the commotion.

Nickolas looks down at Brett, pleased to see the prick lying on the ground like the scum that he is. 'I warned you, didn't I? Next time, you won't be able to get back up.'

Nickolas walks over to Aiden and takes two servings of food. He ignores the feeling of déjà vu that comes over him as he walks back to Finn with a tray in hand. Instead of relishing in the pulsating sensation that's spreading across his knuckles from the satisfying punch, he kicks himself for doing exactly what Brett was aiming for when the asshole made that comment about Finn. After all this time, the countless homophobic, disrespectful, and selfish comments Brett has made, nothing had caused Nickolas to behave like his old self. The person who used to use violence to get his point across. If Brett didn't already have suspicions about him and Finn, Nickolas was positive that Brett would use his outburst as confirmation.

He enters the infirmary, unaware that he had been holding his breath until he sees Finn sitting up in bed, reading a book with a look of concentration. Nickolas's hands stop shaking as he sets the tray down on the overbed table, allowing his emotions to settle.

'Hey, you okay?' asks Finn.

No. The last time I brought us dinner to eat, I walked into a scene from a slasher film.

'Fine. But I'm expecting a phone call from HR later.'

'HR?'

'Human Resources.'

'You didn't?'

Nickolas holds up his right hand so Finn can see the redness on his knuckles from where the 'hate' on his knuckles came in contact with that fuckhead.

'Damn. Wish I could have seen it.'

Nickolas doesn't respond, glad Finn wasn't there to hear Brett's ugly words. 'Hope you're hungry. I made sure Aiden gave us extra.' Nickolas places two plates of lasagne in front of Finn, one of which is for himself, but he's willing to give it up if Finn wants it.

'You eating with me?'

'I'm not going back out there anytime soon, so if you're sharing...'

Finn pushes a plate towards him.

Nickolas takes a chunk of lasagne. Instead of holding the plate in his hand, he lets it stay on the table and risks his food falling from his fork, as he attempts to close the distance from the plate to his mouth. Finn does the same in a much more delicate manner.

'Don't they need your help out there?' Finn asks.

'Sounds like you're trying to get rid of me.' Nickolas takes another bite.

'No, it's just, I don't want you to get in trouble by staying with me.'

Is Finn saying this because of what Dot said?

'Do you want me to go?'

'No, I don't want you to go.'

'Good. Then shut up and eat before it goes cold.'

They sit in silence, enjoying the food and the company. Once they are finished, Nickolas moves the plates to the side, making sure Finn's utensils are accounted for.

'So, the doctor said you can't get your bandages wet for the next forty-eight hours, which means you get a sponge bath,' explains Nickolas.

'You've got to be kidding me.'

'It'll be quick. Just a wipe down of your body and arms. The rest can wait.'

'Oh.'

Nickolas cocks his eyebrow. He can't work out if that was a relieved 'Oh' or a disappointed 'Oh'.

'I'd normally say skip it, but you kind of have blood on you still. I figured you'd sleep better if you got to clean yourself up.'

'You're probably right.' Nickolas watches Finn try to stand, but weak shaky legs get in the way.

'Easy there. You're still not back to full strength.' Nickolas wraps his arm around Finn's waist, helping to support his weight while standing. The catheter must have been removed while Nickolas was doing the paperwork, and the needle where Finn had his blood transfusion is also gone.

'You always hear those stories of how tragic it is when someone takes their life, but you never hear about those that survive a suicide attempt and the struggles they have to go through afterwards,' says Finn.

'Finn...'

Should I be worried?

'No, I'm not...I'm just saying, society has this image that people who try to take their lives are weak. That they can't fight or hold on anymore. But the strength someone has to have to come back from a suicide attempt, that speaks volumes. The weakness from the blood loss, the embarrassment of knowing you once again failed at something while deep down realising that someone higher up decided it wasn't your time to go. The fact that, if you aren't found quick enough, then you could suffer brain damage or wake up with the depression being worse and simply leading to you wanting to try again.'

Nickolas stops walking, concern on his face.

'I may have done some research a few years back,' Finn explains.

'Why?' Nickolas's question is fearful, not harsh.

'My mum, she, ah, she slit her wrists on our kitchen floor. I wasn't sure what she'd be like once we found out she survived, so I looked it up.' Finn looks down at the floor, not meeting Nickolas's eyes.

'I'm sorry. That must have been really traumatic for you.'

Finn doesn't answer, simply pushes forward. They make their way towards the bathroom within the infirmary. It has a drain in the floor with a shower head and a toilet to the side, and an empty bucket and sponge waiting for them.

Nickolas lowers Finn onto the toilet seat to rest while he fills the bucket with water. 'You need help undressing?'

'One day I'll say yes, and on that day, you'll be getting undressed with me.'

'That so?' Nickolas keeps his head down, focused on the bucket of water, hiding the blush that is seeping onto his face. He imagines their bodies naked together under the spray of hot soapy water. This shift between them, whether it happened after admitting they're friends or something more if their situations were different; however it happened, this place they are in now with the jokes and flirting, it's exciting and Nickolas can't get enough of it. He turns the water off as it reaches the top of the bucket. Nickolas spins around and walks towards Finn, who is now only wearing boxers. He places the bucket down and then kneels before him, picking up the sponge and squeezing out the excess water so it doesn't drip everywhere.

Nickolas takes Finn's right hand and holds his arm out as he gently wipes down his lightly freckled skin. The water glistens under the lights, making Finn's freckles look like speckles in soft white sand that the sun catches, bringing a sparkle to the ground. It's beautiful, captivating, and Nickolas has never found someone's skin so alluring before. He dips the sponge back into the bucket, the water turning a soft pink as the blood rinses out. He wipes the same arm down again, making sure to not get close to the bandages, before he rinses the sponge out and repeats his actions on Finn's left arm.

'You seem to know what you're doing,' says Finn.

'This isn't my first sponge bath.'

'And here I was thinking I was special.'

Nickolas rinses the sponge out again, Finn's legs next to be cleaned. He rubs the sponge in soft circular motions as he works his way up Finn's lean and muscular leg. Red hair darkens as it gets wet. Nickolas manoeuvres Finn's boxers so he can clean all the way up to the hip bone. He squeezes a little around the sponge, gripping Finn's thigh in the process.

He wrings the sponge out once again, the water more red than pink, and goes back to washing Finn. Cleaning his chest, Nickolas starts at the top, rubbing around Finn's neck then carefully makes his way down a well-toned torso. A small gasp escapes Finn's lips as Nickolas brushes over hard perky nipples. Nickolas tells himself it's from the mix of the warm water and the cold air, but the look in Finn's eyes says otherwise. As he cleans over Finn's abs, getting a clear look at the phoenix tattoo, Nickolas stops as his eyes land on Finn's lap, a clear tent forming in his patient's boxers.

'I guess that particular side effect has worn off.' Finn sounds just as shocked as he looks, the heat in those green eyes causes Nickolas to break out in a sweat.

Nickolas coughs to break the tension. 'The blood transfusion would have cleaned out the drugs in your system, but hopefully with your new dose, your body will already be used to it. Save you from having to go through the side effects again.'

Nickolas looks away, puts the sponge back in the bucket, and takes it over to the drain so he can tip the water out.

'Fingers crossed. I'll know by tomorrow, I'm sure.'

Nickolas keeps himself busy at the sink while Finn dries off, taking longer than necessary to give Finn the chance to calm down. When he turns back around, Finn is already standing up, fully dressed, a hand on the railing beside the toilet to help keep him steady, waiting for Nickolas to help escort him back to the bed.

'Mr Cunningham. We meet again I see.' Dr Murphy is waiting in the infirmary. Finn gives the doctor a small nod, while Nickolas ignores Dr Murphy completely. He gently lowers Finn back into bed, knowing it's time to say goodbye for the night.

'You need anything else before I go?' Nickolas asks.

Finn keeps his green eyes locked on Nickolas'. 'No...Are you ... are you working tomorrow?'

'Morning shift. And since I'm already running off no sleep, I better get home and try and catch up on it.'

'I'm s—'

'I swear to god if you say sorry one more time...'

'You'll what?'

Nickolas bites his lower lip, cocking his eyebrow. 'James will be by shortly with your meds. If you have any issues, let Dr Murphy know. Most importantly though, you need to sleep, okay?'

'I will.' Finn gives him a soft smile.

'I'm glad you're okay, Finn.'

'Me too, Nick.'

Nickolas gives Finn's ankle a quick squeeze before turning around and making his way out of the room. He walks towards the front desk to leave notes for James about Finn's whereabouts, his medication, and any side effects that may develop from the change. The lithium will knock Finn around for a bit, depending on the dosage, but he hopes it will give Finn a chance to close those beautiful green eyes and rest.

James walks through the doors at ten to eight. Nickolas is already standing with his bag in hand, deciding not to bother changing before he heads home. He waits for James to return to the reception desk before he leaves.

'I'm so disappointed in you, Nickolas,' says James.

He looks at James standing in the doorway, wondering what the hell he had done wrong now.

'You finally punched Brett and I wasn't here to see it?'

Oh. That. Word sure gets around quickly. 'Trust me. The asshole got off easy. I have done a lot worse to guys that have done a lot less.'

'All in good time, I'm sure.'

Brett walks in behind Sam, waiting to be buzzed through to make an escape. The shiner Nickolas left behind is a mere warning of more to come if Brett keeps running that mouth.

Nickolas smiles, pleased that he has left his mark.

'Do I need to escort you boys to your car, or can I trust you both to leave without causing another scene?' asks Sam.

'I think Brett got the message loud and clear. Besides, no one's in the parking lot to see me knock him to the ground.'

Brett is surprisingly quiet.

Nickolas puts his backpack on his shoulder, making his way out from behind the front desk, following behind Hayley who has since joined them.

'James, I've left you some notes. I'll touch base with you in the morning, but get Lydia to look over them too, just in case,' Nickolas explains.

James gives Nickolas a salute as he walks through the automatic doors.

He gets home in record time, giving Socks a bit of extra attention since he never came home between his shifts. He tops up the food bowl with a bit more than usual before he strips and jumps into bed, still wearing the boxers that they provide the patients. He figures the shower he took at work is sufficient enough for him not to take another one before bed. Lying on his stomach, Nickolas sets his alarm for four a.m. before he wraps his arms around his pillow and buries himself into it. Just as he is about to doze off, Socks jumps onto the bed and nuzzles into his side, soft purrs lulling him into a peaceful sleep. Instead of the horrors he was seeing the last time he closed his eyes, his mind envisions soft sandy white skin lying beside him, with hair as bright as the sunrays. Green eyes as cool as the ocean are looking soft and calm as they stare back at him. Finn smiles, telling Nickolas he'll be right here beside him when he wakes up.

8. Tuesday

Once again Nickolas finds himself sitting on the soft sand of a deserted beach. Why his mind keeps taking him to the ocean, he doesn't know. It could be because he's never been, the images in his head are simply created from things he has seen in photos or movies. Maybe it's because he finds the atmosphere of the waves rolling in and out soothing in his somewhat hectic life. Or it could be because white, green, and orange – the colours that make up the beautiful landscape before him – will forever remind him of Finn. White skin, green eyes, red hair. Nickolas never really had a type, until now.

He's sitting with his legs bent, his hands clutching around them to keep them close to his chest.

'Hey, Nickolas.'

He turns to his right and his heart leaps into his throat. He can't believe she is here, sitting beside him, looking as beautiful as he remembers and, most of all, healthy. He wants to reach out and touch her but he's afraid he will wake if he does.

'You're here...' Nickolas is surprised.

'Course I am. Got nothing better to do.'

'But I mean, normally you're...'

'You dream of me looking like that because of the guilt you hold inside. This is me now. Whole. Calm. Finally at peace.'

Nickolas's eyes travel over her body so he can burn it to memory.

'None of it was your fault, Nickolas, and I wish I could've told you that before it all happened.'

He tries to process what she's saying, but words keep pouring from her mouth.

'I never left you, you know. I'm always beside you, watching, screaming into your ear that you need to go live your life. I want you to have fun and to stop feeling like a failure, because you're not.'

She takes a moment and Nickolas wonders if she's finished speaking.

'No matter how much you tried to help me, it was inevitable.'

Tears roll down his cheek. She's smiling back at him, not a single tear or ounce of sadness on her face.

'I miss you, so fucking much,' murmurs Nickolas.

'I know. The only thing I knew I was going to miss when I was gone, was you. But it wasn't enough to keep me around, to keep me going. And that's not on you, Nickolas. If anything, you gave me more time than I was willing to spare.'

Slowly, he takes his hand from his leg and reaches out towards her. She smiles as she takes his hand and the contact causes Nickolas to break down, no longer able to control the tears from falling. He feels her soft delicate fingers slide between his own, her warmth radiating from them.

'How is this real?' he asks between sobs.

'It's all memories, Nickolas. The way I look, sound, feel. It's all there inside of you, but you're forgetting all the good and focusing on the bad.'

'I remember you that way so that I feel the pain. It's what I deserve. Besides, it hurts too fucking much to remember you happy. Healthy. Knowing that you're gone and I'll never get to see you like that again.'

'That's not how I want to be remembered. That's not what I deserve.'

She's right. Nickolas spends every day telling families and patients not to define themselves based on their mental health, and here he is, doing exactly that.

'I'm sorry,' says Nickolas. 'I didn't mean—'

'I know. You've been trying to heal. But you're not alone.'

'It feels like it.'

'Maybe so. But the people you work with, they care about you.'

'They're just colleagues.'

'Doesn't mean they aren't friends.'

Nickolas scoffs, wiping at his eyes so he can see her more clearly.

'You have Finn.'

'What?' His eyes widen at the sound of Finn's name. She lets go of his hand so she can turn her body towards him rather than being side by side like they were.

'I told you, I never left. I've been watching you two, watching him. He's kinda cute. Totally would have gone for him if he wasn't gay.'

'Fuck off.' He says the words but there is no heat behind them. He sniffs back tears and wipes his nose with the back of his hand.

'He's good for you. He's making you feel alive again, showing you that there is more to living than just working all the time.'

'I like my job.'

'And that's great, but you deserve to have someone special in your life. You deserve to have love and happiness. Someone to come home to after work.'

Her words mimic how he's been feeling since he met Finn. Maybe she has been watching over him.

'I know you're scared. But you don't need to be.'

'I found him...like you.' Nickolas's voice breaks at the last two words.

She takes his hand back and holds it between both of hers. 'He isn't me, Nickolas. Finn's a fighter. And he has you fighting alongside him.'

'I fought alongside you too.'

'You did. But you were fighting alone.'

Silence. Her thumb rubbing against his hand.

He closes his eyes as he takes it all in. He sighs. 'He's my patient.'

'True. But one day he won't be. You've waited this long to find someone you can see a future with...what's a little more waiting?'

He shakes his head. Her words are sinking in, but the fear he felt seeing Finn lying lifeless in that bed hits him again. 'I was so scared that he wasn't going to make it.'

She simply nods. 'You know, I said Finn's good for you, but you're also good for him.'

'He doesn't even know me.'

'That's because you won't let him. Finn's opened up to you because he trusts you, so maybe it's time you do the same.'

She turns towards the sun, closing her eyes as the rays cast a glow across her face. Nickolas takes in her beauty and wonders why no one could ever see her the way he saw her. Maybe things would be different if people did.

'It's time for me to go.' She stands.

Nickolas panics as she lets go of his hand. 'Wait. Already? Hold on.' He tries to stand up but he can't seem to rise. 'Wait. Will I see you again?'

She smiles down at him, the sun casting a halo above her head. 'I told you. I'm always with you, Nickolas. But hopefully, if you listen to my advice, then maybe we won't need to see each other anymore.'

'I'll always need to see you.'

'No, you won't, Nickolas. And that's okay. Once you accept forgiveness, accept love and happiness back into your life, then you'll be able to move on. And with that, you'll find other things and other people will make their way into your dreams, and I'll only pop in from time to time. But that doesn't mean you love or miss me any less.' She gives Nickolas a smile. An honest to God, could-not-be-happier smile. 'I promise I'm okay. I just want you to be okay too.'

A tear rolls down his face. He blinks it away and when his eyes open again, she is gone. He holds his eyes closed again, squeezing them shut, willing her to return, only this time when he forces them open, he wakes in his bedroom. The room's still dark due to the early morning, tears are falling onto his pillow.

'Please take me back to her,' Nickolas whispers as he closes his eyes, but the sound of his alarm going off interrupts his pleas. He turns his head into the pillow, softly sobbing as he allows the ringing to continue, masking the sounds of his cries.

Eventually, he finds the strength to shower, his mind holding onto the sight of her smile. The way the sun lit up her face and the way the wind blew her hair – it was the first dream Nickolas has had since she died that made him happy to see her in his sleep. Nickolas was always under the assumption that the idea of ghosts and spirits and the afterlife was simply a ploy to help people move on after they lose someone they love. But something about that dream seems too real. Is she trying to communicate with him through his dreams? She did mention Finn, a person who came into his life after she—

The need to get dressed and ready for work gives him the perfect distraction. He pours a cup of coffee as he exits the kitchen, the towel still wrapped around his waist from his shower. Back in his bedroom, Socks is still asleep, snuggled into the warm patch he left when he got up. He throws the uniform and boxers Dot had provided for him into his backpack and gets dressed in a pair of jeans and a hoodie, with his own fresh uniform already in his bag to change into. Nickolas grabs some food, another cup of coffee, and heads out the door, the night slowly beginning to lift as it welcomes a new day.

He drives, his mind playing over every word spoken in his dream. Reassuring words about being happy and at peace. Advice about needing to trust and live. A part of Nickolas wants to do as she says, take a step into a life he never thought he'd get to enjoy. The other part reminds him that if she doesn't get to live a life of happiness, then why should he?

'I promise I'm okay.' Her voice lingers in his ear.

Parking his car, he lets out a deep breath and decides to forget about the dream for the time being and get himself in the right headspace for work. Darren and Sky step out of their cars as he locks his, the three of them silently making their way towards the entrance, still too early to talk to one another more than they need to. Sam notices the sullen tone on their faces and buzzes them in without so much as a good morning.

Nickolas changes with his back turned to his colleagues so he doesn't have to see the way Darren's eyes roam his body when he gets undressed. He pulls the spare uniform and boxers out of his bag so he can return them, and makes his way to the infirmary, letting the others deal with waking the patients up and getting them to the dining area for breakfast. Hopefully, if all went well during the night, Finn will be able to join everyone. He drops off the dirty uniform and then lets himself into the infirmary without knocking, just on the off chance that Finn may still be asleep. Dr Murphy is nowhere in sight, so Nickolas assumes he is talking to Lexi at the front desk before the shift changeover.

Nickolas walks over to the bed where Finn is still asleep, his body and mind needing the rest. Finn looks so peaceful. Nickolas tries to remember if he's seen Finn like this since being admitted, but nothing comes to mind. Part of him doesn't want to disturb Finn's sleep, but the commotion Lexi will make when stepping through the doors will no doubt startle the sleeping redhead.

'Hey, sleepy face,' says Nickolas.

His voice doesn't even cause Finn to stir. Perhaps the new medication has knocked Finn out.

He tries again, this time with a little more attitude. 'Yo. Rise and fucking shine, Cinderella.'

Finn groans.

Nickolas chuckles at how adorable Finn looks when waking up in the morning.

'Five more minutes.' Finn rolls over, eyes still closed while trying to duck under the blanket.

'Sure. But then Darren will have to come get you for breakfast, and he doesn't know the secret word that will get you extra bacon from Aiden.'

Finn opens an eye to look up at him. Nickolas is smiling way too bright for this early in the morning and it's all Finn's doing. 'You said wake up was seven. It's only just turned six.'

'I started at six, and I figured it's my face you wanted to wake up to, so this is what you get.'

Groaning even louder, Finn sits up in the bed, rolling his green eyes so dramatically Nickolas is surprised they don't fall out of his head.

'How'd you sleep, anyway?' Nickolas asks.

'Surprisingly well. I think the meds knocked me out a bit.'

'Still groggy?'

Finn yaws before answering. 'Not for the moment, but it's only been one dose. Get the next one before breakfast.'

'Any other symptoms?'

Finn holds out a hand, which shows a slight tremor. It's not as obvious as the tremors from the first round of medication, but it's enough to cause some discomfort.

'As I said, hopefully since the previous drugs were already in your system you won't experience the side effects as severely.

However, with the blood transfusion, there's no guarantee.' He offers Finn a small smile for reassurance.

'Good thing this place has such great orderlies that can help if the meds decide to try and knock me down.' Finn winks at him, and Nickolas blushes. Six fucking o'clock in the morning and Finn has him blushing.

'So, you're scheduled for one-on-one therapy today, but no group session. My guess is once Dr Hale sees how you're progressing, she'll allow you to join the group if she feels you're ready.'

Nickolas sits down on the chair beside Finn.

'Does everyone know what happened?' Finn asks.

'Word has probably spread. It's the downside to being a small centre, I suppose,' Nickolas explains. 'Once a patient is missing, they notice straight away, and they ask questions and listen to the things orderlies are saying. It doesn't take long for patients to piece things together.'

Finn sighs and stares at the ceiling.

'You don't have to worry, Finn. Everyone here has relapsed. They know what it's like and none of them are here to judge.'

Finn looks ahead, nodding along before turning towards him. 'Have you spoken to my sister?'

Nickolas thumbs his bottom lip, breaking eye contact for a moment. 'Kinda.'

'Nick?'

'Things may have gotten a little heated between us.'

'Shit. I'm sorry. Jessica just doesn't know when to mind her own business, but I swear, whatever she said she—'

'Finn! Stop.' Nickolas cuts Finn off mid-rant, smiling as the redhead defends his honour. 'I, ah, I may have to be the one to apologise.' He bites his bottom lip.

'What?'

'I was the one that went off at your sister, not the other way around.'

'Wait? Really?'

'I'm sorry if I overstepped. I was just looking out for you and in the heat of the moment, with some of the things she was saying, I kind of snapped.'

Finn smiles, and Nickolas isn't sure why that makes him feel proud inside, but it does.

'No one has ever stood up for me before,' Finn explains. 'Especially not against my sister.'

'Yeah, well. It was about time someone did.' Nickolas's cheeks feel hot.

The door swings open and Lexi walks in, taking the attention off Nickolas and a chance to change the subject.

'Oh good, you're up. Let's change those bandages before you head out for breakfast.' Lexi is bright and bubbly even at this hour of the morning, but Finn doesn't seem to mind. While holding each wrist out for her to unwrap, clean, and bandage back up, Finn's eyes are on Nickolas.

'Stitches are looking good. They'll no doubt start to itch soon, but that's a sign that they're healing,' Lexi explains. 'You'll probably be left with a scar around two inches long, give or take.'

'When can I take the bandages off?' Finns asks.

'Give it another day. We'll see how they go, but it looks like they should be fine after that. The air will help them heal quicker too.'

Finn nods.

'Okay. Well, I have medications that I need to get sorted for the patients, so I suppose I'll leave you two to it,' Lexi explains before walking to the other side of the room.

'What's wrong?' Nickolas asks as Finn sinks into the mattress, eyes cast down as shoulders sag.

Finn shrugs.

'You know you don't have to be ashamed of them.'

'Easy for you to say. For the rest of my life when I go for an interview, or on a date, the first thing they'll see are these scars. Straight away they'll assume I'm crazy, or they'll worry that I'm going to do it again.'

Nickolas ignores the date comment. 'Are you?'

Finn looks away from the bandages and towards Nickolas. 'Am I what?'

'Crazy?'

'No. But this place says otherwise.'

'No, it doesn't. This place says you need help adjusting to a medication that is literally rewiring your brain.'

'That's a nice slogan, you should put it on the front door.'

'Whatever, smartass. My point is, you need to stop thinking about how other people view you, because at the end of the day, how you view yourself is all that matters.'

'You sure you're not a therapist?'

'I'm sure.' Nickolas moves to sits on the edge of Finn's bed. 'So, you're not crazy. But that begs the next question: Are you going to do it again?'

Finn shakes his head. 'No. I never wanted—I don't want to be...No. I won't.'

'Then fuck the outside world. Wear long sleeves to the interview so they hire you before they see them. And if any guy thinks any less of you because of those scars, then he isn't good enough to be with you. The right guy would take his time to get to know you and understand what those scars really mean.'

'...and what do they mean?'

'They mean you're a survivor. They mean you have overcome a hardship in your life that tried to tear you down...but you won. You walked away with these scars to prove that you fought the darkness. Every single person in this world has that voice in their head telling them to give up, to throw in the towel. Some listen to it and never come back, some ignore it altogether. Others, however, have a moment of weakness, just like all human beings do, but right at the end, they decide that what they did was a mistake, and they fight like they never have before to bring themselves back from it. That's you.'

Finn wipes away a tear.

Nickolas knew Finn's question was a setup, fishing for a compliment. But Nickolas would use his last breath to give Finn the support and confidence needed to move forward.

Finn slides his hand into Nickolas's, their fingers intertwining long enough for Finn to give his hand a squeeze before disentangling.

'You hungry?' Nickolas asks.

'Starving,' says Finn.

'Think you can walk?'

'I'll try. Think you can catch me if I can't?'

'Always.'

Nickolas makes his way over to Lexi, collecting Finn's meds from the cart, checking them, and then marking them off before heading back to the bed. He watches Finn swallow them down and goes to grab him some extra water.

'Morning Lexi, cart ready?' Darren asks, stepping into the infirmary.

'It's all yours Darren,' Lexi confirms.

'Excellent. Oh, hey Nickolas. You ran off so fast this morning after you changed, wasn't sure where you went.'

'Dot asked me to look in on Finn, help bring him to breakfast,' Nickolas lies. Dot didn't have to ask him; he wanted to do that all on his own.

'Well, guess I'll see you there.' Darren winks, and all Nickolas wants to do is roll his eyes.

He makes his way back to the bed, pleased that the curtain prevented Finn from seeing any of that cringe-worthy exchange. He pushes the curtain back, smiling at Finn as he hands over another cup of water before helping him stand.

In no rush, Finn swings his legs around and places them on the floor, the shaking not as intense as yesterday. The walk to the dining area is slow and Nickolas keeps his hand on Finn's waist, making sure that Finn is the one taking charge. As Nickolas swipes his key card to the common room, Finn takes in a deep breath before slowly exhaling. Opening the door, Nickolas is relieved to find that everyone is already in the dining area eating, giving Finn a little more time before coming face-to-face with everyone.

When they enter, Cora calls out, smiling. A hand waving for Finn to come over and sit at the table. Finn turns to Nickolas, who gives a nod of encouragement. 'Go sit, I'll grab you some breakfast.'

Nickolas places the tray in front of Finn, the extra bacon he hinted at there on the plate.

Finn is happily listening to Cora babble on about the events that happened over the last few days, but he still finds a moment to look up and offer a smile of thanks.

Nickolas steps away and stands beside Darren and Sky as they watch everyone eat.

'Is he back for good?' Darren asks.

Nickolas tries not to roll his eyes. 'What kind of fucking question is that?' Nickolas makes sure that none of the patients heard him swear, a slip-up due to how comfortable he's becoming when talking to Finn.

'I'm just saying, has he had the all-clear from the doc?'

'Jesus Christ, Darren. He's sitting here eating with everyone isn't he?' Nickolas points out.

There is a silence between them all, but only for a moment.

'Must have been hard for you, finding him like you found—' His colleague stops. The look on Nickolas's face saying Darren has crossed a line.

He wants to smirk at the way Darren takes a small step back, possibly out of fear. Truth be told, after his dream, he wants to talk about her. He wants to tell people how amazing she was and how much he loved her. But those people are not Darren.

'How 'bout you go and start monitoring the return trays,' Nickolas instructs Darren.

'Yes. Right. I'll just...go over there.' Darren rushes off, leaving Sky and Nickolas near the entrance.

'How do you do it?' Sky asks.

'Do what?' questions Nickolas.

'Make someone scared of you, but also want to fuck you at the same time.'

Nickolas's eyebrows shoot to the roof, not used to hearing Sky speak so bluntly, especially since he assumed Darren's infatuation with him was on the down low with his colleagues.

'What's the saying...play it mean, keep 'em keen?' says Nickolas.

'Ha. You sayin' you're keen?' Sky questions.

'Fuck no. But it's fun watching the guy squirm.' Nickolas looks to Finn, not surprised to see green eyes watching him. But when Finn's eyes avert towards Darren and then back towards him, there is questioning look on the redhead's face.

'Can I leave you two to sort this out while I go read over the notes from last night?' Nickolas asks.

'I'm sure we can manage,' says Sky.

Before leaving, Nickolas makes his way over towards Finn.

'I need to check over some things. Are you alright here or did you want to head back to your room?' asks Nickolas. The last thing he wants to do is shove Finn into socialising too soon, but at the same time, he hopes Finn understands there is no reason to hide away.

Finn avoids making eye contact with him. 'I think I'll stay. Thanks. I have my session with Dr Hale soon anyway.'

Nickolas isn't sure he can believe Finn's words without seeing his face, not because of trust, but because he'd hate for Finn to do something only because he thinks it's what

Nickolas wants. During the moment of silence, Alex continues to talk to Finn, so he decides to let it go, knowing the sooner he leaves, the quicker he can return.

When Nickolas steps into the common room, everyone is talking, watching TV, or drawing with charcoal. He makes his way over to Finn and lets him know that it's time to see Dr Hale. He helps him stand; the tremors still present as Nickolas holds onto Finn. They walk in silence. Nickolas can tell Finn is lost in thought, perhaps preparing for the session. As they stop outside the door to Dr Hale's office, Nickolas goes to wish Finn good luck, but he's stopped before he can do so.

'So, you and Darren?'

'Me and Darren what?'

'It's cool. You don't have to – I mean, it's not any of my business.'

'Finn, what are you talking about?'

Finn knocks on the door to Dr Hale's office. 'Play it mean, keep 'em keen, right?'

Nickolas opens his mouth, wanting to explain but the door opens and Dr Hale is standing in front of them. Nickolas wishes he could close the door and ask for a moment alone but Finn steps inside, avoiding Nickolas's gaze.

He spends the next two hours a frantic mess. Finn had a double session, and all Nickolas could do was count down the minutes till he could talk to Finn and explain the misunderstanding. He replaced the bedding for all the patients, as well as providing them with a fresh set of clothes. He made an appearance in the common room, touched base with Ethan who seems to be less on edge today with no new visible bruises, and then read Ethan's notes to make sure nothing had been reported. He and Dot had decided it would be best to examine Ethan's body at night before lights out in case whoever it is decided to get creative with their location, so if anything was found, Lydia would have reported it in last night's notes.

Nickolas looks at the time on his watch. There's twenty minutes before Finn's session is due to finish. Desperate to clear things up with him, Nickolas makes his way toward the therapy room in case Dr Hale lets Finn out early. He paces back and forth in front of Dr Hale's door. The anxious energy rising inside of Nickolas is making him feel sick. The last thing he wants is Finn thinking Nickolas is lying, using Finn as some side piece.

'Today was a good session, Finn. I'd be happy for you to come back and join us in group sessions from tomorrow, based on what we achieved from today's talk.'

'Thank you, Dr Hale. It felt good.'

Nickolas locks onto Finn before quickly averting his eyes to Dr Hale.

'Nickolas, can you please escort Finn back to the common room?' instructs Dr Hale.

'Of course.' Nickolas waits for the door to close before he reaches out and grabs Finn's hand, dragging the redhead through the corridor, ignoring the protests from Finn.

'What the hell, Nickolas?' Finn tries to pull out of Nickolas's grasp, but it's no use. Nickolas is holding on as though his life depends on it.

He shoves the door to the showers open, pulling Finn inside before he closes the door behind him.

'Really, Nickolas?'

'I'm sorry. I just needed to talk to you away from everyone else out there.'

'And you thought the showers were the best place to hide?'

'No windows, and the cleaner has already been, so no one will come in here till tonight.'

Finn looks down. Nickolas can see that this is a conversation Finn is trying to avoid, making it all the more reason why he needs Finn to know.

'Look—'

'No, it's fine.' Finn looks up, face soft, showing no signs of anger or resentment.

But Nickolas can see the disappointment in those beautiful green eyes. 'It's not fine.' Nickolas takes a step closer, holding onto hope as Finn stands guarded.

'You don't have to explain anything. You said it yourself. We can't. I'm your patient so whatever you have going on with Darren is none of my—'

Nickolas lunges forward. His hands grab for Finn's waist and the back of his neck, pulling Finn towards him as he presses their lips firmly together. His mouth catches the small gasp that Finn lets slip and he swallows it down. He instantly feels Finn relax into his arms, melt into the kiss and when a hand holds onto Nickolas's neck, while another rests against his cheek, Nickolas moans into the touch. It causes his lips to open enough for Finn to suck on his bottom lip and the sensation has him weak at the knees. Reluctantly, Nickolas pulls back. He rests his forehead on Finn's, his hand still holding onto his lean waist as they catch their breath.

Nickolas keeps his eyes closed, his heart pounding in his chest. 'I swear to you. The only person I am interested in, the only person I have anything going on with, is standing right in front of me.' He slowly opens his eyes, the ocean meeting the meadow, and his heart begins to settle from the soft smile that appears on Finn's face. He runs his fingers through Finn's silky red hair, right above the nape of his neck, the sensation calming them both.

'I thought you said we can't,' Finn whispers against Nickolas's lips.

'And I meant it. We can't, not yet. But I didn't want you to think I was off with someone else, killing time or something before you and I could be together.'

'You saving yourself for me?' The seduction in Finn's voice makes Nickolas tremble.

'I'm afraid you're a few years late for that. But let's just say it's been a while.' Nickolas chuckles at the quiet 'fuck' Finn lets out under his breath. He moves his hand to the side of Finn's face, gently rubbing his thumb against a blushing cheek.

'I've never wanted something like this before. Never wanted someone for more than just the physical. Not until I met you.'

'You're making it really hard for me not to kiss you again.' Finn's forehead once again rests against his. All Nickolas wants to do is lean that little bit closer so that their lips are touching.

'I know. But I need you to know that this is real.' Nickolas explains. 'I want this, I want you. If you're willing to wait, then so am I.'

'You're worth waiting for, Nickolas,' Finn whispers into his ear.

A loud bang in the hallway causes them to pull apart quicker than if someone had screamed fire. Nickolas turns towards the door, checking to see if anyone was about to walk in, while Finn turns, taking the time to cool down. Nickolas curses himself for being so impulsive and letting his actions speak for him.

'Nick?'

The sound of Finn abbreviating his name covers his body in goosebumps. Nickolas doesn't turn around. One look at Finn, and he'll ignore all the voices in his head telling him to be professional. He's now had a taste and he's already craving more.

'We should head back. People are already talking,' he explains.

Nickolas heads for the door, knowing without looking that Finn is following him. They walk back to the common room, no one around to question their lack of eye contact or the distance between them. Finn has enough strength to be able to walk without Nickolas's assistance, but he still glances Finn's way in case he needs to suddenly reach out and help. He unlocks the door with his key card and holds it open for Finn, making sure not to follow as the redhead walks towards Ryder, Cora, and Alex.

'Sky, can you take Ryder to his appointment with Dr Hale?' Nickolas instructs.

Without question, Sky follows his orders. For the remainder of the morning, Nickolas makes sure to keep himself on opposite sides of the room to Darren, just to further his point to Finn in case there are still any doubts.

Nickolas's mind keeps wandering back to their kiss. He was never much of a kisser when it came to hooking up. Some guys needed it to get themselves going, so Nickolas would indulge them, not really getting anything from it but merely wanting to speed the process along so he could get his release and leave. Others thankfully knew it was all about the physical and didn't bother with any of that foreplay shit. With Finn, though, Nickolas's body is screaming for him to kiss Finn over and over again and never stop. The small kiss they shared on Sunday had sparked something inside of him, a flame burning just for Finn.

With Nickolas focused on whether Finn was going to survive, he couldn't take the time to process the significance of their kiss. But now...now Nickolas has a moment to think about both of their kisses, the most recent one being so simple, yet so mind-blowing. He couldn't help but bring his fingers up to his mouth, feeling the lingering touch of Finn's lips on his.

The sound of the door opening brings Nickolas out of his head. The patients he's sitting with are happy watching TV rather than interacting. Hayley and Eric walk in, ready to start the afternoon shift. Time was going quickly, or did it feel that way with his mind too busy basking in the afterglow of kissing Finn?

'Hey, guys.' Nickolas gives them both a wave hello. 'You mind getting the dining area ready for lunch?

*

While everyone eats, Hayley and Eric begin to set up the common room for group therapy. Nickolas stands to the side, watching over the patients. Finn and Ryder are deep in discussion. A small spike of jealousy runs through Nickolas as Finn leans in close to talk to Ryder. He is quick to shut that down; he doesn't do jealousy. He hears Finn's words in his head – *you're worth waiting for, Nickolas* – and he knows there was no word of a lie in that sentence.

Everyone starts to hand their trays in, Sky checking everything over before they make their way back to the common room to either stay or be escorted back to their rooms. There's always thirty minutes after lunch and before group starts. Enough time for everyone to settle, take any bathroom breaks and get to where they need to be. For the first time, Finn is standing by the door, waiting to be escorted to room thirteen, a look of relief appears on his face as Nickolas moves towards him.

'Kinda glad I don't have to sit through group today,' says Finn.

'Here, I'll drop you off at your room before I head on my break.' Nickolas doesn't have to worry about watching over the other orderlies; he's given them their tasks for the remainder of the day and trusts them to follow through. He walks Finn to room thirteen and when he opens the door, Finn steps inside and stands there, looking around as though expecting to find something.

'You wouldn't even know what happened in here.' Finn walks over to the mattress, trailing fingers over the bleach-white bedding.

'I never saw them clean it, but unfortunately, they know how to handle those types of situations in a place like this,' explains Nickolas.

Finn sits on the mattress, picks up a book from the floor beside the bed, and wiggles in place to get comfortable.

'If you want, I could—' Nickolas stops. He bites his bottom lip.

Finn looks up from the book, waiting for Nickolas to continue.

'I could bring my lunch in here. Maybe sit with you?'

Finn's smile is the only answer he needs. Nickolas smiles back. His head tilts down while his eyes cast up at Finn, hiding the giddy blush on his face. Without another word, he turns around and leaves so he can grab his lunch. He is quick, not wanting to waste a minute that could be spent alone with Finn. He goes to the bathroom, empties his bladder while his food is heating in the microwave, then takes a bottle of water and his lunch to Finn's room, mindful that no one sees him sneaking in.

Quickly closing the door behind him as he enters the room, he finds Finn sitting against the wall with his blanket and pillow laid out on the floor.

'We having a picnic or something?' asks Nickolas.

'I figured this way no one would see you if they walked past the door and looked in,'

'Jesus. I feel like I'm sneaking in your window in the middle of the night.' Nickolas walks towards Finn and takes a seat, telling the voice in his head to shut up so he can enjoy the moment.

'Never had a guy do that for me before. Probably because I live in a double story house...and share a room with my brothers.'

'Back when I was living at home, everyone had to walk through my room to use the bathroom. Never had any privacy.'

Nickolas ignores the cold cement wall on his back and focuses on the heat he feels from Finn's shoulder pressed up against his own. He takes a bite of pasta. Half of it falls from his fork before making it into his mouth.

Finn laughs at the mess on Nickolas's uniform. 'Is this why you are all wearing purple? To cover up the food stains since none of you can eat like decent human beings?'

'Ha. Ha. Laugh it up. We have been taught to eat quickly, in case our breaks get interrupted. That's why we wear purple, because mess can be expected.'

'Wait, really?'

'No, you idiot. They're purple to cover any—' Nickolas focuses on wiping his shirt clean.

But Finn isn't dumb. He pieces it together quickly. 'Blood.'

Nickolas nods. He opens his mouth to speak, but Finn beats him to it.

'Guess that's better than wanting the staff to look like eggplants. That emoji is used as a dick for a reason.'

Nickolas bursts out laughing, which causes Finn to do the same.

'Exactly! That's what I've been saying. Apparently, the colour is soothing or some shit like that, so I guess we're stuck wearing it.'

'Could be worse. Could be in this ugly ass green t-shirt and grey sweatpants. I feel like a bum.'

'Brings out your eyes.' The words fall from Nickolas's mouth before he can stop them. To his surprise, he doesn't go into a panic after his little confession.

'Tell me something, Nickolas.'

'Like what?'

'I don't know. How'd you end up working here? I mean, this doesn't seem like the line of work some kid from the South Side dreamt about having a career in when they grew up.'

Nickolas moves the food around with his fork, no longer hungry. This is it. This would be the time to explain everything. To open up and trust Finn. He can hear her voice in his head again. *'Finn's opened up to you because he trusts you, so maybe it's time you do the same.'* Nickolas drops his fork and turns his body so he is facing Finn rather than sitting side by side. If he is doing this, he needs to be able to see Finn's face.

'I've, ah, I've been coming here since I was eighteen, as a visitor. My sister, Mandy, she was a patient.' Nickolas takes a moment. Saying his sister's name out loud in the past tense always hurts him. He takes a breath and looks up at Finn, who is patiently waiting for Nickolas to continue at his own pace.

'I had my sister committed when she was seventeen for self-harm and severe depression. I would visit every day, only to be told that I couldn't see her until visiting hours on Sunday. After two weeks of me harassing them, Dot would sneak me in so I could see her for an hour each night, right before lights out.'

He thumbs his nose, scratching an invisible itch before continuing.

'Dot noticed how well I cared for Mandy, and not just because she was my sister but because I was aware of her condition, ya know? I knew what she needed and understood how to treat her when she was in certain moods. Dot pulled me aside one day and asked if I ever considered working as an orderly.'

'Of course I laughed at her. I mean, at this stage, I was lucky that I hadn't landed in prison and had outrun the cops quick enough to avoid juvie. If you knew my dad, you'd know that a life of crime was kind of expected of me. Well, 'til he found out I was gay, but that's a whole other story.'

'One day I'd like to hear that story too...if you want to tell me,' Finn says it with such sincerity that Nickolas feels like he could tell him that he killed someone, and Finn would still support him.

Nickolas smiles before continuing with his story. 'I thought the idea was fucking ridiculous. I mean...'

Nickolas balls his hands into fists and points them towards Finn so his tattoos could be read. With a huff, Nickolas puts his hands back in his lap.

'After thinking about it, I thought if I did go down that path, maybe it could help Mandy more. Something I could use in the future, extra knowledge or whatever for when she got out. So, I went back to school since I needed my diploma. Kept my head down and attended my classes. Graduated. Did a six-month course that involved an exam, and here I am. Been working here for almost two years now.'

'Wow. That's...that's great.' There was a slight hesitation in Finn's voice.

'But you said your sister was committed when you were eighteen, so, she's been here for... '

He can tell Finn is trying to do the math.

'I'm twenty-two this year.'

'Right, okay so, if she's been here for almost four years, how come I haven't seen her around?'

Nickolas sniffs. 'She was only here for three years. Mandy...' Nickolas takes a deep breath in and out before he continues. 'I guess what you need to understand is, I spent my whole life trying to protect her. She was my little sister; it was my job. She had just turned sixteen and I wanted to take her out to celebrate. She didn't want to; said she wasn't in the mood, which wasn't like her. Mandy was always the life of the party, hell she was just life itself. The room lit up when Mandy was around. So, I kept asking her what was wrong, why she didn't want to go out, but I got nothing out of her. I, ah, I woke up in the middle of the night to piss and I heard crying. I went to check on her and I found her curled up on the floor in her bedroom with a positive pregnancy test.'

Nickolas runs his hand down his face, willing himself not to vomit as he repeats the next part of the story.

'She...she told me that our piece of shit father would come home drunk and mistake her for our mother.'

A gasp falls from Finn's mouth.

'I stole money from one of my dad's drug deals, not caring if he came after me and beat the shit out of me. He never needed an excuse to do that anyway. All I cared about was helping her get rid of the kid and getting her the hell out of there.

He's so deep into the story now he knows he can't stop.

'We finally got an appointment for her and that day, after we got home, I began working anywhere they would hire me so I could save money and get us a place of our own. If our father was home, I made her sleep in my room and if I had to work, I told her to stay with a friend. When we came back from the hospital though, she just wasn't the same. The light inside her was out. She began drinking more, hanging out with guys that treated her like shit. I came home one day and found her in the bathroom, cleaning her face from a busted lip and a bruised eye and I lost it. Went into her room where the guy was asleep as if beating woman deserved a nap and I kicked the living shit out of him. Mandy had to pull me off, the guy was hardly breathing by the time I was done.'

Nickolas's hands begin to shake as he remembers the feeling of his knuckles burning, aching from the contact of flesh on flesh.

'Over time, doesn't matter what I did or what I said, she lost all self-respect. Jumped from one shitty relationship to the next. Closing herself off from me and those around her. I knew I wasn't strong enough to help her anymore when I came home from work one night and I...I found her in the bathroom, cuts all over her thighs. I could barely see where one cut started and one ended. The blood was just, dripping everywhere. But what scared me the most was how happy she looked afterwards. So, I brought her here.'

It had been a long time since Nickolas had to think about those years. It pains him to remember what life was like for his sister before Mandy was committed. Tears threatening to fall. He wipes them away.

Finn reaches out, takes Nickolas's hand and squeezes it gently. 'You don't have to keep going.'

'I know...but I want to. It might help, actually talking about it.'

Finn gives him a nod and waits for Nickolas to find the strength to keep going.

'For three years she was a patient here. They tried different medications and therapy treatments, but nothing worked. She had attempted to take her life twice while here and at one point they had to isolate her from everyone.'

He looks at his hand in Finn's, feeling the strength pass through him.

'When I began working here, Mandy had already been a patient for two years and the only way they could allow me to work at the same centre was if I was scheduled on for night shifts. They don't allow family to work where family members are being treated, however, they made the exception as long as someone else did her nightly check-ins, so I wasn't technically interacting with Mandy as a patient. Six months into working, something changed. When I'd visit on Sundays, she was no longer in a haze. She was talking and making eye contact. Hell, one day she even laughed at a story I told her.'

A tear rolls down Nickolas's cheek. A smile on his face at the memory.

'Nick...' Finn interjects. 'Why do you keep saying was?'

Nickolas looks up at Finn, the smile falling from his face as he's taken back to that day.

'Because one day they were desperate for staff, and they called me to work the afternoon shift. It was their only option. Gastro was going around and wiping the staff out. Mandy was in her room. She was nauseous from one of her medications so, I brought her lunch so she could eat in private. She asked for some water, saying she had a headache, so I left the room and went back to get her a bottle.' Nickolas's voice begins to shake. 'When I came back to her room, I found the plastic knife had been snapped in half, making the edge sharp enough so she could cut down her wrists on both arms.'

'Holy fuck, Nick.'

Nickolas sits still as Finn leans forward and envelops him in a hug. Tears fall, dampening Finn's shirt as Nickolas buries his face in the crook of Finn's neck. 'If I hadn't left...'

'It wasn't your fault, Nickolas. You need to believe that.'

'I tried, Finn. I tried so fucking hard to save her. But it was too late. I was too late.' Nickolas sobs, the memory in his head as if it were yesterday. 'When I saw you, all I could think of was her. How I failed her, lost her. And how I was about to lose you too.'

Finn pulls back, encasing Nickolas's face between warm, tender hands. 'Nickolas. Look at me. Please, just—look at me.' Finn's voice cuts through to Nickolas. 'I promise that you're not going to lose me. I hate that I put you through that and most of all, I hate that it caused you to relive that day. But you have to believe me when I say that what happened with me, with your sister, none of that falls on you.'

'Fuck. I miss her so much. She was the only family I had that accepted me. The only one that understood me and supported who I was.' He hears Mandy's voice in his head again, *I'm always with you, Nickolas.* His eyes leave Finn's for a moment as they scan the room, seeking out a sign that his sister is here with him right now.

'When did she pass?'

Nickolas presses the palms of his hands into his eyes, the motion causing Finn to let go of his face. 'It's been six months. Being back in this room made it feel like it was yesterday.'

'You mean...?'

'We haven't had to use this room since it happened. Then you walk through the door and suddenly I'm in here, realising this room has more power over me than I thought it did.'

'If there is anything I've learned while being here, it's that the only thing that holds power is ourselves,' explains Finn. 'If you were allowing this room to make you feel something about what happened, it was because you wanted it to. Otherwise, you would have had the power to say it's just a room and what happened was in the past.'

'Seems like those sessions are helping.' Nickolas sniffs, wiping his nose with the back of his hand.

'I can't change my past, Nickolas, but I have the power to learn from it, move on from it and accept that it happened. I have the power to make sure it never happens again, and never allow myself to be in that position again. It's all on me.'

Nickolas takes Finn's hand in his. 'It may be all on you, Finn. But that doesn't mean you can't lean on those around you for support.'

'You need to take your own advice,' Finn says the words so softly.

'Trust me, I've been trying. I think it's gotten to the point where my subconscious is even trying to talk to me in my dreams.'

'What?'

'Never mind.' Nickolas catches a glimpse of his watch, noticing that he has gone over his lunch break by fifteen minutes. 'Shit. I need to get back out there before someone sees me in here.' Nickolas grabs his uneaten lunch and the fork he brought in with him. He stands, legs shaking as he reaches out and places a hand on Finn's shoulder to steady him.

'I'm guessing you're finished for the day?' Finn asks.

'Yeah. I took a late lunch,' says Nickolas. 'After the mix-up this morning I didn't want to leave you, in case...'

He can see Finn piece it all together. Nickolas takes his hand away from Finn, his body now feeling cold after the last hour of being so close.

'What shift are you working tomorrow?' asks Finn.

'Night. I'll see you when I do the rounds with the med cart,' explains Nickolas.

Finn nods, stands, and scuffs a foot against the floor. 'Hopefully with the adjustment, the side effects won't be too intense by then.'

'You seem to be doing okay so far. By tonight you would have had three dosages of the new meds.'

'Thankfully, I'm not nauseous and I guess tonight we'll see if I can sleep. The B12s may be helping me stay awake during the day for a change, but besides the slight tremors, I can't complain.'

'Dot is working tonight. If you need anything, she'll be the best to help you. You're in good hands.'

'You said Dot is the one that let you visit Mandy after hours, right?' Finn clarifies.

'That's right. She's kinda like a mother figure. She saw the potential in me that no one else did. Helped me when Mandy...She lets me bend the rules a little because she knows I bend them to help others, not to hurt them.'

'Is that what you're doing with me? Bending the rules to help.'

'I think by now you know the rule book has been thrown out the window when it comes to you and me.'

Finn's smile is all teeth, which is all Nickolas needed before he left the room.

'Hey, Nickolas.'

With his hand on the door, he turns back to Finn.

'Thank you. For sharing that with me. I know it must have been hard, but it means a lot that you trusted me with it.'

Mandy's voice echoes in his mind, *He's good for you. He's making you feel alive again.*

'See you tomorrow, Finn.'

He closes the door behind him, hoping no one sees how red and puffy his face is as he makes his way to the break room to drop off his uneaten lunch.

'You're still here? We thought you may have left without letting us know.' Eric grabs water from the fridge while waiting for an answer.

'Sorry. Lunch didn't sit well with me. Had to use the toilet for a bit.' The lie seems to work.

He makes his way towards the locker room, Darren staying on to work a double and Sky most likely already gone for the day.

Nickolas doesn't change out of his uniform. He takes his backpack, says goodbye to Jasmine, and sits in his car. He bows his head, his chin resting against his chest as he takes a deep breath in. Finn's scent lingers on his shirt; he can't put his finger on the smell considering all Finn uses is the standard soap that is provided to every patient, but there is something there – something that makes Nickolas think of a warm spring day and the need to eat something sweet. He basks in the smell as he drives home, smiling to himself like a happy idiot.

He shared one of his deepest secrets. The part of himself that he has been holding deep inside for months, as he allowed it to eat away at him. Finn didn't judge him, blame him, or pity him. He simply held him tight and told him the power to move forward is in his hands. Finn made it sound so simple, and it is. But until he had heard it from Finn, the thought of letting the past go seemed impossible, like he was giving himself a free pass.

Nickolas parks his car and rests his head against the seat. Closing his eyes, he takes in a deep breath and feels his body relax. *You're good for Finn, but he's good for you too.*

9. Wednesday

For the first time in a long time, Nickolas wakes up without an alarm blasting in his ear, without any nightmares and without Socks jumping onto his face demanding food and attention. The latter is probably because Socks is curled up beside him, tucked in close. He looks at his phone and is pleased to see it's past nine a.m. His body has finally had a chance to catch up on the missed sleep from all the night shifts and doubles he has been working.

Lying on his back, Nickolas's mind wanders to Finn and whether his redhead slept okay, or did another dose of medication cause further side effects? Those thoughts slip away and are then replaced with Finn's smile, and laugh, and eyes. He remembers the smell of Finn lingering on his body, the way it felt to be wrapped in those arms, and most of all, Finn's soft lips pressed against his own. Nickolas closes his eyes, taking himself back to the shower room and envisioning what could have happened next if the situation between them was different.

He imagines going back in for another kiss, Finn's hands cupping his face as he's pushed against the wall, allowing Finn to take control. Nickolas can feel the ghost of Finn's lips as his hand trails down his body and under the waistband of his boxers so he can hold himself – not moving, just putting weight on his dick as he chases the feel of Finn's lips. Nickolas opens his mouth slightly, giving in to his fantasy of Finn's tongue battling his own for dominance.

His dick twitches to life, craving the attention it would be getting in his fantasy. He opens his eyes, shooing Socks off the bed and in no way feeling guilty when his cat meows at him and scurries off to the living room. Opening his bedside drawer, Nickolas grabs the bottle of lube and his dildo. The silicon dick doesn't even compare to Finn's nine inches, but it will make do with helping him feel whole. Nickolas squirts the lube on his fingers, closing his eyes to envision himself back in the shower room as he leads his hand down to his ass.

He's suddenly bending over the bench that he sits on while Finn showers, but this time, the gorgeous redhead has pulled Nickolas's purple cotton pants down to his ankles in one swift motion, spits into a warm palm as Finn goes for Nickolas's hole.

'How many fingers do you normally use?' Finn asks with dominance in his voice.

'Two.'

'Going to need at least three if you want to be able to take me.' Finn purrs into his ear.

Nickolas moans as he slips a finger inside, envisioning Finn's long freckly fingers doing it for him. It's mere seconds before he adds the second, enjoying the stretch that comes with being scissored open.

'That's it, Nickolas. Open up for me.'

Nickolas pinches his nipple. The pleasure and pain mix together as he pushes in a third finger, sending a shudder down his spine as he brushes against his prostate.

'Fuck.' The burn turns into pleasure, he's ready to take the dildo.

Nickolas opens his eyes quick enough to lather his toy with lube before closing his eyes again, taking his mind back to his fantasy, back to Finn.

Finn lifts Nickolas up, his back presses against the cold hard wall, arms wrapped around Nickolas's thick thighs as Finn holds him in place. They're completely naked with no clothes in sight.

'You ready?'

Nickolas has his arms around broad shoulders. He leans in, devouring soft pink lips as he feels Finn's dick rest against his ass. Finn's body weight pushes into him, pinning Nickolas between muscle and the wall. Finn lets go of Nickolas's thighs and cups his ass cheeks, spreading them apart as he pushes in.

'Fuck, Finn.' Nickolas pushes the dildo inside himself at an achingly slow pace. He bites his bottom lip, imagining his own skin as if it were the soft flesh of Finn's neck. Once the dildo bottoms out, he takes a moment to adjust, loving the sweet feeling of being filled.

'Fuck me, Finn.' Whispering the words to himself, Nickolas begins to move the dildo in and out, feeling it drag against his walls. He clenches his ass tight while he pulls it out, relaxing as he pushes it back in. He claws at the bedsheets, at a freckled back, as he feels Finn push deep inside.

'Fuck, Nickolas. You're so tight.' The force of each thrust takes the breath out of his lungs. The pressure of being pushed into the wall each time Finn bottoms out is euphoric. Each thrust takes his breath away, as Finn's weight presses down on him. It's only when Finn slides out of him, does Nickolas have a moment to breathe. Although he can't quite understand it, the motion creates a sense of safety that Nickolas revels in.

'Make me come, Finn.' Nickolas twists his wrist just enough so the dildo hits his prostate. His legs lock around Finn's waist. Sweat drips down the back of Nickolas's knees as he spreads his legs wider while lying on his bed. Nickolas runs his fingers through sweaty red hair, clasping tight as he feels his orgasm building, pulling Finn's hair just enough to hear a groan in satisfaction.

Nickolas reaches for his dick. It's aching to be touched, precum leaking from the stimulation to his prostate. He begins to match each thrust with each pull of his dick. Finn suddenly has Nickolas standing against the wall, his back against Finn's chest. He rams into him, one hand digging into Nickolas's hip while the other jerks him off.

Finn pants in his ear, whispering how tight he is, how hot he is. He tells Nickolas how he's going to fill him up, stretch him so wide he won't be able to walk. Nickolas moans, and just like that, he releases everything he has into Finn's hand. He holds onto the last visual of Finn coming right there with him, as he holds the dildo in place, clenching tightly around it as he presses it into his prostate.

Nickolas catches his breath, his body sticking to the sheets in all the right ways. As he calms down, he turns his head to the empty side of the bed, wishing Finn was lying there beside him. One day, once Finn is released, it may very well get to be part of his reality. He takes some wipes from his bedside drawer, cleaning himself up just enough so he can walk to the shower without cum dripping onto the floor. He takes the dildo with him into the bathroom so he can clean it, turning on the shower and waiting for the temperature to become hot. The water relaxes his muscles. Nickolas closes his eyes and allows the heat to seep into his skin before he begins to wash away the cum that was starting to stick to his hair.

Nickolas showers till the water turns cold, then gets dressed in a hoodie two sizes too big and sweatpants. Deciding to make himself eggs for breakfast – well, more like brunch, as it's nearly eleven a.m. – he whips together his food and remembers how much he used to enjoy cooking. It was always so calming, being able to move around the space while throwing one ingredient after another into the pan. Cooking was his way of providing for Mandy, making sure she was eating and being taken care of. It felt homely in a home that treated them like they were prisoners. Stuck, with no escape, living in constant fear while their father was around.

While he enjoys his breakfast, Nickolas scrolls through his phone, searching for recipes he remembers making. When he sees that he already has a lot of the ingredients on hand, he quickly cleans up, puts his music on shuffle, and begins to chop garlic and herbs to mix it into some soft butter. He stuffs the butter inside two chicken breasts and then rolls them in flour, egg, and breadcrumbs before putting them to the side to be cooked. He used to make chicken Kiev at least once a week for him and Mandy. It was a meal that warmed his sister's heart, reminding them both of their mother, who would cook traditional Ukrainian dishes while singing in the kitchen. Those were simpler times.

Waiting for the pan to heat up, he imagines standing in his kitchen while Finn sits on the couch, relaxing, calling out about something that's on the TV while Nickolas cooks them a meal. He imagines them curled up on the couch, Socks nestled between them while they watch a movie – no doubt something Nickolas would hate, but he'd sit through it because it's what Finn was in the mood to watch. He imagines them brushing their teeth at the same time, only to then complain about who left toothpaste stuck to the bathroom sink. They'd go to bed, unable to fall asleep unless a part of them was touching the other.

This whole domestic dream that's playing out in his head stops him in his tracks. Why is this happening now? Why with Finn? He's been living alone in this apartment since he began working at the centre. He never saw that 'happy couple' lifestyle as something he could have for himself. Never thought he could explore that type of life with someone the way he is considering right now.

Nickolas turns the chicken in the pan so it doesn't burn, still processing his thoughts. What he feels when he is around Finn, he can't explain it. It's like this magnetic force that is constantly pulling them towards one another. He wants to hear everything Finn has to say and share all of his deepest, darkest secrets. Finn looks at Nickolas the way Mandy did, making him feel like he is worth something. Finn wants to get to know him, the real him, not just the cover story he uses to make it seem like he's lived a life of rainbows and sunshine.

Putting the chicken on a plate to cool down, he saves one for tomorrow and the other for tonight's dinner. This 'lone wolf' lifestyle he is living started when he prioritised his sister's needs over his own. For the last three years, he put Mandy first, and he doesn't regret a single moment. There was no time for a relationship with studying and taking care of Mandy. When he started working night shifts, his days were spent sleeping and completing the list of everyday errands that accumulated over the week. And then it happened. He lost the last bit of family that loved and cared for him, and the thought of a physical relationship was forgotten. If Mandy couldn't live her life with a happy and loving partner, then neither should he.

At first, he was numb. He dove headfirst into work, using it as a distraction to get by. He didn't bother with a funeral, figuring there was no point since they didn't have any family that would attend. Then the anger took over. He went out every night after work, and the first guy that so much as locked eyes with him, Nickolas took into the alley, bent the guy over, and made sure it was rough enough to leave the guy aching when he was done. That didn't last long, though. The emptiness he felt after each fuck was making the hole inside him so big that Nickolas was afraid it would never heal. Finally, the guilt set in. The guilt of Mandy dying on his watch. The guilt of not mourning his sister properly. The guilt of using meaningless sex to escape. That caused Nickolas to feel as worthless as his father had made him feel.

But with Finn, all that is forgotten. The worthless feeling, that hole inside of him caused by his self-destructive behaviour, is closing a little more each day with every smile from

Finn, every touch or stolen kiss. Although the guilt may take longer, in its place he feels cared for and as though he could start living again.

After cleaning up, Nickolas walks towards the wardrobe in the hallway, where he stored Mandy's belongings in the hopes of unpacking them when his sister was released, and where he kept the items he stole from his father, Dominic, that had more value to Nickolas. It's not like Dominic was going to miss any of it. It was mostly sentimental items like awards from school, back when he actually attended; Mandy's favourite teddy; jewellery that belonged to his mum that Dominic hadn't pawned off yet; photo albums of him and his siblings when they were younger, his mum smiling in every single one of them. By the time his mother stopped smiling, the photos had stopped being taken. He doesn't have a single-family photo after the age of eight, when his mother passed away.

He bypasses those boxes and finds the one he is looking for, stashed high enough that he needs a chair to reach it. He pulls the box down and finds his mum's old recipe books. The pages are slightly discoloured but the handwriting is still legible. Nickolas smiles at seeing a piece of his mum on the pages. He keeps hold of the book he was looking for, closes the lid, and steps back onto the chair to put the box away. As he reaches up, he sees a box he had long ago forgotten. It was a simple filing box with 'Mandy Markova' written across it. On instinct, he reaches out and takes the box, then slips the other back in its place.

He sits on the couch, the box in front of him on the coffee table, and just stares at it, waiting for something to tell him he should open it. Socks jumps on the table beside it, a black paw tapping on the lid.

'Guess we're doing this, hey girl.'

Socks meows back.

Nickolas smiles, and Socks leaps onto the couch and curls up beside him as he opens the lid. He takes a deep breath as memories flood his mind. He picks up the journal Mandy was instructed to write in during therapy sessions and runs his hand down the hardcover. His sister told him once that it was filled with poems and drawings, things that used to help express the thoughts that Mandy struggled to discuss with the therapist. He quickly flicks through the pages, seeing a lot of darkness inside. He has never read it and he doesn't feel like he can. Nickolas hears his sister's voice again in his head: *That's not how I want to be remembered.* He flips the journal in his hand, studying the front and back before he puts it to the side. He doesn't want to remember Mandy that way anymore.

He comes across a few items of clothing, most likely what Mandy was wearing when committed. It's impossible, but a part of him thinks he can still smell his sister's perfume lingering on the clothes. He finds a photo and instantly breaks out laughing. It's a selfie of them both scrunching up their face and sticking their tongues out. It's dorky and stupid and he loves everything about it. Nickolas stands up, walks over to his fridge, and displays the photo with a magnet holding it in place. He looks at Mandy's face staring back at him in the photo and decides that's enough for today. He wants to end the walk down memory lane on a high note and nothing could top that photo. As he goes to put the lid pack on, his eyes land on a purple iPod nano.

Nickolas picks up the iPod and does a quick shuffle around the box to see if he can find a charger. No luck. He isn't surprised; if this is everything that Mandy had while committed, the charger would've been a hazard. He had to take it home with him to recharge and bring it back the next time he visited. Looking through the wardrobe, he finds a shoebox full of random cables, surprised and thankful when he comes across the one that belongs to the iPod. He takes it to the wall, plugs it in and waits as it comes to life, the charging symbol popping up on the screen.

Music was a big part of Mandy's therapy. He spent hours loading song after song onto the iPod, from all different genres. Mandy's therapist tried explaining to him how music acts as a medium for processing emotions, trauma, and grief. How it can be utilised as a regulating or calming agent for anxiety and depression. He lets it charge, searching his apartment for a pair of Bluetooth headphones –a spare pair of knock-off AirPods in the key bowl. He puts them in his backpack, which he sets beside the iPod so he doesn't forget to pack it.

He puts all the boxes away, takes his mum's recipe book, and reads over the notes while making a list of ingredients he'll need. He still has time to head to the gym and hit the store before needing to get ready for work.

*

His workout is intense. All his excess energy is used to do a cardio session as well as a round on the punching bag. Remembering Finn's comment about his ass, Nickolas also does a few sets of squats before his cool down. Dripping with sweat, he heads to the store near his apartment, buying the ingredients he needs as well as a few Reece's Peanut Butter Cups that are on special and some Snickers bars. Nickolas refuses to believe his choice in chocolate has anything to do with Finn's love for peanut butter. Barry or Brent, or whatever the fuck the guy's name was, is once again at the checkout. Nickolas is pleased to see the clerk looks down, scans all of Nickolas's items, and makes no comment about his food choices or appearance.

He returns home and unpacks, has a quick shower and eats one of the Chicken Kievs with a premade salad he picked up at the store. By seven, Nickolas is in the car and on the way to work.

He parks, having arrived earlier than he normally would. Nickolas locks his car and makes his way inside. Dot is talking to Jasmine out the front, a scowl on his boss's face aimed directly at him.

'I left you alone for five hours on Monday and I come into work today to find Brett with a busted nose and only one person who could have given it to him,' scolds Dot.

Nickolas leans on the counter, arms crossed. 'Let's be honest, Dorothy. Although I'm flattered that I'm the first person that comes to mind, there is a queue of people begging to punch Brett in the face bigger than the lines at Krispy Kreme when they give away a year's supply of free donuts. So really...it could have been anyone.'

'Mhm. You're lucky he isn't going to HR with this, Nickolas.'

'That's because if he did, I'd have to tell them everything he said that led to me punching him in the face.'

'So, you admit it.'

'It's going on my resume under achievements.'

Jasmine giggles and buzzes the door open for him to walk through.

'If I were you, I'd make yourself scarce till he clocks off,' suggests Dot.

Dot's words travel down the corridor as Nickolas heads into the locker room to change into his uniform. Dot's request is easy enough. Once he's dressed in purple from head to toe, he shoves a few items in his pockets and heads out towards the corridor. The only person he wants to see before his shift starts is in room thirteen.

Nickolas knocks on the door, waits a few seconds before he hears Finn's voice carry through. 'Come in.'

Nickolas steps inside. The sight of Finn with damp hair sitting on the bed, smiling up at him is enough to make his day one thousand times better.

'Hey. Missed you today,' says Finn.

'You did, did ya?' Nickolas puffs his chest with pride.

'I mean, without you, I had to deal with Darren who, now that I've gotten to know a bit better, I can see is totally not your type.'

Nickolas chuckles. 'Really? And what's my type?' He takes a few steps closer.

'Hmm...tall. Green eyes. You're totally into redheads that are way too confident for their age, with a slight case of mental illness.'

'Sounds exotic. Know where I can find someone like that?' Nickolas sits on the end of Finn's bed. Their soft laughter fills the space between them.

Finn gives him a small push. 'I did, however, enjoy seeing Brett's busted-up nose all afternoon. He seemed to keep his distance.'

Nickolas isn't sure if he's relieved at hearing this news about Brett or if he should be worried. Brett has never been the type to back down. However, this is the first time Nickolas has used violence to shut Brett up. Perhaps his warning was enough for the guy to step back.

'Sky and Dorothy helped me today,' explains Finn.

'That's why I'm here. Brett still has twenty minutes left of his shift and I'm under strict orders to not cross paths with him,' says Nickolas.

'And here I thought you missed me.'

Nickolas shuffles on the spot, the single mattress not leaving much room between them. 'Who says it can't be both?' Nickolas cocks his eyebrow.

They sit there in silence for a moment, just looking at one another, comfortable, relaxed.

'I, ah, came across a box of my sister's things today,' Nickolas offers. 'I hadn't looked at it since she...since she passed.' His voice is sad, but he doesn't shed a tear. Progress.

The bed creaks as Finn moves closer, only enough to place a hand on Nickolas's knee.

'Her, ah, her journal was in there. I couldn't bring myself to read it. Not yet. But I also found this.' Nickolas reaches into his pocket and brings out the iPod nano with the spare Bluetooth headphones.

'I'm not sure what kind of music you're into, but this has a bit of everything. Her treatment at one stage involved music therapy. She'd get lost in the music for hours, wouldn't even acknowledge I was in the room sometimes, but I think a part of it helped, for a while at least.' He hands the items over to Finn. 'I thought it could help pass the time. Or if you're having trouble sleeping or whatever.' Nickolas suddenly feels self-conscious.

'You sure? Aren't you going to get it trouble if they find out you gave it to me?'

'You can't harm yourself with it and the headphones have no cords. Unless you want to swallow them like Alex, I think I can trust you with it.'

Finn chuckles, turning the device on and giving it a quick scroll through.

Nickolas waits, giving Finn a moment before he opens his mouth to speak again. 'Mandy was the first and only person to know I was gay...at least willingly.'

Finn looks up, placing the iPod to the side so Nickolas has his full attention.

Nickolas runs his hand over his mouth, not sure where this sudden urge to share is coming from. 'Dominic Markova is an abusive, homophobic, Nazi loving rapist, who just so happened to also be my father.' He looks up at the ceiling, amazed that all those things could make up a single person. 'I used to run drug and gun deals with him. He wanted to train me up to take over the family business since my idiot brothers didn't have the smarts for it. Just because I was the favourite though, doesn't mean he didn't throw a fist towards me if I ever fucked up. I swear, the only reason I got into fights with people was because I knew when he hit me, I couldn't fight back, so I took my anger out on those that owed us money or tried to rip us off.'

Nickolas shifts on the bed, turning himself more towards Finn.

'I tried to hide it. I slept with a few girls so my family didn't get suspicious. I was never able to finish, just faked it or whatever. They didn't know the difference. So, one day, Dominic comes home boasting about this fag he just beat the shit out of, and I winced. No matter how many times I took a hit, never have I winced. Of course, he noticed, so he stepped towards me, grabbed the collar of my shirt, and asked if I had a problem with him going after a faggot.'

Nickolas takes a breath.

'I answered no. Said a few things about how disgusting they all were, hoping it would make him believe me more, but the only way Dominic believes a person is through action. He shoved me in the car, drove me to the edge of Boys Town, and we sat there waiting. He spotted a young guy walking alone from a club or a bar, I don't know, but he told me to go beat the shit out of him until he couldn't get back up.'

The slight gasp that comes from Finn breaks a part of Nickolas, but he needs to spill all his secrets, even the darkest ones that made up the person he once was. He hopes Finn will understand the circumstances he was in as he continues his story.

'I, ah, broke the kid's nose. Bruised some ribs and gave him a concussion.'

'How'd you...?'

'I called hospitals the next day asking for him. I stole his wallet, making it look like a mugging, but it was so I had his name, and I could make sure he was okay.' Nickolas takes a deep breath, everything falling out of him like word vomit.

'I got back in the car and there was a proud smile on my father's face. I sat looking out the window on the drive home, my arms crossed over my chest to stop them from shaking because I knew that if he ever found out about me, my fate would be ten times worse than what I did to that kid.'

'What happened?' asks Finn.

'He dropped me off home and went out drinking. I barely made it to the bathroom before I puked everything I had into the toilet bowl, and that's how Mandy knew. She found me crying, vomit around my mouth with blood on my knuckles, and she just crouched down beside me and said, "I hate that you have to hide who you are because of this family. But you never have to hide around me".'

The love and sincerity in his sister's voice echoes in his head as Nickolas says the words out loud.

'I was fifteen and I just broke down, telling her everything. And after that, it was me and Mandy against our family.' Nickolas wipes a tear from his eye. They weren't falling from sadness, but more the relief he remembers feeling at that moment, knowing he had someone on his side. Someone he loved and didn't have to hide from.

'Did your dad ever find out?'

Nickolas nods. 'He had one of his goons tailing me. Saw me hooking up in an alley, and reported back to him. I came home, my room had been raided and there he was, gun in hand with my porn and anal beads. Honestly, I was surprised I made it out alive. Mandy found me unconscious on the floor. I had a skull fracture from him pistol-whipping me and two broken ribs. My nose was bleeding but, thankfully, not broken. I remember him saying how no son of his was going to be a cum bucket, right before I blacked out.'

'Jesus, Nick.' Finn takes his hand, giving it a squeeze.

'I kept my head down, avoided hooking up since I never knew who was watching. He stopped asking for my help with everything, which meant I had no income, so I started picking up odd jobs around the neighbourhood. I had Mandy let me know when he was out of the house so I could come home and shower, sleep. But without me being at home all the time, that's how...that's how he turned around and started going after her.'

For the first time since he started talking, Nickolas looks at Finn. His green eyes are soft and a gentle smile appears on Finn's face when their eyes lock.

'Looks like I'm not the only survivor in this room.' Finn offers.

Nickolas scoffs.

'Nick, you can't do that. You can't expect me to believe your words if you can't believe them yourself.'

'My story is nothing new to all the other people that grew up with shitty parents in the South Side.'

'Maybe it is, maybe it isn't. That doesn't mean it's worth any less. That doesn't mean you're not allowed to feel hatred or sadness. Or pride and strength. And it also doesn't mean that what happened to Mandy while you were gone had anything to do with you either.'

Nickolas opens his mouth, only to close it again.

'If I've learned anything about you over the last week or so, it's that you wear your heart on your sleeve,' says Finn. 'You put those you care about above yourself and hold yourself to blame whenever something goes wrong. The only person who is to blame in any of this is your dad. For what happened to you, to Mandy. You were the glue trying to hold her together, but sometimes the desire to give up overrides the desire to live.'

'Sounds like someone has made progress in their therapy sessions.' His comment is to steer the attention away from himself and Finn is fully aware of it.

'Dr Hale seems to think so. The meds are working. I'm feeling balanced to some degree. We still have a few things to tackle but everything that happened when I was manic, I've...come to terms with it, I suppose. The best I can...considering.'

Nickolas's eyes catch the time on his watch. It's past eight p.m.

'Shit. I'm late for work.' He stands up, rushing towards Finn's door.

'Nickolas!'

He turns around.

'Thanks for telling me. For trusting me with your story.'

He gives Finn a smile before turning back around and leaving the room.

*

Lydia is preparing the med cart, ready to head towards the patients' rooms, as Nickolas walks out towards the front desk.

'There you are,' says Lydia. 'Dorothy said you were already here but I couldn't find you anywhere.'

'Sorry. I had to—' Nickolas gets cut off.

'I know where you were. Just get to it.'

Nickolas stops in his tracks. He isn't used to Lydia being so demanding towards him. He almost finds himself saying 'yes, ma'am' as he takes the cart and checklist, heading back out towards the patient corridor. He makes small talk with each patient, some of them he hasn't spoken to in a while, others simply enjoying seeing Nickolas again. Ethan's quiet while he does a body check, and Nickolas is pleased to see no new bruising has appeared. He asks once again if Ethan is ready to admit who is to blame for the bruises, but Ethan simply takes the medication and lays down in bed to read.

Back in room thirteen, Finn takes the cup of pills from Nickolas, swallows them down with the water, and only then does he notice Finn's wrists.

'Your bandages are off.'

Finn looks down. The stitches are still visible, but the red, risen skin is looking calmer.

'Dr Winslow removed them this afternoon after group. Said the air would help them heal quicker. Plus, it meant I was able to shower by myself. Well, by "myself" I mean wash my own body in front of the other patients. But it's better than Eric helping me. He isn't as gentle as you.'

'He didn't hurt you, did he?'

'What? No. He's more, wham, bam, get dressed, you're done.'

'Good. The only person who should be taking their time with you is me.' His head is bent down towards the check-list, but his eyes are directed at Finn, pleased to see the blush appear across his freckled cheeks. 'Alright. I would say get some sleep, but I'm guessing you're going to ignore that piece of advice and stay awake.'

'And miss out on my ten o'clock check-in? I have music now to keep me entertained, so I'll see you shortly.'

Shaking his head, Nickolas walks out of Finn's room. He returns the med cart and then makes his way into the break room to face Lydia.

'Spill,' Lydia demands.

Nickolas hasn't even stepped over the threshold before Lydia is on him.

'About?' He decides playing dumb is his best defence.

'Come on, Nickolas. Your hourly check-ins end up taking two hours because you stay in Finn's room chatting. You spent the night by his side when he hurt himself and although I never believe workplace gossip, I'm starting to think it's true.'

'What have you heard?' Nickolas crosses his arms over his chest.

'That you are giving Finn more than just "special treatment", if you know what I mean.' Lydia mimics his stance, attitude always being Lydia's way of getting a point across.

'Jesus Christ. Nothing has happened.' Besides a kiss or two, Nickolas reminds himself.

'Ah-ha. You said "happened". As in you want something to happen.'

Nickolas pours himself a cup of coffee, thankful to see there are still apple and cinnamon muffins on the table from Dot. He takes one, walks over to the couch, and sits down. Lydia's eyes are burning into his skull as he takes a bite and washes it down with a sip of coffee.

Lydia takes a seat in the chair at the table, turning the chair so it's facing towards him. 'Are you sleeping with him?'

'NO! For fuck's sake, he's a patient.'

'And you're not his doctor.'

'No, but I still understand how ethically wrong that would be.'

'Good.' Lydia sits back, happy with his answers so far.

'So, what's going on then?'

'Nothing, we're just...talking.'

'Talking?'

'Yeah, talking.'

'Lots of people in the world you could talk to, Nickolas.'

'Not like this.' His voice drops as he looks down, picking the crumbs off his uniform before he continues. 'There are things that people will just never understand. But he...Finn gets it.'

'Things like Mandy?'

'Among other things.' Looking up he catches Lydia relaxing into the chair. The silence between them lingers, giving Nickolas the impression that the conversation has been dropped.

'You haven't spoken to anyone about her since she passed.'

Nickolas can hear in Lydia's voice that she's pieced together how important it is for him to finally be dealing with his sister's death, to be talking about it, while also understanding the significance of whatever he has going on with Finn.

'I don't know what it is about him or how it happened, but we just clicked. I can talk to Finn about it all, and I don't feel like I'm being judged or see pity on his face when I look back at him.' Nickolas scratches at his eyebrow. 'I know you guys are all here for me. Hell, I've known some of you since Mandy was a patient. But none of you know half the shit I've gone through.'

He looks Lydia in the eyes.

'My pain doesn't start and end with Mandy, it goes back years. It goes back to growing up poor in the South Side with shitty parents, having to hide who I am from everyone around me. Finn gets that. Finn lived that. So yeah, I know the world is full of people to talk to, but this world only has one Finn, and I was lucky enough to finally find him. Even if the situation isn't ideal.'

The sound of the ticking clock in the room fills the silence between them. Nickolas begins to count each tick to help ease his mind as Lydia keeps looking at him.

'Okay,' says Lydia.

'Okay?' questions Nickolas.

'Okay. I get it. If you swear to me that nothing physical is going on between you both, then I'll cover for you.'

'I swear.' And Nickolas means it. As much as he wants more to happen, and although they have kissed twice, he knows everything else needs to wait until Finn is no longer a patient.

'Then I believe you.'

Nickolas exhales, leaning back into the chair.

'You know, they taught us that one treatment won't work for everyone,' Lydia explains. 'You could have three patients that all have the same mental illness, and yet individually, they all need a different form of medication, a different form of therapy, and even a different approach to getting them to open up and talk, to heal.'

Nickolas waits for Lydia to continue.

'Finn is the method of therapy you need. You need to talk to someone who has walked a similar path as you. You need to share your demons with someone who has their own, because it makes you feel like an equal. Put you in a room with an actual therapist and your body would shut down, feel inferior, and no matter what advice you were given, you'd automatically assume it was a way for them to push you out of the room and be done with your mess.'

He sits up a little straighter, feeling extremely exposed by how accurate that sounds.

'We've been working together for almost a year, Nickolas and the only thing I remember on my first day was Dorothy pulling me aside and saying how you come across tough, but you have a heart of gold when it comes to these patients. She told me to take my time with you and eventually, you'd come to me.'

Lydia's words hit Nickolas deep down, as well as the knowledge that Dot had said those things about him. 'I swear that woman is going to destroy my reputation.'

They both chuckle.

'Well maybe so. But I think having a reputation for going the extra mile in helping these people heal and helping them become better versions of themselves outweighs any street rep,' says Lydia.

Nickolas leans forward, resting his elbows on his knees as he clasps his hands in front of himself. 'I do it for Mandy. Every single one of these patients that get to go home smiling, it's for her.'

'But what do you do for yourself?'

'You practicing your schooling on me now? Pretty sure you're not a licensed therapist yet.'

'Humour me.'

Nickolas exhales, thumbing his nose as he tries to think of something, but only one thing comes to mind. 'I survive.'

Lydia head tilts to the side.

'I get up every day knowing that that's one more day I have over my father,' Nickolas explains. 'He'd rather I be dead, not Mandy. But the fact that me being alive means I'm winning, that's enough for me to keep going.'

'One day though, Nickolas, that's not going to be enough for you. Then what?' Lydia asks.

Hopefully, when that day comes, he'll have Finn. But he doesn't say that. 'I'll cross that bridge when I come to it. Until then, I take one day at a time. But waking up, knowing I have that power over my father, and someone that makes me smile when I talk to him, well, that makes things a little less shitty.'

Lydia's gentle smile is enough for him to know she understands. 'Go.'

Nickolas cocks an eyebrow.

'It's been an hour. Do the rounds. And if you don't come back, I won't come looking...at least for the next two hours.' Lydia gives him a wink.

'Thanks. You going to study?'

'Nope. Sat my exam yesterday. Now I just have to wait.'

'I'm sure you killed it.'

Lydia flicks her hair to the side, showing no sign of doubt or hesitation. 'I made that exam my bitch. I have my last one in four months and then I'm done.'

Nickolas laughs as he exits, making his way to touch base with each patient before heading towards Finn. He peeks in the window, the soft light of the iPod screen reflecting onto Finn's face, still awake, as Nickolas suspected. He unlocks the door, letting himself in as he watches Finn be consumed by the music.

'Jesus Christ, Nick. You scared the shit out of me.' Finn puts a hand over his heart, the fright making Nickolas chuckle rather than apologise. Finn takes the AirPods out, pausing the music.

'Guess you found a few songs that you like,' says Nickolas.

'More than a few. Mandy had good taste in music.'

'Actually, I put the songs on there for her.'

'Really?'

Nickolas nods, slowly stepping closer towards Finn.

'Do you remember them all?'

'Fuck no. I barely knew half of them. Most of the time it was just a song or two that I wanted to add, trying to give her different genres, but I found I was too lazy to sort through it all so I just added the whole album on there.'

'I um...can I...there is a song that kind of reminds me of you.' Finn is nervously rolling the AirPods between slender fingers. 'Can I show you?'

Finn looks up, his green eyes meeting Nickolas's in the darkness of the room.

Nickolas gives a small nod before taking one of the AirPods, the other going back into Finn's ear. Finn shuffles over to the edge of the bed and Nickolas sits beside him. The single mattress is barely big enough for them both, but the close proximity is comforting. Finn turns the screen back on and presses play to the song.

A soft melody begins to play. The tune of a piano fills his ears and warmth spreads throughout his body. He listens intently to the words, the male voice singing about moments of loneliness and having someone to help you through your fears. The beat begins to increase as it builds up to the chorus, though nothing too overpowering on bass or drums. As the chorus breaks, the lyrics filter through and goosebumps litter Nickolas's body. He takes Finn's hand, unaware he is shaking until he is holding onto Finn for support.

A wave of emotions crashes over him as he pieces together what this song means, what Finn is trying to share with him. Nickolas takes the AirPod out of his ear before it breaks into the second verse. He doesn't have the capacity to put words together. Finn must sense that as he begins to speak.

'*Saving Grace* by Kodaline,' Finn offers. 'It was the third song that played when I pressed shuffle, and I've had it on repeat ever since.' Finn pauses, his hand still clutching Nickolas's. 'I don't...I don't know when I'll get out of here, or what will happen between us when I do. But I do know a part of me wouldn't have survived this place without you.'

'Finn...'

'No, please, let me...I don't just mean the suicide attempt. I mean me. I was so broken when Jessica brought me here to be committed and I honestly felt like I had nothing left to offer. You showed me that I had more inside of me. You're my saving grace, Nick.' Finn squeezes his hand to emphasise his point. 'This place helped me, but you're the one that saved me. I'll forever be grateful, and I'll forever remember that, even if we part ways when I leave this place...'

A few tears trickle down Nickolas's face before he lets go of Finn's hand to wipe them away.

'Nick?'

'What are the odds?' He sniffs back the tears.

'I don't...'

Nickolas stands.

Finn goes to speak, but stops as Nickolas begins to lift his purple cotton shirt over his head.

Confusion is written all over Finn's face as Nickolas stands in a black tank top in the darkness of the room. He turns around, his back facing Finn as he removes his top.

The clouds move in the sky. The reflection of the full moon shines into Finn's room, casting a glow onto Nickolas's body and his tattoo.

Wings.

Beautiful angelic wings across Nickolas's back, spreading over his shoulders and down a quarter of his arms. The sleeves of Nickolas's uniform cover the tip of the feathers, hiding them from those around him.

Nickolas hears the sound of bedsprings. He quivers as fingers touch his skin, gently tracing over the feathered wings. He can envision his tattoo from the way Finn moves over every detailed line with a phantom touch.

He closes his eyes. 'Mandy had a song for us. Some Pete Murray song that she used to sing to me when she was having a good day. Said it got her through dark moments, knowing I was the light waiting for her. That I was her...her saving grace.' Nickolas slowly turns around, his chest now on display.

Finn's eyes catch the tattoo inked over his heart.

'My hand will forever be grasping hers. Keeping her from falling.' Nickolas explains the meaning of his tattoo. It's not as detailed as his wings, a mere outline of two hands grasping each other over Nickolas's left pec muscle. 'I got the wings a year after she was committed. The hands I got a day after she passed away.'

'They're beautiful, Nick. But I, I feel like that isn't the right word to use to describe them. Not when they have so much love and meaning behind them.'

Nickolas looks down at his shoes. 'Out of every single song on that iPod, a song titled *Saving Grace* is the one that reminded you of me. How is that—'

'Because, Nick, doesn't matter how many times we tell you, how many times you try to deny it, you're the one that's trying to save us all. This world is dealing out shitty hands, one after another, and when none of us have the strength to keep fighting, you're the one holding our heads above water, telling us to paddle just a little bit longer.'

Nickolas looks up at Finn, feeling the truth behind every word.

'What amazes me even more is, after hearing what happened to you, what your father did to you, you still see the world as a place that can have beauty in it, that can have good.'

Nickolas doesn't know what to say. Instead, he puts his tank top and purple uniform back on, not wanting Lydia to suddenly walk in and assume he lied because he's standing half-naked in a room with Finn. 'It's not the world that I see beauty in, Finn. It's the people in it.' Nickolas takes a step closer, his hands latching onto Finn's hips, their foreheads resting against one another.

'Do you have to leave?' Finn whispers.

'Lydia gave me another hour.'

'Gave you an hour?'

'To talk. She knows we're...friends.'

The silence of the room wraps them up in their own little world.

'Come to bed with me?' Finn asks.

Nickolas pulls back, the words catching him off guard.

'Lie with me, that's it.'

Finn slips a hand into Nickolas's, pulling him towards the bed and onto the mattress. Finn scoots as close to the edge as possible, giving Nickolas enough room to lay down beside Finn. They face one another, foreheads touching, their legs entwined as they hold hands.

Finn's eyes start to droop.

'It's okay. You can go to sleep.' Nickolas whispers.

'I can't. If I fall asleep holding onto you, I don't think I could handle waking up without you.'

'Even if you wake up and I'm not beside you, you know that this is where I'd rather be.'

Finn's eyes slowly close, the grip loosening in Nickolas's hand as Finn's body relaxes.

Nickolas doesn't want to leave. He wants to stay the night holding Finn against his body, wake up beside him, and watch the morning sun shine through the window as his green eyes slowly flutter open. But Nickolas also doesn't want that here. He doesn't want to experience a moment so intimate in a place that feels so clinical. He wants to save those precious moments for when they are free of these cement walls. He stays until the very last moment, knowing he needs to get back and do another check on the other patients before returning to Lydia, as he promised. He carefully extracts himself, making sure not to disturb Finn as he rises from the mattress. He pulls the blanket up over Finn's body, watching the redhead nuzzle into the warmth. Nickolas bends down, lays a soft kiss on Finn's forehead as his fingers comb through his red hair, and whispers, 'I'll be your saving grace, Finn...because you're mine.'

Nickolas stands outside of Finn's room, his heart pounding against his chest. He hadn't realised until that moment that, sometimes, the person you save is also the same person that can save you.

10. Thursday

Nickolas looks out the car window, his fingers drumming mindlessly against the steering wheel as he tries to find the courage to open the door and get out. He has been sitting inside his car for a good twenty minutes since he parked. He tells himself that if he doesn't get out right this second, then he'll have to just head back home and get ready for work – even though it's three hours till his shift starts. Nickolas exhales and puts his hand on his car keys, ready to turn the ignition back on when he stops. Mandy's voice rings in his head.

This is me now. Whole. Calm. Finally at peace.

He pulls the keys out, steps out, and locks his car. There is no turning back now. He has only been here once, but he still remembers where to go. It's sad to see how much has changed in six months. How much more has been added.

Nickolas stops walking, realising he has reached his destination. There in front of him lays a small plaque attached to a stone. His sister's name, two dates, and the words 'May peace be with you' staring back at him. Nickolas doesn't remember picking the words that would forever be engraved beneath Mandy's name, but the phrase seems fitting after the suffering his sister had endured while alive. He wishes the tombstone could have more of a grand gesture to it. At the time, it was all he could afford. Now it looks abandoned, the grass overgrown, covering part of the plaque.

Nickolas coughs. 'Hey, sis.' He shoves his hands in his pockets, not sure what to do with them. 'I'm, ah, I'm sorry it's been so long since I visited. There's no excuse. Doesn't matter how hard I—fuck.' He coughs again, rubbing his thumb over his nose. 'Doesn't matter how hard it is, I should have come sooner.'

He looks at the plaque, his own face reflecting back at him. He never noticed until now just how similar his facial features are to his sister's. It's as though Mandy is looking up at him from the grave. He scans the cemetery. No one else is around. He takes a seat on the grass, pulling his legs up to his chest and wraps his arms around them as he gives himself a moment.

'I realised that, for the last six months, I've been going about this all the wrong way. I've been torturing myself for letting it happen instead of actually thinking about why it happened.'

He thinks over what dream Mandy said to him and remembers Finn's words about the desire to rest overriding the desire to live.

'I get it. You being alive, living each day, hurting like you were – that was me being selfish. It was me wanting you here, in any way I could have you, just so I wouldn't be alone. But you weren't living, Mands. You were trapped. Trapped in a world that didn't treat you right. Trapped in a body that you could no longer look at and trapped in a mind that was telling you this was the life you were dealt and it was never going to get better.'

Nickolas sniffs back the tears that he can feel rising to the surface.

'I could sit here and tell you that I wish you had just kept fighting. That you had me to fight alongside you. You know I would have searched the ends of the earth to help you find whatever it was you needed so you could realise that everything you were feeling, everything you were thinking, it was just your brain lying to you. But there is only so much fight within a person.'

He wipes the few tears that had fallen on his cheek.

'You're at peace. You're happy. Fuck, that's all I've ever wanted for you, Mands. And I know that's all you've ever wanted for me. And I—I think I've finally found it.'

A soft smile appears on Nickolas's face as Finn seeps into his mind.

'His, ah, his name is Finn. I swear you two would have been inseparable.'

Nickolas chuckles at the thought of arguing with Mandy about hogging all of his boyfriend's spare time, about Nickolas never getting a moment alone with Finn. His heart speeds up as he realises the error he just made. Finn isn't his boyfriend. He is merely a friend, who is a boy, who he has feelings for. He pushes the thought aside, not needing to add to his emotional rollercoaster at the moment.

'He makes me happy. Happy in a way I never thought I'd get to be. And I'm not just saying that because of the guilt I've been carrying around, but because of the fuckin' life we were given. Growing up the way we did...I mean, to find someone that would want to spend their life with me, that actually cares about me...what are the chances?'

Nickolas shakes his head in disbelief.

'Finn makes me believe that maybe what everyone needs to survive this fucked up world is the right person beside them.'

Nickolas runs his hand over his chest, tracing the outline of his tattoo, knowing exactly where each line starts and ends.

'He called me his saving grace.'

He smiles.

'I know that's what you used to call me, but when he said it...I don't know. It's like...it was like all the pain he had ever felt, I was ready to take it from him so he wouldn't have to feel it anymore. And yet at the same time, he's this light that turns everything around me from black and white into colour. Jesus. I probably sound crazy. I know it's crazy. I've only known him for ten days, if that'—Nickolas takes a moment— 'I guess when you know, you know. You know?'

He suddenly remembers that Mandy isn't actually able to reply to him. He lets go of his legs, the tightness of them around his chest not helping the way his lungs are starting to feel restricted.

'No matter how much time passes, I'm never going to forget you, Mandy. I'm going to love and miss you till I'm buried right here beside you. You're my family. The only family that I've ever truly had. The only family that's mattered. From here till eternity, you're going to be stuck with me. So, enjoy the time to yourself because once I meet you up there, you ain't getting rid of me.'

Nickolas wipes at his face. He quickly stands so he can set his body into motion and hopefully stop the tears from falling.

'I'll visit again soon, sis. I promise you won't have to haunt my ass to get me over here. But, uh...either way, I know you're always with me.'

He quickly squats down, placing his hand to his lips and then to Mandy's name on the plaque. He stands back up and makes his way towards the car, his chest feeling open and light, as though a small piece has been put back in the hole that has been gaping inside of him longer than he can remember.

*

Nickolas parks his car and spots Dot juggling enough items to be classed as a safety hazard.

'Here, let me help.' He jogs over and takes the plate of still-warm chocolate and white choc chip cookies from Dot's hands.

'I'd say thank you but I know you're just after a cookie.' Dot chuckles.

'I'm hurt that you would even suggest that the survival of these cookies outweighs helping you from your car into work,' says Nickolas.

'Mhmm.' Dot side-eyes him as he slips his hand under the Saran wrap and takes a cookie.

Darren is getting buzzed through and holds the door open for them both.

'Thanks,' Nickolas mumbles with his mouth full of the delicious cookie.

'You know I generally don't mind someone talking with their mouth full, but that's not a pleasant look.' says Darren.

Nickolas wants to roll his eyes so hard that they'd probably fall out of his head, but instead, he swallows, licks the crumbs from his lips, and gives Darren an annoyed glare.

'So glad it's almost the end of the week,' Darren chimes in.

'Not really classed as a weekend when you have to work it like the rest of us.' Nickolas changes quickly, eager to start work and to see Finn.

'Touché, but tomorrow I work the morning shift which means Happy Hour in Boys Town.'

'Have fun with that.'

'You could join if you want. Make it extra fun.'

'Working.'

Nickolas closes his locker door and walks out. He makes his way to the break room to drop off his food, goes to the bathroom to take a piss, and then beelines for the common room. As Nickols opens the door to a room full of patients, Finn's laughter fills the room and Nickolas is suddenly home.

'Giggles McGee. Could hear you laughing all the way out into the corridor,' Nickolas states as he puts his hands in his pockets and stands beside the group Finn is laughing with. Cora and Alex have tears falling down their faces while Ryder looks somewhat embarrassed.

'Hey!' Finn looks at him with a smile as bright as the day.

'That would be my fault,' Cora cuts in between fits of laughter. 'We were swapping stories about how awkward our first time was and Finn here couldn't control himself when I explained how mine involved a rickety old table at a party that ended up collapsing under me, resulting in my ass being covered in splinters.'

'The fact that you kept going though,' Finn chimes in, still laughing.

'What can I say. He was good at what he did. I wanted the D more than I cared about the pain in my ass,' says Cora.

The group once again erupts into fits of laughter.

'Speaking of pain in the ass. Finn, what's your story?' Ryder's question has the group turning towards Finn. A question that also spikes Nickolas's interest.

'Who says I'm a bottom?' Finn interjects.

'Oh, gold star top, are we?' asks Ryder.

'Well...' The laughter dies down as Finn's behaviour goes from happy to solemn. All of them attend the group sessions, well aware of Finn's past trauma.

'It's okay, Finn,' Alex chimes in. 'That doesn't count. You're still a gold star.'

Nickolas puts his hand on Finn's shoulder, giving it a quick squeeze before removing it and placing his hand back in his pocket.

'Joe Richards. He was happy to be called Dick. It was the boys' locker room at school. Saw him checking me out and I took the gamble. Nothing awkward or embarrassing about it.'

'Well, that's boring.' Cora's look of disappointment makes Finn chuckle.

'What about you, Nickolas?' Alex asks.

'I don't think so. I'm not involved in this conversation,' says Nickolas.

'Don't be shy. Think of it as another group session,' Alex states.

'There is a reason orderlies don't attend those sessions.' explains Nickolas.

'Come on, Nick. I shared mine,' says Finn.

Nickolas looks at Finn, scratching the corner of his right eyebrow. 'Alice Redford. She was pretty much known for saying yes to anyone. Drank half a bottle of bourbon beforehand and left straight after.' Nickolas knows it's not the best story and it paints an image of him being a complete asshole. But it got his dad off his back once people were talking about it.

'Okay...but what about your other first time.' Cora cocks an eyebrow.

Nickolas opens his mouth, closing it again as he looks around. It's not a story that he is particularly proud of, nor one he thinks he should share with people who are supposed to feel comfortable coming to him for help.

'Okay everyone, please make your way towards the dining area for lunch,' Dot calls out.

Nickolas could not be more relieved.

'Finally. I'm starving.' Alex walks towards the dining area. Cora gets up and winks at Nickolas while Finn slowly stands, in no rush to leave Nickolas's side.

'Alice Redford, hey?' Finn confirms.

'Had to keep my dad off my back, man.'

'I get it. But, uh, I'd still like to hear the other story.'

'Trust me, it's not any better.'

'Let me decide that.' Finn walks off, leaving Nickolas to stand alone in the common room, collecting his thoughts.

*

Dot sends Hayley, James, and Sky on a break while everyone has lunch.

'Nice to see Ryder is eating again,' Nickolas says to Dot.

'Almost everyone in this room will have their good days and their bad. Some will be able to push past those bad days on their own, while others will need help and assistance. Ryder pushed through it, that's what matters.' Dot's voice sounds so proud that Nickolas can't help but look towards Ryder and smile. Dot steps away, heading towards some patients at the far end table, leaving Nickolas standing to the side by himself. His eyes land on Finn and, as if the redhead can sense him watching, he turns around and smiles back at him.

'So, I realised something,' Darren says, walking towards him.

'What's that?' Nickolas plays nice for the eyes and ears in the room.

'You're a "tell it as it is" kind of guy. Say it upfront, no hints, just give it to you straight...so to speak.'

'Right. And?'

'Right. So, because of that, I'm just going to say it.'

Nickolas opens his mouth to speak, but Darren cuts him off. 'Do you want to go out sometime? With me. Like, on a date.'

Nickolas figured one day Darren would ask, but he didn't think it would be in a room with another sixteen other people. Maybe that's why Darren did it, so the pressure of everyone around them would make Nickolas cave and say yes, and Darren could avoid the awkwardness of rejection. He considers agreeing and then pulling out at the last minute, saying he is sick or working another shift. It's a shitty thing to do, but Darren asking him while he's working, in front of all these people, is also a shitty thing to do.

Nickolas scans the room, hoping for an answer, and he finds it when he sees Finn looking back at him. The small frown on Finn's face and the sadness in those green eyes makes the answer as clear as day.

'Look, Darren, you need to back off.'

'What? I'm just—'

'I tried to play it off, let you down easy, but it ain't going to happen.'

'But—'

'I'm seeing someone, okay?' Nickolas so desperately wants to look over and watch Finn's face light up as a small blush appears on the redhead's face. If he does that, there is no denying Darren would catch on to who that someone is.

'Oh. I wasn't aware you—'

'It's new. Besides, didn't feel like parading my fuckin' private life around at work.'

'I'm sorry. If I had known, I wouldn't have...'

Nickolas nods.

'I hope it goes well for you.'

'Me too. I, ah...' He looks to his feet, thumbing his lip in the hopes that it covers his blush. 'I really fuckin' like him.' To avoid further questions, Nickolas walks away. He grabs a bottle of water from Aiden in the kitchen and sneaks a side-eye glance at Finn. Just as he suspected, his redhead heard it all and the freckled face is beaming with joy.

*

Nickolas stands near the lunch cart, taking note of each patient's tray as they return it, pleased to see all the utensils are accounted for. Finn is once again the last in the queue.

'How was your lunch?' Nickolas asks.

'Give my thanks to the chef,' says Finn.

Nickolas chuckles and takes Finn's tray, giving it a quick once over.

'So, should I back off?' Finn questions.

'What?' Nickolas cocks an eyebrow.

'This guy you've been seeing. Don't think he'd like to know I've been going after his man.' Finn winks and Nickolas can't help but to blush and laugh.

When did this become his life?

'Oh, he'd knock your teeth out if he knew.' Nickolas says.

'I've gotten into fights over less important things.'

'You callin' me important?' He bites his bottom lip. A small groan escapes Finn's mouth from the action. Finn takes the smallest of steps towards Nickolas, fully aware that they are out in the open, as those green eyes look down into his.

'I really fuckin' like you too, Nick.'

The air leaves Nickolas's lungs. Finn's arm brushes against him as he walks away, heading back to the common room, while Nickolas stands frozen in place. He's a twenty-one-year-old male whose heart is racing as if he were a thirteen-year-old girl who was told the boy she has a crush on likes her back.

He pushes the cart into the kitchen, chatting to Aiden briefly so he can calm his breathing before stepping back into the same room as Finn. If he just so happens to eat a chocolate pudding or two while doing so, Aiden wouldn't be one to judge him.

*

The room is set up for group, and Nickolas helps escort the patients who aren't scheduled for the session back to their rooms, feeling eyes on him every time he walks in and out of the common room. Darren stands by the door during the session while Dot and Nickolas attend to the mundane tasks, giving them a chance to casually talk and catch up.

'I went to the cemetery this morning.' Nickolas keeps his head down, focusing on retrieving the files Dot had asked him to get.

'Are you okay?' Dot stops writing notes.

'Yeah...surprisingly. It felt...'

'Like a goodbye?'

'No. No, more like a "see you soon".'

Dot looks alarmed.

'Fuck—no! Not like that. I just meant, shit, I meant that for once it felt like she wasn't *gone* gone, ya know? Like visiting was a way for me to just talk to her. I don't know. I'm probably making no sense.'

'You're making complete sense, Nykolai. People process grief differently. It can take longer for some than it can for others.'

He takes a seat across from his boss.

'Any chance a certain someone has helped you move past that guilt you were torturing yourself with?' Dot questions.

'Why ask the question that you already know the answer to?'

Dot looks smug. He suspects his boss had suspicions, which explains the one-on-one discussion she had with Finn.

'I'm glad. Really, I am. I can see the difference in you both.' Dot reaches across the table and places a hand on top of his. 'But you still need to be careful, Nykolai. He is still a patient, and you are still his orderly.'

'I know, Dot. I'd never—'

'I never said you would.' Dorothy gives his hand a soft pat, then continues writing her notes.

'We're friends. That's it.'

Friends that really fucking like each other. But right now, all they can be is friends. Especially in the eyes of those around them.

'Just be sure he knows that too. Patients can get the wrong idea. But regardless, I trust you, Nykolai.'

A pit of shame opens in Nickolas's stomach. The minute his lips landed on Finn's, with every touch and caress that followed, it shattered that trust. Lying on the same mattress as Finn slept, every comment and look, it's all been tainted with the knowledge that he was being unprofessional. He fought so hard to make sure that he didn't do anything unethical, but then Finn kissed him, and then almost died, and suddenly Nickolas didn't see the point in fighting with himself any longer.

*

At three o'clock, Hayley, James, and Sky head home as everyone shuffles out of the common room. Many look exhausted, a sign of an intense session, and one of those faces belongs to Finn. Nickolas ducks into room thirteen and waits.

Finn exhales while entering the room, and stretches out his neck.

'You okay?' Nickolas asks.

Finn sighs. 'Better now.'

'Can I do anything?'

'What are the chances I could get a hug?'

Nickolas bites his bottom lip and eyes the door. He tilts his head towards the bathroom, a smile instantly breaking out on Finn's face.

Hidden away, Nickolas wraps his arms around Finn's shoulders, gives the redhead's nape a quick squeeze while running his fingers through the soft hairs at the bottom of Finn's head.

Finn inhales, nose pressed into the crook of Nickolas's neck.

'Better?' Nickolas asks.

Finn simply nods. Reluctantly, Nickolas pulls away, walks into the middle of the room and waits for Finn.

'We talked about coping mechanisms today.' Finn sits on the mattress, Nickolas still standing, keeping his distance. 'We discussed healthy ways to handle things when situations get rough...you know, for when we get out. But we also talked about the unhealthy coping mechanisms we had used when we were struggling.'

'It puts a whole new perspective on the saying "take a walk down memory lane", doesn't it?'

'Ha. That's for sure.'

'Facing it is the only way you can move forward from it though, Finn.'

Finn's head tilts to the side. 'You read Mandy's journal yet?'

'Wow!' Nickolas crosses his arms over his chest.

'Sorry, sorry, I didn't mean...' Finn exhales, exhaustion evident.

'No, I get it. I shouldn't be pushing you when I can't even take my own advice.'

'It's completely different circumstances, Nick.'

'It's fine. You're making progress. It's showing, not just with me but with everyone. You're doing great and that's all that matters.'

A proud smile spreads over Finn's face.

'I'll, ah, I'll let you rest up.' Nickolas turns to leave.

'Nickolas. When you're ready, as hard as it will be, I'm sure reading Mandy's journal will have the answers you need to give yourself closure.'

Nickolas doesn't reply. He simply watches Finn lay back onto the mattress, closing eyes and entwining his long fingers over his chest.

*

Near the end of his shift, Nickolas collects the med cart from the reception desk with plans to see Finn one last time before he goes home. He does the rounds, relieved that Ethan has no bruises, but does seem reserved as Nickolas says good-night, locking the door behind him. Finn is already lying in bed, the blankets pulled up.

'Hey...you awake?' Nickolas whispers.

'Just resting. Big day, ya know?' Finn mumbles.

'Here. Take these.' Nickolas sits on the edge of the mattress and watches Finn take the pills with no argument, then lies back onto the pillow.

'You feeling okay?' Nickolas brushes a few strands of damp hair from Finn's forehead.

'Yeah. It's not the meds, just thinking.'

Nickolas hums in understanding.

'You still owe me a story about your first time,' says Finn.

Nickolas pulls his hand away, groaning. He'd hoped Finn had forgotten. 'I don't know if now is the best time for that, Finn.'

'Please. It will help me get out of my head.'

Nickolas sighs and runs a hand down his face. 'It was two weeks after Alice. I was dealing for my dad and this guy was a regular customer. Everyone knew he was gay, but I dealt with him so Dominic didn't beat the shit out of him.' He pauses. 'One day he asked if I wanted to share a joint with him, I had nothing else to do and he had already paid me, so I figured if the guy wanted to waste the product on me then that was his choice.'

'We were smokin' up on the football field at the school. It was dark out, just talking shit, when he puts his hand on my knee. I pushed it away, internally freaking out, but he didn't move. He sat there, waiting, and as I looked around the field seeing just how alone we were, I pushed him onto his knees, and he knew. He took off his pants, got on all fours, and well, you know how it is.'

'That doesn't seem so bad,' comments Finn.

'Story isn't finished.'

'Oh.'

Nickolas coughs a couple of times to clear his throat. 'When it was over, we pulled our pants up and the guy turns to me, smirking, and says, "Always knew you were gay." And, I don't know, maybe it was hearing someone call me gay for the first time or the internal panic of someone knowing my secret – I just, I lost it. I punched him, the shock kept the guy down long enough for me to straddle him and I kept laying punch after punch. Even as I'm doing it, I hate myself for it, but a voice in my head kept saying, "better him than you".'

Nickolas looks down at his hands, envisioning the blood staining his knuckles.

'I got up, watched the guy roll to his side as he's spitting out blood...I don't even remember how I was able to stop hitting him. Anyway, I, ah, I told him, "I ain't no fag and if you tell anyone about this, next time I won't stop till your heart does" and then I left. Never saw the guy again.'

Nickolas jumps as Finn places a hand on his knee.

'Hey. I get it,' says Finn. 'What happened, why you did it. I'm not going to judge you for a mistake you made while living in fear.'

Nickolas puts his hand on Finn's and gives it a gentle squeeze.

'I, ah, I have to go,' says Nickolas.

'Nickolas, no. You don't have to leave.'

'I don't want to go, but I have to. My shift is about to end and if I'm not back out front in time they're going to come looking.'

Finn lets go.

'Thank you. For not...' *For not hating me*, Nickolas thinks.

'You never have to worry about something you did in the past changing how I feel about you, Nick. Just like I know my past doesn't change the way you feel about me.'

'Nothing could change that.' Nickolas gets up, making his way to the door.

'See you tomorrow?'

'Of course.' Nickolas closes the door and heads back towards the front desk with the med cart. He changes out of his uniform, grabs his bag, and stays at the front desk till the clock strikes eight, chatting away with Dot and Sam. Brett is working the night shift with Lydia, and Dot is making it a point to keep them separated as much as possible.

'Let's get out of here.' Darren says as Lydia and Brett step through the gate. Nickolas makes eye contact with Brett, daring his colleague to say something. To Nickolas's surprise, Brett stays silent.

Nickolas asks Lydia to do the first few night checks, in case Finn is still awake. He can trust Lydia to let it slide, knowing Finn would eventually fall asleep. Lydia promises before saying goodbye.

*

Nickolas walks through his door, greeted by purring and meowing as Socks does a figure eight around his feet. He grabs a beer and takes a seat on the couch. Socks leaps onto his lap, demanding love and affection, which Nickolas is more than happy to provide. He runs his hand from Socks's head to her spine and chuckles as the purrs increase in volume while Socks arches into his touch.

Deciding that's enough, Socks jumps off Nickolas and onto the box that is still sitting on the coffee table. He managed to put the rest away after retrieving the iPod charger but got preoccupied and left this one out. He cocks an eyebrow as Socks perches on top of the box. Nickolas takes a sip of his beer, then another while he watches the furball scratch at the lid.

Nickolas shakes his head in disbelief. 'You and Finn been talking to each other behind my back, have ya?'

Socks meows in response.

He puts the beer beside the box and lifts his cat off. He removes the lid and picks up Mandy's journal. He stares at the hardcover as though it might bite him.

He runs his hands down his face, then grabs his beer and chugs it. With the journal in hand, he leans back against the couch and opens the front page, but the dark scrawl of Mandy's handwriting has him close it again.

'Nope. I...yeah, I'm not ready for this.'

He grabs a second beer from the fridge and chugs half of it down. He knows Finn is right, that he needs to read it. The closure he's been seeking since Mandy passed is in that journal. But he can't do it. He storms back to the coffee table, puts the journal inside the box and closes the lid.

Visiting Mandy's grave was a big enough leap for one day, he doesn't want to push himself with too much too soon. But the damn box is calling to him like the beating drums of the Jumanji board game. He grabs his keys and jacket and walks out the door. He doesn't know where he's going, he just knows he has to keep walking. But the sound of the busy streets and passing cars isn't enough to drown out the battle going on in his head.

The truth of the matter is that he's scared. Scared of finding out something about his sister that he was never meant to know. Scared of the image he has of Mandy forever being tainted. He's scared to get a glimpse into his sister's mind, even though he knows that seeing the way Mandy struggled will help him come to terms with why Mandy took her life.

His lungs burn with each ragged breath of cold air. He looks around and is shocked to see he's made it all the way to Boys Town. He doesn't exactly live far, but he sure as hell isn't close enough for it to be an easy walk. He considers hailing a cab, but the loud music from a club is enough to silence his racing thoughts. With no line, he enters and heads straight to the bar. He has walked off the two beers and will need his blood alcohol concentration to be much higher if he hopes to keep his thoughts at bay.

Nickolas takes a seat at the bar, flags down the bartender and orders a whiskey. He downs it and signals for another before the bartender has a chance to serve anyone else.

'Trying to drown your sorrows?' Some guy yells in his ear, appearing suddenly at his side.

The music covers Nickolas's groan. He doesn't bother to reply and continues to sip his drink, hoping the guy will take the hint and walk away.

'You know, there are more exciting ways to help you ease whatever it is you're trying to drink away,' the guy continues.

'Not any I'm interested in,' Nickolas spits out.

'How'd you know until you give it a try?'

A hand slides up Nickolas's thigh. He slams his hand on top of it, giving it a not so gentle squeeze as he removes the hand from his leg. 'Take the hint. I ain't interested.'

'Jesus, fine. Sue me for wanting a little fun.' The guy scurries off to the dance floor as the song changes.

'What's the matter? Wasn't your type?' The bartender pours him a third drink without Nickolas requesting it.

'Not what I came here for,' Nickolas explains.

'That's what everyone says. Till the right person comes along.'

'Already got the right person. Just needed a drink.'

'If that were the case, you'd be drinking with him, not in some bar in Boys Town on a Thursday night.'

'Trust me, no place I'd rather be than spending my night with him, but circumstances prevent that. So, it's either at home with my thoughts, or here with the shitty music that's loud enough to drown everything out and enough booze to shut everything up.'

'Fair enough. Want me to leave the bottle?'

'Better not, gotta work tomorrow.'

The bartender fills another glass up for Nickolas, placing it beside the one he is still sipping, and gives him a wink before walking away. Guess the guy felt sorry for him. Nickolas's ears become accustomed to the music, allowing him to tune in to the conversations around him. People complaining about their love life, others wanting to blow off some steam after a big week of work. A few celebrate, whether it be a birthday or a raise. One guy is trying to get over a broken heart, friends assuming the best way to do so is for him to get laid. Nickolas doesn't make eye contact with anyone in that group. The noise and drama are enough to push thoughts of Mandy back into the box Nickolas has been keeping his sister in until he is ready to open the lid back up.

Nickolas finishes his fourth drink. Time to get back home. He is working a double tomorrow, which means he needs to be well-rested. As he throws some bills onto the counter, along with a tip, he picks up on the conversation between a businessman in his mid-to-late forties and what looks to be a few work colleagues.

'I swear, he was the easiest ass I've had in months. If only all the twinks around here were that willing to give it up.'

Something about the way the guy is bragging causes the hairs on the back of Nickolas's neck to stand up.

'I had him begging for it. He couldn't get enough. He was kinky, too, wanted it rough and shit,' the guy continues to gloat.

'Fuck. Should have seen if he wanted to make it a party,' one of the colleague's chimes in.

'No way was I going to share. But here, I got photos.'

'Oh, shit, pass them over.'

Nickolas moves behind the group to see the phone screen as the guy clicks into a folder within a folder within a folder till the photos appear of...Finn!

As the guy swipes the screen, the story of what happened plays out before him.

Finn naked, face down on the bed, out cold.

Swipe.

Finn tied to the bed.

Swipe.

Waist down of the guy pushing inside of Finn.

Swipe.

Finn's eyes opening in shock.

Swipe.

Panic on Finn's face.

Swipe.

Hands gripping tightly onto Finn's hips.

Swipe.

Cloth being tied around Finn's mouth.

Swipe.

Cum seeping out of Finn.

Swipe.

A close-up of Finn's face, eyes closed in pain as tears fall.

Swipe.

A full body shot of Finn passed out, bruises on his hips and cum on his back and thighs.

All Nickolas can hear is the laughter and commentary coming from these assholes; the way this rapist pig is twisting the story of what these pictures show to make Finn out to be some greedy whore when, really, Finn was begging for the guy to stop, to let him go, screaming in pain after being drugged, tied up, and raped.

Nickolas taps the guy on the shoulder.

'Hey, man. Couldn't help but notice the nice piece of ass you're showing around there,' says Nickolas.

'What's it to you?' the business questions.

'I just figured your friends might want to know the full story.'

'What?'

Nickolas puts all the force he can into his punch. His knuckles connect with the guy's nose, and the force sends Finn's rapist stumbling backward. Height is against Nickolas, but he has the strength. As the asshole wipes the blood dripping from his nose, Nickolas's fingers claw at dark hair, gripping tightly before slamming the guy's head into the bar counter.

'You want to tell all your friends how you raped that so-called "twink"?'

Murmured voices begin to gossip behind him.

'You want to tell them how you drugged him? Tied him up? Forced him?'

The guy struggles underneath his grasp. 'Li-lies. He fucking begged for it.'

Nickolas thumbs his nose.

The bartender is watching, making no rush to call over security.

'Begged for it? Okay. Guess I'll tell everyone how you begged for me to beat the living shit out of you then.'

Nickolas pulls the guy off the countertop and knees the lying scumbag's groin. The guy falls to the floor. Nickolas gets down and presses his knee into a wheezing chest.

'You piece of shit.' Nickolas slams his right hand into the guy's cheekbone, then the jaw. 'I don't remember being told in school to keep going when someone screams stop.'

He breaks the skin on the guy's lip, blood spreading across the face of Finn's attacker with each new blow. Nickolas gives his right hand a break as his left hand goes for the guy's ribs.

'Rapist pigs like you deserve to be buried six feet under.'

Nickolas is surprised that the colleagues who were drooling over Finn's photos aren't coming to the rescue. Either they believe what Nickolas said or they know they wouldn't stand a chance against him.

He eases up when he notices the guy has stopped struggling a good thirty seconds ago. Nickolas leans back onto the balls of his feet and searches the assailant's pockets while catching his breath. He finds a wallet, pulls out the ID, and grabs the asshole's jaw, forcing dazed and confused eyes to look up at him.

'See this? Hey, fuckhead, look at me.' Nickolas slaps the guy's bleeding cheek before gripping his bruising jaw, squeezing it tight to make sure Nickolas has his attention.

'I know your name and your address. I'm taking your phone and if you even think about going to the cops about this, just remember that I know where you fucking live.'

'What—' The guy coughs. A few splatters of blood land on Nickolas's face. 'What are you going to do?'

'I'm going to ask my boyfriend if he wants to report your ass now that we have the proof.'

'If he does that, you'll get arrested for assault.'

'Think I give a shit? After what you did to him, I'd happily kill you and go to jail for it.' Nickolas spits on the guy's face. He stands, pockets the ID, and snatches the phone from the work colleagues who are still standing there in shock. Nickolas sees if the phone can be unlocked, and of course, not even a passcode is set up.

Nickolas nods to the bartender, who gives one back and continues cleaning the glasses, ignoring the mess on the floor. The cold air hits Nickolas's face as he exits and he breathes it in. God, what he would do for a cigarette right about now. The streetlights give him a clear view of his hands; drying blood and cracked skin tell a story without the need for any words. He hails a cab and gives the address of his apartment, keeping his hands out of sight.

Within minutes Nickolas is heading up to his door. It's past midnight as he steps inside. He needs to shower. He needs to drink a glass of water. He needs Finn. In the bathroom, he washes away the evidence on his hands. Besides the one punch he threw Brett's way, it's been years since his hands looked like this, and to be honest, he was hoping they would never look this way again. But Nickolas wouldn't have been able to live with himself had he just walked away from the guy who hurt Finn, who took advantage and then bragged about it like Finn was some prized conquest. That rapist asshole had thought he got away with it and no doubt had plans to do it again. Nickolas should have cut his dick off.

He barely has his hands dry before he hears his phone ringing. Tired and ready for bed, he quickly hits accept, too exhausted to question who could be calling him this late at night.

'What?'

'Oh, thank God. Nickolas, you need to get here. Now!' The panic in Lydia's voice sobers him up.

'What's wrong?'

'It's Finn. I told Brett not to do it, but he wouldn't listen and—just, hurry up, okay?'

Nickolas hangs up. He grabs his keys and heads straight for his car. His tyres skid on the road as he reverses out of the car-park and swings the car around. He tries not to break any road rules, as his blood alcohol concentration would be over the limit if he got pulled up. Nickolas's heart is racing. Whatever Brett has done, if he has hurt Finn in any way, Nickolas knows he won't be able to hold back.

He double parks out the front and he runs through the doors of the centre.

Lydia is waiting for him at the desk. 'I'm so sorry. I tried to stop Brett but—'

'Lydia, where's Finn?'

'In his room. Nickolas, wait—'

He is already running through the open gate towards Finn's room. He gets to the door without his key card.

'You need this.' Lydia is beside him, swiping the card, and Nickolas bursts through the door.

Finn's sobs are the first thing Nickolas can hear. He steps closer towards the mattress and his heart leaps into his chest. Finn's wrists are restrained above his head.

'Fuck.' He crouches down making quick work of unfastening the buckles. 'Finn. It's okay, I'm here. Hey, look at me.'

'You promised, Nickolas.' Finn lets the words out in-between sobs.

Nickolas feels like he took a punch to his heart. 'I'm so sorry, Finn. This never should have happened.'

'You promised you'd never restrain me.' Arms now free, Nickolas notices a few stitches have torn from Finn pulling at the restraints, skin red and blood smeared around the wounds. Finn's arms press into his chest, curling into a ball as Nickolas carefully reaches out to run his fingers through red hair.

'What happened?' Nickolas's voice is stern. It's directed at Lydia as his eyes stay focused on Finn, his heart breaking at the soft whimpers that fill the room.

'Finn woke up screaming. He had obviously had a nightmare. I tried to calm him down, but he was calling out for you, pacing the room saying he couldn't go back to sleep.' Lydia's voice is filled with remorse. 'Brett came in, pinned Finn against the wall so he could try and sedate him, but Finn knocked the sedation out of Brett's hand. Brett, he...he pinned Finn down on the bed and restrained him.'

Nickolas closes his eyes, his anger has him ready to erupt like a volcano.

'That's when I called you.'

'I'm going to kill him.'

'Nickolas.'

'No. I specifically wrote in Finn's notes that he wasn't to be restrained due to past trauma and now look what's happened.' The way Finn is shaking makes Nickolas question whether he should hold Finn now and kill Brett later, or come back with the news of Brett's death to make Finn feel better.

'I'm sorry, I tried to unfasten them, but Brett—'

'It wasn't your fault, Lydia.' He leans forward, placing a soft kiss on Finn's forehead before whispering in Finn's ear.

'I'm so sorry, Finn.'

'I trusted you, Nickolas.'

'I know. I'm going to make this right. I swear on my life.' Nickolas stands, his fists ready for round two.

'Stay with him.' Nickolas makes his way towards the door.

'Nickolas!' Lydia calls out.

He stops, but keeps his eyes in front.

'He's in the break room.'

All Nickolas can see is red. Every comment Brett has ever made, every insensitive remark about the patients, every homophobic slur Brett has directed toward him, it's all fuel for the fire burning inside of Nickolas. But what Brett did to Finn was enough to tip him over the edge. He storms into the break room and spots Brett sitting at the table, back turned towards the door. Nickolas kicks the chair from under Brett, watching as he tumbles to the floor. He picks up the chair, throws it to the side so it can't get in the way or be used as a weapon.

'I fucking warned you.'

He lays a kick into Brett's stomach, strong enough to have his colleague gasping for air.

'You're a sadistic piece of shit.' He kicks Brett harder than the first time. 'I should have done this a long time ago.'

He aims his next kick for Brett's face, connecting his boot perfectly to the mouth that Nickolas had warned to stay shut. Brett's head tilts back from the sheer force of the kick, blood spills and the sound of coughing fills the room as Brett chokes on metallic liquid.

Nickolas grabs a fist full of Brett's hair and pulls so their eyes meet.

'This about that faggot, isn't it?' Brett spits out. 'I knew something was going on with you two.' The blood smeared around Brett's mouth and the hint of joy in his eyes reminds Nickolas of The Joker.

'You're still not seeing the full picture here.' Nickolas talks calmly, even with the anger running through him.

'Sure it's got nothing to do with the way I pinned that psycho to the bed while he screamed out for you? Thrashing around while I fastened those restraints so tight that his fingers turned purple?'

Nickolas bites the inside of his cheek. He knows Brett is baiting him and it's working; that's why he's enjoying the way Brett's blood is leaving a stain on the carpet.

'Nah. This is because I don't fucking like you.' He lands a punch to Brett's nose, positive that this time, it is broken.

'This is because someone like you doesn't deserve to take up space on this earth.' He throws another punch, landing on Brett's cheekbone.

'This is because you're a worthless, good-for-nothing piece of shit that takes pleasure in hurting the innocent.' He pushes Brett's head so it thuds against the floor.

Nickolas feels arms pulling him away from Brett's beaten and broken body, and he doesn't fight it.

'I think he's had enough, don't you, kid?' Sam's grip is tight in case Nickolas decides to go back for another round.

'You ask me, he deserves a lot more than what I gave him.' Nickolas pulls away and turns around, leaving the room and all the evidence of what happened within it.

He heads back to Finn's room to find Lydia still sitting beside the bed. Her worried eyes focus on Nickolas's hands, once again covered in blood, though he isn't surprised to see the way Lydia gives him a small nod of approval. Nickolas kicks his shoes off, hoping Finn will allow him to be close.

'Finn?'

'Nick?' Finn's voice sounds tired, broken, hoarse from screaming.

'I'm here. I made things right. Just like I promised.' Finn turns towards Nickolas, tear stains on his scared, freckled face, eyes red and puffy. Nickolas crawls onto the bed, sitting up against the wall and opening his legs so Finn can lay between them. Finn's back presses against Nickolas's chest, his body curling into a ball as Nickolas wraps his arms around him.

'It was happening all over again...my dream. I was back in that hotel, and he was—'

'Shh. It's okay, Finn. I promise it was just a nightmare.'

'I could feel the pain all over my body.'

Nickolas holds back tears. After seeing those photos tonight, he knows exactly what type of pain Finn would have been feeling. 'I promise you're safe. What you were feeling was just muscle memory, Finn. But you're not there. You're here, with me, and no one is going to hurt you like that ever again.' He lays a kiss on Finn's head, taking in a deep breath as his nose buries into red wavy hair. 'I swore on my life that I would make things right and I did.'

Tonight, he was Finn's saving grace in every sense of the phrase. Was it a coincidence that he ran into Finn's rapist the same night Finn had a nightmare? Perhaps. Would he have attacked Brett if his body hadn't already been in fight mode from the club? Maybe not. But would he have done any of it differently? Fuck no. The anger inside of Nickolas that caused him to lash out was a part of the person he used to be, using violence as his way to get a message across. But perhaps it wasn't the fact that Nickolas had changed over the years that made him retire his fists. Perhaps it had more to do with the fact that Nickolas didn't need to fight anymore because he had no one he needed to protect.

The beatdowns he gave on behalf of his dad were a way for Nickolas to protect himself. When Mandy was committed, his sister was safe from their family, they both were. Safe from the horrors they were hiding from. He no longer had to use his fists for their survival. With Finn though, he would gladly bring his fists out of retirement and fight all of his battles if it meant Finn was safe and protected. That's what you do for the people you love.

'I'll come to get you before shift change so you can sneak out,' explains Lydia.

'I'm not leaving him,' Nickolas whispers, pleased to see Finn had drifted off back to sleep in the warmth and safety of his arms.

'I'm sure the punishment for assaulting Brett will be bad enough. Don't let this go against you too, Nickolas. Think about Finn.'

'I'm always thinking about Finn.'

'Exactly.' Lydia's voice is still low but it's stern. 'He needs you, and if you get fired, then what? A fight with a co-worker, who had it coming, if you ask me, could result in a warning, maybe a suspension. But you know the risks are greater if the wrong person sees this.'

Only the night before, he swore to Lydia that nothing physical was going on between him and Finn. There is no way Lydia would believe that now. And yet, his colleague is still protecting him from losing his job.

'Wait, you're still going to cover for me?' Nickolas asks.

'I can see what this means for you both. It's not an orderly sleeping with a patient, or you abusing your power to get something from Finn. You're connected. It's still not right and it's still risky, but the physical aspect of what you two have is more about feeling safe and loved than it is about sex.'

'He's changed me, Lydia.' Nickolas runs his fingers through Finn's hair, who relaxes further into his touch.

'I've noticed. You're good for each other. But I only work nights. I can't cover for you if you slip up during the day.'

'I know.'

With that, Lydia stands and walks towards the door.

'I'll be back just after five to come and get you. Should give you enough time to say goodbye and head into the break room. I'm sure you'll have a big day ahead of you tomorrow.'

Lydia isn't wrong. Who knows what tomorrow will bring for him once they find out what he did to Brett.

Lydia closes the door behind her. Nickolas squeezes Finn tight as he closes his eyes and tries to get some sleep, finally being able to hold Finn in his arms as he does so. He just wishes it was under better circumstances.

11. Friday

Nickolas wakes to someone gently shaking him from his warm slumber. As his eyes open, taking in the bare walls, glass windows with the light beginning to shine through, and Finn curled in his arms, peacefully asleep beside him, the events from the night before come rushing back.

'Hey,' Lydia whispers.

Nickolas turns his head, keeping his body as still as possible so he doesn't disturb Finn.

'It's five. Thought I'd come to get you before Darren, Hayley, and Sky show up.'

Nickolas pinches the bridge of his nose with the hand that was wrapped around Finn's waist. The arm Finn is using as a pillow may be a little harder to get free.

'Thanks.' He keeps his voice low. 'Where's, ah, where's Brett?'

'Break room. He's playing the victim card so be prepared. Dorothy has been called and so has HR. Brett thinks he has the upper hand.'

'Why the fuck did he call Dot? It's her day off.' Nickolas is still whispering. Patients aren't due to wake up for another two hours and considering Finn had a restless night, he needs those extra hours.

'He wants Dorothy on his side before you convince her otherwise.'

'Once I explain what Brett did, not just last night but all the other shit I've kept to myself, he'll be lucky to have anyone on his side.'

'If you need someone to back you up, let me know.'

'Thanks.'

Lydia walks out, leaving the door open so he doesn't get locked in. Nickolas turns his head away from the door and back down at Finn, asleep in his arms. Although his muscles felt stiff, it was still the best sleep he's had in a long time. Finn slept peacefully in his arms for the remainder of the night, during which Nickolas went from sitting up against the wall to curling behind Finn, engulfing his body like a security blanket.

Nickolas runs his fingers through Finn's red hair, leans down, and presses a gentle kiss to his temple. Finn stirs but doesn't wake.

'I have to go,' Nickolas whispers.

'Please, stay...' Finn's eyes are closed, body still exhausted.

'Trust me, I don't want to go. But I can't be seen here...I'll see you when I work this afternoon, okay? I promise.' With great difficulty, Nickolas extracts his arm from under Finn's head, who shivers from the lack of warmth that Nickolas's body was providing. He pulls the blankets over Finn's body and takes one final look before walking out of the door.

At the front gates, Nickolas signals for Sam to buzz it open.

'How's the kid?' Sam asks.

'Better. He was pretty shaken up, so I sat with him to make sure he was okay,' Nickolas explains.

'You don't got to lie to me.'

Nickolas leans on the reception desk, cocking an eyebrow towards Sam.

'After the way you came in last night all frantic, and how you kicked the living daylights out of Brett, I figured the complicated situation you were telling me about was the same guy you went running towards.'

Nickolas runs a hand up and down his face a few times, giving himself a moment to think.

'Jesus, is it that obvious?'

'No. But I've been around the block a few times, I notice things that others wouldn't.'

'Then how come you haven't noticed Dot?' He changes the subject on purpose, not needing to worry about the consequences of so many people knowing about his feelings for Finn.

'I've noticed her plenty, but we aren't talking about me right now.'

Nickolas deflates. 'I'm *so* going to get fired.' He bends his head down, and groans.

'I doubt it. Nothing actually happened between you two, right?'

'Right. But shit like that doesn't matter.'

'Maybe so. But who knows? And I'm not talking about rumours or gossip, I'm asking who actually knows that Finn is more than just your patient?'

'Lydia, you...Darren knows I'm seeing someone, but that's it. Needed to get him to back off...'

Sam chuckles.

'Dot knows we're close, but not that close.'

Sam nods in understanding. 'Okay, so you know Lydia and I aren't going to say anything. So as long as you keep it professional, then you're in the clear.'

Professional. Does he even know the meaning of the word anymore? Kissing Finn in the shower room is not professional. Holding Finn while sleeping is not professional. Spending his day off sitting by Finn's side, holding hands, and talking about his deepest secrets is not professional. But Sam's right. Only he and Lydia know that there is something more than just a friendship between them. He just needs to keep it that way a little longer.

'I'm going home.' Brett's voice breaks the silence.

Nickolas looks up and glares at Brett.

'The fuck you still doing here?' Brett questions him as they lock eyes.

Nickolas doesn't have a chance to answer before the automatic doors open, and a woman in her forties steps through wearing a black business suit that is cut perfectly to shape her body. Heels click on the floor as the woman walks towards the front desk.

Nickolas steps aside, the woman's presence alone makes him feel like a stain on someone's shoes.

'From the state of your face, I'm going to assume you're Brett Phillips,' the woman says.

Brett stands tall. 'How's that any of your business?'

'Well, considering I was woken up at a God-forsaken hour to hear that there was an altercation between you and a colleague—the second altercation, I might add, both ending in a physical assault—I'd say it damn well is my business.'

Nickolas has never met anyone from HR before. They come and go when they are needed. This somewhat small facility that he takes pride working at is only one of many that are owned by the same company.

Brett gives Nickolas the side-eye.

The woman from HR turns, attention now focused on Nickolas. 'I'm going to assume you're the colleague.'

'Yes, ma'am.' Nickolas would have said it was a lucky guess, but he's betting the bruised knuckles and dry blood he has yet to wash off them, were a dead giveaway.

'You're not going anywhere. Take a seat. You,' the woman points towards Brett, 'follow me.' She walks to the gate and one look back at the desk has Sam buzzing the gate open. The woman walks towards the rooms that are used for one-on-one sessions with the therapists.

Nickolas turns his attention back to Sam before realising he may as well head to the break room. It's going to be a long-ass day.

*

Nickolas pours himself a cup of coffee and sits down. Lydia has gone home, but not before mentioning that Mrs Monroe – apparently that was the name of the tough HR lady – had asked Lydia to share her version of the incident later that day. Brett was going to be in the wrong in terms of the treatment given towards Finn; what had Nickolas concerned was whether he was leaving today with his job or not.

'Nickolas? What are you doing here?' Darren questions while walking into the room.

He raises his cup to Darren. 'Needed a coffee, and I knew no place could compare to the stuff we kept here.' His comment brought a chuckle to everyone in the room, but it was clear they wanted to know the real reason. 'HR needs to speak to me... about Brett.'

'Wait, what?' Sky moves towards Nickolas, waiting for him to elaborate.

Nickolas pinches the bridge of his nose and decides to get it all out. 'I'm sure you'll hear about it soon enough, so what the hell. Brett mistreated a patient last night after their file specifically stated not to take a certain course of action. The patient was inconsolable, so Lydia called me. I came in and after seeing the state of the patient, I may have acted with more than just my words.' Nickolas keeps it anonymous. He speaks professionally, figuring it is good practice for when he needs to speak to Mrs Monroe regarding his side of the story.

Darren slumps into a chair, sulking like a baby. 'You mean you kicked his ass, and once again, I wasn't here to see it?'

'Well, shit.' Sky leans back, taking in Nickolas's words.

'Shit indeed.'

Nickolas turns to the door, surprised to hear such language fall out of Dot's mouth.

'I must say, getting called in on my day off is not something I am pleased about. But learning why I was called, well, let's just say I'm surprised to hear Brett is still walking.'

Darren hands Dot a cup of coffee, and she takes the cup and sits down beside Nickolas. Now on the clock, Darren, Sky, and Hayley scurry off to prepare for the day. Nickolas and Dot sit in silence for a few minutes.

'Is Finn okay?' Dot asks.

'I'm not sure. He was shaken up when I saw him last night, but I haven't seen him since.' He hates lying to Dot, but he takes Sam's words to heart. If anything happens, Dot can't get reprimanded for Nickolas's behaviour or actions.

'Surprised you stayed here all night then.' His boss takes a sip of a coffee.

'Lydia told me Brett called HR. I figured I was going to get called in. Plus, I wanted to make sure Finn had settled during the night.'

'Hmmm.'

'Mr Markova?'

Nickolas turns to the sound of his name. Mrs Monroe is in the doorway, Brett standing behind the woman, a cocky smirk on the assholes face.

'Follow me, please.'

Dot gives his leg a tap of encouragement.

Nickolas follows Mrs Monroe into the office. The door closes behind him and for a brief moment, he takes a look around, envisioning what it must be like for all the patients who come in here to discuss their feelings, their issues.

'I spoke to Mr Phillips, and he informed me that over the last week or so you have threatened him, pushed him up against the lockers, punched him in front of the patients in the dining area, and then last night assaulted him after he restrained a patient for their own safety. Is that correct?' Mrs Monroe pushes closer into the desk as Nickolas takes a seat.

'Yes, but—'

Mrs Monroe holds a hand up, silencing Nickolas. 'I'll get to your side of the story. Until then, is Mr Phillips's account of your behaviour accurate?'

'Yes, ma'am.'

'Before we continue, please know that I have asked Miss Fraser, who was on duty last night, to inform me of the situation as she is the only witness to the incident.'

Nickolas simply nods.

Mrs Monroe picks up a pen and then looks towards Nickolas. The silence is his only cue to know he is free to talk.

'While I understand that my behaviour was unacceptable, inexcusable, and unprofessional, I'd like to make known that my actions were due to Mr Phillips repetitively abusing his power and not changing his actions once spoken to. I acted out of frustration and anger, and it was wrong of me to do so.' Nickolas has never been happier than he in that moment to have a decent poker face.

'So physical violence was your way of getting your message across?'

'...Yes.' Nickolas sighs as he watches Mrs Monroe take notes.

'Can you please elaborate on the behaviour that caused you to act out?'

'On multiple occasions, I, as well as other colleagues, have heard Mr Phillips use offensive language towards the patients. He—'

'Such as?' The question cuts him off and it takes a second to register what has been asked.

'Calling them crazy. Using homophobic language, and referring to one of our patients as Jekyll and Hyde...among other things.'

'Will this patient be willing to speak against Mr Phillips?'

'I don't...Maybe. Patients can be a little fearful when it comes to speaking out against Brett's behaviour.'

'And why is this?'

'Probably because he is a sadistic piece of—' Nickolas remembers who he is addressing and cuts himself off from continuing. 'Sorry.' He takes a moment to lower his anger 'Mr Phillips treats these patients like they aren't worth saving. Like they're helpless. He makes comments about their mental illness and how it's just an excuse they use to justify their past actions, which can sometimes be of a sexual or addictive nature. He makes inappropriate jokes in front of the patients about their disorders. I've heard him call a patient we have with Pica, Frankenstein. He offered to give a patient we have with tremors, due to medication side effects, maracas so they could play music for him.'

Mrs Monroe takes notes.

Nickolas can't hold back his emotions any longer. 'Mr Phillips calls this place the Arkham Asylum, threatening to leave patients to urinate on themselves if they don't use the bathroom when he asks, and using the patients' pasts as a way to gossip about them behind their backs.'

'I see. And what was the incident that led to you punching Mr Phillips in front of the patients?'

'One of our patients was in the infirmary due to self-harm, it was...touch and go for a while. When I went to retrieve a meal for the patient, he made a comment about the patient needing to "get it right" the next time.'

Mrs Monroe stops writing, the magnitude of Brett's comment no doubt a shock. Nickolas waits for Mrs Monroe to prompt him to continue.

'Last night. From what I've been told, you were not working, and yet Miss Fraser called you. Why is that?'

He shuffles in his chair a little. 'Miss Fraser called me after she tried to reason with Mr Phillips. When I answered the phone, she was frantic due to the patient being in distress, knowing that Mr Phillips's treatment was only making the patient's fear escalate. The patient's file specifically stated that he was not to be restrained due to past trauma and that the best course of action is to talk to the patient and help calm him down, with sedation being the last resort. Miss Fraser was in the process of talking to the patient when Mr Phillips barged into the room. He had gone against what was written in the file, even after Miss Fraser tried to stop him by explaining the process of his treatment plan. When she went to release the patient from the restraints, she explained to me that Mr Phillips got aggressive and demanded that she leave the patient in that state. So, she called me for assistance.'

'So, when you arrived, what happened?'

'Mr Phillips was nowhere in sight, and Miss Fraser was waiting for me at the reception desk. She led me to the patient, who was at risk of slipping into a depressive state due to being restrained. The patient's stitches from his current wounds were slightly torn, but not to the point of causing additional damage. He was scared and, at the time of trying to talk to the patient to calm him, Miss Fraser explained what had happened that led to the patient being in that state of mind.'

'That then caused you to assault Mr Phillips?'

'Yes. I had warned hi—'

'Threatened.'

'*Warned* Mr Phillips multiple times about his behaviour. I suppose anger got the better of me after everything I had witnessed over the last week or so.'

'You suppose?'

All Nickolas could do is nod.

'So, you sought out Mr Phillips, kicked him from his chair where you repeatedly kicked his ribs, stomach, his face, with a final punch to the face before you were pulled off his body.' Mrs Monroe read from the notes written from when Brett was being interviewed. Nickolas was hoping, now more than ever, that the prick's nose was broken. Brett probably wouldn't have stayed to finish work though if it was.

Nickolas nods, palms sweating.

'From what Mr Phillips explained, the patient was aggressive and screaming for you when Mr Phillips tried to assist him. Any idea why that may be?'

Shit. Nickolas acts quickly. 'The patient had a nightmare about a traumatising moment he suffered a few weeks back. From what I know, I'm the only orderly aware of this due to the patient confiding in me. My best guess is he was scared and hoping I was around to talk to about the nightmare.'

'Mhmm. And do patients do that often? Confide in you?'

'Sometimes. This place can get pretty lonely. They tend to feel as if the only time someone wants to listen to them is when they have a session. Even then, it might not be a preferred topic of discussion. I try to talk to the patients. To make sure they don't lose the parts of themselves that keep them connected to the outside world. It's easier for them to adjust when they get released if they don't feel as though they will forever be seen as a patient.

'This patient. Am I right in assuming it is the same one Brett made a comment about that led you to punch him in the dining area?'

'Yes, ma'am.'

Mrs Monroe writes another note. 'Mr Phillips seems to believe the reason this patient was calling your name was due to a physical relationship you have formed.'

Fuck. Nickolas scratches his eyebrow. 'Mr Phillips thinks, just because the patient and I are both gay, that any kind or friendly behaviour that I have expressed means we must be fucking. As I said, he's a homophobic moron who only sees in black and white.'

Mrs Monroe coughs. 'Final question. Mr Phillips has higher authority due to him working here longer than you; however, Miss Fraser still felt the need to call you.'

'As I said, Mr Phillips's actions were causing more harm to the patient than good. Higher authority or not, he was acting out of line, and Miss Fraser, who I have been training, saw the signs of mistreatment. So, she called me for help and assistance.'

'Thank you, Mr Markova. I'll be sure to speak to Miss Fraser, as well as some of the patients, before making my final decision.'

'If I may, does one of those patients happen to be the one that caused the disagreement between myself and Mr Phillips last night?'

'Yes. I will be speaking to Mr Cunningham at some point today. Will that be an issue?'

Nickolas shakes his head before the words leave his mouth. 'No, no, not at all. I'm just not sure the state he'll be in after last night.'

'I understand. I'll be sure to be delicate in my questioning.'

Nickolas gives a nod and stands once Mrs Monroe rises, who then opens the door and exits, expecting Nickolas to follow. Back in the break room, Dot is knitting a scarf and Brett is sitting at the table, cowering in pain, not speaking a word or looking at anyone in the room.

'Ms Whittle, if you wouldn't mind finding Finn Cunningham for me, I'd like to have a word with him if that's okay?' instructs Mrs Monroe.

'Of course,' says Dot.

'Also, it has come to my attention that other patients may have some information they may care to share. If any of them would wish to speak to me, please let them know that my door is open, and that any information will be confidential and anonymous.'

Brett's head shoots up, eyes locked on Mrs Monroe before they flick to Nickolas, a glare so cold that under anyone else, they would tremble. Nickolas takes it as a sign of fear.

'Mr Markova, I believe you're not working till later today. So, you're free to go home. If I need to speak with you again, I'll do so when you return for your shift. Mr Phillips, go home. I'll call if I need to speak with you further. In the meantime, I'll be speaking with Miss Fraser after I have spoken with the patients as well as you, Ms Whittle.' And just like that, Mrs Monroe turns around to leave.

Brett stands, bag in hand and walks out. It's the first time Nickolas has had the pleasure of seeing the guy go home silenced.

'Do you know which other patients Mrs Monroe was referring to?' Dot asks.

'Ethan, Alex. Those are just the ones I was witness to Brett tormenting,' Nickolas explains.

Dot hums. 'I'll go around, see if anyone else wants to speak out. You better head home. Get your clothes. Are you going to be okay to work a double tonight?'

'I got some sleep last night. I should be fine.'

Without another word, they both leave the break room, Dot heading towards the patients while Nickolas heads back out to his car. He's surprised to see it's still parked with no ticket on the windscreen after leaving it at the entry, right beside the fountain late last night. Nickolas only has two hours before he is due back to start his shift. A lot can happen in two hours when it comes to deciding the fate of his career. He tries not to think about it as he drives home and walks inside his apartment.

He quickly gives Socks a cuddle, lifting the furball into his arms as she purrs into his neck. Nickolas places his cat on the bed as he grabs a fresh uniform. He will have to do a load of laundry tomorrow before his shift starts – that's if he still has a job. He showers, eats, packs some food in his bag, and then gets back in the car to make the drive over to the centre.

*

Once changed, Nickolas makes his way towards the common room. Everyone is going on with their day as if nothing has happened. In hindsight, besides Finn and the orderlies, no one would be aware of the mess that is unfolding behind closed doors. But Nickolas also isn't sure how many patients have spoken to Mrs Monroe since he left, if any, and word can spread quickly between patients when things happen outside of routine.

Dot is crouching down in front of Ethan. Alex and Ryder are casually chatting away. Darren is doing craft with some of the other patients while Sky and Hayley are setting up for lunch. Finn is sitting in a corner, curled into Cora's side, not a word being said between them. Nickolas wants to go over to Finn so badly, but right now, all eyes are on him. He needs to wait for the right moment. Instead, he tells Darren to go on a break, sending Hayley off as well. Eric walks through the common room doors, working the afternoon shift alongside Nickolas. Sky's working a double, so he figures she will want a break later in the day to help space out the shift.

'Lunch is served, slowly make your way into the dining area to collect your tray,' Nickolas calls out. Finn hasn't looked his way since he walked through the common room door. He hopes whatever happened with Mrs Monroe isn't the reason for Finn ignoring him. Lunch is a simple pumpkin soup with bread and butter. Nickolas eyes the room, hoping he'll lock eyes with Finn for a brief moment, long enough to be able to get a sense if he's is okay or not, but that moment never comes. Dot signals for Eric and Sky to keep a watch while she ushers Nickolas back into the common room to talk. Dot points for him to take a seat and suddenly his mouth is dry.

'So far, five patients have spoken up about Brett. Finn, Alex, and Ethan included in that mix.'

'Who else?'

'Sasha and Chris.'

Nickolas doesn't know much about Chris. The patient keeps to himself and is not very talkative when Nickolas has tried to include him in conversations, but if Chris is speaking out about Brett, that could be why he was always hesitant towards Nickolas.

'Jesus.' Nickolas rubs the back of his neck.

'I've spoken with Mrs Monroe and so has Lydia. As much as Brett wants to throw you under the bus, and don't get me wrong, this does not excuse you for acting the way you did, at this point, it does look like his actions speak greater than yours.'

Nickolas exhales, unaware that he had been holding his breath this whole time. He nods, taking a moment to process that he may still be walking away today with his job intact. 'How's, ah...how's Finn?'

'He's shaken up. Reserved. He did well with Mrs Monroe, but until about an hour before you arrived, he didn't even want to speak with his friends.'

'Did he go to his session with Dr Hale?'

Dot nods.

Now more than ever Nickolas wants to be able to pull Finn aside and see for himself that he is okay.

Conversation over, Dot goes to the break room, since today is technically her off day, leaving Nickolas to set up the common room for group while everyone finishes eating.

In a world of his own, thoughts racing through his mind, Nickolas doesn't even notice that lunch is finishing up until some of the patients take their usual seats in the room. Finn is walking towards him, head low, arm in arm with Cora. There are too many people around to be able to talk to Finn, so Nickolas offers to help escort the other patients back to their rooms. As Dr Hale walks through the door, Nickolas sends Sky on break. He asks Darren to stand guard while Hayley and Eric are on laundry duty. Nickolas goes to the bathroom, his bladder screaming at him to take a piss. When he comes out, he grabs a bottle of water and is about to read over some paperwork when Mrs Monroe comes back into the room.

'Ah, Mr Markova. Just who I was looking for.' Her tone gives nothing away.

Nickolas gulps the water down and follows Mrs Monroe back to the therapist rooms. He takes a seat across from her.

Mrs Monroe sorts some papers before clasping her hands together and places them on top of the desk, then holds Nickolas's gaze longer than he feels comfortable with.

'As of today, Mr Phillips no longer works for this centre and I will see to it that he never gets hired in this field of work ever again.'

Nickolas's eyebrows shoot up. That was not the result he was expecting but one he is more than happy with.

'After speaking with you, I spoke with Mr Cunningham. His recollection of last night's incident matched up with yours and Miss Fraser's story more than Mr Phillips's. After then speaking with Alex, Sasha, and Chris, who on multiple accounts could recall mistreatment or offensive language directed towards them or about them, it was evident that you were telling the truth regarding your testimony towards Mr Phillips. What was most upsetting was to hear that Mr Phillips has been physically abusing one of your patients...Ethan, I believe his name is.' Mrs Monroe reads the notes to make sure the patient's name is correct before continuing.

Nickolas's mouth gapes open. 'Wait...Brett is the one who has been leaving bruises on Ethan?'

'Yes, I believe so. Ethan claimed that Mr Phillips would grab him and throw him around, trying to antagonise him in the hopes that one of Ethan's alters would make an appearance to protect him from Mr Phillips.'

'Holy shit.' Nickolas covers his mouth.

Mrs Monroe gives him a moment to process the information.

'In regards to your behaviour, after speaking with Ms Whittle, who spoke the world of you, as well as Miss Fraser and the patients, we have decided to write you up with a warning. However, due to the magnitude of this incident, if anything else were to be reported against you, you will be joining Mr Phillips in the world of unemployment, Mr Markova.'

'Yes, ma'am.'

'We do not tolerate violence of any kind, even when the means seem justifiable.' The look in Mrs Monroe's eyes suggests that Brett deserved more than the beatdown Nickolas gave him. But he understands from the stern tone that rules need to be followed.

'Yes. Understandable. It won't happen again.'

'Good. You are free to return to work. I hope I won't be seeing you in the near future, Mr Markova.'

Nickolas gives a polite nod and makes his way to the door. He goes looking for Dot to share his news, but after no success, he asks Jasmine, who informs Nickolas that Dot left for the day. He decides not to call. Most of Dot's day off has already involved needing to be at work, the exciting news can wait till tomorrow. He continues with the paperwork he had planned to tackle before Mrs Monroe pulled him into the make-shift office, completing it just as group is finishing, meaning Darren and Hayley are now heading home for the day.

Nickolas asks Eric to put the common room back in order, letting his colleague know that once finished, it might be best to float around and check in on everyone, especially those that may have spoken with Mrs Monroe today. He waits ten seconds after Eric and Sky are out of his sight before he heads towards Finn's room. This time Nickolas knocks and waits.

After a beat, Nickolas walks in, eyes landing on Finn curled into ball on the bed with headphones in his ears. Finn's back is to the door. He walks around so he is in Finn's line of sight and smiles when their eyes lock onto one another.

'Hey.' Nickolas stands there, his hands in his pockets.

Finn removes the AirPods and carefully sits up on the mattress, focusing on a loose string on the bedding rather than on Nickolas.

'I, ah, I tried to get a chance to speak with you today, make sure you were doing okay,' says Nickolas.

'I'm fine,' says Finn.

'Good, that's...I was worried. I mean, after last night...'

'It's whatever.'

'Okay. I guess I'll leave you to it.' Nickolas heads towards the door, walking slower than usual, hoping Finn will stop him.

'I'm sorry.'

'What?' Nickolas turns around, confused.

Finn's knees are pulled into his chest, arms wrapped around them. 'I'm sorry. If I hadn't—because of me you're going to get fired, right?' Finn's voice is beginning to break.

'Finn...'

'I called out for you. I know I shouldn't have, but I did. And then, and then when he—I had to fight back. I didn't want to be like that again – tied down and helpless. But now you're probably going to get fired because I was too scared to know the difference between my dream and reality. If I had just let him do it, then none of this—'

'Hey, hey, Finn. No. Listen to me, okay?' Nickolas kneels down. He doesn't touch Finn even though his body is screaming out for him to do so. 'I'm not getting fired.'

Finn's head rises, making eye contact.

The stormy green eyes finally looking back at him makes Nickolas's heart flutter.

'Brett got fired, not me. But even if I had been fired, I wouldn't have changed anything I did.'

'Nick—'

'I'm serious, Finn. I love my job, I do. But I—' He stops himself. He takes a breath and slowly reaches for Finn's hand, pleased that Finn doesn't pull away. 'What Brett did, he knew that went against your treatment plan and yet he did it anyway. When I saw you hurt and scared, I just had this anger inside of me and, honestly, Brett got off easy if you ask me.'

'I'm not worth losing your job over, Nickolas.'

'Yeah, you are.' Nickolas cups Finn's cheek and uses his thumb to wipe away a tear.

Finn closes his eyes and leans into Nickolas's palm.

'Is that why you were avoiding me today?'

Finn nods. 'Figured if you were leaving, I might as well get used to not speaking to you, or seeing you. Cora thought it had to do with what happened with Brett, so she stuck beside me like we were conjoined twins.'

'Finn. If today was my last day, I would have made sure I spent the whole day with you.' Nickolas lets those words sink it. He needs Finn to know how much he cares. 'Because of what happened though, I'm going to have a lot more eyes on me for a while. Which means...'

'Which means you can't be seen always talking and being around me.' Finn deflates.

'Yeah...' Nickolas takes his hand away.

Silence falls between them.

'Thank you...for staying with me last night. It was kind of nice, considering...'

Nickolas tilts his head down to mask his blush, his eyes casting up at Finn as a playful smirk appears on Nickolas's face. 'I didn't take you for a little spoon kind of guy, but...it was nice.'

Finn pushes at his shoulder and they both let out soft chuckles.

Finn blushes. 'Probably the best sleep I've had in a while.'

'Me too.' Nickolas notes the time on his watch. He stands, Finn's eyes watching every move he makes. 'I better go. But I'm working night shift, so...'

'So, I'll see you tonight?'

'Course.'

Finn smiles, face lighting up. It's the first real smile Nickolas has seen all day.

'You still got enough power on that thing?' Nickolas points at the iPod.

'Should last me till tonight. Then it might need charging.'

'I'll take it home with me before I leave in the morning. Bring it back when I come in for work.'

Nickolas leaves Finn's room and, for the first time that day, he feels calm and at peace.

*

Dinner goes smoothly. Ethan opens up to some of the patients, smiling and laughing with them. It's the first time Nickolas has ever seen Ethan interact like that. Nickolas catches Finn's eye once or twice, looking down and scratching his bottom lip with his thumb in the hopes that no one catches him smiling back.

*

With the patients showered and back in their rooms, Nickolas makes his way towards the reception desk. As he begins checking off the med cart, Sam and Lydia walk through the doors and the phone rings. With Sam not yet on the clock, Nickolas answers, putting on his best customer service voice.

'Nickolas? It's Jessica.'

'Oh. Hey.'

'How's Finn?'

'He's, uh, he's doing really well. His wounds are healing and the adjustment to his meds seems to be working. He had a nightmare last night which had him a bit shaken up, but other than that, he's doing good.' Telling Jessica what happened after the nightmare would only cause questions to arise regarding Finn's fear of restraints, and that wasn't his story to tell, it was Finn's.

'That's amazing.' There is a hitch in Jessica's voice. 'Can you, can you tell him we miss him? And that we love him more than anything?'

'Sure.'

'Is, ah, can we come up and visit him on Sunday?'

'Did you have a think about what I said?' His tone is harsh. He doesn't mean for it to be, but Finn is improving and the last thing his patient needs is a setback because Jessica and the rest of his family are behaving selfishly.

'I did. And trust me, I'm not used to being told what to do. I've had to take charge for so long that following orders took me a while. But you were right.'

'I get it. He's your brother. But the Finn you know and the Finn that came in here are two different people. The Finn that has to learn to deal with being bipolar, the one that will be taking medication for the rest of his life while tracking his moods and learning to trust people enough to confide in them with his diagnosis, that's the person you're going to have to learn to live with too. And that doesn't mean baby and coddle him. It just means learning to accept things are going to be different and there is nothing wrong with being different.'

Jessica sniffs a couple of times. 'You're right. I've kinda been fucking up in that area.' Jessica huffs out a laugh.

'Guess I'll see you Sunday then.'

'You will. Thanks, Nickolas.'

Sam comes out, taking a seat at the front desk, with Eric and Sky following behind as they take their bags and leave for the night. Nickolas waves them goodbye, gives Sam a pat on the shoulder, and takes the med cart towards the patient corridor. When he gets to Ethan's room, Nickolas hands over the anti-depressants while trying to find the right words to say.

'It's okay. You don't have to say anything,' Ethan interjects.

'No, Ethan. It's not okay. I can't—I'm—' Nickolas stumbles.

'It's not your fault that it happened.'

'But it's my fault that we didn't stop it. That we didn't even notice what was happening.'

'Nickolas. You can't control everything that happens in this world. I know you try, but Brett had ways around it. Ways to make sure no one noticed.'

'Don't excuse his actions.'

'I'm not. Trust me. I was so scared every time he was working and it wasn't because I was worried about the new bruise that would arise. I was worried that one day it would work, that one of my alters would take over, and suddenly I'd be lost again, fighting to come back.'

'Do you—did he say why he was trying to get one of your alters to appear?'

'Why does anyone have a reason for anything they do when it comes to hurting someone...?' Ethan looks down at the empty paper pill cup. 'He was just another abusive asshole that took pleasure in hurting people in any way he could.'

'It's a fucked up world full of people just as fucked up, if not more. Still, that shouldn't have happened. And I'm sorry none of us were able to protect you from him.'

'Thank you...'

Nickolas shuffles on the spot a little. 'Well, if you need anything, I'm here.'

'I know.' Ethan gives a polite smile and goes back to reading his book.

Finn's room is Nickolas's final stop. A warm smile greets him, compared to the sombre look Finn had earlier today. He swallows his meds without complaint.

'Your tremors have eased up,' Nickolas points out.

'Finally.' Finn sighs.

'Everything else okay?'

'I think so. I can sleep, eat, jerk off.'

Nickolas blushes.

Finn throws a cocky smile Nickolas's way.

He coughs, thinking of Dot in a bikini to get his brain to stop sending blood to his dick. 'Did you—did you talk about the nightmare in your session today?'

Finn nods. 'Dr Hale believes it was due to the deep discussion we had in group that day. My mind was open to the past, causing me to feel vulnerable, ashamed, perhaps even scared of it happening again. I think it was more the shock of what happened after the nightmare than the nightmare itself that set me off. I was trying to remind myself where I was, that I wasn't in that room, with him; and then, to have Brett storm in and force me into restraints, just like that night...well, Dr Hale was extremely apologetic for what happened, but was pleased to see I was able to bounce back from it quicker than she thought I would.'

'Of course you would. You're a fighter.'

'Maybe. But I also had you by my side all night. And when I woke up, I felt safe. Calm.'

Nickolas sits on the end of Finn's bed, mindful of the time. He takes a deep breath. 'There's something I need to tell you.'

All of Finn's attention is focused on him 'Every time someone starts a sentence like that, it's never good news.'

Nickolas shuffles, nervous. 'I went to a club last night. Before I got called here, I, ah, I went out to drink because I didn't want to be alone at home with my thoughts.'

Finn's face shifts from panic to concern.

'Anyway, there were these guys.'

Finn's face drops. He knows what Finn must be thinking.

'One of them, he was bragging about this guy he had...fucked. Mostly talking out of his ass, but something about it caught my attention. He...' Nickolas bites his lip. 'He started to show some photos on his phone, to prove his story to his friends, and that's when I saw...that's when I saw pictures of...of you.'

Finn's face goes from confusion to realisation to something that looks like fear and sickness rolled into one.

'Photos...o-of me.'

'From that night.' That's all Nickolas has to say for Finn to understand. 'I confronted the guy and he may have left with a bloody nose, some bruised ribs along with no ID or phone. But I couldn't let him get away with what he did.' Nickolas rests his hand on top of Finn's, giving it a gentle squeeze.

'My saving grace,' Finn whispers the words, a single tear rolls down a freckled cheek.

Nickolas offers a soft smile. 'If...if you want, you can report him. His phone has the evidence, his ID has his name and address. This fucker deserves more than the beatdown I gave him.'

Whether Finn decides to file a report today, tomorrow, or in a week's time, those photos are enough to charge the asshole with rape and assault.

'Did you see them all? The photos?' Finn's voice is soft.

'Yeah.' He gives Finn's hand another squeeze, reassurance that what he saw doesn't change the way he feels about Finn.

'What did you see?'

'It doesn't matter. That's not what's important.'

'It is to me.' Finn's voice has dominance back in it.

'Finn.'

'Tell me. I need—I need to know.'

Nickolas takes a breath and relays to Finn the montage of photos. He leaves out no details, being completely honest, because that's what he'd want Finn to do for him.

'Fuck.' Finn removes his hand from Nickolas's, running fingers through his freshly washed hair, head down, as tears begin to fall.

'I can't believe you saw me like that.' Finn hides in shame.

'Don't do that. When I look at you now, I don't see what I saw in those photos. I never have.'

'I...I need to get tested. You said you saw...'

'We can do that. I can organise Lexi to give you a blood test.'

Finn nods, taking a deep breath in and out before making eye contact with Nickolas.

'What do you think would happen? If I report him?' Finn's eyes are red and puffy.

'If he's found guilty, he'd get locked up for up to thirty years. They'd have to prove it, though. Not just with the photos but with video surveillance footage from the clubs, maybe some witnesses. But I don't think that should stop you from at least trying. Run his name through the mud so he's put on the sex offenders list. Let everyone out there know what this fucker has done to make sure it never happens to anyone else again, ya know.'

Finn nods. 'I'll think about it.'

'There's no rush, Finn.' Nickolas goes to stand. 'I should probably head back.'

Finn reaches out and grabs his wrist. 'Wait.' Finn doesn't let go. 'Before you go, can you tell me why you went out? What thoughts you were running away from?' That look of fear is back on Finn's face.

'If you're thinking it had to do with you, then stop.' Nickolas smiles.

Finn's face relaxes.

'I was trying to read Mandy's journal. But I couldn't. And being in the house with it sitting there, taunting me. I just had to get out.'

'I can help.'

Nickolas cocks an eyebrow.

'I can help with reading her journal. If you want. I can either read it for you, or to you. I can read it and tell you what it says, or even just sit here with you while you read it, just in case.'

Nickolas bites his bottom lip.

'Think about it. All I'm saying is that I'm here for you too. And if, if it's something you can't do alone, just know that you don't have to be.'

Nickolas changes the subject. 'Are you going to be okay? For me to leave, I mean.'

'I should be. You're here all night so, I have that to comfort me.'

'I know what I told you is a lot, and I hate that I added more on top of everything after what happened yesterday, but I couldn't keep it from—'

'Thank you. Thank you for telling me, for doing what you did. You could have gotten arrested and yet you still went after him.'

'I may not be able to erase what happened, but I'd sure like to help you move forward from it...same way you're helping me.' Finn lets go of his wrist. 'Oh, one last thing. Jessica wanted me to tell you that she misses you and that she loves you.' Nickolas's heart flutters as the L-word leaves his lips.

Finn smiles.

Nickolas pushes the med cart back towards the reception desk. He's in a world of his own as he walks into the break room, thinking about what Finn said. Maybe having Finn beside him while he reads Mandy's journal might not be such a bad idea.

He takes a can of coke out of the fridge and microwaves his food. He stands in silence, watching the numbers count down, lost in his thoughts. Once he is sitting at the table with his drink and food, Lydia decides to speak.

'What happened?'

Nickolas takes a bite of his food to buy himself time. 'Brett got fired. I got a warning. One more and I'm out.' He keeps his eyes down, knowing that an email will be going out to the staff tonight so everyone will be aware of the situation. They'll be short-staffed for a while, but as of right now, none of that is Nickolas's concern.

'That's, that's amazing. Right?'

'Right.'

'Then why are you acting like someone told you to pack your bags?'

'Because that fucker got away with so much before someone actually pulled him up on it.' Nickolas drops his fork, the metal making a clanking sound against his plate. 'These patients come here for help. They come here to get away from the people who mistreat them. The people who try to take advantage of them because they don't understand their disorder, or worse, people who do understand and think they can get away with abusing them because they are different.' Nickolas clenches his teeth. 'They...they trust us to help them, and yet Brett got away with betraying them. He said terrible things, he...he did things, and it would have kept happening if it weren't for...' He exhales.

'If it weren't for you worrying about Finn.' Lydia finishes Nickolas's sentence. 'You think this would have kept happening if Finn hadn't been hurt.' Lydia's voice drips with sadness.

'If Brett had done that to any other patient, you never would have called me. I never would have beaten the shit out of him and all those patients that were being hurt or mistreated never would have come forward. Ethan...God, Ethan would still be living in fear every time Brett was working.'

'Not true. If I witnessed Brett go against a treatment plan for any of these patients, I would have called someone. Maybe not you, but someone who could have helped with the situation.'

Nickolas ignores Lydia's words, too busy feeling the rage build inside of him.

'Nickolas.'

'I'm angry, okay? I'm angry because it happened. I'm angry because he got away with it for so long and I'm angry that it took someone I care about getting hurt to make me step up and do something about it.'

'Hey. It wasn't just you that prick was fooling. It was all of us. So, you're not the only one allowed to carry all the guilt. Not this time.'

'But why now? Why didn't I report him when he called Ethan "Jekyll and Hyde"? Or every time he made some "fag" comment towards Darren, or myself?'

'Because you love him.'

Nickolas's eyes shoot up, looking like a deer's been caught in headlights.

'You took the jokes and the hate because you could handle it. And when you couldn't handle it, part of you thought you deserved it. But once you saw Brett go after someone you care about, someone you love...There is no stopping someone when they want to protect the person they love.'

Nickolas looks down, pulling a loose thread from his top. Is that what he feels when he is with Finn? When he thinks about Finn and his chest tightens and a smile forms on his face. The only person he has ever loved is Mandy, but love between family is different from love between two people, two strangers. Can he still call Finn a stranger? It's been just over a week, but Finn knows more about him than the people he has worked with for over a year. Finn knows more than any person

Nickolas has fucked and any family member that wasn't his baby sister. Whether it had been two minutes, two days, two weeks, or months. Nickolas just knew. He knew Finn was important to him. Sometimes it just takes longer for the head to catch up to the heart.

'You going to tell him?'

'What? No! I can't. I don't even—what if—'

'Nickolas. You'd have to be blind to think Finn doesn't feel the same way. I was with you both for five minutes and what I saw was deeper than anything I've experienced in my life.'

Nickolas sighs. 'What if it's just this place?'

Lydia looks confused.

'What if, once Finn leaves, he realises it wasn't me he liked, just my company.'

'Love comes with risks. The fear of finding out if the other person loves you is one of the hardest parts. But it's also the most rewarding.'

Nickolas shakes his head. 'I can't. Not...not while he's here. The last twenty-four hours have been a lot for Finn. Throwing this at him, it wouldn't be fair.'

'And that right there shows just how selfless you are. Putting his needs before your own.'

Nickolas scoffs. He goes back to eating, the food now cold, and his stomach no longer hungry, but he needs to eat. He downs his coke, belching from the fizz, and takes his plate to the sink.

'I'll do first check,' says Nickolas.

Lydia smirks. 'Say hi to Finn for me.'

'That's not...whatever.' Nickolas huffs out of the room.

A few of the patients are still awake, lying in bed, looking up at the ceiling or outside their window. Nothing too alarming, so Nickolas lets them be. When he gets to room thirteen, he stops. Finn is fast asleep, turned towards the door so Nickolas can see the softness on Finn's face, his head on the pillow with the blanket pulled up. Nickolas decides he'll retrieve the iPod in the morning before leaving, so he doesn't disturb Finn from his sleep. He's pleased to see him finally resting.

As he makes his way back towards the break room, Lydia's words play over in his head. He isn't ready to label this feeling he has for Finn. He's not sure if it's because he's too scared or if it's because he has nothing to compare it to, but he does find himself wondering if this feeling is what others call love.

What he does know is he has spent his whole life running. Running from who he is, who he was, and who his father wanted him to be. He has been running from the pain, the guilt, the regret. There are billions of people in this world and yet here he is, just doing his job and all it took was one person to come into his life and make him want to stop running.

12. Saturday

Nickolas barely makes it to his bedroom before he falls face first onto the mattress. Finn was still sleeping when it was time for him to leave, and Nickolas didn't have the heart to wake his sleeping beauty. He was able to sneak in and take the iPod so he could charge it and lay a soft kiss on Finn's forehead before walking back out.

At Sock's persistent meowing, Nickolas gets up to fill her food bowl. He then decides to quickly shower before he crawls under the blanket, Socks curling up beside him, falling asleep the second his head hits the pillow.

*

His bladder feels like it's about to explode. Nickolas isn't even sure if he has the ability to stand and walk towards the bathroom or if he should just piss the bed and deal with the clean-up. Once he wakes up enough for his common sense to kick in, he makes his way towards the bathroom, sighing in relief as his stream hits the water in the toilet bowl. He throws his washing in the dryer and then heads into the kitchen for a glass of water. His eyes catch the time on the microwave, and he figures he could still get a few more hours of sleep that his body desperately needs to catch up on. He heads back to bed, only needing a few minutes before he's softly snoring again.

Around five p.m., Nickolas stretches in bed, his body feeling refreshed and ready for the night ahead. It's been a while since he's been able to get eight hours of sleep, but his body is thankful for it. He shuffles into the kitchen, making a pot of fresh coffee and cooks a couple of eggs. Nickolas sits down to eat, turning the TV on in the background. The evening news is discussing some shooting. The reporter moves on to a robbery, and by the time Nickolas is finished eating they're mentioning a murder that took place in the North. The stories have one thing in common, they are all about those in privileged areas. 'Typical' Nickolas chides. Almost all the kids in the South Side are being abused, where is that story? What about the night a gay kid got put in the hospital due to Nickolas's father's instructions? That never made the news. A gun goes off every hour like clockwork in the South Side, not a word about it gets mentioned. Those are the stories they need to report on because those are the issues that will make a difference if the right people step up and help. As the weather report comes on, his eyes land on the box with Mandy's belongings. Nickolas drops his fork, leans back in his chair, and simply looks at it. He doesn't know what he is expecting. Perhaps it will vanish into thin air. Maybe the lid will miraculously spring off, Mandy's journal landing open in front of him, leaving him no choice but to keep looking through it. Socks meows at him, breaking Nickolas out of his thoughts. He pushes his chair back; the legs screeching against his floorboards and makes his way into the kitchen to clean up and pack himself food for dinner.

The beep of the dryer goes off. Nickolas folds his clothes, ninety percent of them being purple uniforms while the rest are his boxers. He puts them away, but packs one set in his backpack, and sets out to brush his teeth and do his hair. By the time he's ready to leave, Nickolas puts the iPod and food into his backpack before heading towards the door. With his hand on the doorknob, he stops. If he overthinks it, he'll talk himself out of it. He'll be late for work if he waits any longer, so Nickolas turns around, pushes the lid off the cardboard box, takes Mandy's journal, shoves it into his backpack and storms out towards his car, feeling as though he's carrying bricks inside his bag.

*

Dot and Jasmine are chatting at the front desk, too busy looking at paperwork to see Nickolas walking towards them.

'Honestly, I don't even know where to begin,' says Dot.

'With what?' Nickolas chimes in, his eyes glancing at what looks to be résumés.

'Finding a replacement for Brett...and Jasmine.' Dot sighs that last part.

'It's not like I won't be back,' offers Jasmine.

'I know, but in the meantime, I have to find someone that can live up to your workmanship,' explains Dot.

'Anyone good?' It'll be Nickolas's job to train whoever Dot decides to hire, so he'd like to see who he'll be dealing with before the final decision is made.

'Define *good*.'

Jasmine buzzes Nickolas through. He changes into his uniform, and as he pulls his food out of his bag, Mandy's journal is staring at him. He shoves his bag into his locker and tells himself to ignore it. The break room is empty as Hayley and James help the patients finish up with their showers and get the med cart ready. Nickolas puts his food away, eyeing what looks to be banana bread on the table, and cuts himself a slice.

Enjoying the sweet flavour of banana, maple syrup, and coconut, he shoves the last bite into his mouth as Dot steps into the room.

'I figured you could use a treat after yesterday,' explains Dot.

'You're rewarding me?' asks Nickolas.

'As disappointed as I am that you used your fists once again while working, I am relieved to see Brett gone.'

There is a compliment in there somewhere, but the words still cut him deep. He looks up to Dot, and the last thing he would ever want is to let her down. That's why hiding what's going on between him and Finn is killing him. Dot is the one person he wants to tell most in the world and yet, he can't bring himself to face what his boss and friend might say about it if he does.

'Everything seems in order for tomorrow. Darren and Sky will help with the visitors, and you have James helping you for the first hour.'

'Why do I feel like I'm being spoken to as if it's my first time being left unattended?'

Dot stops moving around and looks towards Nickolas.

'Because last Sunday was rough. Not only on Finn, but on you too. And this time I'm not going to be here to help.'

Nickolas swallows so hard he's sure Dot can see it. Does tomorrow really mark a week since he walked into Finn's room, finding him lying in a pool of blood? A shiver runs down his spine. So much has happened within a small timeframe that it causes Nickolas to feel light-headed.

'I'll be fine.' His voice sounds weaker than he wants it to be.

Dot steps closer, making sure not to crowd Nickolas's personal space. 'I know you will. And I know you'll have Finn's back if his family visits again and things go haywire.'

'You don't think he'd—'

'No. No, Dr Hale strongly believes it was an imbalance of his medication and he has been making wonderful progress in his sessions. However, that doesn't mean tomorrow will be easy. It'll be the first time seeing his family since the incident and, how they react could cause a trigger. So, just...'

Dot doesn't have to finish the sentence. They both know that he'll make sure Finn feels in control tomorrow. Nickolas will be ready to help take Finn out of any situation that may be upsetting.

Laughter from James and Hayley snaps Nickolas out of his thoughts as they walk past the break room, heading towards their lockers to grab their belongings and head home.

'Med cart is checked, either yourself or Lydia can go and deliver it,' Dot explains.

Nickolas nods as Dot gives his arm a gentle squeeze for reassurance.

'I'll see you on Monday,' Dot calls out to Nickolas while exiting the room.

Lydia slides past Dot while making a beeline for the coffee machine. 'I tell ya, nothing better than spending your Saturday night working instead of going out drinking and dancing with friends.' Lydia drinks half of the freshly brewed coffee in one gulp.

'Even if I wasn't working, I wouldn't be doing that,' states Nickolas.

'Right. Sorry. You're not into the whole "going out and having fun" kind of thing.'

'Have you met me? In what world would dancing with friends be classed as fun?'

'Fine, going out drinking and getting laid.'

'That sounds more like my Saturday night.' Nickolas thumbs his nose. 'But I still wouldn't be doing that if I had the night off.' He rushes towards the door so he can grab the med cart.

'Because of Finn?'

Nickolas freezes, hoping everyone's already gone home and didn't hear what Lydia said. He turns back around, not surprised to see a smug look on her face. 'Not that it's any of your business, but I haven't been...'

Lydia cocks an eyebrow.

'Even if...I'm not saying...For fuck's sake, it's been a while, okay. You happy?'

Lydia's smirk says it all. 'Well, I'm sure the wait will be worth it once you and Finn...connect.'

'Jesus Christ, I'm leaving.' He walks out of the room, but not quick enough, as he can still hear Lydia's chuckles.

'It's cute how you're saving yourself for him.'

He gives Lydia the finger and it only makes her laugh louder.

Nickolas tries to shake off the blush before he gets to Sam at the reception desk.

'How're things going tonight, Sammy?'

'Well, I'm here. So that's a good sign, I guess.'

Nickolas chuckles. He pats Sam on the back and heads off to do the rounds. It's quick. All the patients seem to be tired or not in the mood to chat, which works for Nickolas.

As he enters Finn's room, it's almost as if he's coming home.

'Hey, stranger.' Finn smiles up at him and suddenly, all his worries vanish.

'Whatever. It hasn't been that long since I was last here. Besides, I actually need to sleep if I want to function, which means I have to go home at some point.'

'If I recall, you slept here just fine the other night.'

Nickolas recalls perfectly. But it's not something they can do again while Finn is still a patient.

'Either way, it feels like it's been forever since I saw you. Especially when you sneak into my room early in the morning and don't even say goodbye.' A playful smile appears on Finn's face.

'Don't know what you're talking about.' Nickolas hands Finn his meds, the cup of water and notices some tape on Finn's inner arm. 'You got your blood test today?

'Yep. Dr Winslow said I should have the results back by Monday.' There's hesitancy on Finn's face. Nickolas decides for a more playful topic of discussion.

'So, would you have rather me sneak into your room or leave you with a dead iPod?'

Finn acts as though the question is a tough decision to make.

Nickolas tries to ignore how cute Finn's facial expression is.

'Fine, iPod please.' Finn holds his hands out.

'I may have left it in my locker.'

'Well, what are you waiting for then?' The tone of Finn's voice lets Nickolas know it's all a game, but he can't help rolling his eyes at the way Finn's arms cross over his chest, acting like a child.

'What's in it for me?' Nickolas cocks an eyebrow.

'You saying my charming personality and dashing good looks aren't enough?'

Nickolas smiles at the adorable dork, watching Finn's eyes turn playful with a hint of lust in them. He looks at his watch, relieved he still has fifteen minutes before lights out. 'Fine. Let me take the cart back and I'll grab it for ya.' He smiles ear to ear from the look of joy that spreads across Finn's face.

Nickolas takes the cart back, then heads to his locker to retrieve the iPod. Mandy's journal is the first thing his eyes land on. He picks up the book which feels heavier than before and tucks it under his arm so he can get the iPod. He shoves his bag back in his locker, pushing down the anxious energy bubbling inside of him as he walks out with both items in hand. Nickolas lets himself into Finn's room, not bothering to knock.

'That was quick.' The playful smile falls from Finn's face while shuffling to the edge of the bed. 'Nick? You okay?'

Nickolas looks at the items in his hand. 'Can you—I need—fuck, um...this is Mandy's journal and, and I'm scared shitless to read it in case what I find tarnishes the memories I have of her.' His heart pounds in his chest. Tears threaten to fall, but he holds them back. 'Do you think you could...'

Nickolas doesn't know when Finn stood up and walked towards him. Finn's hands rest on top of his own, stopping them from shaking as he holds the journal so tight that his knuckles are turning white.

'Nickolas.'

How can the sound of Finn saying his name calm him instantly?

He looks up. Finn's emerald eyes match the colour of his t-shirt.

'Would you like me to read it for you?'

All Nickolas can do is nod.

'Then I will. Let me help you with this. You don't have to do it alone.'

Nickolas loosens his grip as relief washes over him. His hands slip away from the journal, leaving Finn to hold the weight of it. He exhales as he looks wordlessly into Finn's eyes, hoping the gratitude he feels is evident on his face.

Finn runs a hand down the hardcover, delicately, aware of how important the journal is, before taking Nickolas's hand and leading him to the bed.

The minute Nickolas's ass hits the mattress he can't sit still, too anxious.

'Listen to music.'

'What?' Nickolas turns towards Finn.

'Listen to some music while I read it. It'll help keep you distracted.' Finn hands over the AirPods.

'I can't...I should get back.' Nickolas's hands are sweaty. He rubs them on his legs but it doesn't help.

'Okay.'

If he wants to run, he knows Finn is going to allow it. But Nickolas is tired of running. He takes a deep breath and reaches out for the AirPods with shaking hands.

The lights go out and Nickolas takes comfort in being able to hide away in the darkness. The moon shines through the window, allowing Finn to still be able to read the words on the pages.

Finn settles back against the wall as Nickolas shoves the AirPods in his ears. He puts the iPod on shuffle, and turns the volume up as loud as his eardrums will allow. He lays back vertically on the mattress, his legs still touching the floor as he closes his eyes and gets lost in the music. Unaware of how much time has passed, he feels a sudden tap against his arm. On instinct, Nickolas's hand grabs for the arm, his eyes shooting open as they lock onto Finn. He quickly releases his grip, relieved to see Finn isn't startled or afraid that Nickolas grabbed him. He sits up, taking the AirPods out, and waits.

'You should read this,' says Finn.

Nickolas shakes his head. 'No. I—just tell me.'

'Do you trust me?'

He'd trust Finn with his life if he had to. 'Yes'

'Then you should read it. It's...dark, but I'm right here if you need me.' Finn holds the journal out.

Like ripping off a band aid, he takes the journal from Finn and opens it up to a random page. His eyes scan the paper, taking in every sketch and drawing, trying to analyse what it represents. He runs his hand over the words, some messy like they were written in anger, others soft, showing the sadness that was evident at the time of Mandy writing them.

Some of the pages are chaotic, making it seem as though Mandy's mind was trying to process everything at once and she couldn't get it onto the page quick enough. He wished that his sister would have opened up to him at least once about all the battles that she was fighting in her head. As he turns the pages, they get darker, a sign of Mandy giving up, feeling more trapped and alone. He stops as he gets to a page, their father's name scribbled at the top.

~~Dad~~

Dominic,

I don't know why I'm writing this, some part of my therapy or whatever, but I doubt it will fucking do anything. 'Write a letter to express how you feel about what your father did to you.' Yeah, cos a letter will fucking help. If me screaming at you, begging you to stop won't work, what's a letter going to do?

What the hell, have to show I'm trying, I guess...

So, I suppose I'll start by saying FUCK YOU, you worthless piece of shit. Our lives were bad enough having to grow up in the fucking South Side, trying to find food to eat and a way to keep warm, but then that wasn't enough. You had to take the one thing left that kept me separated from you. I WAS YOUR DAUGHTER! You were meant to protect me, but instead, you used me. Used me for your own sick, twisted pleasure till there was nothing left of me. You made me a shell, dead inside.

You made me feel worthless. Like I was a piece of trash that any guy had the right to use and throw away. God, this is so fucking stupid. What's done is done now. It can't be taken back. It can't be changed. You raped me! I got pregnant, and then I got an abortion all before the age of sixteen. Lucky me...

No one was ever going to love me once they found out the truth anyway...and in the meantime, I get to live with the pain of everything that happened. Live with the scars inside and outside of my body. Live my life knowing nothing will ever get better...

You know
my name,
not my Story...

Hold on
Hold on
Hold on
Hold on

Stay Strong

Be happy
Be happy
Be happy

I'm sorry
I'm such
a fuckup. I'm
sorry. I'm sorry.
I'm sor
I'm suc
a fuckup. I'm
sorry. I'm sorry.

I'm sorry
I'm such
a fuckup. I'm
sorry. I'm sorry.
I'm
I'm such
a fuckup. I'm
sorry. I'm sorry.

LIFE BEGINS AT THE END
HELP ME!

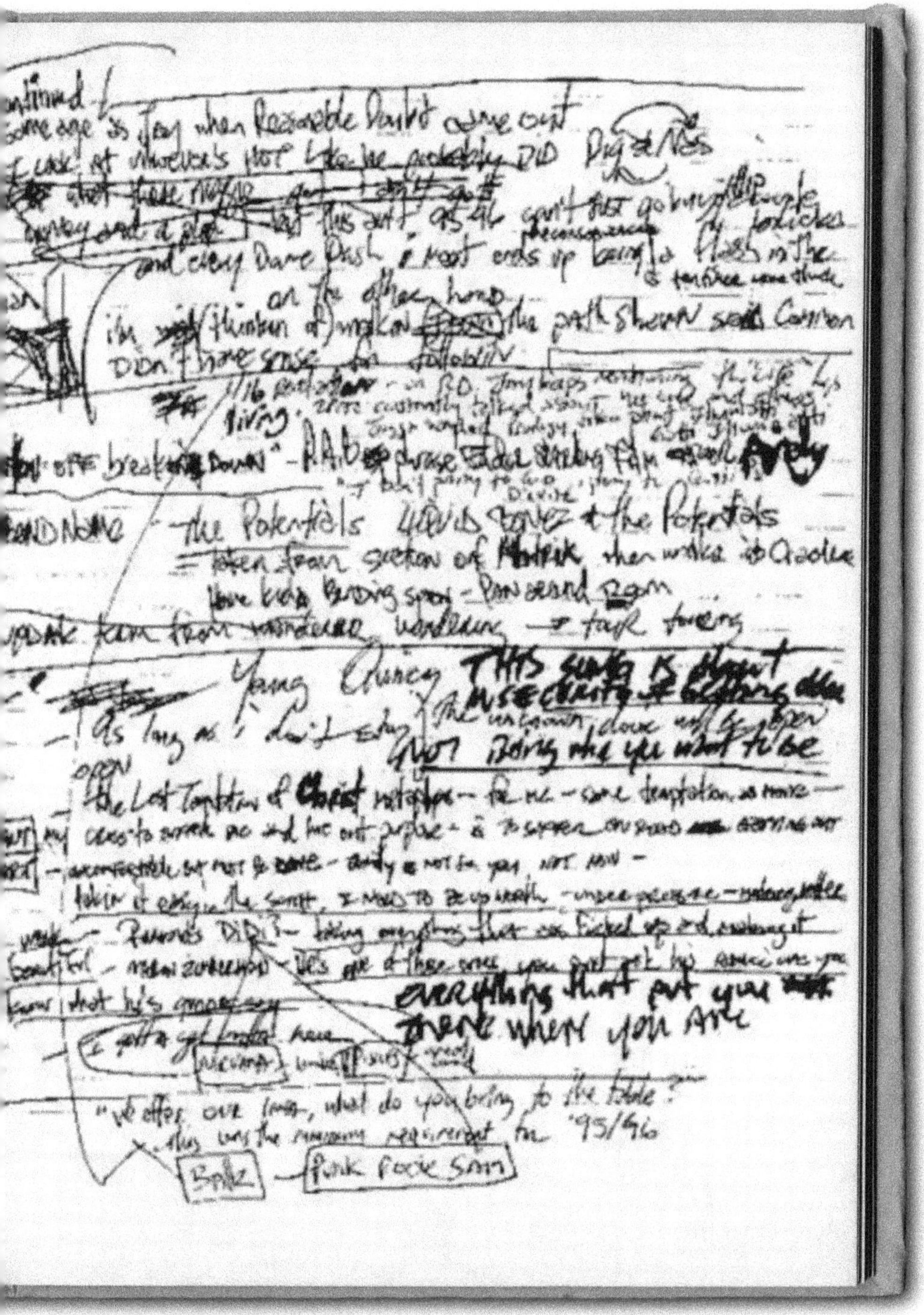

no
No
No
no
no
No
No
no
No

NEVER MIND

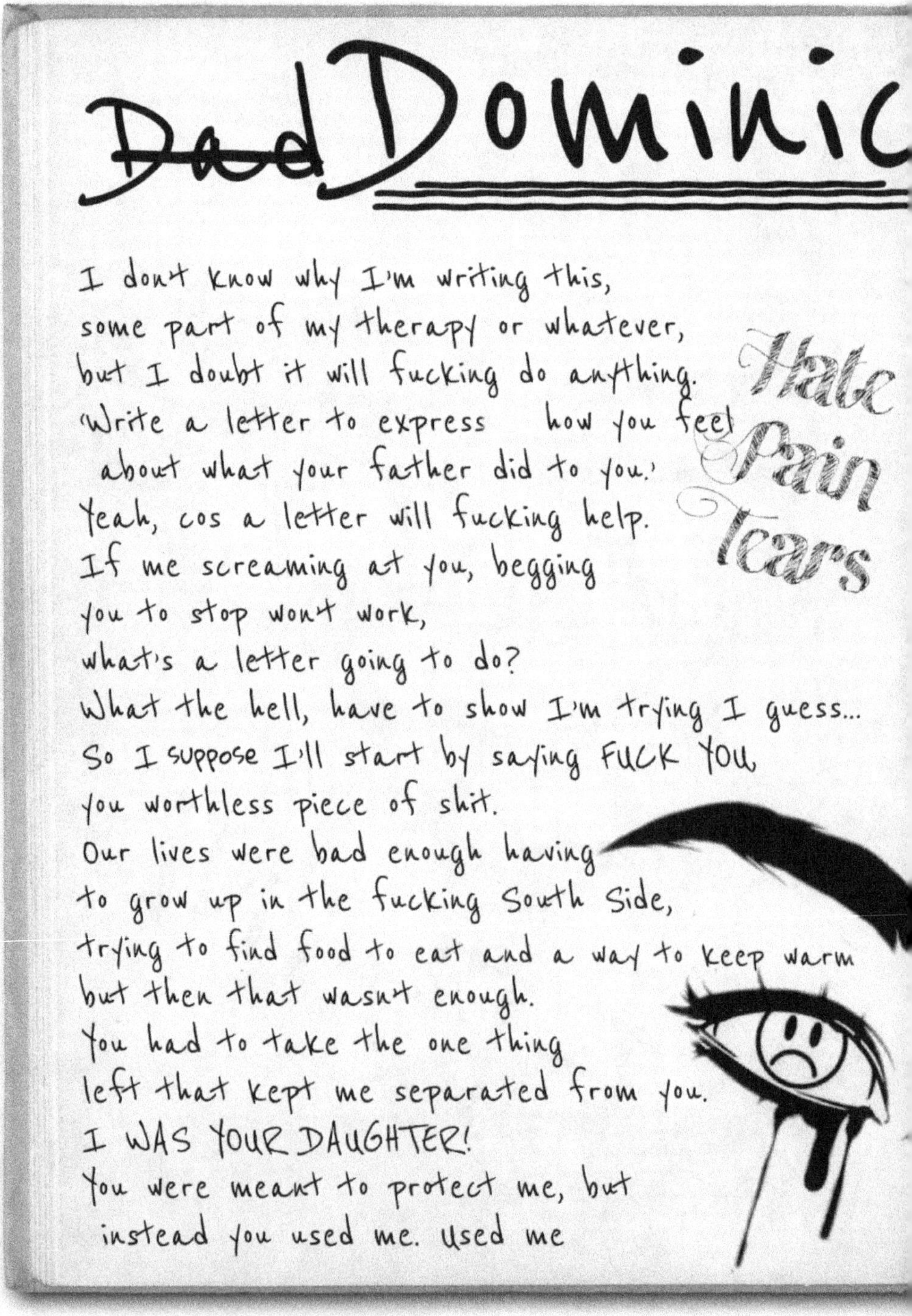

~~Dad~~ Dominic

I don't know why I'm writing this,
some part of my therapy or whatever,
but I doubt it will fucking do anything.
'Write a letter to express how you feel
about what your father did to you.'
Yeah, cos a letter will fucking help.
If me screaming at you, begging
you to stop won't work,
what's a letter going to do?
What the hell, have to show I'm trying I guess...
So I suppose I'll start by saying FUCK YOU,
you worthless piece of shit.
Our lives were bad enough having
to grow up in the fucking South Side,
trying to find food to eat and a way to keep warm
but then that wasn't enough.
You had to take the one thing
left that kept me separated from you.
I WAS YOUR DAUGHTER!
You were meant to protect me, but
instead you used me. Used me

for your own sick, twisted pleasure
till there was nothing left of me.
You made me a shell, dead inside.
You made me feel worthless.
Like I was a piece of trash that
any guy had the right to use and
throw away. God, this is so fucking
stupid. What's done is done now.
It can't be taken back.
It can't be changed. You raped me!
I got pregnant, and then I got an abortion
all before the age of sixteen.
Lucky me...

SCARS SCARS
SCARS

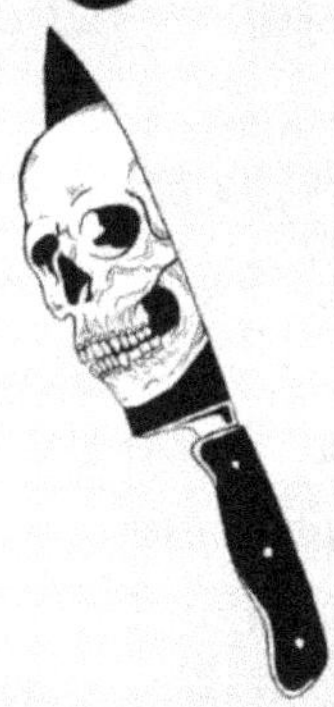

No one was ever going to love me
once they found out the truth anyway...
and in the meantime, I get to
live with the pain of everything
that happened. Live with the
scars inside and outside of my body.
Live my life knowing nothing will ever get better...

'I hope he gets what he deserves in prison. I hope someone makes Dominic their bitch and then slits his throat when they're done using him.' Nickolas's words are coming out ragged. 'He deserves to slowly choke on his own blood after what he did to her...to me...'

Finn lays a hand on Nickolas's knee, rubbing a thumb gently over his pants, and gives Nickolas the time he needs to process everything that's going through his mind. Nickolas lets out a breath and keeps reading. The pages get darker. Sadness. Anger. Hate. All those emotions bleeding through the pages and expressing the downward spiral his sister was heading towards. He gets to a page with a sketch of two hands clasping one another, exactly like the tattoo he got over his heart, and for a second, he can't breathe. He traces the outline just like how he does on his own body. He always told Mandy he would never let her fall; little did he know his sister drew it as a reminder of his promise. The rest of the page causes a knot to form in Nickolas's stomach and when he turns over to the next page, a gasp falls from his lips. Wings. Beautifully sketched angel wings in the centre of the page, with his name written at the top in Mandy's handwriting.

Nickolas,

If you're reading this, then it means I'm free. It means I finally did it and I'm now at peace. But if I know you, and I feel like I know you better than I know myself sometimes, then I know you're blaming yourself right now. So, I'm going to say this loud and clear, DON'T! Don't blame yourself for any of this. None of this is your fault, big brother. Not what Dominic did. Not what happened afterwards with the guys and the drinking. But most of all, not for me taking my own life.

You tried to save me, Nickolas. Over and over again, but each time you did, there was nothing left of me that was worth saving. I spent three years trying, for you, but I didn't have any fight left inside of me. It was hurting me each day I was alive, and I couldn't take any more pain. I'm sorry that I left you alone, that's my only regret, but deep down I know someone is out there who will make you feel whole again.

You were my guardian angel, big brother. My saving grace. And I know you'll help so many others from the darkness that is trying to consume them, but the light at the end of my tunnel is the one I'm not going to wake up from...

Just, please promise me that you'll stop running and start living. Fuck what Dominic said and fuck our good-for-nothing brothers. You're who you're supposed to be. You're the best thing about this fucked up world and one day you'll find someone who gets to share their world with yours. When that day comes, they'll be pretty fucking lucky.

It's okay if you're angry at me. It's okay if you hate me. I won't be upset if that's how you feel. I will be upset if you waste your life away. You're allowed to be happy, Nick. You're allowed to have a life. I'll be there watching, every step of the way, because nothing in this world could ever bring me the joy that I'd feel from seeing you happy and free.

So...I guess this is goodbye, big brother. It's okay...I'm okay with this decision. Nothing has ever made me feel more peace than knowing my time is finally coming to an end. Thank you for being the best brother a little sister could ever ask for.

Love you always, Mandy xx

EVERYTHING SUCK
everything feels empty now
Please Stop hurting me...

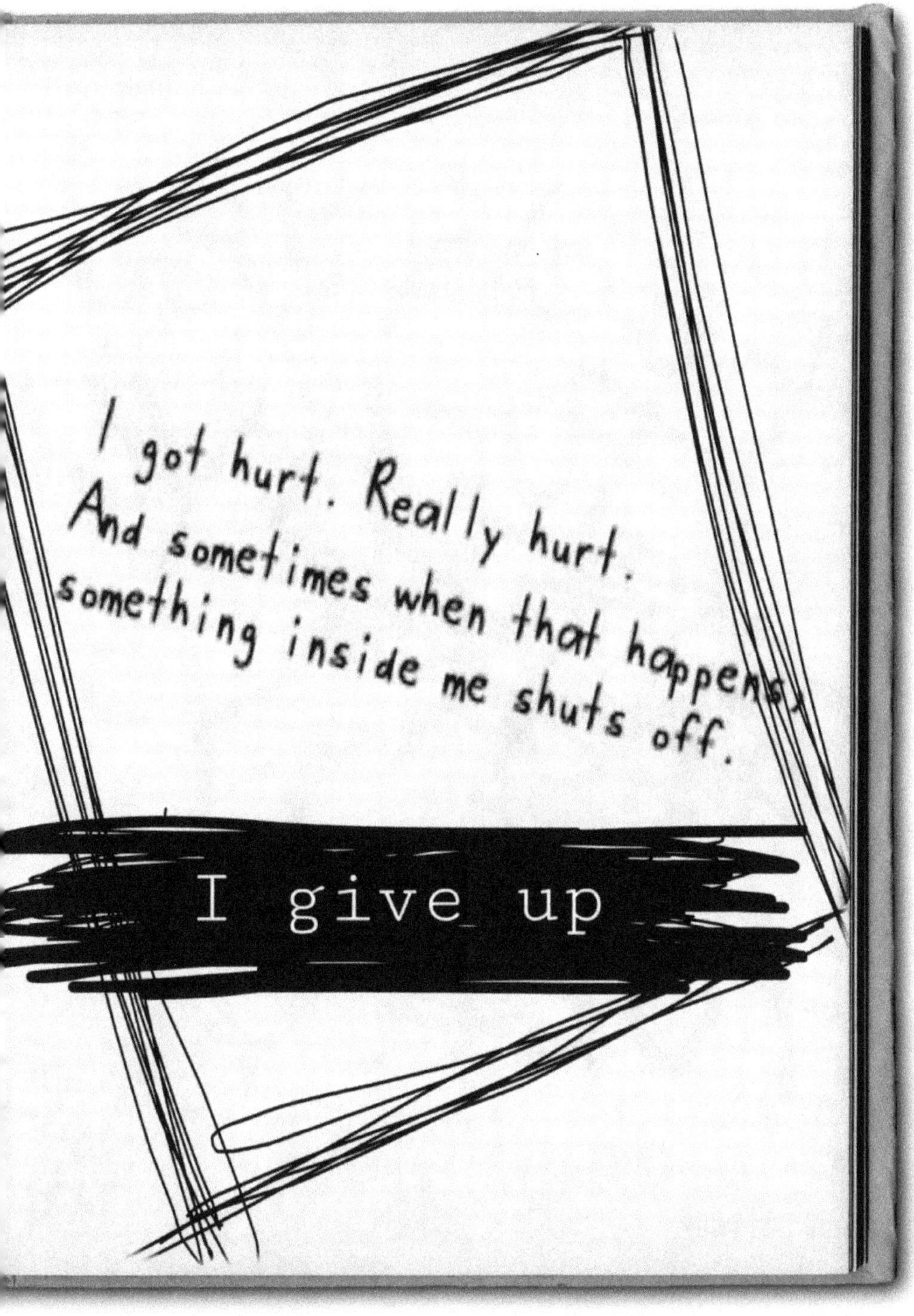
I got hurt. Really hurt.
And sometimes when that happens,
something inside me shuts off.
I give up

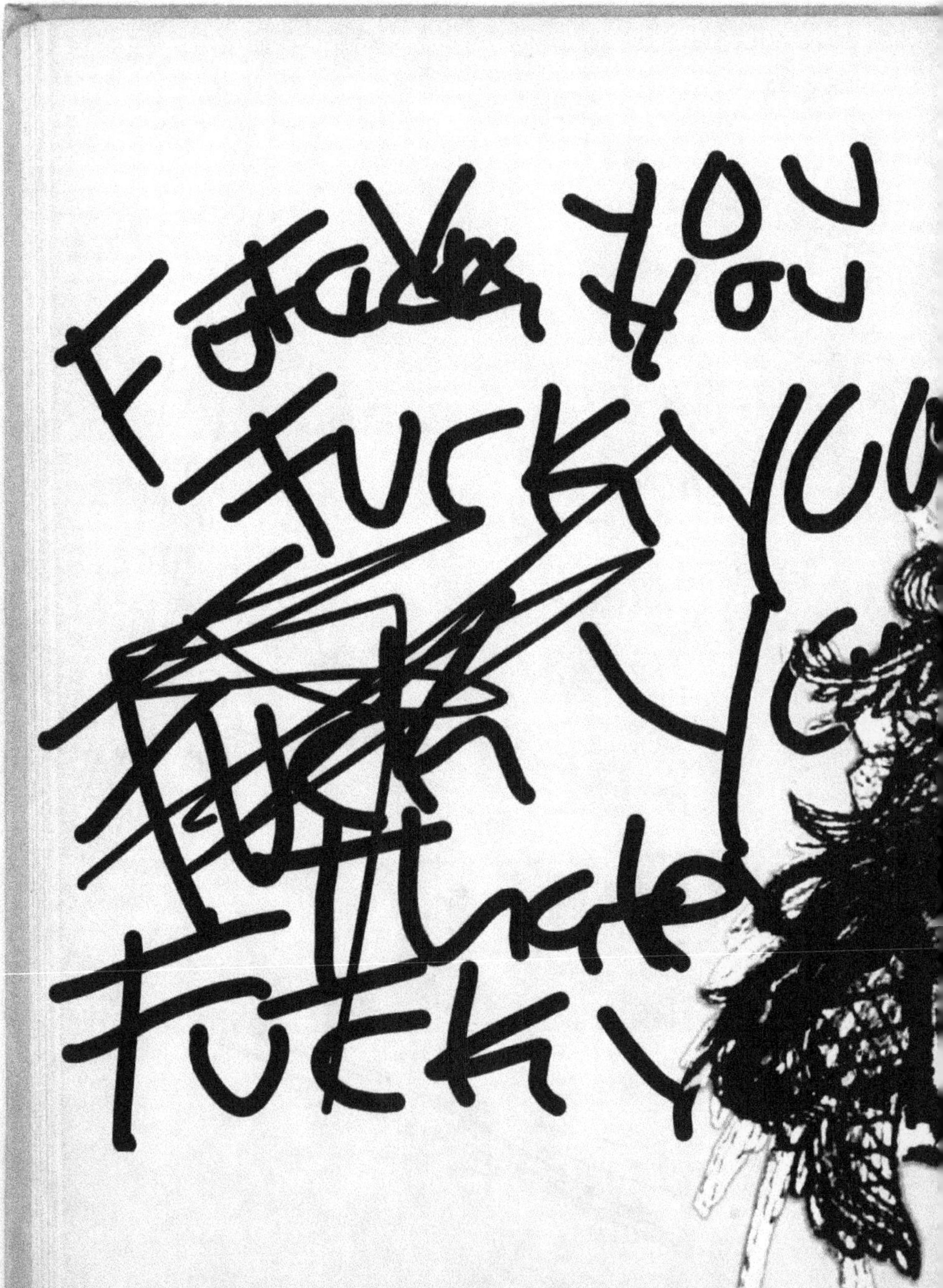
Fuck you
I hate

YOU
YOU
YOU
YOU

I'M FINE
ALWAYS
TIRED.

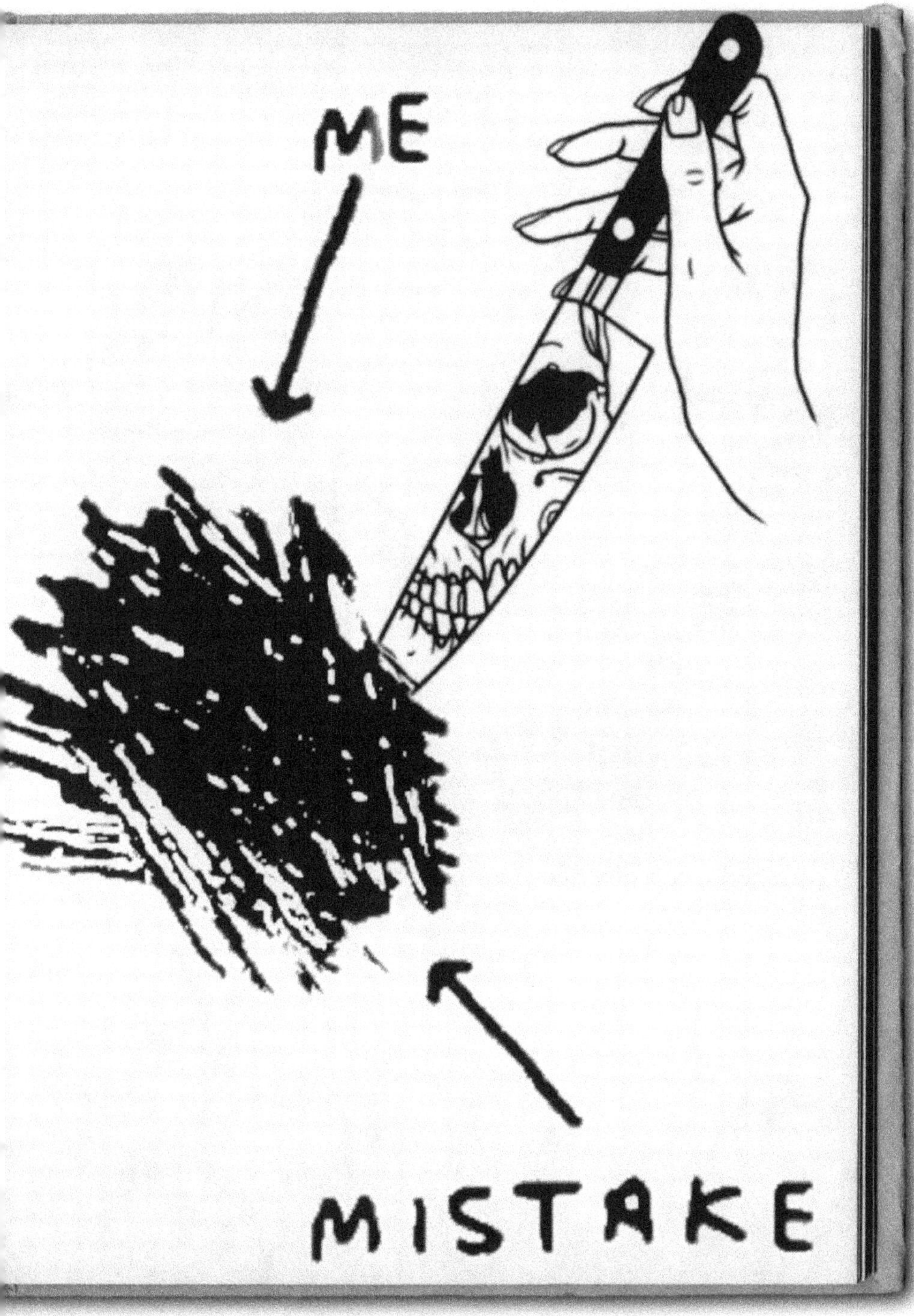
ME
MISTAKE

Stop
stop
stop
Stop
stop
STOP

Alone
BUT I
AM
GOOD
ENOUGH

Are you happy?
Are

happy?
Are you happy?
:Numb

Nickolas

If you're reading this, then it means I'm free.
It means I finally did it and I'm
now at peace. But if I know you,
and I feel like I know you
better than I know myself sometimes,
then I know you're blaming yourself right now.
So I'm going to say this loud and clear, DON'T!
Don't blame yourself for any of this.
None of this is your fault big brother. Not what
Dominic did. Not what happened afterwards with the guys
and the drinking. But most of all, not for me taking my own life

You tried to save me, Nickolas. Over and over again,
but each time you did, there was nothing left of me
that was worth saving. I spent
three years trying, for you, but I didn't have any fight
left inside of me. It was hurting me each day
I was alive and I couldn't take any more pain.

I'm sorry that I left you alone,
that's my only regret, but deep down
I know someone is out there
who will make you feel whole again.

You were my guardian angel big brother. My saving grace.
And I know you'll help so many
others from the darkness that is trying to consume them,
but the light at the end of my tunnel
is the one I'm not going to wake up from...

Just, please promise me that you'll stop running and start living.
Fuck what Dominic said and fuck
our good-for-nothing brothers.
ou're who you're supposed to be.
ou're the best thing about this fucked up world
nd one day you'll find someone who gets
o share their world with yours.
When that day comes, they'll be pretty fucking lucky.

It's okay if you're angry at me.
It's okay if you hate me.
I won't be upset if that's how you feel.
I will be upset if you waste your life away.
ou're allowed to be happy, Nick.
ou're allowed to have a life.
I'll be there watching, every step of the way, because nothing
n this world could ever
ring me the joy that I'd feel from seeing you happy and free.

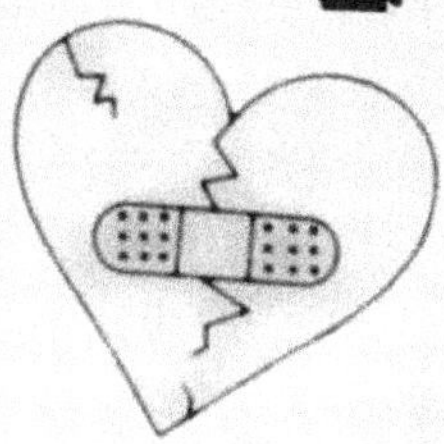

So...I guess this is goodbye big brother.
It's okay... I'm okay with this decision.
Nothing has ever made me feel more peace than
nowing my time is finally coming to an end.
Thank you for being the best brother
a little sister could ever ask for.

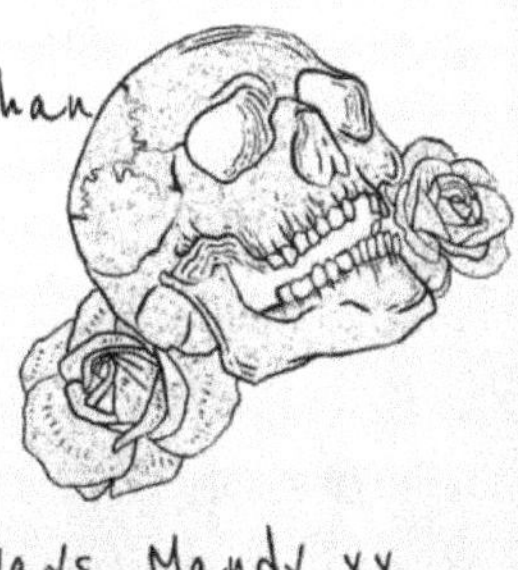

GoodBye.

Love you always, Mandy xx

Nickolas can barely make out Mandy's final words, tears clouding his vision. His quiet sobs are ripping him apart.

He's suddenly wrapped in Finn's arms, and Nickolas leans his head on Finn's chest as he lets everything go. Although part of him is breaking, the other part of him is relieved. This is the closure Nickolas has so desperately been chasing for the last six months. This is the goodbye he never got to have. He could hear Mandy's voice in his head as he read every single word. It was like his sister was standing beside him, reading the note out loud.

'I'm always beside you, watching, screaming into your ear...'

Nickolas pulls away from Finn's hold to ease the restriction in his chest. He leans forward, pressing the palm of his hands into his eyes as he sniffs back the tears and wills for them to stop falling.

'Fuck. Why couldn't she have left this out instead of hiding it away?'

Finn rubs soothing circles into Nickolas's back.

How much of a difference would this letter have made six months ago? By some act of fate, was this how it was meant to be? Did Nickolas need to find the strength in himself to forgive and allow himself to heal before he found Mandy's note? A part of him always questioned how clear-minded Mandy was when she took her life, but after reading the note, it's evident that Mandy was pretty fucking clear.

'Tell me what I can do...' Finn whispers into Nickolas's ear.

He trembles. 'You're doing it. Just...being here, that's all I need.' And it's true. Finn is that someone Mandy was referring to, that person that brings him happiness. That person who makes him feel like he's living, that makes him want to live. Finn's that person who's made Nickolas feel whole again.

'I understand now...why she did it. And—' Nickolas takes a deep breath to control his voice from breaking. He's still looking down at his knees but the tears have slowed down. 'And as much as I miss her, this, what she had here, that wasn't a life worth living. Mandy deserved more than this place.' Nickolas sniffs, finally looking up and making eye contact with Finn. 'You deserve more than this place too.' Nickolas puts a hand on Finn's face, stroking the soft, freckled cheekbone.

Nicolas looks down, needing to break eye contact with Finn before he does something stupid, something that he promised he wouldn't do until Finn was released. His eyes catch the time on his watch and he curses. He's been in here far too long. Lydia will be doing the hourly checks soon and his colleague is no doubt starting to question why Nickolas has been gone since he delivered the meds.

'I hate this...but I have to go.'

'I know...' Finn sounds sad. 'Are you going to be okay?'

Nickolas nods. Words suddenly lost on him.

'You know where to find me if you need to talk.'

A soft smile appears on Nickolas's face.

'Thank you. I don't—fuck, I don't think I could have done that alone.'

Finn takes Nickolas's hand. 'I'm glad you came to me for help.' He gives a gentle squeeze. 'Did it, though? Help you, I mean.'

'You, or reading it?'

'Either. Both?' Finn looks down.

Although the moonlight is all they have, Nickolas can see the slight tinge of red on Finn's cheeks.

'You helped. Reading it was...it was rough, but it's what I needed to be able to say goodbye to her. That's all I ever wanted... to say goodbye.'

They sit in silence for a little longer.

'I wish I could kiss you right now,' Finn confesses.

It's Nickolas's turn to blush. 'I wish you could too.' He gives Finn's hand a final squeeze before standing, Mandy's journal in hand. He makes his way over to the door, his legs heavier with every step he takes away from Finn.

'I um, I decided I'm going to report that guy. For what happened to me. For what he did,' Finn states. 'Will you come with me? When I get out of here, will you come to the station with me?'

'Of course. Anything you want, Finn. I'll be there every step of the way,' says Nickolas.

Finn smiles.

Nickolas smiles back, wishing he could give Finn so much more at this moment. 'Get some sleep. Big day tomorrow.'

'Ha. Doubt my family will be happy to see me after last time.'

'You know I'll be there to help if you need someone to lean on.' Finn's soft eyes are the last thing he takes in before Nickolas turns and leaves.

He walks around the corridor, doing a quick check of the other patients before making his way back to the break room. He sits on the couch, Lydia taking one look at him and knowing not to ask where he has been. His eyes are heavy and sore from shedding so many tears and are no doubt still red.

'Did the rounds. You can grab the next one,' Nickolas states.

'Sure thing.'

Lydia goes back to her books and Nickolas sits there in silence. Mandy's words ring through his head so clear it's as though his sister is sitting beside him. He leans his head back against the cushion, looking up at the ceiling and the bright fluorescent lights.

'Thanks for saying goodbye, sis. I miss you,' he whispers. It is crazy, but deep down, he knows Mandy has heard them.

13. Sunday

Fucking Brett. Nickolas is not going to lie, he's glad to see the asshole gone, but the scheduling is a mess while they try to find a replacement. Nickolas clocked off at six a.m., drove home, and crashed in his bed, well aware that he had to be back at work by twelve p.m. If he was lucky, he'd get four hours of sleep before he had to be up, showered, and on his way back to the centre.

Thankfully, he was able to get a couple of hours of sleep last night while Lydia took charge. When he woke, he offered for Lydia to get some rest, which gave him the chance to look over Mandy's journal again while she was asleep. Within the silence, Nickolas analysed each sketch and drawing, impressed with the talent his sister was harbouring within the pain that littered the pages. He had no idea this was what Mandy created during her therapy sessions. He'd always figured it was more a diary of sorts. A way to speak when Mandy couldn't find her voice. This journal, these pages, this was his sister. This was Mandy's story. Mandy's suffering. Mandy's journey. And as hard as it was to see some of the things written on the pages, to see his sister's struggles and emotions drawn out in the sketches, he valued every part of it.

When he walked through his apartment door, physically and emotionally tired, he only had enough energy left to set an alarm before sleep took over. And for once, his dreams aren't filled with pain, guilt, sorrow, or regret. Mandy was at peace, and now Nickolas can be too.

*

Nickolas's groaning and grumbling causes Socks to hiss. He sits up, his head feeling as though he spent the night drinking. Thankfully he only has three more days of work before he gets some time off. Working two weeks straight is a lot, but the money is good, and it helps the staff that have families. He takes a quick shower, not being able to enjoy the pleasure of the water like he normally would since he decided the extra sleep was more of a priority. It occurs to him as he's getting dressed that if he and Finn actually decide to see each other once Finn is released, then maybe he won't be taking as many shifts as he's used to. The thought of prioritising work over the time he could spend with Finn feels like a punishment. He used to get so much joy working extra shifts so he could spend more time with the patients. He still does, except they're not Finn.

He doesn't have time to pack a meal, but he can get some leftover food from Aiden after dinner has been served to the patients. He leaves food and water for Socks, quickly refreshes the litter box, and then heads out the door. For a Sunday, traffic is unusually busy. He parks with ten minutes to spare, rushes inside and says a quick hello to Jasmine as he gets buzzed in. Nickolas changes into his uniform, fixes his hair after pulling his shirt off messes it a little, and then takes a deep breath to calm himself down. Sky walks in to get changed as he leaves the locker room, and makes his way towards the exit and into the patient corridor.

Nickolas scans his key card and walks into the common room. The atmosphere is light. Everyone seems to be relaxed and smiling. A day with no therapy can do that but it's also the excitement of being able to see family that sets the mood. It's the reason why Nickolas loves to work on Sundays.

'See, told you it would be Nickolas.'

The sound of Finn saying his name catches his attention. Finn is sitting with his friends, a smile of delight shining his way as Nickolas walks over.

'Whatever. That doesn't mean anything. Everyone knows Nickolas works the Sunday afternoon shift.' Cora playfully pushes Finn's arm.

'She's right. Going to have to do better than that,' says Alex.

'Better than what?' Nickolas says.

'Finn is trying to convince us he can predict the future,' states Cora.

'I CAN! Not all the time, but with small things,' says Finn.

Ryder's hand moves in a jerking motion, convinced Finn is talking bullshit.

'Fine.' Finn's eyes close, pretending to meditate. 'Nickolas is seeing someone.'

Everyone turns their head towards Nickolas for confirmation. He decides to play along.

'What—how did you...no one knows that except Darren.' He knows it's risky having Finn say this to the patients, but if gossip queen Darren knows, then he's sure the patients would eventually overhear.

The small cocky smile that appears on Finn's face, thanking him for playing along with the ruse, causes Nickolas's heart to beat a little too fast for someone standing still.

Everyone looks between Finn and Nickolas, trying to wrap their head around it.

'Bullshit!' Alex calls. 'Nickolas must have told you.'

'Why would I tell Finn? I keep my private life private, and now, thanks to your voodoo magic,' Nickolas points dramatically at Finn, 'the whole damn centre is going to know.'

'Wait, why would Darren know? Oh my god, is it Darren?' Cora says the last line a little too loud.

'God, no. I mean,' Nickolas lowers his voice, knowing he shouldn't act so repulsed about a fellow colleague, 'No, it's not Darren.'

Everyone looks like they're watching a game of tennis, bouncing their heads from left to right as they study one another's facial expressions. It's getting harder for Nickolas to keep a straight face and not break out into fits of laughter.

'Well, fuck.' Ryder looks starstruck.

'Do me, do me. Tell me something about my future.' Cora gets giddy, bouncing in the chair.

'Sorry. It doesn't work that way. I just get random images in my head before things happen or as they're happening.'

Nickolas puts his fist to his mouth, wanting to laugh at the pure bullshit Finn is spilling to the group. Finn catches his eye, and that's enough for the redhead to crack, no longer able to play the charade, bursting into a fit of laughter.

'You dick!' Cora pushes Finn off the chair.

Finn happily lays on the floor, laughing while everyone else mumbles about being played.

'And you. How can we trust you now after you played us like that.' Alex points a finger at Nickolas.

Nickolas raises his hands in surrender, playing the victim role. 'I'm innocent. I was promised chocolate pudding if I played along.'

'Like hell I'm giving you my chocolate pudding.' Finn stops laughing, a playful tone still evident in his voice.

'Wait, wait, wait. *Are* you seeing someone?' Cora interrupts, more interested in the gossip than Finn's game.

'Ah,' Nickolas scratches his eyebrow. 'Yeah...yeah, I am. But it's new, so, we're just taking it slow.'

'Okay, everyone. If you could slowly make your way towards the dining area, lunch is ready.' Darren's voice echoes throughout the room. Everyone begins to stand, including Finn, who is purposely taking longer to get up and head off with the others.

'Thanks for playing along. It was nice being able to joke around and enjoy a laugh for once,' says Finn.

'No problems. I wasn't joking about that pudding though. Fair is fair,' Nickolas states.

'And here I thought you'd want to help me out of the kindness of your heart.'

'I mean, sure, but who can say no to extra chocolate pudding?' Nickolas bites his lip. He likes the way it causes Finn to blush.

'Fine. I'll give you my pudding. You're lucky I like you enough to hand it over without a fight.' With that, Finn walks away.

*

Nickolas sends James off to have a break and asks Hayley to organise the common room for the visitors. He casually chats with Sky and Darren about having to find new staff and needing to work around the new hours till they do. Nickolas takes point in counting the utensils as everyone returns their tray once they've finished eating. He watches as the patients happily scurry back to the common room, finding a place to sit alone while they wait for their family to arrive.

No surprise to Nickolas, the last person to hand in their tray is Finn. He counts everything before putting the tray aside, looking back at Finn in question.

'As promised, one chocolate pudding to say thank you.' Finn's hand appears from behind his back, holding out the pudding on a flat palm.

Nickolas cocks an eyebrow, taking the pudding from Finn's hand, and without saying a word, he peels the tub open and licks the chocolate pudding off the back of the lid.

'Mmm, I do love that creamy, gooey texture coating my mouth. Nothing better if you ask me.' Nickolas gives Finn a wink and takes off to get a clean spoon, enjoying the way Finn adjusts his pants before walking into the common room to join the others. Nickolas stays behind to help Aiden clean up for a few minutes, enjoying the sweet taste of his dessert while doing so.

As the clock gets closer to two o'clock, Nickolas sends Hayley off to have a break. Darren and Sky will wait at reception to escort the families while he and James keep an eye on everyone in the room. He takes a seat with Finn while they wait, watching as the redhead studies his stitched wrists.

'You nervous?' Nickolas asks.

No answer, but Nickolas can read Finn's body language.

'I wish the stitches could have been removed before they saw me.'

Nickolas looks down, watching the way Finn is rubbing at the skin around the scars.

'Finn, if they can't look past your scars then that's on them. You know what they represent. You know that they make you a survivor, and no one should ever make you feel any less because of it.'

Finn looks up, green eyes vibrant from the sun-filled room. 'I know that's what these scars mean. I could tell my family a hundred times over that it will never happen again, but I know them. They'll look at my wrists and it's gonna be one more reason for them to think I'm like Cassandra.'

'Your mum, right?'

Finn gives a single nod.

'Tell you what. How 'bout we have a code word and if you need me to bail you out from talking with them, you can just say it in a conversation and I'll make up some excuse for you to leave.'

Finn looks at him, amused. 'A code word?'

'Yeah. Like, chocolate pudding.'

Finn cocks an eyebrow.

'Work that into a sentence and I'll know you want an out.'

There is no time to respond as a hand gently grips Finn's shoulder. Looking up, Finn's eyes lock with Jessica's.

Nickolas realises that's his queue. 'I'll leave you guys to it. Just let me know if you want any chocolate pudding, okay Finn?'

He can see Finn is struggling with words now that he is once again reunited with family.

Nickolas thumbs his nose and as he steps away, he feels a hand grip his arm. Turning around, he's surprised to see Jake holding him back, more interested in speaking with him than saying hello to Finn.

'I wanted to say, thanks, man. For everything,' says Jake. 'This isn't easy on us, but what you said to Jessica was right. You know, about this not being easy on Finn either.'

He looks past Jake long enough to see Jessica and Finn hugging. The redhead suddenly looks so small in comparison. He can see Jessica is whispering in Finn's ear who is nodding along. This is what Finn needs.

Nickolas gives Jake a polite nod. It's all he can offer without saying more than he should. Jake releases his arm and Nickolas sets off to monitor the room, watching patients reunite with family as they hug and kiss hello. It's always an emotional time for everyone involved.

*

It's been an hour, and everything is going smoothly. Hayley comes back from break, so Nickolas sends Darren off. Meanwhile, James and Sky's shift has finished for the day. Every single patient has someone visiting and it warms Nickolas's heart to see how much of an impact it has made on them. He floats around the room, checking in, being pulled aside by parents or loved ones who want to thank him or ask a question. He hears Jessica talking to Finn about their siblings, and the stories make Finn's face light up, only for it to then fall, the realisation that he's missing out on sharing these memories in person.

'Hey, it's okay. You have all the time in the world to spend with them when you get out. All they care about is seeing you get better.'

Nickolas is pleased to hear those words come from Jessica. Their chat has obviously paid off.

He is speaking with Alex's family when his attention gets pulled back to Finn.

'You can ask you know. I've noticed the way your eyes keep looking down at them. So just say whatever you want to say,' says Finn.

'I don't—I'm just...Do they hurt?' Jessica asks.

Finn scoffs. It's obvious that's not what Jessica actually wanted to ask. Even Nickolas could work that one out.

'Not anymore. Just tight and itchy. Stitches should be out soon.'

Nickolas begins to bounce his knee a little. He is focusing on the story being told, acting polite towards Alex's family, but it feels like this could be a 'chocolate pudding' moment and he doesn't want to miss his cue.

'I know you're not Cassandra, Finn,' says Jessica. 'I know that you're trying, which is more than she ever did. You're taking the meds instead of riding the highs and crashing with the lows. That alone already makes you different. Makes you better.'

Nickolas fakes a cough, turning to the side as he covers his mouth, giving him a view of Finn as Jessica reaches out, a smile on Finn's face as he takes Jessica's hand.

'What you did, hurting yourself...it isn't on you. We know that. And everything from before, we don't blame you. We love you and we're here for you. Whatever you need,' says Jessica.

Nodding his head along to what Alex's mother is saying, Nickolas wishes he could see Finn's face to gauge how he's feeling.

'You're doing so great in here, Finn. We can see that, and the doctors can too. That's probably why they called us yesterday to let us know that you're ready to come home,' says Jake.

Nickolas whips his head around so fast he feels a few bones in his neck crack.

Finn's eyes open wide in shock. Body frozen in place. 'What?'

Jake pats Finn on the arm. 'I thought you'd be excited, man. We asked the shrink if we could be the ones to tell you after they gave us a call. Come Tuesday, you're a free man.'

Nickolas turns back towards Alex's family, hiding the internal freak out building inside of him.

'Sorry. I thought I heard someone call my name.' It's a bad lie but it's the best he can do. 'Sounds like you kept your folks busy, that's for sure.' He hopes his little input will show he has been paying enough attention that they won't ask him any follow-up questions because he has no idea what they've been saying this whole time.

'I'm...I can go? They're letting me go?' There is hesitation in Finn's voice.

If Finn is getting released, then that means—

'Your medication is balancing out. Your therapy sessions have been going great. They mentioned how you're making an effort, opening up, and even noticing things that you need to work on before the doctor has to prompt you for it,' explains Jessica. 'She said as long as you find a therapist that you visit once a week to help keep an eye on your dosage, she doesn't see why you can't go home.'

Thankful that the conversation with Alex's family is at an end, Nickolas politely stands up and explains that he needs to check on something in the kitchen before hurrying off. He walks past Finn, whose eyes quickly flick up at him before looking back towards Jessica. Nickolas reaches the dining area and closes the door behind him as he leans against it. His hands tremble as they move to cover his mouth, and his brain begins to process the information.

Finn is getting released. He's going home. All the promises of them being something more once Finn is no longer a patient are finally coming true. Only now, it's not a matter of when because, in two days, Finn will be free. With that thought, panic suddenly sets in.

By the time Nickolas has pulled himself together so he's able to step back into the common room, Darren is helping to walk families back out towards the exit and Hayley keeps an eye on the patients. Nickolas stays in the common room, watching loved ones kiss and hug goodbye as they make promises to come back next week, giving words of encouragement before they walk out the door. He casts his eyes over to Finn for a split second, long enough to see Jake pulling Finn in for a one-arm brotherly hug, giving a pat on the back before letting go.

'We'll be here at nine a.m. Tuesday to pick you up.' Jessica's smile is beaming.

'Can't wait,' says Finn.

Darren walks back in, offering to help walk Jessica and Jake back to the reception desk.

Jessica stops walking and looks in Nickolas's direction. 'In case we don't see you, thanks again, Nickolas. It's nice to see people working in these places that actually give a damn, you know?'

'I get it. My sister used to be a patient here, so I know what it's like to be on the other side of that mesh gate.'

'I'm glad it helped her too.'

Darren leads them out the door and Nickolas is left standing in the middle of the common room. He blinks a few times, bringing himself back to reality as he hears Ryder's mother laughing way too loudly. He spins around, ready to get back to work, freezing as he sees Finn standing right in front of him.

'Hey,' says Finn.

'Hi,' says Nickolas. *Why is everything suddenly so awkward?*

'Guess I didn't need any chocolate pudding.'

'Guess not.' Nickolas bites his lip, stepping around Finn so he can collect the extra chairs and put them away.

'So, guess you heard the news.'

'Yeah, man. That's ah. That's great.'

'You don't seem that excited for me.'

Nickolas stands still. There is one family left and Darren is about to lead them out. Everyone else is off in their own groups again, sharing stories while Hayley walks around to check in with them. Why no one is paying attention to him and Finn standing like two statues in the middle of the room, he has no idea, but he's thankful for it.

'Can we not do this here?'

'Do what?' Finn's voice rises just enough to cause Nickolas to panic.

'Would you—fuck.' He quickly looks around. 'Grab some fucking chairs and follow me.'

Finn folds up three chairs, carrying them while following Nickolas to a closet off to the corner of the room, out of sight from everyone else.

'Well, isn't this poetic? Putting me back in the closet, are you?' says Finn.

'What are you talking about?' Nickolas huffs as he drops the chairs, Finn doing the same.

'I thought you'd be excited. I'm getting out, Nick. I thought that's what we wanted, what you—' Finn takes a moment, voice lowering. 'I thought that once I got out, that meant that we could...'

Nickolas runs a hand down his mouth. This is it. Finn's right. It's the moment they've been waiting for, and now that it's here, Nickolas is fucking petrified. He doesn't know what to say, where to start, and the longer he makes Finn wait, the more Nickolas can see the worry appear on that beautiful face.

'Course that's what I want, Finn. I just wasn't sure if that's still something you wanted.'

The confusion on Finn's face is enough for Nickolas to know that Finn was not expecting that answer.

'Everything I said was true. The way I feel about you. How much I want you. The fact that I was willing to wait for however long I needed to. But—' Nickolas scratches his bottom lip with his thumb, nervous to say the next sentence. 'But what if you realise that I'm not what you want.'

'*Nickolas.*' Finn takes a step forward as he takes a step back. Keeping a safe gap between them.

'You've been stuck here for almost two weeks, Finn. This place can get lonely, and I understand that sometimes...sometimes we latch onto things we normally wouldn't latch onto.' Nickolas looks down at his shoes. 'Besides the other patients and the doctors, I'm the only one you've really been talking to. It would make sense if what you thought you felt...that once you leave, and you have everyone else in the world around you, then maybe you'll see that I'm—'

'Nickolas!' Darren calls out.

Their bubble is broken as Nickolas snaps back into reality. He shouldn't be doing this. Not here. Not now. This isn't a late-night visit while everyone is asleep. Nickolas panics, walks away from Finn without another word, and heads towards Darren.

'Hey, need help moving this TV set back,' explains Darren.

By the time the room is back to normal, Nickolas decides to get the dining area set up, needing to distance himself from Finn as much as possible. At five, he calls everyone in to get dinner, using that moment to take a break so he can sit alone with his thoughts. He realises the minute he sits down to eat how horrible of an idea this is. His mind is racing, thoughts spiralling out of control as he sits alone in the silence of the break room. He begins to analyse every single touch shared between him and Finn. He thinks back to every conversation, trying to decipher who said what. Trying to remember which one of them made the first move. Did Finn see that Nickolas was interested and decided to play along to pass the time? Or did Finn show interest first? He's so confused. This is what he was afraid of. This is why he doesn't open up to people – the fear of learning that everything he thought was real is in fact all one-sided.

By the time he is due to get back to work, he has barely touched the food Aiden prepared for him. He steps into the corridor, where patients are getting escorted to their rooms to collect their belongings before heading off to the showers. Only two more hours before he can go home.

He walks the corridor, keeping his head down and his ears alert for anyone that may need help. He's lost in his own thoughts, something he doesn't like to do while working because it distracts him and can lead to mistakes. That's exactly how he's caught off guard by a hand grabbing at his shirt and pulling him into an empty room. He's pushed up against the wall as wide hands with long thin fingers cup each side of his face. Nickolas goes to speak but the words get caught in his throat as lips press onto his.

Finn's lips. The way they feel is burned into his brain because it's unlike anything he's ever felt before. Nickolas moans into the kiss and Finn gladly swallows it down. He opens his mouth and Finn understands it's an invitation. Finn's hands tighten their grip on Nickolas's face as his tongue enters Finn's mouth. It's primal. Needy. Full of want and heat. Finn presses a knee between Nickolas's leg and the pressure on his dick causes him to gasp.

Finn pulls away, their foreheads instantly resting against one another. The heavy breathing coming from each of them as they catch their breath feels like they are filling each other's lungs with air. There is barely any space between their lips and Nickolas is fighting every part of him that's screaming to go back in for more.

'Whether I met you on the street, in a club, at my first job or in this place, it wouldn't change how I feel about you.' Finn's whispered words feel loud in the quiet of the room. His fingers trail from Nickolas's cheek to the back of his neck, gently combing through the nape of Nickolas's jet-black hair. 'There is a lot that's still uncertain to me, Nickolas. I'm taking it one day at a time. But you...being with you. I've never been more certain of that.'

Nickolas would have buckled to the ground with how weak his knees suddenly felt if not for Finn's hands holding onto him.

'I'm not perfect, Finn. Far from it,' whispers Nickolas.

'Neither am I.' Finn admits. 'But I think that's what makes us perfect for each other.'

Nickolas grabs onto Finn's hips, digging his fingers into the flesh and holds on tight. He can't speak. He can't move. He just hopes at this moment that Finn knows what he's trying to say through his actions. Nickolas slowly nods his head, making sure that Finn understands that he is agreeing to them giving this a try.

'I hope you know what you're agreeing to, Nickolas. Because once I have you, I don't think I'm ever going to be able to let you go.'

'Who said I want you to?'

He gives Finn's hips one final squeeze, using every bit of strength he has left to push Finn away, fighting against his instincts that are telling him to pull him in closer. From the look on Finn's face, Nickolas can tell that he knows he's not pushing him away as a rejection. This alone makes Nickolas wonder when they began to read each other's body language so clearly.

'I better leave. Darren will be coming around to collect you soon for a shower and he still thinks I got a guy on the outside,' Nickolas explains.

'In two days, you will,' says Finn.

Nickolas blushes. He steps out of Finn's room, running his fingers through his dishevelled hair. He makes himself look busy as Darren steps around the corner, knocking on doors to get the patients out and ready to shower. Hayley isn't far behind, leading the females while Darren assists the males. Nickolas keeps his eyes down, feeling the heat of Finn's touch all over his body, savouring every minute of it. He feels a hand brush against his as someone walks past, knowing in his heart that it's Finn.

He sets off towards the infirmary to collect the med cart, knowing he can use this time to go over the checklist so Eric or Lydia don't have to.

At eight o'clock, he clocks out, along with Hayley and Darren. He's disappointed that he doesn't get to say goodbye to Finn but he figures that they said everything they needed to say with that kiss. Walking back to his car, he feels like he's floating. He hasn't kissed many guys. He never wanted to, but kissing Finn was different. Is different. It's something his body craves long before it wants any other physical affection. Since he got a taste, his world has exploded into colour and everything has changed.

A kiss from Finn spoke volumes. It said hello and goodbye all at once. It said I want you, I need you, I care for you, and I want to protect you, all within one breath. Nickolas gets in his car, and he knows in his heart that if he ever lost the ability to speak, Finn would be able to understand exactly how he was feeling through kiss alone. And now, all he has to do is wait two more days and he'll be free to kiss Finn whenever and wherever he wants.

14. Monday

Nickolas wakes up feeling refreshed, calm, and dare he say it, giddy. He wants to punch himself in the face the moment he thinks of *giddy* as a way to describe how he's feeling, because a word like that makes him sound like some schoolgirl getting all excited over a boy because he's said, 'I like you'. But truth be told, he is excited. Finn is getting out tomorrow and all the visions he's had for them will become reality. He even woke up and decided to clean his apartment. Once he had moved into his own place, Nickolas realised just how much filth he was living in back home. Sure, his apartment is no mansion, but in comparison to the thick layer of scum in the bathroom sink, the worn-down carpet, and the constant pile of cigarette ash, beer bottles, and guns on the table in the house he grew up in, he figures his apartment is a step up.

He pulls out the vacuum. After rolling it over a section of the carpet, he notices how the remainder of the room is a darker shade due to the layer of cat hair that has settled on top. He does the same to the couch, vacuuming the fabric to help bring colour back into the furniture. He cleans the toilet, bathroom sink, and bathtub, constantly having to push Socks away from wanting to play with the scrubbing brush that is soaked in cleaning chemicals.

The dishes are mostly clean since whenever he has cooked, he cleaned as he went. He packs away the box of Mandy's belongings but decides to keep her journal in his bedside drawer.

He cracks open his bedroom window just enough for air to come through, but not wide enough that Socks can get out. Looking around his apartment, Nickolas feels accomplished with the work he did. It isn't until he finally sits down to eat that he realises he's gone and given his apartment a full spring clean like people do when they're expecting someone. That someone being a tall, handsome redhead with kind, green eyes, who makes Nickolas weak at the knees every time his name leaves Finn's plump pink lips.

'Jesus Christ, this is pathetic.'

Nickolas finishes his bowl of cereal and then takes a moment to spend time with Socks, lying on the floor as the furball stretches beside him. He runs his hand down her stomach. She purrs in approval and playfully paws at his hand to keep it in place.

'You're going to like Finn. I mean, you have the same hair colour, so you'll probably think you're related.'

A quick meow in response makes Nickolas smile.

'Just, be nice, okay? I know you've only ever had me around, so don't go attacking him just 'cos he's new. I like him, which means you have to like him.'

After a few more minutes, Nickolas gets up and heads to the bathroom to shower. He shaves the small amount of stubble he has growing on his face and then gets dressed. Packing his uniform in his bag along with some food, Nickolas heads out the door with a spring in his step that he would deny to anyone that asked him about it.

*

There are a few people in the waiting area as he walks in. It's rare to ever find people waiting unless they are picking patients up, admitting them, or it's visitors day. From the looks of them, they're not here for any of those reasons.

'Hey, Nickolas,' says Jasmine.

'Hey. What's with the crowd?' Nickolas places his arms on the counter, leaning towards Jasmine so his voice doesn't travel.

'Replacements. Dot's been trying to fit in interviews with them all morning while running around to get things done.'

Nickolas gives the receptionist a nod of understanding. He looks over his shoulder, sussing them out for himself since there's a chance he could be working with one of them soon. He turns back towards Jasmine who buzzes him in, and he heads on back to change. Hayley is already in the change room, tying up shoe laces as he walks in.

'Did you get a look at the fresh meat out there?' asks Hayley.

'They look scared shitless. This ain't the place for people with no backbone.' Nickolas shoves his backpack into the locker and starts to change.

'I'm sure it's just the interview they're nervous about.'

'We'll see. Dorothy will be able to see right through 'em if they try and bullshit their way into the job.'

Hayley chuckles while walking out, Nickolas following shortly after. He drops his food off in the break room and is about to leave when Dot steps in.

'Nickolas. Excellent, you're here. I've been running around like a headless hen all morning,' explains Dot.

'How can I help?' asks Nickolas.

'I need to be able to do these interviews without any interruptions.'

'Of course.'

'Great. I tell you, some of these applicants better be as good in person as they make themselves out to be on paper.'

'From my experience, the paperwork tells the lies more than the person does.'

'Yes, well. We don't need another situation like we had with Brett, so I want to be thorough with them.' Dot turns around and heads back towards the reception desk.

In the common room, everyone is around the craft table, laughing and smiling.

'Is there a party going on that I didn't know about?' Nickolas asks Sky who is smiling along with the patients.

'Hey. Finn had his last session with Dr Hale today who confirmed that he gets to go home tomorrow, so everyone decided to make him a goodbye card he can take with him.' Sky hands over a piece of folded paper and a crayon, indicating that Nickolas also has to make a card.

Finn already has a small pile of cards, which he's begun to look through. They make him smile and sometimes laugh while he reads over the messages inside. Nickolas takes a seat next to Sasha so he can join in, pleased to see everyone so at ease. Finding out someone gets to go home can bring a sense of hope to those that are still obligated to stay.

Nickolas casually chats with Sasha as he draws on his paper, adding silly little doodles that have a special meaning behind the time spent with Finn. Eric's voice cuts through the chatter as his colleague directs everyone to the dining area for lunch.

Chairs scrape against the floor and a flood of bodies make their way to the doorway. Nickolas finally locks eyes with Finn. He sends Sky on a break, and Hayley follows everyone into the dining area where Eric is waiting. That leaves Nickolas to clean up the table, alone, with Finn.

'So, Dr Hale gave you the all clear?' asks Nickolas.

'Yep. We mostly spent today talking about how I felt after seeing my family yesterday, considering what happened last time, and she referred me to a few therapists I could see when I get out. But besides that, I'm good to go,' explains Finn.

Nickolas stands up straight, looking directly at Finn. 'That's, that's really great, Finn.' He takes a small step closer.

'It is great...' Finn takes a step towards Nickolas. Their bodies are only a step away from being pressed up against one another.

'Here.' Nickolas hands Finn the card he had spent the last twenty minutes working on. Finn takes it, smiling at the doodles of bath sponges, music notes, iPods, and angel wings. A laugh erupts from Finn when his eyes land on the sketch of a chocolate pudding cup that's got a speech bubble saying how sweet he tastes. When Finn spots the drawing of a phoenix, Nickolas preens at the impressed look on his face.

'You remember what my tattoo looks like?' Finn asks.

Nickolas shrugs.

Finn opens the card, and Nickolas can't help but notice the contrast between the crimson paper and Finn's porcelain white skin. 'Proud of you. See you on the outside.' Finn reads the words out loud as if Nickolas hadn't been the one to write them. Their eyes meet and all Nickolas wants to do is lean in and kiss him.

'Nick—'

'Go eat. I have to finish in here.'

Finn puts the card with the others in a neat pile, and heads off to get some food. Nickolas cleans up the craft table, sets up the chairs for group, and then takes the cards to Finn's room so they don't get damaged or forgotten.

*

At three p.m., Nickolas and Hayley walk back out into the patient corridor, relieving Eric and Sky who are finished for the day and ready to go home. In the common room, Nickolas puts the chairs away while Hayley helps everyone head back to their rooms. Nickolas overhears Dr Hale give Finn some last words of advice.

'There is still a long road ahead, Finn. But your time here has shown me that even though you lost the map, you're willing to stop and ask for directions.'

Finn nods. Dr Hale pats Finn on the shoulder and heads towards the offices. Nickolas gives Dr Hale a nod hello as they walk past one another, making his way closer towards Finn.

'So, did you sing kumbaya for your final group session?' Nickolas thinks back to the comment Finn made before his very first group session.

'Oh yeah. We all stripped naked and held hands while swaying from side to side. It was very moving,' Finn jokes.

'They mustn't have liked you very much. Normally after the getting naked part, they play a game of twister and things can get a bit handsy.'

Nickolas can't hold a straight face any longer, breaking out into a smile from Finn's faux hurt expression.

'Alright, you going to help me or what?' Nickolas gives Finn a small nudge, causing a chuckle to escape from the lips he can't stop thinking about. After folding the chairs and returning them to the corner he and Finn hid in only yesterday, Nickolas makes his way towards the exit so he can escort Finn back.

'Nick.' Finn reaches out, taking Nickolas's wrist to stop him from leaving.

The warmth of Finn's fingers spreads throughout Nickolas's body. He lets himself be pulled back, their bodies facing one another. Finn's fingers intertwine with Nickolas's, offering a gentle squeeze. He looks down. He doesn't trust himself to look Finn in the eye without leaning forward and capturing those perfect pink lips with his own. Finn rests his forehead against Nickolas's, and they take a moment to breathe one another in.

'I'm actually getting out of here, Nick,' Finn whispers. 'We can finally be together.'

Nickolas's heart skips a beat.

'When I walk out of those doors at nine a.m. tomorrow, I'm taking you out,' says Finn.

'I have to work tomorrow. I don't finish till three,' Nickolas whines. *Who is he?* Not once has he ever whined like this. He doesn't even know who he is at this point, already behaving like a kid that's been told no.

'Well, then I'll come have lunch with you and then we can go out once you finish your shift.'

'Is this you asking me out on a date?' Nickolas pulls back and cocks an eyebrow.

From the corner of his eye, Nickolas sees a shadow walk past the door. He pulls away as though a cold bucket of water has been tipped on him. He remembers that they're standing in the middle of the common room where anyone can see them.

'What's wrong?' Finn asks.

'Nothing, nothing. I just, I forgot that we're pretty open here, so...you know.' Nickolas thumbs his bottom lip, nervous energy taking over. 'We better get you back to your room.'

He doesn't say a word as he walks Finn back, the concern about being seen outshining the desire to say goodbye as he closes the door behind him. At the reception desk, a tired-looking Jasmine says goodbye to the last interviewee of the day.

'How'd it all go?' Nickolas asks.

'Haven't seen Dorothy yet to ask, but some of them couldn't even look me in the eye when I was talking to them,' Jasmine explains.

Nickolas shakes his head wondering why people like that try working in an industry that relies heavily on social skills.

'Nickolas – you have a minute?' Dot calls.

He whips around and eagerly follows his boss. In the break room, Dot is standing by the door, waiting for him to enter and then closes it behind him. As the door clicks shut, Nickolas waits for the intel.

'How long?' Dot asks.

'How long what?' questions Nickolas.

Dot crosses her arms. 'How long have you been intimate with Mr Cunningham?'

Nickolas freezes. His feet feel like they've been dried in a cement block, locking him in place. 'I'm not—'

'I saw you, Nykolai. So don't you dare lie to me. Not me.' Dot points at her chest to emphasises their bond.

'Dorothy, please. If you let me explain.'

'Explain? Do you know what could happen if HR found out about this? Hell, what about what they'll do to me if they find out that I knew and didn't report you?'

'It's not what you think.'

'Really? Then enlighten me.'

Nickolas takes a moment to collect his thoughts. He sits at the table, but Dot doesn't attempt to join him.

'Nothing physical has happened between us.'

Dot looks as though she can smell bullshit.

'I'm serious. It's not like that between us. It's...' He realises the only way he can explain it is if he starts from the beginning. 'I was someone Finn could talk to. I was trying to encourage him to open up during his sessions so that he wasn't stuck here longer than he needed to be. He, he confided in me.'

'Patients confide in us all the time, Nickolas. It's our job not to get attached, especially if they get attached.'

'This isn't him seeking out someone to keep him company. This was about both of us helping the other to see the light again.'

Dot sighs, taking a seat at the table across from him.

'I spoke to Finn...about Mandy. Since she died, I haven't been able to speak her name to anyone, let alone talk about what happened. But with Finn I knew, I knew he'd understand in a way none of you could.'

'How do you know that? You never tried to talk to us, even when we offered.'

'You knew her. And if you didn't, you knew me. You knew me as her brother. As an employee and a friend. Finn was a clean slate. I could share my story from my point of view and know whatever he said was an unbiased opinion. The regret, the guilt, the self-hatred, he helped me sort through all that pain and helped me breathe again.'

Dot sits back in the chair and exhales.

'I never wanted to pursue anything with Finn because he was my patient. But something between us clicked, and it was getting harder and harder to walk away from him.'

'You should've come to me. I would have taken you off his services and put someone else on to assist him.'

'And have what happened with Brett happen again? Scrap all his progress and have him start from scratch?'

'Yes!' Dot's voice rises. 'Because what happened with Brett could have been avoidable had Finn not been involved with you.'

'Oh, that's bullshit and you know it. Whether he woke up screaming for me or his own sister, Brett still would have acted the way he did.'

'Is that why Lydia called you? She knew what was going on and she rang you to help?'

Nickolas exhales, waiting for himself to calm down. 'Yes.'

'Sweet Jesus.' Dot looks up at the ceiling, unable to look Nickolas in the eye.

'As I said, it's not physical.'

'Didn't look that way when I saw you before.' When their eye's meet, Nickolas's knows there is no way out of this.

'So we hug. And touch. It's not in a sexual way.'

'Oh, Nykolai. It would almost be better if it were just sex. But this, this goes deeper. You care for him.'

'Course I do.'

'Which means you need to let him go.'

'What?!' Nickolas can't believe what Dot is saying right now.

'Listen to me.' Dot's voice is calm, waiting for Nickolas to calm down also. 'I'm not happy about this. Far from it. And you and I will be talking about this again once he leaves tomorrow.

But right now, you need to understand that what has happened between you two has jeopardised his whole treatment.'

'Wh—how?'

'The point of Finn being committed was for him to learn to take care of himself, for himself. But now, his whole recovery is questionable on whether or not he was learning to cope for himself, or for you.'

A cold shiver runs down Nickolas's spine.

'He had a reason to get better, Nickolas. You. You were his prize for leaving this place. What happens if it doesn't work out between you two? Does he relapse and come back? Does he run off again, leaving his family wondering if he is safe or alive? Finn needed to be able to complete his treatment with the prize being his release, knowing that he has the strength and power to handle his bipolar on his own. Without his family...and without you.'

Nickolas stands up, pacing the room while his boss sits with a look of sadness. Dot's right. Of course, Dot's right. He runs a hand down his face. Too many thoughts racing through his mind.

'I'm not saying what you have isn't real. And I'm not saying you shouldn't pursue it. What I am saying is you have to wait.'

Nickolas stops pacing. He leans against the corner sink and looks down.

Wait.

Dot wants him to wait.

The question is, how long for? A month? Six months? A year?

'When Finn leaves tomorrow, it's going to be a whole new world for him. It's not going to be like how it was before he was committed and it's not going to be like the world he had in here,' Dot explains.

'I know that,' Nickolas spits.

'Do you? When he leaves, he has to willingly take his pills, not have someone watch over him while they hand them to him. He's going to have to build a routine around his life. Find work, adjust to triggers like stress or things from his past. He can't have you there to run to whenever things get rough.'

A sick feeling begins to rise in the pit of Nickolas's stomach.

'I don't want to see you get hurt, Nykolai.' Dot rests a hand on his arm, and Nickolas wonders when his boss got up and walked towards him.

'But Finn is our patient and it is our duty to put his well-being above all else...even our own.'

'You're right.' Nickolas barely gets the words out before his voice begins to break. He collects himself, making a mental promise that he can break down later because right now, he needs to make things right. He looks up, the expression on Dot's face making him feel small.

'I'll talk to him,' says Nickolas.

'I think that's best.'

He rubs his hand under his nose. Silence falls between them for a few minutes before Dot speaks again.

'In other news, I met some promising applicants today. Might be able to hire a couple more staff than the ones we need to replace Brett and Jasmine. Could help. Give you a break from working so many shifts.'

Nickolas nods. He wants to hear more, but he's not in the mood to discuss work.

'I'll give you a minute,' offers Dot. 'Take your time, we can handle dinner without you.'

The quiet of the room is deafening.

*

By the time Nickolas has calmed his racing mind and beating heart, the patients are halfway through eating dinner. He joins Dot and Hayley in the dining area, keeping close to the door so he doesn't lock eyes with Finn. The only chance Nickolas is going to have to talk to Finn is right before he leaves for the night, once everyone settles back in their rooms following their showers.

Dot signals for him to head into the common room so patients who are finished eating can enjoy a bit of downtime for the night. Nickolas wanders around the patients, lost in his own world, making himself look busy so he isn't cornered by Finn, forced to make conversation when, within the next hour, Finn will want nothing to do with him.

The TV gets turned on, a game show catching everyone's attention as they scream out movie titles that are nowhere close to the movie being described. He can feel Dot glancing his way and he ignores it the same way he ignores Finn.

They start taking everyone back to their rooms to collect their belongings, and then to the showers. Nickolas chats with the other patients to keep himself busy. The minute they hit the shower room, Finn purposely positions himself in Nickolas's eyesight. He sits down, trying to avoid catching a glimpse of Finn's beautiful body while keeping an eye on the patients. Ignoring Finn is torture. This is his punishment. This is his hell.

Everyone is cleaned, dressed, and making their way back to their rooms. This is it. Nickolas stands in the middle of the empty corridor, everyone settled in for the night. With his hands in his pockets, he takes in a few deep breaths. Then he knocks on Finn's door.

'Come in,' says Finn. 'Oh, it's you. Since when do you knock?'

'Always have. I kinda stopped, which I realise was unprofessional, so, sorry about that.'

'Right...I'll make sure when I leave my review that I comment on how rude you were for not knocking.'

It's a joke, but Nickolas adds it to his list of mistakes when it comes to his behaviour around Finn.

'Listen. About tomorrow.'

Finn sits up a little straighter, attention fully on Nickolas. There is worry in those soft green eyes, and he has to look down to keep himself from backing out.

'When you get released tomorrow, I think it's best if we don't see each other for a while.' Nickolas swears he hears glass shatter. Maybe it was just his heart.

'Wh-what?' Finn's voice quivers.

'I think we moved too fast. We got caught up in it all and when you step outside those doors tomorrow, you're going to see that too.'

'Nickolas, what are you talking about? I already told you, it's you I want. No one else.' Finn stands up, but doesn't make a move towards Nickolas.

'You say that now because I'm here. I helped. But tomorrow is going to be like starting from scratch. New job. New routine. New you. There's no room for me in that.'

'Yes, Nickolas. Yes, there is. I'll make room. I'll—'

'Well maybe I don't want you to, okay?' Nickolas looks up, locking eyes with Finn. There is heat in his voice and he hates it because he isn't angry at Finn, he's angry at himself. But the only way he is going to be able to walk away is if Finn hates him. 'I don't want to be your nurse, Finn. I took care of you in here because it was my job. But I don't need to leave my work at the end of the day only to come home and take care of someone else.'

'I'm not asking you to take care of me. I'm asking you to be with me.'

'And maybe one day we will be. But that can't be today.'

'I don't believe you. You made sure nothing happened between us until I got out to prove that it's real. That this is real. That it wasn't just a fling. If you didn't care, you wouldn't have stayed by my side all night making sure I didn't die.'

Nickolas flinches. It's true. Every word Finn's saying is true. And so is everything Dot explained to him.

Finn takes a few steps towards him, voice strong and powerful.

'No. This isn't you talking. This is someone else. And you know what, fine. If you want to run from this, from us, then be a coward. Keep running. But don't make out like I'm the problem. You know how much I hated my siblings having to take care of me, having to baby me. You think I want to throw that responsibility onto you? Hm? So, whatever has you scared, own up to it because I don't believe for one second you would have told me about your past, your fears, or risk your career for me, only to turn back around and act like I'm not what you want.'

Finn is practically towering over Nickolas, pushing a finger into his chest to prove a point. Finn may not believe Nickolas, but that doesn't matter because right now, Finn is hurt enough to allow him to walk away.

Nickolas knows he is going to have to be the one who has to take that step and leave, especially since Finn is still stuck here for one more night. He takes one final look into those green eyes, the hurt masked by rage, and sends Finn a silent apology.

'Whatever. Believe what you want to believe.' Nickolas turns around to leave. Tears threaten to fall, and if they do, Finn won't believe a single thing he said.

'Dr Hale told me today that although I got lost and didn't have a map, I'm no longer afraid to stop and ask for directions,' Finn explains. 'Whichever way I go, Nick, it's going to lead me back to you.'

Nickolas walks out and closes the door behind him as his vision blurs from the tears streaming down his face. He pushes the palms of his hands into his eyes, willing the tears to stop long enough for him to collect his belongings, get in his car and drive home. His body begins to tremble. He takes a couple of deep breaths and makes his way for the door into the back rooms so he can leave. He can't be here any longer.

Collecting his bag, he walks out still wearing his uniform. He keeps his head down as he pushes past Sam, who is walking through the gate.

'What's with the rush?' Sam calls after him, but Nickolas doesn't reply.

'Nickolas. Nickolas, wait,' Dot calls for him.

But he doesn't wait, he can't speak to Dot right now. He sniffs back the tears that are fighting to fall. He just needs to get to his car and then he can let go.

'Nickolas. Are you okay?' How Dot was able to catch up to him he has no idea, but hearing Dot's concerned voice so close to him makes him freeze.

'Nickolas...'

'Don't. I did what you asked, okay.' He can't look at his boss.

'I'm sorry you're hurting. But you did the right thing.'

'For who?' Nickolas spins around. 'From where I was standing, Finn looks worse than before and that's on me.'

Dorothy's mouth opens to respond but then closes it again.

'That's what I thought...see you in the morning, Dorothy.' Nickolas heads to his car. He closes the door and lets himself break down.

The conversation he had with Finn plays over and over in his head on a constant loop. He sees the hurt on Finn's face each time he relives it. He can barely control the shaking in his hands as his emotions take over. This is why he's always so scared to open up to someone, to let someone in. He's scared of disappointing them. Scared of the pain if they got hurt, or worse, if he hurt them.

He hopes that one day Finn will forgive him for his hurtful lies.

15. Tuesday

Nickolas startles from the loud knock echoing in the confined space of his car. He groans. His head is pounding. His eyes are struggling to open at the sight of the early morning sun, dry from the tears he shed the night before. Pinching the bridge of his nose, the repetitive knocking pierces through his skull and Nickolas is ready to punch whoever is adding to his headache. With squinting eyes, he catches Lydia standing outside his car window, a cup of coffee in hand. He steps out, regretting the decision to sleep in his car.

'Figured you might need this,' Lydia explains.

'Thanks,' Nickolas grumbles. He takes the takeaway cup from Lydia and enjoys the way the liquid burns his throat as he swallows. 'Guess I'm late for my shift.'

'Not yet. I asked if I could finish an hour early today. I have a role-playing assignment for school. They give us a patient and we have to determine their diagnoses from the scenario they read out to us.'

'Good luck, not that you need it.'

'Ha, thanks.'

Nickolas takes another sip. 'Say whatever you need to ask so I can get it over with.'

'I don't need to ask. From the look of you, the look on Finn's face when I delivered his meds last night, and the chat Dorothy gave me before she left, I was able to piece it all together.'

'He—he okay?'

Lydia shrugs. 'He's been quiet. I couldn't tell if he was sleeping last night or just lying perfectly still.' There is a pause. 'What happened to you last night?'

'Went for a drink at that dive bar around the corner. One drink may have turned into seven. Decided, instead of catching a cab home and another back to work this morning, I might as well sleep it off in the car.'

'Sure. Because coming to work hungover, smelling like stale beer, in yesterday's work clothes after a shitty sleep in your car, makes way more sense than paying a cab fare.'

Nickolas gives Lydia the finger. The truth is, if he went back to the apartment he put time and effort into cleaning because he was hoping Finn would be making a visit over the next couple of days, he would have drunk everything in his apartment until he blacked out. At least at a bar, the bartender was able to cut him off before he got too intoxicated, even if sleeping in his car made his back hurt and his neck stiff.

'You going to be able to work today?'

Nickolas takes another gulp of coffee before answering. 'I'll shower inside. Pretty sure I have a spare uniform in my locker.'

'That's not what I was asking.'

He exhales. He's tired. Tired from the lack of sleep. Tired from working fourteen days straight with crazy hours. Tired of running. Of fighting. Of crying. Of being scared. Today was meant to be the start of something new. Funny how a lot can change in a blink of an eye. 'I'll be fine. Only have to work three hours before he gets released. 'M sure I can avoid him within that time.'

Lydia nods.

'Guess I'll see you in a few days then. Try and enjoy your time off, okay?' says Lydia.

'Thanks.'

Lydia walks towards her car and stops, turning back around. 'For what it's worth, I was happy for you both. I know what

Dorothy said makes sense, but I also know you'd never do anything that would risk Finn's mental health. Dorothy may think she knows what's best for Finn, but you're the one that knows Finn.' Lydia unlocks the car, gets behind the wheel, and drives out of the parking lot.

Is Lydia trying to tell him that Dot is wrong? That what his boss made him do was a mistake and he should fix it? No, he can't go down that rabbit hole. Not today. What's done is done. He downs the rest of his coffee before opening his car door to grab his backpack from the front seat. After standing in the fresh air, the stale smell of alcohol makes him want to gag.

As he steps inside, Sam looks up from the desk and gives Nickolas a silent nod before buzzing the side door open. Nickolas hates that people know what has happened. It's why he always keeps his life private, because the minute people know about anything good, it means they'll know when everything decides to turn to shit. He doesn't need them to feel sorry for him. He doesn't want them offering an ear if he needs to talk. He just wants to move forward.

Nickolas grabs his spare uniform and steps into the employee shower. Turning the hot water on, he allows the room to fill with steam. He takes a few deep breaths, the warm air opening up his pores, helping him sweat out whatever alcohol he has left in his system. In the shower, Nickolas leans against the wall and envisions the water washing away every trace of Finn that is left on his skin. Finn's breath against his ear while whispering to him in the common room, the pressure from his fingers entwining with Finn's. Nickolas needs it to be gone. It's the only way he's going to be able to survive.

Drying himself off, he sees his tattoos in the mirror. Saving grace. That was meant to be between him and his sister, but now Finn's words will forever be a whisper in his ear, haunting him.

You're my saving grace. This place helped me, but you're the one that saved me.

'Fuck.' Nickolas grips the sink. He doesn't know why he's trying to fool himself into believing everything is going to be okay, it's a waste of energy that he needs to preserve to get through the day. He takes a few deep breaths, reminding himself that feeling is a sign of living, then he gets dressed.

Dot and Hayley are putting their belongings away in their lockers, freezing as they lock eyes on Nickolas.

'Good morning, Nickolas,' Dot speaks first.

'Morning.' Nickolas looks at Hayley as he says it, stepping past them both so he can put his clothes from last night back into his bag before he walks out. He's planning to sneak in to see Aiden so he can grab some food, his stomach rumbling at the thought. He hadn't eaten last night, his last meal being around two p.m., when he had his break.

The radio is playing softly as Nickolas steps into the kitchen. Aiden is in a world of his own, shuffling along the floor, dancing while whisking pancake batter.

'Lady Gaga? Really?' Nickolas teases.

Aiden spins around with a fright. Nickolas chuckles from the look on Aiden's face. He ducks to the side in time to avoid the pancake batter Aiden flings in his direction.

'Jesus. You scared the shit out of me.' Aiden collects himself. 'What do you want? Breakfast isn't for another hour.'

Still chuckling, Nickolas makes his way towards the fridge. 'Just needed something to eat. Didn't get a chance this morning.'

'Help yourself.' Aiden gets back to cooking, brushing Nickolas off while humming along to the music.

Nickolas fills the biggest bowl he can find with cornflakes, a banana and milk. He stands against the counter, eating his food in silence.

'Hey, how's that guy going?' Aiden asks.

Nickolas holds the spoon mid-air, mouth open. So much for avoiding all things Finn. He takes a bite, using it as an excuse to buy himself some time.

'He's good. Getting released today.'

'That's great. I was worried for a minute, you know, with the whole...' Aiden shakes a wrist in the air, causing Nickolas to roll his eyes. This is why Aiden works in the kitchen and not with the patients.

'We all were, but he pulled through.'

'That's awesome. I see all the patients every time they come and get a meal, I hear bits and pieces about how they're going, but I never actually get to find out when they make it out of this place. Sucks sometimes, ya know?'

Nickolas simply nods. It's all he can offer in his current state. Aiden nods back, focusing again on the task at hand. To offer his thanks, and to avoid Finn just a little bit longer, Nickolas cleans his dishes and helps with the ones that are already waiting in the sink. Drying off his hands, he catches the time on his watch. 7.15. He steadies his breathing while he starts lining up the trays and utensils. Aiden begins to lay out the food, ready to hand it out to each patient as they make their way into the dining area to collect a plate.

One by one, patients make their way inside. Nickolas stands at the end, watching them collect their food and then find a place to sit in the room. His heart pounds with each patient that enters. He wouldn't be surprised if everyone could see the outline of his heart pushing against his ribs as it tries to burst out of his chest.

He gives Cora a smile and a nod hello as she walks past him to find a table. Suddenly, it feels as if all the air is sucked out of the room. Nickolas holds his breath, trying to keep his eyes anywhere that isn't on Finn. Despite his attempts to go unnoticed, Nickolas feels eyes on him. He knows from the way his body responds that it's Finn who is staring him down. He breaks out in a small sweat as heat pools in his stomach. Not wanting to look like a coward, he averts his eyes back up towards the line, and there Finn is, ruffled hair and dark eyes from lack of sleep. Eyes that are on him.

Nickolas wants to reach out and hold Finn. He wants to tell him he's sorry and admit that Finn was right. Finn knows him well enough to see through the lies. He wants to beg Finn for forgiveness. What he said was cruel. If he were Finn, though, he wouldn't be so quick to take him back, even if he did apologise and explain why he said those things. Instead of doing any of that, he simply watches his patient collect the food before walking right past him as if Nickolas were a ghost.

Honestly, the way Finn ignored him hurts more than if he looked at Nickolas with hatred in his eyes and spat in his face. At least then he'd know Finn was angry, but being ignored, it's as though he isn't even worth Finn's time. He rubs at the back of his neck and makes his way towards the door, needing to get out of there. Being in the same room as Finn used to feel like breathing in that first breath of fresh air after being trapped within the centre's walls all day. Now he stands here feeling like he's suffocating. His eyes catch Finn looking up from the tray of food as he walks out. Dot reaches out to stop him, but he dodges his boss, makes his way out of the dining room, and heads straight for the patient corridor.

He looks around the empty corridor, anxious. The walls are closing in around him. There's no escape, no exit. He's trapped and for the first time in almost four years, he understands how the patients must sometimes feel.

'Nykolai?'

Nickolas spins around. The concerned look on Dot's face distracts him long enough to settle his panic so he can focus on his breathing.

Dot reaches out, gently taking Nickolas by the arm, and guides him to the door that leads into the back rooms. Dot scans the key card to unlock the door and nudges Nickolas inside. He pulls himself out of his boss's grip, making his way towards the break room, hoping that Dot will take the hint and leave him alone. Of course, that doesn't happen.

'Do you need to go home?' Dot asks.

'No.' Nickolas paces the break room. He can't look at Dot. He knows none of this is her fault, not really, but right now his emotions are heightened and he's afraid he'll say something he'll regret if they lock eyes.

'I hate seeing you like this. I thought—'

Nickolas stops, watching Dot exhale before continuing.

'I thought once Finn was released, that you'd forget him. That he'd become a memory like all the other patients you've helped. I figured what happened between you both was more of an infatuation, but clearly, after seeing you like this, I was wrong.' Dot's hands clasp together, placing them in front of herself.

'What?'

'I was trying to protect you. Protect your job. You deserve to be with someone that isn't a burden to you.'

'A burden?!' Nickolas balls his hands into fists.

'The whole time I have known you, you have been caring for someone. It's what brought you here. You were caring for Mandy, helping her. Then I see you do it all day with these patients. Now Finn? When is someone going to take care of you, Nykolai?'

'HE DID TAKE CARE OF ME!' He has never raised his voice to Dot before, until now. 'He helped me open up and learn to live again. All I was doing was working in this place. I had no life, no family, no one to share myself with. I was a fucking shell, Dot. Finn cracked me open. I was able to let go of all the pain and guilt and hate I had inside of myself, telling me I didn't deserve all of those things because of my past. He made me feel...' Nickolas runs a hand down his mouth, giving himself a moment to calm down. 'And now none of that matters. Because I did what you asked and I hurt him. And what's worse...what's worse is I know the fucking pain and suffering he has gone through, and in comparison, with what I said, someone he trusted and confided in, I know nothing I say will ever be enough for him to forgive me.'

He needs a drink. Hard liquor. But the best he can do right now is the can of coke sitting in the fridge. He cracks it open, chugging half of it down.

'You love him,' Dot whispers.

Nickolas can't deny it. Not anymore. He looks down at the can in his hand and nods.

'I didn't know,' says Dot.

'You weren't meant to know. No one was. Not even he knew.' He scratches his bottom lip, his eyes still locked onto his drink. He chugs the rest of the can, then crushes it in his hand and throws it into the bin.

'What I said yesterday, about his treatment...I'm still concerned that his recovery was influenced by you, but perhaps I've been following the rules for too long,' explains Dot.

Nickolas looks up, a frown on his face.

'I've seen how the system works. Sure, I've allowed you to bend the rules to help patients open up so that they communicate better, especially since it can be daunting for them to speak to a stranger about their fears, their past, their condition. But times have changed. Medicine has changed and maybe that means it's time for me to change too. Have a more open mind to what people need in order to recover.'

Nickolas's head is spinning. Dot is saying this *now*? After he was forced to walk away from Finn. Maybe he can blame Dot's behaviour yesterday on the shock of seeing them together, being blindsided, and causing his boss to panic about Finn's treatment as well as both of their careers. Dot's words should be giving him comfort right now, but how could they when it's too little, too late.

'It doesn't matter now. As you said, he'll be getting picked up in the next thirty minutes and then I won't ever see him again.' He sniffs a few times, holding back the pressure behind his eyes. 'If you need me, I'll be changing the bedding in the patients' rooms.' He walks past Dot and heads straight for the laundry room.

*

He keeps his mind focused on the job. As he walks out of the third room, he hears the buzz of the mesh gate being unlocked. On instinct, he looks over, and there Finn is, standing by, ready to walk through and forget about this place, forever. Finn pushes the gate open but doesn't walk forward. Nickolas holds his breath, watching. Finn looks back over his shoulder, eyes landing directly on Nickolas, and without another word, Finn turns back around and leaves.

Nickolas wipes the small tear at the corner of his eye and moves onto the next room.

*

He walks into the last room. Finn's room. Sitting on the pillow, like a parting gift the cleaners leave at a hotel, is Mandy's iPod. Beside it are the AirPods, sitting on top of a piece of paper. He slowly walks towards the mattress, like it's a sleeping animal and if he moves too quickly it could wake and attack him. He picks up the iPod and headphones. The paper underneath is the goodbye card he made. Finn left it behind, keeping all remnants of Nickolas locked away in this place to be forgotten.

Nickolas opens the card one more time. His stomach churns as he reads 'see you on the outside'. He folds the card and puts it in his pocket so he can throw it in the bin later. He pockets Mandy's iPod and begins to strip the bed. He doesn't place any clean sheets on the mattress since room thirteen is now vacant. He returns the bin of dirty laundry so it can be washed and collects the trolley of clean clothes that needs to be distributed to every room.

Once finished, he takes his break, not bothering to let Dot or Hayley know of his whereabouts, considering he has been absent since he started work this morning. He goes to the break room, remembering that he didn't have any food and is left snacking on whatever he can find in the cupboards. It hits him that this is the first time Dot didn't bring any baked goods to share.

He finds a few muesli bars, a packet of chips, and an apple in the back of the fridge that he claims for himself. He sits and eats in silence, not allowing his mind to focus on anything besides the sounds of his biting and chewing. When he's finished, he makes his way to the common room with Eric and Sky, their shift starting for the day. He steps inside and the room feels different. Cora, Alex, and Ryder are sitting in a corner, keeping to themselves, the room deprived of the laughter and warmth it held over the last few days. Finn was a ray of sunshine that lit up everything and everyone he touched.

He lets Dot and Hayley go on break and sets up for lunch while Sky and Eric try to liven up the atmosphere in the common room.

*

The remainder of the day leaves Nickolas working on autopilot. He ticks things off in his head, making sure all tasks are complete as they go through the process of lunch, setting up for group, and escorting those who aren't involved back to their room. He isn't in the mood to strike up a conversation with anyone and only gives the bare minimum response when asked a question. Patients that he would happily spend his day interacting with, he decides to let them be, figuring he won't be great company today with how he is feeling.

Eventually, the clock strikes three and Nickolas is ready to hightail it out of there. He collects his bag so he can go home, get drunk and spend the next two days curled up with Socks in the darkness of his bedroom. He bangs his locker door closed, stopping in his place when he sees Dot blocking the doorway.

'Before you leave, I just want to say that I'm sorry,' says Dot.

All Nickolas can do is stand there. No energy left to fight.

'Everything that happened with you and Brett, between the incident and him being fired, having to find a replacement for not only him but for Jasmine too...I just...I behaved irrationally.' Dot sighs.

'You behaved how a boss should behave when they learn that their employee was breaking rules and protocols with a patient.' Nickolas sounds robotic.

'Perhaps. But when have I ever questioned the way you bend the rules around here, Nykolai? And if I do recall, I bent them first when I allowed you to visit Mandy at night.'

He recalls. But now, as he stands in the middle of the locker room, body exhausted from talking, feeling, hurting, he's ready to just go home and be alone.

'I hope one day you can accept my apology.'

Nickolas sighs. He knows he will. Dot is like his mother and sometimes a parent's actions are misguided, thinking of what's best for their child's interests, but not realising what's actually best for the child.

'I'll see you on Friday. Please don't call me in,' says Nickolas.

Dot chuckles. 'I won't. Scout's honour.'

He hikes his backpack over his shoulder and makes his way past Dot, accepting the pat on his back as he leaves. He waves goodbye to Jasmine as she buzzes the door open and heads for the automatic doors, squinting as the bright afternoon sun shines down on him. The doors close behind him, and he stops. Nickolas looks up to the sky as he takes a minute to enjoy the breeze through his hair, the sun on his face, and the feeling of being free.

After a few deep breaths, he brings his head back down, trying to blink away the dots he sees in front of his eyes as they adjust to a natural amount of sunlight. He stops blinking once the dots have cleared, only to blink again as he questions the sight in front of him.

It can't be. Sitting on the edge of the fountain is Finn. Green eyes are looking back at Nickolas, Finn's elbows resting on his knees, his red hair styled as though it's meant to be messy. Finn's wearing a maroon long sleeve top, which is hugging his body in all the right places, and dark blue jeans with a pair of Converse. Finn looks beautiful. Healthy. Put together. And Nickolas is pleased to see some of the purple under those beautiful eyes has gone. Stuck in place, unable to move, whether from the shock of seeing Finn or from fear that it's a hallucination, Nickolas's breath hitches in his throat.

Finn stands up and takes a few steps towards him, stopping with only a couple of feet between them. He shoves his hands in pockets and gives Nickolas a small, shy smile.

'Hey, Nick.'

Two words. That's all it takes for Nickolas's knees to go weak.

'Hey.' He thumbs at his lip, scared to know if seeing Finn right now is a good sign or not.

'What...what are you doing here?'

'I, ah, I forgot something. I came back to get it.'

'Oh. Well, I—I cleaned out your room, man. Nothing was left behind.' He doesn't bring up the iPod or the card. The way they were strategically placed, it was obvious they were left behind on purpose. 'But you can go in and Jasmine can take a look for you.'

'No need. What I left behind is standing right in front of me.'

Nickolas's heart begins beating so fast he's sure Finn can hear it. The rush of blood to his ears makes him wonder if he heard Finn correctly. A hand cups Nickolas's face, and he can't help but lean into the touch, the warmth of Finn's palm feeling as good as, if not better than, the sun on his face.

'I spent the last fourteen days rewiring my mind and my body,' Finn explains. 'I spent all that time learning how to deal with a mental illness I'm going to be living with for the rest of my life. I also learnt that just because I'm bipolar, that doesn't mean it's the end for me.'

Nickolas takes in every word, unsure where Finn is going, but hope still bubbles inside him.

'The one thing I didn't expect in those fourteen days, Nickolas, was to find someone that opened up my world.'

'Finn—'

'No, let me finish. Please. I thought being bipolar was a death sentence and, fuck, if I hadn't started taking the medications or had people around me to help while it was balancing out, then it could have been. I don't want you to take care of me, not like the way you take care of everyone inside of this place. I want us to take care of each other the way you take care of someone you're falling in love with.'

Nickolas gasps.

'I've been slowly falling in love with you each and every day I was here. Each time you came to check on me, each time you sat by my side while we talked. I could feel something growing between us.'

Nickolas is speechless, which is probably for the best since he doesn't want to interrupt what Finn has to say.

'You saved me, Nick. Not only physically, but metaphorically too. Because of you, I started to believe that there was a life waiting for me when I got out. A life worth living. A life filled with friends and family, with a decent job I can enjoy. A life that would one day open the doors to me getting my own place, maybe a dog so I have someone I can take running with me in the mornings.' Finn looks down, breaking the eye contact between them. 'But it isn't enough.' Finn looks back up, green eyes locking on Nickolas's. 'It's missing you. I want all those things and I want to share them all with you, Nick.'

Nickolas searches Finn's face, looking for any lie behind the words. All he can see is hope. Soft, green, cloudy eyes filled with hope and love. Nickolas holds back his tears. 'What I said...'

'Was because of Dorothy.'

Nickolas shoots his eyebrows up.

'She told me. Before I left this morning, she pulled me aside and explained what she did, what she said. It all made sense after that.'

'It doesn't matter if it was because of her. I still said it and I hate that I hurt you like that. I didn't mean any of it.' A single tear falls down Nickolas's cheek and Finn wipes it away with his thumb.

'I know.' Finn closes the gap between them. Their foreheads rest against one another, and Nickolas closes his eyes and breathes Finn in.

'I don't know when it happened, but I realised that I want to share everything with you,' explains Finn. 'My life. My world. My heart. And once I realised that, I knew I was in love with you. All of you. The good, the bad. To me, you were perfect...*are* perfect.'

Nickolas looks up into Finn's eyes and closes the final gap with a soft kiss. Nickolas feels as though he is having an out-of-body experience, watching the kiss between himself and Finn from afar. They take their time, no longer needing to rush in fear of being caught. No longer feeling as though what they are doing is forbidden. Their lips move slowly, sensually, taking turns in sucking the other's bottom lip before releasing it and doing it again. Nickolas moans and Finn swallows it down. As

Finn's tongue presses against his own, Nickolas knows that nothing in his life has ever tasted so good. Heat begins to build in the pit of his stomach as Finn's hand moves from his cheek to the back of his neck, pulling Nickolas in closer. After what feels like hours, Nickolas pulls away. He's dizzy, feeling as though he's floating, and needs to take a moment to come back down to earth.

'Did you get my card?' Finn keeps Nickolas close.

'Card? You mean the one I made you?'

'It was my way of saying I'll be here waiting.'

See you on the outside. This whole time, Nickolas thought Finn was angry at him, when in actual fact, he hadn't stopped fighting for them.

'How long have you been waiting out here?' Nickolas asks.

'Around three hours.'

'What? I told you what time I finished work today.'

'I know. But after I saw you this morning, I wasn't sure if you were going to stay on and finish your whole shift. I didn't want to risk missing you.'

Nickolas brings his hand up from Finn's waist, holding the back of Finn's neck so he can run his fingers through soft, fiery hair.

'When I saw you at breakfast, all I could do was blame myself,' Nickolas explains.

Finn brings him closer, the extra contact settling his nerves. 'When Jessica picked me up, I went straight home to see my siblings. I showered, went to the pharmacy to get my prescription filled out and I called one of the therapists Dr Hale recommended to make an appointment for tomorrow.'

Nickolas pulls back so he can see Finn's face.

'It's okay. I'm okay. I did it because I want to do this right. Us. Keep up with my meds. Keep up with my therapy so everything doesn't fall on my family, or you. So, once I did that, I asked Jessica to drop me off here.'

'Bet she had a few questions about that.'

'She said after you two shared a heated conversation over the phone, she had her suspicions that you weren't just my nurse.' Finn smiles a cocky smile.

Nickolas scoffs to hide the blush spreading over his face. 'Bitch, I'm nobody's nurse. I'm an orderly. It's different.'

'Ah, ha...you know, defending my honour to my sister is pretty fucking hot.'

'Oh really?' Nickolas smirks.

'So, what do you say, should we make this thing official?' Finn asks.

'Thought you'd never ask.'

Smiling like two lovesick teenagers, they kiss again. Finn's arms wrap around Nickolas's waist to lift him off the ground and spin on the spot. Nickolas laughs. It's the gayest, most embarrassing thing that has ever happened to him, but he doesn't fucking care. He's happy. He's in love. Everything else is just white noise in comparison.

16. The Months That Followed

The setting sun is beaming on Nickolas's face. He tilts his head back, his eyes closed against the golden glow so it doesn't blind him, as he takes a deep breath in. He's made it. After all the dreams he was having, he finally found the time to drive down to 12th Street Beach.

It's not a luxurious beach. The sand isn't starch white, and there are no palm trees or people drinking from coconuts. But it's the closest thing he has, which doesn't say much since this is the first time he's visited the ocean. As he sits on the beige sand that has more weeds and rocks than sand, he's still able to enjoy the calming sound of the waves crashing onto the shore, the green water still reminding him of the beautiful eyes that belong to the man he loves. Finn.

The last three months have been like nothing he could have expected, yet everything he has ever wanted all wrapped up in one. Since the day Finn was waiting for him at the fountain, his world has been tipped upside down. For the better, of course.

*

Nickolas can't believe this is real. Finn walked out of the centre only six hours ago, and yet here he is, sitting in the passenger seat of his car. He keeps glancing at Finn as he drives them to his apartment, so Nickolas can change before they go on for their first official date.

'Take a seat anywhere; I promise I'll be quick. I just don't want to go out smelling like a hospital,' Nickolas explains.

'You know, I never understood that phrase until I got home and realised my clothes smelled like sterilised equipment.'

'It's from the products the cleaners use at night,' Nickolas yells out to Finn as he runs the water for his shower. He gets under the spray before it's even warm, too eager to clean himself and get back to Finn in case he steps out and realises it was all a dream. As the water runs down his back and the soap lathers up his skin, he hears Finn's love confession in his head, as if he were standing in the bathroom with him, repeating the words again and again. He can feel the firmness of Finn's hand on his hips and the softness of his tender lips on his own. If none of it is real, he's going to have to give his mind praise for concocting such a detailed hallucination.

He steps out of the shower, dries himself off, and wraps the towel around his waist. He opens the bathroom door, and all he can hear is Finn's voice, a few octaves higher than Nickolas is used to hearing it.

Cautiously, Nickolas steps out and makes his way into the living room, where he can see Finn sitting on the couch, back turned towards him.

'Well, aren't you a cutie? Yes, you are, and you know it too. Look at you. Personally, I'm into boys, specifically your daddy, but I think I'm going to have to make an exception for you.'

Nickolas can't help but smile as Socks meows and starts purring.

'Socks, that's your name, right?'

Another meow.

'Does your daddy have a thing for gingers? I'm just asking because, between the both of us, I couldn't help but—'

Nickolas clears his throat. Finn spins around quickly, the movement causing Socks to jump up onto the back of the couch.

'I see you met Socks.'

'I have,' says Finn. 'She shook me down, gave me the whole "if you hurt my dad, I'm going to scratch you to pieces" speech. Very intimidating.'

Nickolas can't help but chuckle. 'I bet. Is that why she was rolling all over you?'

'Well, I mean, we gingers have to stick together. And since you took so long in the shower, we had time to bond.'

All Nickolas wants to do is step over and kiss the dork he is so madly in love with. Instead, he makes his way into the bedroom, quickly gets dressed in his black skinny jeans, which have so many rips that it shows more skin than they cover. He puts on a black tank top and his red and black flannel, which he leaves unbuttoned, and rolls the sleeves so they stop at his elbows. He puts on a fresh pair of socks, and he takes a deep breath before stepping back out into the living room.

He looks up as he hears a whistle. Convinced Finn is playing with Socks, a blush creeps up onto Nickolas's cheeks as he notices Finn is in fact looking at him, evidently undressing him with lust-filled eyes, which he finds ironic since he was standing before Finn in nothing but a towel only moments before.

'You look...wow. I mean I liked you dressed as an eggplant, but this is...'

Once again, Nickolas laughs. He flips Finn off, but it's not serious. He loves the way the redhead can make him laugh and smile out of nowhere. He has laughed more in the last few weeks with Finn than he has in his whole life.

'Whatever, you love my eggplant uniform,' says Nickolas.

'I mean, I love eggplants, but the uniform is neither here nor there.'

Nickolas makes sure Socks has food and water before grabbing his keys, phone, and wallet.

'So, where you taking me?' Nickolas asks.

'That will spoil the surprise.'

'Okay, then how will I know where to drive to?'

Finn holds a hand out, indicating that Nickolas isn't the one driving, and without hesitation, he rolls his eyes and gives the keys over.

*

Finn first makes a stop for food. They learn that they both love olives on pizza. According to Finn, it would have been a deal-breaker if Nickolas had said no. Finn parks the car, and Nickolas recognises where they are. They step out and make their way onto the pier at the North Ave Beach scenic spot, a place Nickolas knows well but has never visited. Although there is sand, it's more of a lookout, with the pier being the main attraction of this part of Chicago. Nickolas doesn't think he can tick 'visiting a beach' off his bucket list, especially since his feet have yet to touch sand.

They walk down the concrete path in silence, passing a few people, but for a late afternoon on a Tuesday, it's mostly dead. Thankfully, there isn't a strong wind and the sun is still out, so as they take a seat on the ground with the water and Chicago skyline as their view, Nickolas opens the pizza box and enjoys the peacefulness of their destination.

They eat in silence, but the lack of conversation doesn't make Nickolas feel awkward; however, he does suspect Finn is feeling as nervous as he is.

'I've been meaning to ask if, if you got into trouble at work...because of me.' Finn throws a burnt crust into the pizza box. 'After Dorothy explained things to me, I was worried that...'

'No. No, it's okay. I didn't get fired or suspended or whatever. The worst of it was that night, when I said those things to you.' Nickolas takes a piece of pineapple off the top of his pizza, needing something sweet in his mouth. 'Dot had no intentions of reporting me, even if sometimes I feel like she should have.'

'What?'

With his appetite suddenly gone, Nickolas throws the half-eaten pizza slice back into the box, dusts his hands off, takes a deep breath, and turns towards Finn, giving the redhead his full attention.

'Did you...did you follow through with your treatment for me?' asks Nickolas. 'Did you only do it knowing that it meant we could be together when you got out?'

'Honestly? Maybe at first...' Finn confesses.

Nickolas sits up straight, dread coursing through him.

'But I promise that didn't last long.'

Nickolas waits for Finn to elaborate.

'When I woke up in the infirmary, I understood my situation...my diagnosis – it wasn't something I could ignore anymore. I didn't want to live like my mother, but I was also scared of what the medications were going to do to me. I mean, even when I was taking them, they still made me want to try and kill—' Finn stops.

Nickolas reaches over, taking Finn's hand, knowing he can do so without having to worry about anyone seeing.

'I woke up, and I decided that I wanted to do things right. For me. Not for my family, and not for you. I wanted to be able to know I had things under control. That I had my life back. So, after that moment, whether you were waiting for me at the finish line or not, I wanted to cross it on my own. That way, once I did it, I'd know that I could cross any other finish line that came before me in the future.'

'You know, if you need help, I'm here. Not in the way that makes you feel like you're incapable of doing anything, but if you're having a rough day or unsure if you're slipping and may need an adjustment to your meds, you can come to me,' Nickolas offers.

Finn nods. 'I know. As I said, I want us to take care of each other as any couple without a mental illness would.' Finn smiles to try and make things seem less intense.

But Nickolas only notices one word in that whole sentence. 'A couple, huh?'

'Yeah, a couple. You know, partners, lovers, boyfriends. All of that...if that's okay with you.'

'I think I'm more than okay with that.' Nickolas leans forward, placing his lips on Finn's, and he can't help but smile against those perfect soft lips as he realises he can do this whenever he wants, wherever he wants, loving it more and more each time he does.

'There is something else I should tell you,' Finn interjects.

Nickolas pulls back just enough so he can see Finn's eyes.

'My family wants you to come over for dinner.'

Nickolas can't help but groan. Not because he doesn't want to – okay, a part of him doesn't want to, but it's more because he has never had to do the whole 'meet the family' thing before, and considering how he and Finn came to be, he isn't thrilled about possibly getting yelled at, especially after the ear full he gave Jessica.

'There is no way of getting out of this, is there?' Nickolas asks.

'Afraid not. And you can't use work as an excuse because Jessica will literally pick a breakfast, lunch, or dinner to work in with your shifts,' explains Finn.

'Ugh. Can I at least enjoy my two days off first?'

Finn chuckles. 'Of course. But don't put it off for too long. She's persistent and might end up visiting the treatment centre while you're on your break.'

The thought of that makes Nickolas panic. He suddenly yawns, and although he'd love nothing more than to keep spending time with Finn, he needs to get home and start catching up on sleep.

'Come on, big guy. Let me take you home,' offers Finn.

Finn drives them back to Nickolas's apartment, returns the keys, and although Nickolas would love nothing more than to invite Finn up so they could fall asleep beside one another, Nickolas figures it's probably too soon.

'I think we should take this slow.' It's as though Finn had read his mind. 'Dr Hale mentioned that I need to take it easy in regards to starting a new relationship, and as much as I want to do everything with you that I've spent the last fourteen days dreaming about, I also don't want to ruin this by going too fast.'

'I think slow is a good idea. This whole relationship thing is new for me too, so going slow is probably the best for both of us.'

'Okay.'

'Okay.' Nickolas leans down, his position on the first step of his apartment stairs giving him a slight height advantage. He gently cups Finn's cheek and kisses his lips, enjoying one final moment before going inside. It's so soft that he would have sworn the kiss never happened. He leans his forehead on Finn's, waiting for his heart to slow down.

'I wrote my number into your phone while you were driving. Figured it's easier than you waiting for me at work,' Nickolas explains.

Finn pulls away, smiling like a goofball, and Nickolas burns the image into his memory as he turns and walks up the remaining steps to his apartment, trying not to look back, knowing he wouldn't be able to continue forward if he did. Once inside, he walks into his bedroom and lays on his bed, smiling as he plays the entire day over in his head.

*

On Wednesday, he sleeps in, and when he wakes, he goes grocery shopping. For the first time in a long time, he buys everything fresh. Meat, vegetables, and fruit. Bread, cheese, and eggs. Goodbye to eating frozen meals for one. He plans to cook; even if most of the time it's just for himself, he knows sometime in the near future he'll be cooking for Finn too.

Once he's home and has everything unpacked, a sudden 'ping' fills the room, and Nickolas looks around to work out where it came from. Socks is curled on the couch, so the noise couldn't have been the bell on her collar. It goes off again and Nickolas registers that the noise is in fact, his message alert tone. It's been a long time since Nickolas received anything but a phone call, so when he sees Finn's name next to a message notification, he can't help but smile.

Finn: Can't stop thinking about you.

Nickolas's thumbs hover over the keyboard. He doesn't know how to respond to that, especially with the way he can feel his heart pounding in his chest. He's never had this, never wanted it until now. The vibration in his hand brings him out of his head as another text comes through.

Finn: Sorry. That was for Socks. Got your numbers mixed up.

Chuckling to himself, Nickolas walks over to Socks, snaps and photo, and sends it back to Finn.

Finn: There's my girl...tell your daddy I miss him.

Nickolas pockets his phone, his cheeks warm as he continues unpacking. He does a load of laundry, getting his uniforms ready for the days ahead. He makes himself some lunch and then decides to give his wardrobe a clean-out of anything that doesn't fit or is too raggedy to wear anymore. Around a quarter to three, Nickolas's phone pings again.

Finn: I heard back from Dr Warnock, the therapist Dr Hale suggested for me. I have an appointment with him this week. Just an introduction so he knows my situation and can get a copy of my prescription in case it needs changing.

Nickolas doesn't hesitate to reply.

Nickolas: That's great. He's been mentioned a few times at work, all good things.
Finn: Whatcha doing?
Nickolas: About to watch a movie.
Finn: Want some company?

Nickolas isn't even ashamed of how quickly he writes 'yes' back to Finn.

When Finn arrives, Nickolas loves the way his redhead greets him with a quick kiss on the lips before taking off his shoes and sitting down on the couch.

'Alright, what are we watching?' Finn asks.

He smiles as he makes his way towards the couch, loving how comfortable Finn feels in his apartment.

Nickolas can't remember anything about the movie, mostly because fifteen minutes in, he fell asleep with his back against Finn's chest, his long legs on either side of Nickolas's body with Socks curled on his lap, keeping him warm. He wakes up to the feeling of slender fingers softly running through his hair, which is so comforting, it makes him want to fall back asleep.

'Hey, the movie's over, sleepyhead. And I kinda need to piss,' says Finn.

Nickolas moves just enough so Finn can worm his way out from under him, and takes a moment for his body to fully wake after his peaceful nap. Nickolas rubs open his eyes as Finn makes his way back into view.

'I, ah. I better get home,' Finn explains.

It's obvious to Nickolas that Finn doesn't want to leave, and he can't deny that having Finn go home is nowhere close to what he wants right now, but they agreed to take it slow.

'Do you want a ride home?' Nickolas offers.

Finn shakes his head 'no', and a part of Nickolas is disappointed that they won't get the extra time together. The afternoon sun is shining outside, which helps ease the worry he has about Finn walking the streets alone. Still lying on the couch, Nickolas watches as Finn walks towards him, steps slow and calculated. Finn crouches down, keeping his beautiful green eyes locked on Nickolas.

'You probably won't believe this, but I had fun tonight,' Finn offers.

'Sure you did.' Nickolas can't help but roll his eyes. 'I used you as a body pillow while I slept.'

'I've been used for a lot worse, Nick. For once, it was nice to have someone want to be close without wanting anything from me.'

Finn's words hit Nickolas like a knife to the chest. He hasn't forgotten about Finn's trauma. It's more as though his mind separated the Finn at the centre from the Finn that's now squatting in front of him. He knows he can't do that though, because they are the same person, both still struggling with the past, and both still learning to adjust to a new lifestyle.

'You know I'd never try to—' Nickolas begins to explain, but his words get cut off by Finn's soft lips. It's not sexual, simply tender, loving, and the motion causes Nickolas to freeze. Finn pulls away sooner than Nickolas would like, and he has to take a deep breath before he can find the ability to speak again.

'I know. I just wanted to let you know that it was nice.' Finn stands up and lets himself out without saying another word.

*

As Nickolas lays in bed that night, it dawns on him that he's in no rush to be the one to take their relationship to the next level. For at least a week now, they've had to navigate around the sexual tension that's been building between them, not to mention the fantasies and dreams that have plagued his mind. But regardless of all that, he knows Finn has to be the one who initiates anything between them. Nickolas doesn't want to risk what they have by complicating it with sex, which means if he needs to wait another month or two, he is more than willing to do so because Finn is worth the wait.

*

When he wakes, he checks the time on his phone only to notice a message from Finn. Eyes still struggling to open, he reads the text, and the words warm his chest.

Finn: So apparently, I can only have a decent sleep if I have the weight of your body on top of me.
Finn: Not in like, a sexual way, but I mean, that's not a bad thing either. I just meant like, cuddling.
Finn: And if you're not into cuddling then that's perfectly fine too. What I'm trying to say is, after our couch session, I may now have some expectations for our relationship.

Nickolas doesn't know what to say. He doesn't want to sound too eager and admit he rolled around for a few hours trying to get comfortable once Finn went home, eventually drifting off to sleep after his thoughts regarding the speed of their relationship quietened down. But now he wants to make sure he doesn't say the wrong thing, so Nickolas figures the best option is to reply with a sarcastic comment.

Nickolas: Not surprised, luxury is hard to walk away from.

The second he presses send, he wants to delete it. He sounds like a self-absorbed idiot, and, considering his history, he is nowhere close to being able to label himself as luxurious. His hands begin to sweat as he tries to think of a comment to cover his tracks when his phone vibrates with another message.

Finn: Don't see myself walking away anytime soon ☺

Nickolas's heart skips a beat.

While making breakfast, Nickolas can't help but read over the messages to make sure he didn't dream them up. He goes to the gym after he finishes eating and does the longest workout he's ever done since working at the centre. He does an hour of cardio, then uses the punching bag for a good thirty minutes before working on his legs, making sure he leaves himself with enough energy to fit in some squats and lunges. By the end of it, his body is aching, and he knows that by tomorrow he'll be cursing himself while he stands on his feet all day at work.

The minute he walks through his apartment door, Nickolas makes his way towards the bathroom to soak his muscles under the spray of a hot shower. As his body relaxes, his mind once again takes him back to Finn's messages from this morning. One of the things he's noticed since Finn left the centre is how he's more open. The last few days before Finn's release, he'd seen glimpses of this side of Finn: talkative and lively. But now, it's as though the freedom is allowing Finn to open up, and Nickolas is finding it intoxicating. Finn is this spark that lights up everything around him, and Nickolas can't help but want to be in Finn's orbit twenty-four-seven.

Nickolas gets dressed and makes himself something to eat before sitting down to spend some time with Socks.

'So, you met Finn, huh? What'd ya think?'

Socks meows, pawing at Nickolas, so he'll move the plate from his lap, allowing Socks to sit in its place.

'Yeah, I like him too.'

*

For Nickolas, returning to work in the absence of Finn is a blessing and a curse. He loves that whenever he thinks of Finn, he can now picture the redhead on his couch or standing outside in the parking lot; his memories no longer confined to Finn being within these cold white walls. However, it makes his days drag. He still has Ryder, Cora, Alex, and Ethan to talk and joke with. Some of them even ask about Finn while Nickolas plays it off as though he has no idea how he's going, but the looks Cora throws his way make him think that she knows he's lying.

His breaks are different. Before they were spent in silence, maybe the occasional conversation with whoever was taking their break with him, but now he sits down and has an influx of messages from Finn waiting to be read, most of them an incoherent string of thoughts.

Finn: Woke up thinking about you.

Finn: What time do you finish work? I think I'm having Nickolas cuddle withdrawals.

Finn: Jessica is on my ass about this dinner. Trust me, rip off the Band-Aid, Nickolas. It will be better for both of us this way.

Finn: My appointment with Dr Warnock went well.
He seems to be happy with how I'm adjusting and pleased that I have some form of routine.

Finn: You're officially looking at the new store clerk for a little bookstore not far from you. My dashing good looks and charming personality won me the position.

'Happy looks good on you,' compliments Dot.

Nickolas looks up from his phone as his boss sits at the table across from him. He'll make sure to reply to Finn before he walks back out onto the floor.

'Don't make it a thing, Dot.'

'Make what a thing? The fact that you're seeing someone and you're happy and smiling.'

He groans, feeling like a little kid whose parents are teasing him about his schoolboy crush. 'It's new. We're still getting to know one another, so don't go gettin' ahead of yourself.'

What Nickolas said is true. It's been a little over a week since Finn was released, and due to his work schedule, they have only been able to see one another twice. But regardless, being able to speak to Finn outside of work hours has made a difference. It's given them space to get to know each other outside of the centre. Finn even surprised Nickolas at work. They ate outside beside the fountain, memories of that day flooding back to them both.

They show affection, and the other night they enjoyed a steamy make-out session in front of the TV that never went further than their tongues exploring each other's mouths. They're going slow, just like they agreed to do.

'I'm glad you're not rushing into anything. I know it's been a while since I dated, but I still remember what it's like when you start a new relationship. How it makes you feel like nothing else in the world matters besides them and all you want to do is explore everything right then and there.'

Nickolas knows those feelings well. He's had them since Finn was his patient, but he doesn't think he should remind Dot of that. He was concerned that his boss may have put him on probation after what happened, but perhaps Dot figured, now that he and Finn are dating, and Finn is still following a routine outside of their relationship, that her outburst may have been unnecessary. His time currently consists of training the new employees, Mary, Alice, and Emmett, who were hired to work the floor. The extra employees have given them the opportunity to cut back on the number of double shifts everyone was working. Ted's replacing Jasmine while on maternity leave, meaning that's one less person Nickolas had to train.

As he takes one of Dot's chocolate chip scones, he can't help but confide in Dot, knowing he has so few people in his life he can do so with.

'We're taking it slow.'

Dot nods.

'Like, really slow.'

'Oh...*Oh*.'

'I've never been in a relationship before, and from what Finn has shared, neither has he. At least, not a healthy one.' His mind goes back to the night they recently shared, where Finn opened up about his past, one that involved much older men. Men, who, at the time, Finn believed to be in love with. And thought loved him back. Now, with the help of Dr Hale, Finn understands that those men were using him. Grooming him to the point where Finn believed that's what love was. Nickolas's only stories were the unpleasantries of randoms he would hook up with, never wanting more than a quick fuck. But Finn never judged or questioned his choices, the same way Nickolas never did with Finn.

'His sister wants me to come over for family dinner,' explains Nickolas.

'Nervous?' Dot asks.

'Shit scared.'

They both chuckle.

'I don't know. I mean, part of me is worried about what they will think about me falling for their brother while he was a patient, but I guess the part I'm mostly concerned about is what they'll think of me, of who I am.'

'You seem to forget that the person you are today is someone any family would be proud to have dating their son, or in this case, brother.'

Nickolas takes another bite of the scone, never able to take a compliment.

'You have your own apartment. You have a steady job in a respectable field. What is there not to like? You don't smoke, you don't gamble, and you drink responsibly. Anyone else that had been brought up in your shoes could have taken a one-eighty and found themselves going down a very different path.'

Once again, Dot is right. He took the shitty hand he was dealt and turned those cards into aces. He made something of himself not only to prove his father wrong or so he could support his sister, but he also did it so he could become the person no one ever believed he could be.

'Tell Finn you're free next Friday. You have the morning shift that day, and then you're working the night shift on Saturday, so you have no excuse.'

Dot gives him a stern look as if to say 'you've got this' before standing up to clean the lunch dishes. Taking a deep breath, Nickolas picks up his phone and replies to Finn's exciting news before he gives his boyfriend some more.

Nickolas: Proud of you. Maybe now you can take me out on a real date 😉

Finn: I'm planning to put my first pay check towards it.

Nickolas: Pizza on the pier is more than enough.

Nickolas: Also, better make sure you have next Friday night off if I'm going to be having dinner with your family.

His phone starts vibrating in his hand as Finn's name appears on the screen. He accepts the phone call, well aware of the dopey grin on his face before he even hears Finn speak.

'Seriously? You're coming to dinner?' Finn sounds so excited.

'Of course,' says Nickolas. 'It's important to your family, and they're important to you, and, well, you're important to me.' Nickolas is sure he can hear the hitch in Finn's breath, but he doesn't comment on it. 'I finish work at three on Friday and have the night shift on Saturday, so I figured it was the best timeframe.' He feels a tap on his shoulder and turns to see Dot walking out, signalling that his break is over. 'I have to get back to work.'

'Right. Go. I'll let Jessica know.'

'Okay.'

'Okay.' Finn's tone of voice makes it clear how excited he is.

Smiling and not wanting to hang up, Nickolas waits a few more seconds to allow the quietness between them to settle his racing heart. 'I'll see you tonight.'

He hangs up, puts his phone back in his locker, and counts down the hours till he finishes work and can go home and spend the evening cooking dinner for Finn.

*

That night, Nickolas cooks Finn chicken and mushroom carbonara and listens to the full story of how Finn got his new position at the bookstore. Nickolas sits there, watching how excited his boyfriend is to have found a decent job that isn't going to trigger him. Nickolas mentions that everyone from his work says hi and how they are pleased to hear Finn is doing well, and then cleans up before they sit to watch a movie together.

The second they press play, Nickolas notices that Finn is fidgeting, unable to stay focused, turning to look his way before looking back at the screen. He doesn't push, hoping that whatever it is, Finn will share when he's ready, but as the movie goes on, Nickolas can't help but feel frustrated by Finn's constant moving.

'What's up? You don't want to watch the movie?' Nickolas asks.

'What? No, that's not...' Finn sighs. 'Would it maybe be okay if...if I stayed the night?'

'Oh.' That isn't what Nickolas is expecting to hear. His one-word reply seems to have put Finn on edge. He tells himself to play it cool as he clarifies his response. 'Sure. I mean, if, if that's what you want...'

'That's what I want.' Finn relaxes, sinking into the couch beside Nickolas. They hold hands, their fingers intertwining as they focus back on the movie.

*

It's an adjustment having someone in bed beside him. Socks is pacing up and down. Her usual spot against Nickolas's chest now occupied by Finn. And it's not that having another human being beside him is making it hard to drift off to sleep; it's the fact that it's Finn beside him. He spent nights dreaming of a time when he could fall asleep with Finn in his arms, listening to his soft breathing as it lulls him to sleep, and it is finally about to be his reality. Socks eventually settles down at the end of the bed near their feet. He gives Finn a gentle squeeze around the waist before laying a kiss on the back of his boyfriend's neck and whispering goodnight.

*

Not sure of the time, but aware it's early morning since it's still dark out, Nickolas wakes to the sound of whimpering as Finn rocks beside him; at some point their bodies naturally rolling away from each other. He wants to reach out and wake Finn, to bring him back to reality, soothe him, and remind him everything is okay, but Nickolas knows from his training that he shouldn't. Waking someone from a nightmare can do more harm than good. They can wake up agitated, aggressive, confused, and, most of all, scared.

Nickolas sits up, pained by the helpless sounds coming from Finn. The commotion wakes Socks, who crawls towards Finn and rubs her soft fur against his face and neck. The tender touch has the tension seeping out of Finn's body, and his green eyes flutter open and lock onto Socks, who is sitting between them.

'Hey, it's okay,' Nickolas whispers. 'You're in my bed, at my apartment. Everything's okay.' But he doesn't make a move to touch Finn. He watches as he sits up, leans against the bed frame, and gently runs his fingers through Socks's fur.

'Sorry that I woke you,' Finn murmurs.

'Don't apologise.' Nickolas waits a moment. 'I didn't know you were still having nightmares.'

Finn shrugs. 'Sometimes. Not all the time. I'm working on it with Dr Warnock.'

'Is it about that night?'

Finn nods.

Nickolas exits the room to retrieve a glass of water for Finn, and when he returns, he makes sure to sit himself flush against Finn's side, knowing the small amount of body contact will do some good. Finn sips the water and then places the glass on the bedside table.

'I haven't gone to the cops yet. Because to do that, I have to tell Jessica what happened, and telling Jessica is like...it's like admitting I needed her to take care of me. To keep me safe.'

'Finn, hey. That is not at all what it is.' He gently takes Finn's hand, relieved at the squeeze he gets in return. 'What happened had nothing to do with your mental illness. You could have been having a night out, decided you wanted to go home with the guy, and it still may have happened. Needing a place to sleep because you had nowhere else to go did not result in your attack.' Nickolas lets go of Finn's hand and leans towards the bedside table on his side of the bed. He opens the drawer and retrieves a mobile phone. He sighs as he hands it to Finn.

'This was his. You can take it to the police, you can smash it, or you can just put it aside until you know for sure what you want to do. But I think you should have it.'

He watches Finn flip the phone around in his hand, studying it as if he's never seen an iPhone before. But then Finn turns the phone on, and Nickolas watches as the guy's picture appears on screen, looking all happy standing beside a wife and kids.

'That's him, and yet he looks so different.' Finn unlocks the phone and then stops. 'Where are they?'

Nickolas isn't sure if Finn should look at them so soon after a nightmare, but it's not his choice to make. He isn't Finn's doctor or therapist; he is his boyfriend. He is going to support Finn's decisions no matter what. He takes the phone, noticing the small tremor in Finn's hands as he pulls it away, and goes into the hidden folder the guy clicked into that night at the club.

The second Nickolas sees the first picture appear, he glances over at him quickly, to make sure this is what Finn wants before handing the phone back. Nickolas doesn't need to look at the screen to know the order of the photos. He had only seen them once, that night at the club, but it was all it took to burn the images into his brain.

Finn suddenly stops and zooms into a photo, letting out a shaky breath before he passes the phone back to Nickolas.

With a quick glance, Nickolas sees that Finn has zoomed onto his own face, the image showing a flow of tears streaming down his red cheeks, his mouth gagged. The pain and fear are evident without needing to see what is happening in the rest of the photo.

'Sometimes it's not even him in my dreams,' Finn begins to explain, 'Sometimes it's Brett. Sometimes it's a person with no face. A few times, it's been multiple men just passing me around like a rag doll. No matter the scenario, I can feel the way my body ached, how it was screaming for him to stop.'

Nickolas throws the phone to the end of the bed and takes Finn into his arms, holding his boyfriend, keeping Finn safe. They sit like that for a moment, neither one of them speaking as Nickolas runs his fingers through Finn's beautiful red hair.

'I'll tell Jessica at dinner,' says Finn. 'If I'm going to do it, I need you next to me. It's the only way I'll be able to get through it.'

Nickolas gives Finn a kiss on his head, a silent agreement that he will be beside Finn every step of the way. They settle back down under the blanket. Finn nuzzles into Nickolas's chest, and they hold onto one another as they try to fall back asleep.

*

In the following days, Finn and Nickolas are inseparable. When Nickolas has to work, his phone is flooded with messages that make his heart beat faster and his face blush. When Finn has to work, Nickolas goes to visit, perusing the bookshelves while sneaking glances Finn's way as his boyfriend serves people behind the counter. Whenever Nickolas doesn't have night shift, Finn stays over. They make out, their hands roaming over each other's bodies, but nothing ever below the waist. The heat and sexual tension they create from their kissing are enough to leave them panting. Then they fall asleep in each other's arms, some nights they're woken by one of Finn's nightmares, while others they sleep peacefully and undisturbed.

Suddenly, it's Friday, and Nickolas is outside the Cunningham house, leaning against his car while trying to convince himself not to leave and call Finn on the way home to say he suddenly has pneumonia. Moments like this make him wish he still smoked. He sends Finn a message to say he has arrived, not feeling confident enough to knock on the door and have someone that isn't Finn answer. Dot made him an apple pie to take, saying it's rude to arrive empty-handed when invited to dinner.

The front door opens, and his boyfriend walks out in the same jeans Nickolas saw Finn wearing that day by the fountain, along with a navy-blue t-shirt. Nickolas is glad he hadn't decided to go with the button-up shirt he had put on and off at least three times before deciding to wear the maroon long sleeve that had thumb holes in the arms.

'Hey, you made it.' Finn beams down the front porch steps towards him.

The smile alone causes Nickolas's worries to fade away. 'Course I did. What, ya think I was gonna make a run for it?'

'Mexico came to mind, but then I figured your pale ass would burn too much.'

They both chuckle and, just like that, Nickolas is relaxed.

'You baked?' Finn asks.

'Dot did, but she said I can tell your family it's from me. Try and earn myself some brownie points.'

'Don't worry, they're going to love you, just like I do.'

Nickolas melts as Finn's lips press against his. If he looked at his life a few years ago, he never would have pictured himself standing outside in the streets of South Side Chicago proudly kissing his boyfriend before meeting said boyfriend's family. Amazing how quickly things can change.

They enter the house holding hands, and the first thing Nickolas notices is the noise. The TV is going, and there are two kids around the age of thirteen or fourteen running after one another while arguing. A toddler no older than three or four is sitting in a highchair, and Jessica is cooking in the kitchen while Jake sits at the counter.

'Jessica?' Finn tries to grab his sister's attention.

As Jessica turns around, her eyes landing on Nickolas, he squeezes Finn's hand a little tighter to brace himself for what's to come. To his surprise, Jessica embraces him in a hug, and Nickolas has to let go of Finn's hand in order to accept it.

'Thank you,' Jessica whispers.

Nickolas doesn't know how to respond, but thankfully Jessica keeps going, so he doesn't have to.

'I've never seen Finn this happy before, and I know it's not just because he's stable.' Jessica pulls back, winks, and all Nickolas can do is give a small smile in return.

'You want a beer, Nickolas?' Jake calls out to him, and Nickolas has to cough to find his voice before responding with a 'yeah, thanks.' Finn walks him further into the room so he can take a seat at the table.

'Nickolas brought us dessert,' Finn says, placing the pie on the counter.

Jessica looks towards him in shock. 'You made that?'

As much as he wants to impress Finn's family, he doesn't want to start off by lying to them.

'I would have, but I didn't have the time due to work, so Dorothy made it and gave it to me to bring.'

Jessica chuckles. 'I was going to say, if you can bake a pie, then my store-bought lasagne isn't going to be a satisfying dinner for you.'

'Oh, Nickolas is a great cook. Some of the best meals I've had,' Finn boasts. '...Sorry, Jess.'

Nickolas blushes at Finn's compliment. Jessica nudges Finn and retrieves a packet of salad out of the fridge.

'Kate! Luke! Come and sit at the table,' Jessica yells up the stairs.

Dinner is pleasant. It's mostly small talk with some background information about Finn's siblings. No one comments about how or when he and Finn started dating, and for that, Nickolas is relieved. He was at least expecting an earful from

Jessica, but Finn's sister held a smile for the whole night. When the attention turns towards him, Jessica and Jake are impressed to hear how long he's been working at the centre. They don't ask how he began working there, and he isn't sure if that is because Finn had asked them not to or if it's because they already know. Either way, Nickolas is pleased that he doesn't need to mention Mandy when he knows tonight's topic of conversation is about to get heavier.

Jessica stands up, taking the plates away and refusing any help from Nickolas. As Finn's sister begins to dish up the apple pie for everyone, Nickolas gives his boyfriend's hand a supporting squeeze as Finn asks Jessica if the kids can eat in front of the TV so they can speak alone.

Kate and Luke take a bowl of apple pie, look back at the table and shrug before running off to watch TV with their dessert. Jessica sits back down, handing everyone a bowl while keeping eyes on him and Finn.

'Why do I feel like dinner is about to take a turn?' Jessica questions.

'I promise it's not bad. It's just...something I need to tell you,' Finn explains.

'Finn, you don't have to protect them. Be honest.' Nickolas encourages his boyfriend, ignoring their curious looks.

Jake leans his elbows on the table, and Jessica pushes the bowl of pie away.

Finn draws in a deep breath and takes one last look at Nickolas. 'I need to tell you something that happened when I ran away. Dr Warnock is helping me through it, and so is Nickolas, more than he probably realises. But, to fully be able to start moving past it, there's something I need to do, and I can't do it until I first tell you what happened.'

Nickolas shifts a little closer to Finn.

'The night the police found me, the night you were called...when I was committed, I remembered how I ended up there, dumped in the alley.' Finn takes a few deep breaths. 'I went to a hotel with a guy. It was how I was able to find places to sleep, by going home with whoever was offering. But, ah, but that night was different.' Finn looks up from the table. 'That night I was drugged, tied up, and raped.'

'Holy fuck.' Jake's words are barely a whisper. Jessica places her hands in front of her mouth, unable to speak.

'I woke up during the attack, and I...I begged him to stop, but instead, he gagged me and kept going. I eventually passed out and woke up in the alley.' Finn quickly wipes away any sign of tears.

'It's okay, Finn. You're doing great.' Nickolas says.

'I wasn't lying when I said I didn't remember,' Finn continues. 'It wasn't until I was restrained at the treatment centre that the memories came back. It was like I blocked them out until I was triggered again.'

'Jesus Christ. Do you know who did it?'

Nickolas turns to Jake, deciding to answer the question to give Finn a moment to regroup.

'It was only by pure coincidence that I ran into him.'

'Ran into him? The fuck's that supposed to mean?' Jake questioned.

'I was at a bar, and this guy was running his mouth, showing photos to his friends, and when I looked over...they were photos of Finn.'

'Wait, photos?' Jessica finally speaks.

'I took his phone once I saw the photos. His name, address...I told Finn that if he wants to report the guy, we have all the proof we need.'

'I don't want to know how you got all that, do I?' Jessica asks.

Nickolas gives a look, silently answering the question.

'Is this why you told us? Because you're thinking of going to the police,' Jessica chimes in.

'Yes.' Finn confirms.

'Would you have told us if you weren't going to report him?'

Nickolas wants to slap Jake across the head for asking such a question, but instead, he sits still, Finn's hand still in his, as Nickolas rubs his thumb in calming circles.

'Probably not,' Finn admits. 'Part of me is still trying to convince myself that this happened not because I ran away while unmedicated, but because it was simply wrong place, wrong time. The other part of myself keeps saying if I had done what you guys said, then it never would have happened, and I wouldn't be waking up in the middle of the night screaming.'

Nickolas lets go of Finn's hand so he can pull him in close and lay a kiss on his temple. He whispers kind, reassuring words into Finn's ear, soft enough so it feels like a secret between them. He doesn't care that Jake is looking at him as if a different person is suddenly sitting at their dinner table, and he ignores Jessica's tears, knowing that how Jessica may be feeling is nothing in comparison to Finn.

'Look,' Nickolas focuses on Finn's siblings, keeping his arms tightly secure around his boyfriend. 'I understand this is a lot for you guys to take in, but Finn needs your support. He doesn't need you to feel sorry for him or give him pity, because he's stronger than that. He just wanted you guys to know, so when he reports this fucking asshole, he has you standing by his side.'

There isn't much that happens after that. Hugs are shared with some whispered words that Nickolas doesn't question Finn about, and Nickolas is once again surprised that some of those hugs are then offered to him. They eat their apple pie, and when the night comes to an end and Finn asks to spend the night with Nickolas, he doesn't hesitate in saying 'of course'. He stands in the living room, leaning against the threshold as Finn collects a few things in a bag.

He's focused on the TV, but his body is always in tune with Finn. So as Finn walks down the stairs, and Jessica pulls him in for a quick chat, Nickolas can't help but listen in on the conversation.

'I get that Nickolas is your boyfriend, and I suppose at this stage, your support person too, but please be careful. After that kind of trauma, it's easy to attach yourself to someone who makes you feel safe and—'

'Jess, I promise, it's not like that. Yes, Nickolas is there for me, but that's not what brought us together. He sees me – all of me. The good, the bad, the messy. He saw me at my worst, and he's still here.'

Nickolas blushes.

'Just, be safe...I know I don't have to worry about teen pregnancies but still—'

'Jesus. Stop. No. You don't have to worry about that either.'

'Finn, you don't have to pretend you're not—'

'Jessica, I'm serious. We haven't...not yet. We're taking it slow, okay? Happy now?'

'Wow. You guys really do care about one another.'

'We do. I love him, Jess.'

Nickolas quickly wipes at his nose, sniffing back the emotions that Finn's words brought to the surface while hiding away so he's not caught eavesdropping.

*

Back at Nickolas's apartment, Socks greets them at the door, with Finn being the first to get attention. As Nickolas watches his boyfriend lift and cuddle his furball, he knows at that moment he has lost Socks. He can't be mad, though, Finn *is* irresistible.

'I'm going to take a quick shower,' he says.

'Okay.' Finn is more focused on giving Socks a scratch behind the ear than directing his words towards Nickolas.

He lets the water run down his body; the temperature perfect for the slight chill that had set in as it got later into the evening.

'Nickolas?'

The sound of Finn's voice calling his name in the echo of the bathroom startles him.

'Yeah?'

'Mind if I join you?'

He freezes for a moment. It's not the question that puts Nickolas off; it's more the fact that sharing a shower means Finn would be seeing him naked, an experience they have yet to share. Although Nickolas has seen Finn's body, the circumstances were different. But now, now Finn's body will be wet, naked, and standing flush against his in the confined space of his shower. For the sole reason of wanting to be close to him.

'Sure.' He tries to make his voice sound confident, even though he feels like a ball of nerves.

Finn pulls the curtain back, steps into the shower, and Nickolas holds his breath as he keeps his eyes focused on the shower curtain in front of him. The moment Finn's naked body presses against his back, Nickolas lets out a sigh of relief at how perfect it feels. Arms wrap around Nickolas's waist, hands gently gripping his hips. Finn's head leans on his tattoo-covered shoulder, his lips turning into Nickolas's neck, and he shudders from the feeling of Finn's hot breath ghosting over his skin.

'This okay?' Finn asks.

Nickolas relaxes into the touch. 'Yeah, I've just...never been naked in front of someone before.' With their positions, Finn can't see the embarrassed look that's appeared on his face from his confession.

Hands run up and down Nickolas's chest, keeping above the waist like they always do when they make out.

'Really? What about when you've been with other guys?' Finn asks.

Nickolas closes his eyes, enjoying the way Finn's hands feel on his body. 'It's always been a quick fuck. Nothing that involved more than unzipping my pants.' Nickolas gasps as Finn tweaks his nipple, a sensation he never knew he'd like until now. Finn's dick presses against his ass. Finn's soft, but it still feels better than any hard dick he has had poking into him.

He feels pressure on his waist as he realises Finn is trying to slowly turn him around. As Nickolas's body begins to face Finn, he opens his eyes and reminds himself to breathe. The water has turned Finn's hair a deep reddish-brown. He likes it, but he already misses the bright red colour that would catch his eye every time he went to work.

Finn moves his hand up Nickolas's side. Gently brushing over Nickolas's ribs, across his left pec muscle, where his tattoo sits over his heart. Finn's hand stops when it reaches the side of Nickolas's face.

'Makes me feel kinda special that I'm the only one that's gotten to see you like this.'

'There is a lot I've done with you that I haven't done with anyone else.'

Finn leans towards Nickolas for a kiss. As their lips touch, electricity shoots up his spine. With the water cascading over them and the way they are embracing each other's naked bodies, this feels more intimate than any sexual encounter Nickolas has had in the past. He moans, Finn's tongue massaging his as he tastes the remnants of apple pie.

They're both semi-hard at this point, but they ignore it, allowing their dicks to press against one another. Nickolas pulls back, not because he wants it to stop, but because he needs to catch his breath.

'Thank you for tonight,' says Finn. 'I don't think I could have done it without you there beside me.'

Finn's hand begins to slowly travel down Nickolas's body, slipping past his hip and getting awfully close to his dick. With the anticipation of feeling Finn's touch, something suddenly clicks, and Nickolas pulls out of Finn's grasp.

'This isn't because...you don't, you don't feel like you have to thank me, do you?'

Finn's sudden silence makes Nickolas turn cold. It could be because the hot water is beginning to run out, but either way, he shuts it off and exits the shower.

He storms into the bedroom, water still dripping off his body, with the towel wrapped around his waist. As he pulls on a pair of boxers and sweatpants, Finn enters the room.

'Nickolas, wait. That wasn't what I was—'

'I'm not angry at you, Finn.' Frustration is in his voice.

'You're...you're not?'

'No.' He slams the drawer closed as he pulls out a tank top, huffing in annoyance. He turns towards a tense Finn and puts his hands on his hips. 'I'm angry because after you ran away, you were forced to believe that if someone showed you a kind gesture, you were expected to offer them sex in exchange for a thank you.'

Finn exhales, looking as though he wants to curl into a ball.

'I'm not them, Finn. And you sure as shit don't have to do that anymore. Not for me. Not for anyone.' He takes a step towards him, placing his hands on either side of Finn's face so his green eyes are forced to make contact with his own. 'I helped you because you needed me to and because I love you. If I do something for you, it's because I want to, and I'll never expect anything in return.'

Finn's glistening tears rip Nickolas apart inside. He rests his forehead on Finn's, aware that even clothed, his body is as wet as Finn's.

'Doing things for someone you love is what being in a relationship is all about.'

Finn sniffs. 'I guess I'm not used to having a boyfriend.'

Nickolas chuckles. 'Well, I'm not used to being one, so looks like we're both learning as we go.'

They pull apart so Finn can get dressed, the cold night air causes Finn's body to tremble. It's not overly late, but they are both emotionally exhausted. Getting under the covers, Finn curls into Nickolas, who lays soft kisses on his head.

'I'll talk to Dr Warnock about it in my next session,' offers Finn.

'Yeah...that might help,'

Silence falls between them. As Nickolas begins to drift off, Finn's words wake him.

'I'm sorry about before, but I'm not sorry I got to see you naked.'

Nickolas huffs in amusement, his eyes still closed, too tired to open them.

'You're beautiful, Nick...just thought I should tell you that.'

*

Things start to get busy for them both. Nickolas no longer has to work doubles due to the extra staff, but he still has a fourteen-day roster, something Dot is trying to adjust so everyone can get a decent amount of down time between shifts. Finn's been working every day as one of the other employees at the bookstore has gone on a two-week vacation, which means the only time Nickolas can see his boyfriend is when he's not working night shifts, and Finn can come over for dinner and stay the night.

When Nickolas gets to the end of his fourteen-day roster, he goes to the police station with Finn to report Mr Brody Gibbs for assault and rape. The officer who's taking Finn's statement is caring and understanding, not once judging the situation Finn was in at the time of the attack and refrains from pushing when Finn needs to take a moment.

When the time comes, Nickolas hands over the evidence, not ashamed to admit the truth behind how he obtained it. If they want to book him, he doesn't care, as long as the rapist fuck gets arrested alongside him.

*

A few weeks later, when Nickolas is working the night shift with Lydia, he gets a call from Finn.

'Hey, you.' Nickolas smiles into the phone.

'He confessed, Nick.'

His smile drops as he hears Finn's soft, dull tone.

'He what?' Nickolas doesn't even need to ask who 'he' is.

'He confessed. Apparently, he's been out of town for work, but they brought him in tonight for questioning after his plane landed, and he confessed to the whole thing.'

Nickolas runs his hand down his face.

'He's going to do five years. I mean, with good behaviour, he'll probably do less, but it worked. He's...he's getting put away. His name will be all over the news, and his family will know the truth about who he really is.' Finn's voice is shaking but full of relief.

'I'm so proud of you, Finn.'

Finn sniffs. 'Fucker didn't even want to press charges against you. He just accepted his punishment.'

Nickolas is not going to lie and say that he isn't slightly relieved to hear that, but regardless, he would have owned up to what he did, not regretting his actions at all.

'I wish you weren't working right now,' says Finn, desperation in his voice.

'I know...me too. You're with your family though, right?'

'Jake is here, and Jessica should be back from her date any minute now. She messaged, requesting a fake family emergency to help get her out of it.'

'That's good – not the date thing, but I don't want you being alone right now.' Nickolas doesn't want to hang up, but the hourly check-in is coming up, and Lydia has done the last two. 'I'm sorry, but I have to go.'

'Got someone in a room waiting up to talk to you?'

'Nah. Everyone is asleep. The only person I want to be talking to is right here on the phone.'

Finn lets out a contented sigh. 'Love you, Nick.'

'Love you, too.'

Nickolas ignores the way Lydia is watching him, aware that she has heard the whole conversation. He walks out of the room, not saying a word as he does the hourly check.

When he returns, Lydia is slowly stirring a cup of hot chocolate, and Nickolas knows she's about to play twenty questions with him, and he has no way out of it.

'You're happy,' Lydia points out.

'Is that a question or a statement?' He opens the fridge, looking for a distraction.

'Statement. I can see that you're happy, Nickolas. To be honest, it's the best look I've ever seen on you.'

Nickolas shrugs. 'He makes me happy, Lyds.' Considering everything she already knows, there is no point in hiding the truth. Honestly, there is no point in hiding the truth from anyone, not anymore.

'You met his family yet?'

'Yeah, when they came to visit.'

Lydia kicks his shin.

'Jesus. Ow. Yes, okay, I had dinner with them.'

'They okay with how everything went down?'

He shrugs. 'It never came up, but that doesn't mean they didn't have some thoughts on the matter.'

'Well, even if they're not okay with it, fuck 'em. If you and Finn are happy, it doesn't matter what they think. Unless they become your in-laws.' Lydia winks, and for a split second, Nickolas has a flash of him and Finn standing at the altar wearing matching suits while holding hands, and surprisingly, the thought doesn't scare him.

'You going to try and work less now that Finn is in the picture?'

Nickolas nods his head. It's something that he's been considering for a while now, hoping he can cut down to five days a week so he and Finn can have more time together.

'I'm hoping once these new guys have passed their probation period, Dorothy may give them some extra shifts so I can cut back.'

'Reducing your workload to spend time with your man...either you really love him, or the sex is amazingly mind-blowing.'

Nickolas bites his bottom lip, keeping his focus on his hands, wishing Lydia didn't know how to read him like a book.

'You...Oh, wow.' There is neither judgement in her voice, nor shock about his silent confession. Lydia's face shows understanding. 'You really do love him.' Lydia says, slightly surprised. 'Not whatever that feeling is when we think we love someone, or that first love sensation, or what we *think* is love when it's just infatuation. No, this is the real thing. The deep, passionate, soulmates written in the stars type love.' Lydia gives Nickolas her full attention.

'I don't, I can't even explain it.' Nickolas picks at his nails. 'When I'm not with him, it's like a part of me is missing. But then when we're together, I feel as though it's still not enough. Like I need to be constantly touching him in order to feel grounded, and when I finally have that feeling, the whole outside world is forgotten and the only thing that's important is Finn.'

Lydia smiles at him proudly.

'So yeah, we haven't...not that I haven't wanted to, but, considering everything, I don't want to rush it...rush him.'

Lydia stands up, walks towards him, and wraps him in a hug. He isn't sure why a hug is necessary after their little discussion, but he likes how it feels, so he allows her to hold him until she is ready to let go.

*

Nickolas doesn't pry when Finn has a session with Dr Warnock, giving him the same privacy he did when Finn was his patient and had mandatory therapy. He leaves it up to Finn to decide what to share and what to keep private. Recently, though, Finn has begun to call him after each session or come over to his apartment if he isn't working at the centre. It's not only so Finn can talk to him about what was discussed in the session, but more for the comfort and affection that they crave from each other.

Tonight, however, as Nickolas dishes up their holubtsi, another traditional dinner dish his mother used to cook, Finn begins to talk about therapy.

'I had a good discussion with Dr Warnock today.'

Nickolas places a plate in front of Finn, studying his boyfriend's face to understand if it's a statement or if Finn is trying to open a line of communication.

'That's great. I'm really glad that things are working out with him.' He takes a seat opposite Finn, picks up his fork, and begins to dig into his dinner. After a second bite, he notices that Finn has yet to eat anything. 'Things are working out with him, right?'

'Hmm? Oh, he's—he's great. I was just...he thinks that...or more so mentioned that I need to find a way to...overpower Brody.'

Nickolas stops eating when Brody's name falls from Finn's lips; this is the first time he's heard him refer to the rapist by name.

'I need to find a way to get my power back. We ran out of time before we could throw some ideas around, but I thought maybe saying his name out loud could be a start. It might help me be less afraid of, of Brody if I make him out to be just like any other person.'

Under the table, Nickolas hooks his leg around Finn's, the touch instantly improving his boyfriend's mood.

'You know, whatever you decide, I'll support you. I'm here to help...if you want it.'

'I know.' A gentle smile spreads across Finn's face.

For the remainder of dinner, Nickolas listens to Finn share a story about a sixty-year-old woman who came into the bookstore requesting Fifty Shades of Grey. Only, the customer didn't know the name of the book, and Finn had to stand behind the counter with a straight face as the woman explained in detail many scenes that took place within the novel.

Nickolas laughs, and as he keeps listening to Finn speak, he thinks about how much he loves his life. It's been almost two months since Finn was released, and here they both are, sitting in his apartment, sharing meals and stories about their day. Nickolas gets to cook for Finn and wakes up with him curled in his arms. It's the bliss he has been searching for, and he never wants it to change.

*

Nickolas wakes up to the bed rocking and instantly thinks it's an earthquake. But he then remembers that those are rare in Chicago and he can't hear any rumbling. As he becomes more lucid and takes in what's going on around him, Nickolas realises it's Finn who is thrashing left and right beside him in the bed. It's another nightmare, the first in weeks, but this one seems worse than any Nickolas has seen in the past. Finn punches the air and kicks at the blankets. Nickolas's heart breaks for him. The man he loves is in pain, stuck in the horrible memories that plague his mind. If there's one thing Nickolas can understand, it's nightmares. For months following Mandy's death, he couldn't escape them whenever he closed his eyes.

'No. No, please. Don't,' Finn begs.

Nickolas looks around the room, hoping that an answer will jump out with how he can help.

'It hurts. Please. Please stop.' As tears fall from Finn's eyes, Nickolas decides that even though he knows he shouldn't wake someone having a nightmare, he can't stand to see Finn trapped with those memories. He leans forward, trying to get his body as close to Finn as possible without getting in the crosshairs of a punch or a kick.

He wraps an arm loosely around Finn's waist and begins to speak in his ear.

'Finn. It's okay. You're safe. You're with me.'

'No...no, no, no, no—' Finn's eyes shoot open while gasping for air.

Nickolas keeps Finn close. He tries to pull out of his grasp, but Nickolas uses his voice and his words to try and calm him down.

'Finn, you're safe. It was a nightmare.' He can tell it's helping, but Finn is still agitated. 'You're in our room. In our bed. No one else is here except me and you. It's okay. It wasn't real.'

Eventually, Finn stops fighting, but the sounds of whimpers and sobs still fill the darkness.

'Make it stop, Nickolas. Please.'

A cloud passes over the moon, and a sudden burst of light comes through the open blinds. Nickolas nuzzles into the back of Finn's neck, leaving soft kisses against freckle-dusted skin.

'Tell me what I can do to help. I'll do anything.'

Finn slowly turns in his arms so that they're facing one another. Nickolas wipes the tears from Finn's cheeks. He looks into Finn's beautiful green eyes, hoping that the love he feels is shining back through his own.

'I want you to fuck me,' Finn whispers.

Nickolas doesn't know what to say. He needs to choose his words wisely.

'Finn, I don't think—'

'Nickolas...please.' Finn's eyes are pleading.

There are so many reasons for Nickolas to say no. Forcing the body to do something the mind isn't ready for can be damaging, and that's the last thing he wants for Finn, especially since there is only a small chance this could help take Finn's pain away. The idea of their first time sleeping together under such circumstances also doesn't sit well with him. But the main issue for Nickolas is that he doesn't want to add to Finn's trauma. If he agrees to this and it turns south, it could cause a setback in Finn's recovery. On the other hand, Nickolas knows that Finn wouldn't be asking this of him unless he had been considering it for some time. Perhaps it's something that's been discussed with Dr Warnock.

'Are you sure? I don't want you to do anything you're not ready for...I don't want to hurt you.'

Finn rolls over, lying on top of him. Nickolas places one hand on the left side of Finn's cheek and uses his other to brush the hair off his face.

'You could never hurt me, Nickolas. That's why I'm asking you to do this for me, please.' Finn looks away for a moment before his green eyes lock back onto Nickolas. 'I need him gone. And only you can scrub him from my body.'

Nickolas can read the honesty in Finn's eyes, and that's enough for him to know this is what Finn wants. What Finn needs. With no further words, he nods.

'You'll do it? You'll fuck me?'

'No.'

Finn's face drops.

'I'm going to make love to you.' Slowly, he brings Finn towards him so their lips can connect.

The moment their lips touch, they are once again in a world of their own. Nickolas softly holds the back of Finn's head, making sure his grip isn't too firm, so Finn doesn't feel trapped. He moves his hand down a well-toned back, his fingertips trailing Finn's spine, which quivers under his touch. When he reaches Finn's hips, he doesn't squeeze them or put any pressure on them that could mimic being grabbed. Instead, he moves his hand under the waistband of Finn's sweatpants and gently palms his ass.

As they continue to kiss, Nickolas feels Finn hardening. He tests the waters by thrusting his hips up, and his semi-hard dick presses against Finn's pelvis. Finn doesn't pull away, freeze, or panic. He only moans in pleasure.

'These need to come off,' Finn says, panting.

Nickolas reaches for his pants until he realises Finn has beaten him to it. Finn pulls Nickolas's sweatpants off and trails that lush mouth down his bare thighs.

'Finn.' The feeling of those lips against his thighs makes Nickolas feel weak. He closes his eyes and basks in the sensation. The touch is soft, yet it has more heat behind it than the sweatpants he was wearing. Suddenly, Finn disappears, and Nickolas opens his eyes in case something has gone wrong. He's met with the sight of Finn, naked, throwing sweatpants to the side of the room before crawling back onto Nickolas's hips.

Green eyes lock on him. Nickolas once again takes Finn's face in his palm, his emotions clear as day: desire, nervousness, love, and fear.

'We can stop at any time you want. I won't mind. I don't want you to force yourself into enjoying this.'

'I promise.'

Nickolas turns towards the bedside table. He takes out the bottle of lube and reaches for the condoms he has stashed at the back, hoping they haven't expired. He places them on the bed beside them, but Finn reaches for his wrist to stop him.

'We don't need that.'

'Finn, you need lube.'

'No, I mean, we don't need that.' He follows Finn's eyesight to the silver condom packet he has in his hand. 'I was tested, remember? I'm clean. So...if you're...'

He waits for Finn to finish the sentence. With what's happening between them right now, Nickolas needs Finn to be crystal clear and communicate what he wants and needs.

'I trust you, Nick. And for this to work the way I'm hoping it will, then I need to feel you. All of you. And...and I need you to remove any and all parts of him that are left inside of me.'

Nickolas swallows. If the situation were different, Finn's words would almost seem romantic. But that's not what this is. This is Finn wanting his rapist to be erased.

'I'm clean. I—I haven't been with anyone since after Mandy...' He stops. Bringing up his deceased sister isn't the best topic for the bedroom. He also realises that this is the first time he's mentioned to Finn when he was last with someone, and that causes him to blush.

Finn lets go of his wrist, taking the condoms from his hand and throwing them onto the floor.

'I guess that settles it then,' says Finn.

Picking up the lube, Finn pops the cap open and squeezes some onto Nickolas's fingers. It's cold, but he makes sure to warm it before he reaches around, positioning himself near Finn's ass.

'I'm going to go slow. Just try to relax and breathe, okay?'

Finn nods, and Nickolas keeps his eyes locked on Finn as his index finger presses against his rim. He can feel Finn tense, and he instantly stops.

'You okay?'

'I'm good. I didn't mean...it was unexpected, that's all.'

'How 'bout I talk you through it?' Nickolas strokes Finn's face, who nods in agreement. He pulls Finn in so their foreheads are touching. 'I'm going to slowly start inserting a finger inside of you. I want you to exhale as I push in.'

As Nickolas circles Finn's rim with lube, he begins to very slowly push his index finger inside. Finn breathes out as Nickolas pushes in. Once he is three knuckles deep, he slowly pulls his finger out, but not to the point of removing it completely. 'Want me to keep going?'

'Ye-yeah.'

He pushes his finger back in, this time swirling it around once he's inside. 'That's it. You're doing great.' Nickolas figures that words of encouragement will help keep Finn present, grounded.

Finn begins to pant a little, relaxing into the sensation.

'I'm going to insert a second finger now.' Nickolas waits for Finn's acknowledgement before his middle finger enters alongside his index. He gently slides them in and out, Finn slowly loosening up. Nickolas scissors his fingers open, and Finn quivers on top of him.

'I—I think I'm ready, Nick.'

'I'm going to do one more, Finn, just to be sure. I don't want you to be too tight, okay?'

Finn groans, and Nickolas isn't sure if it's out of pleasure or annoyance. Either way, he places his ring finger against Finn's entrance and explains that he is about to insert the last finger. As he goes to push in, he leans forward, their lips crashing together, biting down on Finn's bottom lip.

'Oh, shit. Nickolas.'

'I'm not hurting you, am I?' He stops.

Finn shakes his head. 'N-no. It's good. I p-promise,' Finn says, panting against Nickolas's lips. Nickolas goes back in for a kiss, using it as a distraction for any stretch or burn the third finger may be causing.

As Finn pulls away from his lips, Nickolas removes his fingers. 'What happens next is all up to you. You're in control, Finn. Use me however you need.'

Nickolas wipes his lubed hand on the sheets and cups Finn's face. He's rock hard – the feeling of opening Finn up was all it took – his dick now sitting flush against Finn's ass. He watches Finn squeeze lube into his hand and moves to grip his dick. The sensation of the cool gel rubbing up and down his shaft makes Nickolas breathless, but then it stops, and with a firm grip, his dick is guided to Finn's entrance. Nickolas keeps his eyes locked on Finn so he can see his reaction as he pushes inside. Finn is kneeling above him, slowly lowering himself down onto Nickolas's dick.

Out of all the sex Nickolas has had, he has topped at least ninety percent of the time. He's a bottom man, but finding someone he is willing to bend over for is not easy in the South Side. Out of those many experiences, the feeling of a tight ass around his dick has been enough to get him off, but not enough to settle the itch inside of him that makes him feel as though he's had a satisfying release. However, as Finn sinks down, all those experiences fade away, and suddenly, the only experience he can recall is the one he is having right now.

The moonlight makes Finn's pale skin look like crystal, a beautiful contrast against his bright red hair. Finn's eyes are closed, and it gives Nickolas a moment to study every inch of his body. Red pubic hair has grown back since Nickolas saw it neatly trimmed that first night Finn was committed. It looks natural and doesn't take anything away from Finn's glorious size. Freckles litter his boyfriend's body: chest, thighs, and there are even a few on Finn's dick. Nickolas longs for the day he can take his time and count every single freckle with a kiss.

Lost in his thoughts, Nickolas suddenly groans as he feels Finn's ass press flush against his hip bone, aware that he is now fully inside of the man he loves.

'*Fuck*, Nick.'

'Don't move just yet. Take a moment to adjust.' He places his hands on Finn's thighs, slowly rubbing them up and down.

'Whenever you're ready, there's no rush. I'm just going to lay here for you to take your pleasure.'

'I want you to enjoy it too.'

'Finn, I'm already loving this more than any experience I've had with anybody else, and you haven't even started to move.'

Finn blushes, and waits only a minute before moving, lifting up and down, causing Nickolas to bite his lower lip to keep himself from exploding then and there. The sensation of Finn's tight ass teasing him at such a slow pace is mind-blowing.

Finn's eyes are still closed. Sweat slowly drips down both their bodies as Finn begins to pick up a little speed, now comfortable with Nickolas's size.

As Nickolas focuses on the face above him, he realises that what he thought was sweat on Finn's cheek is in fact tears.

'Finn?'

No response, but Finn's moaning is lost, now replaced by whimpers.

'Finn, hey. Look at me.' Nickolas moves his hands from Finn's muscular thighs to cup his face.

Finn's green eyes shoot open, quickly looking around the room, as though he had forgotten where he was.

'Look at me, Finn. It's me. You're with me.' He pulls Finn down, and their noses touch as the rocking of their hips continues. 'You're here with me. I'm the one inside you.' Nickolas whispers.

A tear falls from Finn's cheek onto Nickolas's. He considers stopping, but through the tears, he notices Finn is beginning to pant again, realising that these sensations are neither bad, nor painful or forced.

'I want you to feel good, Finn. I want you to feel how you make me feel just by being in my life.' He whispers as if they are in a room full of people. A few moans slip from Nickolas's mouth. He can't hold on much longer. The fact that it's been so long since he's had sex, mixed with the love he feels for Finn, along with the tight drag of his boyfriend's ass, it's enough to bring him close to the edge. 'I love you, Finn. I'm yours—*ungh*—all yours.'

'*Nickolas...*'

The way his name falls from Finn's lips is pure ecstasy.

'Finn, I c-can't hold it...much longer.' It doesn't help that the rawness of feeling Finn's walls tighten and relax around him while dragging against his dick is heightening every sensation. Or that he's never experienced sex bareback until now.

'Come for me, Nick. Come inside me, please. I want to feel it. I want—I want to be yours.'

Nickolas gently pushes Finn's face away so their eyes lock as he lets himself go.

'Finn...*fuck*, oh, fuck.' He comes inside of Finn, the release so intense that, for a second, he thinks he's blacked out. Nickolas can feel his cum coating tight walls, his dick pushing it deeper inside the more Finn rides him. His release triggers Finn's, who shoots thick ropes of cum over Nickolas's chest, his eyes closed as he rides out his orgasm.

Cum begins to drip down Nickolas's dick, his load having nowhere else to go after filling Finn's ass, whose thrusts slow down until Finn collapses on top of him.

'Hey, handsome.' Nickolas moves the hair off Finn's sweaty forehead so he can see clearly into those eyes he loves so much. 'You okay?'

Finn nods. 'More than okay. That was...I've never felt—'

'Me neither.' Nickolas can't keep the smile from his face.

Finn turns his head to lay a soft, gentle kiss on his lips. It's nothing more than a peck, but it's still strong enough to cause his heart to flutter.

'I love you, so much,' Finn whispers. 'For a moment, I felt like I was there again, and then suddenly I heard your voice, and he was gone. Like a ghost, he just...vanished. And after that, I was here, with you, and what I was feeling turned into pleasure because it was between you and me.'

Nickolas is still inside Finn as they carefully roll onto their sides, neither making an effort to pull apart, using the cum to glue themselves together. They lay there in each other's arms, their eyes having a silent conversation in the quietness of the room. Neither of them wants to break apart, forgoing the need to clean up and not caring that they'll be sticky in the morning.

Nickolas's dick slips out naturally as it goes soft. His cum slowly leaks out of Finn and drips onto peach fuzz thighs and ruffled sheets. Finn curls into his chest, and they hold one another as they have the most peaceful sleep either of them has had since they met.

*

When Nickolas wakes up, Finn is still curled up and asleep in his arms. He can't help but smile at how peaceful he looks. A weight on his side makes Nickolas turn his head to look over his shoulder, not at all surprised to see Socks perched on his hip, her tail gracefully swishing back and forth as she watches him and Finn sleep.

'Can I help you?' states Nickolas.

Reow.

'Can you wait for us to wake up first?'

Reow.

Socks paws at Nickolas's arm. He leaves a soft kiss on his boyfriend's forehead before carefully extracting himself, trying his hardest not to wake him. He throws on his sweatpants and a baggy hoodie, only realising as he makes his way into the kitchen that his pants are Finn's. He gives Socks food, cleans out the litter tray, and begins to make breakfast. Flashes of last night enter his mind as he scrambles a few eggs, fries the bacon, and prepares some French toast.

He puts the food on a tray, unaware that he owned one until he'd gone looking, and then walks into the bedroom with a cup of coffee, black with two sugars, just how Finn likes it, as well as a glass of apple juice.

'God, that smells amazing,' Finn murmurs.

He smiles and stretches his long limbs as he wakes the rest of the way up. Nickolas sits beside his gorgeous boyfriend, presenting the morning feast he prepared.

'Wow. Is this the service you give all the guys you sleep with?' Finn asks.

'Only the ones I love.' Nickolas places the tray on Finn's lap and leans against the headboard.

Finn takes a bite of the food and sips the coffee.

'How are you this morning? Are you sore or have any...regrets?' asks Nickolas.

Finn bites into a piece of bacon, swallowing before answering. 'No, Nick. No regrets. Never.' Finn reaches out and takes Nickolas's hand, rubbing soothing circles into his palm. 'And although I had prepared myself for maybe feeling a little tender this morning, I'm good.'

'Good?'

'I'm good.' Finn clarifies. 'Nothing hurts or aches, and when I woke up this morning, I felt kinda...free.'

Nickolas kisses Finn's hand, then releases it so he can continue to eat.

'There is something that I wanted to ask though, about last night?' Finn's cheeks blush.

'Oh?'

'You, ah...you said "our".'

Nickolas cocks his head to the side, trying to recall what Finn is referring to.

'When you woke me from the nightmare, I heard you say "our room"..."our bed".'

Now it's Nickolas's turn to blush. He rubs the back of his neck. Some part of him had hoped that Finn hadn't heard. But all he can do right now is shrug.

'It just happened. I don't know. In that moment, I was worried about you. I wanted to get you out of your head, and I guess that's what came out.'

Finn nods.

It's not like what he said isn't true. That's exactly what he was trying to do at the time, but subconsciously, Nickolas has slowly been seeing his apartment as their apartment. He's rarely in his bed without Finn beside him, and when Nickolas is alone, it doesn't feel the same. But he knows it's too soon to mention any of this.

So instead, Nickolas allows Finn to finish eating so they can enjoy the time they have before he has to get ready for his night shift at the centre.

*

Three weeks later, Dot finally approves Nickolas's request to cut down to five days a week. His two days off will vary each week, depending on the availability of the other staff, but Nickolas makes sure that Dot keeps him rostered on for the afternoon shift every Sunday during visiting hours.

He has yet to share the news with Finn, wanting to save it for the date he has planned for them tomorrow night. With their work schedules, they haven't had an opportunity to go on an actual date since the pizza they shared on the pier almost three months ago. Though in that time, Nickolas has joined Finn's family for dinners, and they've established a routine where Finn gets up in the morning to go for a run while Nickolas makes them breakfast because no way is he getting up at the crack of dawn to exercise – he'd rather do that once he's had his morning coffee.

Over time, more of Finn's belongings began to appear in Nickolas's apartment. First, it was Finn's meds and that was not at all an issue for Nickolas. He'd rather they be kept at his place so Finn has easy access to them morning and night. Next was a toothbrush beside Nickolas's in the little cup he has on his bathroom sink. Then one day, Nickolas was doing the laundry and found Finn's items were mixed in with his, and instead of returning them, Nickolas simply washed them, folded them, and placed them in a drawer on Finn's side of the bed – because Finn has his own side of the bed.

They call or text one another while at work, and once or twice Nickolas has been surprised to come home and find Finn has prepared dinner for him, which mainly consists of Finn holding a bag of takeout while waiting for Nickolas on the steps of his apartment building. But still, the thought alone makes him smile.

*

Nickolas pulls up to the Cunningham house and this time, he walks up to the front porch steps without any concern about knocking on the door. He's dressed in black skinny leg jeans with no rips – he decided to go out and buy himself a new pair just for the occasion – and a dark blue V-neck, thankful that the night isn't cold enough to need a jacket. He knocks on the door, and Finn opens it before he has time to bring his hand back to his side.

'Well done, Markova. Right on time,' comments Finn.

'Have I ever been late?' Nickolas questions.

'No, but there's a first time for everything.'

Finn stands before him in dark blue jeans and a grey t-shirt with an emerald-green shirt unbuttoned over the top. The colour makes Finn's hair pop and his eyes shine.

'You, ah, you look good,' says Nickolas. 'Really good.'

Finn smirks. 'Was about to say the same about you.' Finn turns around and calls out. 'Jessica, I'm going. I'll see you tomorrow sometime.' Then he walks out and pulls the door closed.

Nickolas takes Finn's hand. 'Planning to stay the night, are ya?'

'You can act like you don't want me to stay, but I know for a fact you sleep better when I'm beside you.'

Nickolas gives Finn's hand a squeeze and lets it go as they get in the car.

'So, where're we going?'

'That will spoil the surprise.' He repeats the words Finn said to him all those months ago, loving the smile it brings to his boyfriend's face.

*

They park the car and Finn looks around. Nickolas has brought them to Hyde Park. The sun is beginning to set, and the fairy lights set up within the trees are illuminated. Hand in hand, Nickolas leads Finn down the path that winds around the lagoon. Most people have gone home for the evening; a few are walking in the opposite direction to get back to their cars, but Nickolas pulls on Finn's arm to lead him off the footpath and onto the grassland. He can't help but find the curious look on Finn's face adorable. Lydia suddenly comes into view.

'Finn, you remember Lydia, right?' Nickolas asks.

'Of course,' Finn offers. 'It's nice to see you outside of the centre.'

'Likewise. And I must say it's nice to see you thriving in the outside world,' compliments Lydia.

'Amazing what the right medications and a therapist can do,' says Finn.

'Sure, because that's all it took.' Lydia gives Nickolas a smirk and a wink.

He pinches the bridge of his nose, silently regretting asking her for help.

'Anyway, Lydia here was just leaving, weren't you, Lydia?'

'Please, it's my first night off in what feels like forever, I'm not wasting it hanging around you two.' Lydia flips her hair over her shoulder. 'Goodnight, boys...enjoy.' She winks before walking away.

With Lydia out of sight, Nickolas gives Finn a chance to take in their surroundings. A large picnic blanket is laid out on the grass close enough to a tree so they can use the fairy lights as their own.

'Nickolas?' Finn questions.

'I had Lydia pick up dinner and set it up for us so it didn't go cold...and so the surprise wasn't ruined,' Nickolas explains.

Finn removes his shoes, steps onto the blanket, sits near the basket of food, and pats the ground beside him. Nickolas quickly joins him.

'I didn't know I was dating such a romantic.' Finn says.

Nickolas scoffs. 'If it's romantic, then that's a coincidence. This is the first time I've had to plan a date, so I didn't have a lot to go on.'

'So instead of a restaurant or a movie, your brain went for a picnic in the park by moonlight and fairy lights?' Finn's head tilts.

Hearing it explained like that does make it seem as though he took the romantic route when all he wanted was someplace quiet for the two of them to be together.

'Whatever. Open the basket before the food goes cold.' Nickolas shakes off his embarrassment.

Finn chuckles and lifts the lid to find Chinese containers, a few beers, and sodas, since drinking isn't allowed with Finn's medication.

'It's perfect.' Finn smiles.

Finn hands out the food, and they begin to eat, first enjoying their own favourites before shoving their chopsticks into one another's container and eating what the other had ordered.

'How was work today?' Finn asks.

'Good. Ryder has finally been given a release date, and Cora's new medication seems to be making some real improvements.' If it were anyone else, Nickolas would never be sharing patient information with them. But Finn knows these people, knows these patients just as much as he does.

'That's so great to hear. Maybe once they get out, I can try and get in contact with them.'

Nickolas looks up from his food and smiles. 'I'm sure they'd love that. They ask me about you every day.'

'Well, we are the "it" couple. It's not every day that a patient and an orderly start dating.'

'You'd want to hope not.'

Finn gives Nickolas a nudge. 'You know what I mean.'

'Ha, well, as far as they know we bumped into each other and that's how we began dating.'

'Okay. I can work with that lie.'

Nickolas flips Finn off, but he's smiling as he does it.

'Anyway, Dot spoke to me yesterday.'

'Everything alright?'

Nickolas keeps his head down. 'She, ah, she's cutting back my shifts.'

'What? Why?'

'She didn't say, but I suspect it might be because of what happened.'

'You mean with us?' Finn puts down the food, a look of shock and frustration appears on his boyfriend's face. 'No. There is no one better for that job than you. And after what she said to me, I thought she understood. We didn't—Nick we didn't do anything wrong. Not really.'

Nickolas can't help but enjoy the way Finn is rambling on about him.

'That's it! Tomorrow, I'm going down there and I'm—'

'Easy, tiger. Calm down. It wasn't because of us. I just wanted to yank your chain a little.'

'What?'

'I was the one that asked for fewer hours.'

'You?'

'I figured this way we'd get more time to spend together. With my shift work clashing with your roster, I thought if I had at least two days off a week, then we'd get—'

'But your patients, Nick.'

'I'm still going to be there for them. I'll still work every Sunday afternoon during visiting hours, but it's time I had a life outside of the treatment centre, and I never thought I'd have that or want that...not until I met you.' He sits there, seeing the love in Finn's eyes shine back at him. 'Which is why, I, ah...look, I know I'm probably going against our whole "taking it slow" thing, but I thought maybe you might want to...move in.'

'Really?' Finn sounds excited.

Nickolas shrugs. 'You spend almost every night at my place – not that that's a problem. And you're always talking about how crowded your house is and how you have no privacy because you have to share with your brothers. I mean, I like having you around. Coming home to you, sharing my apartment with you. And I know Socks will be thrilled to have another ginger as—'

Nickolas suddenly lands on his back as Finn tackles him with a hug. Having Finn's body weight on top of him prevents Nickolas from being able to get any oxygen back into his lungs, but he'd rather struggle to breathe than ask Finn to get off him.

'I don't know how I got so lucky to have you in my life, Nick, but you're the best thing that's ever happened to me.'

'I could say the same. I was broken when you found me, and now I feel almost brand new.' Nickolas runs his hand up a freckled cheek and brushes red hair from Finn's face.

'If you have nothing else planned for this wonderful, romantic evening, I'd like to take you back to our apartment, and head straight for our bedroom,' says Finn.

Nickolas finally catches his breath, only for it to be knocked out of him again. They haven't slept together since the night Finn woke from a nightmare, but they have explored each other's bodies, giving one another dirty blow jobs or jerking each other off as they make out like two horny teenagers.

He nods, and Finn scrambles off of him to help pack up. Their walk back to the car is more of a slow jog as the excitement creeps up on Finn's face. Nickolas is also eager to get home.

*

Stumbling through their front door, Nickolas navigates Finn to their bedroom through the dark apartment as they shed each other's clothes, not once wanting to break the desperation of their kiss.

'Jesus, Nickolas. I want you so badly.'

That's the first time he has ever heard someone say they want him when it's come to sex. In the past, it was more about finding someone who was available and willing to keep a secret. Kicking his shoes off so he can remove his pants without tripping over, Nickolas successfully sits on their mattress wearing nothing but his boxers.

He's panting as he looks up, Finn standing before him naked, unaware of how that happened.

Nickolas voices his inner desires. 'One day I'm going to kiss every freckle on your body.'

Finn cups his face. 'We have all the time in the world to make that happen.'

This time, when Nickolas's lips touch Finn's, he feels as though he's home. His whole life, he's never felt settled until now. Finn is his person, his missing half. Nickolas slowly lays back onto the mattress as Finn's body covers him.

Finn begins to kiss down his body, long, slim fingers roaming until Finn's hands reach his boxers, and Nickolas moans as he begins to mouth at his dick.

'God, Finn.'

His boxers disappear, his dick springs free, angling towards his stomach, and Nickolas begins to shuffle up the mattress till his head is on the pillow. Finn bends over to retrieve the lube, then kneels in front of him.

'I want to open you up...can I do that?'

Nickolas nods, speechless. He has always been the one to open himself up before a hook-up, but the thought of Finn's gorgeous long fingers pushing inside of him is almost enough to make him come then and there. Nickolas bends his knees as Finn shuffles forward and squeezes the lube onto his slender fingers. He warms it up before reaching down towards Nickolas's ass. With Finn's chest pressed against his legs, Nickolas keeps his eyes locked on him as he feels a finger push inside.

'Fuck, I've missed this.' The words slip out before he realises he's said them.

'Have I scored myself a needy bottom?' Finn slips a second finger in while asking the question.

Nickolas can hear Finn's excitement. He decides not to answer, knowing that actions speak louder than words. He whines as Finn scissors him open, and just as Nickolas begins to get comfortable, Finn hits the spot.

'Holy fuck.' Nickolas bucks off the bed. The electrifying sensation that runs through his body is a feeling he's dearly missed.

Leaning forward, Finn's left arm cages Nickolas in as it rests against his head.

'You told me that you needed to trust someone in order to bottom.' Finn is panting along with him.

'In case you haven't noticed, ah, *fuck*...I trust you with my life.' A third finger pushes inside, and the slight burn feels amazing as it mixes with the sensation of Finn twisting and curling all three fingers. 'You know wh-who I am, Finn. My past. My mistakes. No one else knows the real me...no one except you.' He goes to moan, but Finn's lips crash onto his, stopping it from escaping.

Finn bites his bottom lip, but it's not enough to distract him when three fingers pull out of his ass, leaving Nickolas's hole gaping and feeling empty. He begs until the tip of Finn's dick lines up with his entrance. As Finn begins to push inside him, Nickolas's hips lift off the mattress, and Finn cups his face, their eyes locked onto one another as they finally become one.

'Holy fuck, yes,' Nickolas moans.

With their foreheads touching, and Finn's hand still holding his face, forcing their eyes to stay locked onto one another, Finn begins to slowly thrust in and out. Nickolas has never been fucked bareback, and he wonders if it felt this amazing when their roles were switched. He can feel Finn's dick drag against his walls, his body opening with each thrust so it can take all of Finn's incredible nine inches.

'Jesus, Nickolas. You're so fucking tight.'

'Perks of not bottoming for a while.'

'God, your ass is going to milk me dry.'

Finn begins to pick up the pace, shifting slightly to the right, and that's all it takes for Nickolas's body to erupt with pleasure as his prostate gets rubbed with each thrust.

'Finn. *Oh, fuck.* Finn.'

'You're perfect, Nickolas...and you're perfect for me.'

Talking during sex never held much appeal for Nickolas, but Finn's confessions are causing his orgasm to build fast. He can feel his balls tighten as his dick throbs against his stomach, precum dripping out. With each nudge into his prostate, electricity courses up his spine, and he knows he doesn't have much left in him.

'I'm close, I can't—I don't think I can—' Nickolas can barely string a sentence together.

Finn's fingers, those fingers that Nickolas is obsessed with, wrap around his dick. Finn doesn't even stroke him, the mere pressure of his grip is enough to send Nickolas over the edge as he comes, shooting on his chest and dribbling down Finn's hand.

'Finn, *ungh*, holy fuck.'

Finn continues to thrust. Nickolas rides that wave as his prostate gets stimulated, well past what he can handle after being milked dry.

'*Nickolas.*' Warm liquid shoots inside of him as Finn whispers his name against his ear. Finn's thrusts ease as cum fills him. Finn shudders on top of him, panting, no longer moving but staying buried inside.

'Has it ever felt like that for you before?' asks Finn.

'Never.' It's the truth. What just happened between him and Finn felt life-changing.

'I don't think I can move.'

'No complaints here.' Nickolas offers. 'I kinda like the feeling of you on top of me.'

Finn places soft kisses on Nickolas's cheeks, forehead, mouth, and anywhere his lips can get to without having to move.

'Hey, Nickolas?'

'Mhmm?'

'Are you touching my ass?'

Nickolas finds the question odd considering both his hands are on Finn's back, the same place they've been throughout this whole experience.

Meow.

Nickolas's eyebrows shoot up as he puts the pieces together. 'SOCKS, GET YOUR PAWS OFF FINN'S ASS.' The sound of a bell collar jingling off into the distance lets them know Socks has run out of their bedroom and back into the living room. Nickolas is at least pleased to hear Finn chuckling while he lies there, mortified.

'She wasn't in here the whole time, was she?' Finn questions.

'God, I hope not,' Nickolas groans. 'But honestly, if she was, she would have interrupted us mid-fuck.'

'She a regular viewer of yours?'

'Fuck no. I kick Socks out for all bedroom activity, which has been solo since I adopted her, but still. She does not need to see her daddy getting it on.'

'Naw, Nick. You called yourself her daddy.'

They both chuckle as he pushes Finn off, only to flip the freckled beauty and pin him under his own body. Eventually, the wrestling and laughter lead to round two; however, this time, Nickolas makes sure the door is shut before they get started.

*

When Nickolas has his first two days off after working a five-day roster, Finn moves in. Nickolas drives his car to the Cunningham house. Finn's belongings are minimal enough to fit in the back, and he stands near the car as he watches Finn kiss and hug everyone goodbye.

'Jess, I'm literally twenty minutes away,' Finn grumbles.

'It's not the same. Promise you'll come over for dinner once a week,' Jessica instructs.

'Yes, I promise.'

'And call to tell me about your day.'

'Okay, okay. Can I go now?'

Finn walks down the porch steps, waving goodbye.

'Make sure he has his daily serve of fruit and vegetables, Nickolas,' Jessica calls out.

'And he has a bath at eight and is in bed by nine,' Jake jokes.

Finn throws Jake the finger, still smiling wide.

In the car, Nickolas turns the ignition on but doesn't make a move to pull away from the curb.

'Anything you got that desperately needs to go back to the apartment?'

'No...why?'

'Wanted to make a stop first.'

'Oh, okay.'

As Nickolas drives off, Finn waves out the window.

*

'This wasn't the place I had in mind when you said you wanted to make a stop,' says Finn.

'Just...follow me,' explains Nickolas.

They get out of the car, and Nickolas takes Finn's hand. It's a short walk and neither of them speak. When they stop, the realisation of what's going on causes Finn to give his hand a comforting squeeze.

'Hey, sis,' says Nickolas. 'I, ah, I want you to meet someone.' He turns to Finn, a surprised yet honoured look reflecting off his boyfriend's face. 'This is Finn. My boyfriend. The one I told you about.' The emotions he feels from introducing the man he loves to the only other person he's ever cared about hit him harder than he was expecting.

'H-hi, Mandy. I'm sorry that we never got to meet, but I want you to know that I love your brother so fucking much.'

Tears begin to well in Nickolas's eyes. Unable to speak, he watches as Finn takes the reins.

'He's told me a lot about you. How strong you were, how brave. You sound a lot like, Nick. But I want you to know that you don't have to worry about him anymore. I'll take care of him from here...we'll take care of each other.'

Nickolas sniffs, wiping the tears away so he can see Mandy's name clearly on the plaque. 'I told you, sis. He's perfect. He makes me happy, and I know that's all you wanted for me, so I thought I'd come and prove it to you so you can rest. There's no need for you to stick around and keep an eye on me anymore.'

Finn lets go of Nickolas's hand and wraps an arm around his shoulder, pulling him in close. They stand there in silence,

Nickolas once again wishing he could have had one more moment with his sister.

'Love you, sis. I'll be sure to visit again soon. I promise.'

Finn lays a kiss on his temple, and the motion causes tears to trickle down Nickolas's face.

'How 'bout one more stop before we head home?' suggests Finn.

Nickolas nods; the distraction is much appreciated as Finn leads him back to the car. He's been wanting to take Finn to visit Mandy's grave but was unsure how to broach the subject of visiting a cemetery so he could talk to a piece of cement. In hindsight, Nickolas knows that Finn wouldn't see it that way, understanding the need to stay connected to a loved one, in whatever way possible. But like everything, when it comes to him and Finn, Nickolas knew today was the perfect day to take the leap. They're moving in together, and he knew if he didn't muster up the courage to do it today, then it was never going to happen.

He sits in the passenger seat as Finn gets behind the wheel and drives them to their final destination. In the corner of his eye, Nickolas swears he sees a shimmer near Mandy's grave float up towards the sun, or perhaps his vision is blurry from the tears.

That's how Nickolas finds himself finally sitting on the beach, Finn leaning against his chest as Nickolas wraps his arms around the man he loves.

'I was planning to bring you here for our next date, but I think coming today was a better decision,' Finn explains.

Nickolas tightens his hold on Finn as a silent thank you.

'I've never been to the beach either. Funny how we both lived so close to it and yet it took us this long to step foot onto the sand,' says Finn.

Nickolas chuckles. 'I guess when we say "beach", this isn't exactly what we envision.'

'I blame Hollywood.'

Nickolas huffs a laugh. 'You know, the reason I wanted to visit the beach so much was because of you.'

Finn twists in his arms so they can look at one another.

'When we first met, I started having dreams that I was on a beach. The sand was as white as your skin, the water as green as your eyes, and the sky was always fiery red, but not in a bad way, more like a deep setting sun.' Nickolas leans his head against Finn's face before continuing. 'I dreamt of you. You took my hand, and we began walking down the beach as you explained to me that I was hurting, as were you, and you thought we could help one another heal.'

'Wow. Dream me sounds so much more level-headed.'

'Dream you was also extremely cocky, that's for sure.'

They both laugh. Now that Finn has adjusted to the medication, Nickolas has noticed that he does, in fact, have a cocky nature that he wouldn't trade for anything.

'But after that, I dreamt of Mandy sitting there beside me,' Nickolas explains. 'She was happy and smiling, and she told me she was at peace.' He takes a deep breath in and then slowly lets it out. 'Ever since then, I've wanted to visit, thinking it might give me some, I don't know, clarity and maybe make me feel connected to her.'

'So, what are you feeling? Right now, in this moment?'

He takes a minute, looking out onto the water as the sound of the waves helps his body relax against Finn's.

'Content.' He moves his eyes away from the ocean long enough to see Finn still looking up at him. 'For the first time in my life, I'm not having to run. I'm not having to hide, and I'm not chasing answers or living in fear. I enjoy my work. I'm able to support myself legally, and most of all, I have you. I honestly never thought I would find myself wanting to settle down with someone, and I figured I'd be chasing those one-night stands for years to come. But I guess for once, luck was on my side.'

'I don't think it's luck, Nickolas. Luck is finding money on the ground or not getting a ticket when you know you've risked parking illegally. We worked for what we have. We earned it.' Finn turns back towards the water, and Nickolas wraps his arms tighter around his boyfriend, who settles back into his chest. 'Dr Warnock told me broken people fix broken people, and after what you said about your dream, my guess is he's right. We fixed one another, Nick. And from there, we found a connection because we understood each other. The struggles of our past were keeping us guarded, yet we still allowed ourselves to drop those walls for one another. If we were only going to be friends, I would have kept so much of myself hidden from you, but that's not what I wanted. It's not what I saw for us...and I think deep down you knew that too.'

Nickolas did know that. He tried. He tried to keep it professional, and then, when that didn't work, he aimed for platonic. But Nickolas's mind and body were screaming for more.

'I know *how* you came into my life wasn't the best, but I don't regret it happening,' says Finn.

Nickolas looks down at Finn, whose words pull at his heartstrings. He can't stand the thought of living in a world where they never met, and if he could erase the pain Finn endured before being committed, he would.

'I'm glad my first visit to the beach was with you.' Nickolas leans down and places a tender kiss on Finn's soft pink lips.

They look back out onto the ocean and take in their surroundings. For three and a half months, they have been in each other's lives, and it astounds Nickolas how much can change in such a short amount of time. Sure, things moved quickly, but why turn away from something good when he's finally found it?

The phrase 'broken people fix broken people' echoes through his mind. Although that was the case for him and Finn, it wasn't how things worked for him and Mandy. Perhaps the pain of witnessing Mandy's suicide was the final straw that shattered him, leaving him in pieces for Finn to help put back together. Regardless, he doesn't dwell on it, knowing he put the past to rest months ago. He came to terms with what his sister did and doesn't blame Mandy for any of it.

What he now has is a chance to look into the future and see possibilities. He can picture his life in one year, five years, or even ten, and when he does, he believes that one day those fantasies can be a reality for him. As he and Finn watch the sun begin to set, there is only one thing he knows for sure about his future, and that's that in every fantasy, Finn is there, living it out with him.

Keep reading
for a new chapter
from Finn's point of view

17. Finn

His feet hit the pavement, and he can hear his deep, calculated breaths over the music streaming through his AirPods. Finn finds it's the best way not to overexert himself, keeping an even pace as he runs anywhere between thirty minutes to an hour every day. Technically, if Chicago is in the middle of a snowstorm, Finn has to forgo the run, making a trip to the gym instead. Or, more often than not, he gets his heart rate up, burning those calories in ways that leave him and Nickolas sweating, their muscles burning, and their bodies aching as they moan each other's names, leaving marks on one another to stake their claim for those around them to see.

Fair to say, his sex life has never been better and for once, it's healthy. Close in age, check. Consensual, check. Sex is not being used in exchange for a favour, and most of all, it's not always sex, sometimes, most of the time, it's making love.

When he said this to Jake one day, his brother rolled his eyes so hard that Finn considered punching his older brother in the nuts. But then Jake smiled, and Finn knew his brother was happy for him.

Running is Finn's release. It's part of his routine, and every morning he wakes up, leaves behind a sexy, sleeping boyfriend, who sometimes is drooling into the pillow, so he can start the day on the right side of his mental health.

It's been a year since walking out of the treatment centre, and each day, he makes sure his choices won't lead him back inside those concrete walls. He ran before he knew he was bipolar, and he ran five, sometimes ten, miles a day when manic, unaware that all the new energy that made him feel invincible and alive was soon going to be his downfall.

So, as both Dr Hale and Dr Warnock suggested, Finn made a routine that included his morning runs. He has tried to convince Nickolas to run with him, but shift work can come with a lack of sleep and hours that mess with a person's body clock. He doesn't push it, though he may use it against Nickolas when Finn decides to one day breach the topic of getting a dog, explaining how it would be the perfect running buddy. Not sure how that would go with Queen Socks. If Nickolas's relationship with Socks is anything to go by, Finn is certain that if they do decide to take their relationship to the next level – marriage and kids, Nickolas would be wrapped around their little one's finger.

But neither of them is thinking that far ahead. Sure, he moved out at eighteen with a boyfriend he had been with for three months, but in the South Side, that's considered moving slowly. With one less mouth to feed, it helped Jessica with the bills, and it gave Finn a chance to not feel trapped under his sister's thumb. Their apartment is quiet; he's no longer waking to his siblings screaming up the stairs. Their bedroom only sleeps them, and Socks if the bedroom activities have come to an end. Their bathroom doesn't have the risk of anyone barging in to use the toilet or brush their teeth while someone else is showering, mostly because Nickolas is in the shower with him.

On the outside, no one would know he has bipolar disorder. His scars have healed to a faint silver hairline, and he rarely catches someone looking, but when he does, Finn offers a half smile as though to say, 'I'm not ashamed, because I came through the other side.'

*

'I hate your gym,' He whines, throwing the gym bag onto the floor while kicking off his shoes.

'Why? It's got everything ya need.' Nickolas calls from the kitchen while finishing up what smells like pasta.

'It smells like a bag with a dirty jockstrap inside that's been fermenting in it over the summer.'

'That's oddly specific.'

'I'd rather pass out from sunstroke than go to that place again.' He sits at their dining table.

'Okay, drama queen, spill. You had me up until the sunstroke because I've seen you run in ninety-five degree heat without complaining.'

Shit. Almost got away with it.

'This new gym is opening up and, I don't know, I thought maybe I or we could join.' Finn waits, watching as Nickolas walks over with their dinner in both hands and places one in front of Finn before he finally speaks.

'You want to waste money on a gym that focuses more on its fruity-ass drinks and steam rooms than the workout itself? Be my guest. I like my ass-smelling gym.' Nickolas argues back.

'What's wrong with wanting a little more for your money?' He tries to reason with his boyfriend without admitting he'd enjoy a protein smoothie after a workout and relaxing his muscles in a steam room.

'There is a difference between wanting more and needing more. I don't need to spend hard-earned dollars on an expensive gym when I'm going to get the same results at the one I've been going to since I left home.'

Finn knows when to drop a topic. Over the years, his time with Nickolas has taught him that he can be a hothead when it comes to change or if Nickolas's values and lifestyle are being questioned or judged. But what he's also learned is that once Finn's temperamental beauty has had a moment to cool down, Nickolas will apologise and then sit and have a proper discussion, which is why Finn leaves it there for the evening.

*

The café is on the West Side. No newspaper or duct tape is holding the glass windows together, and tables and chairs are on offer out the front for customers to use, which are currently occupied by post yoga mums. Inside, near the far corner sits Cora, Alex and Ryder. Finn rushes over, not at all ashamed at how fast he pulls each of his friends into a hug, no longer doubting that the group before him are indeed his friends.

'Finally, we almost ordered without you.' Cora sing-songs.

'You didn't have to wait. My session ran over and then traffic to get here was a nightmare.' He explains, taking a seat beside Alex.

'No stress. Gave us time to stare at the cutie behind the counter.' Ryder points out while Alex and Cora all take another look. Meanwhile, Finn keeps his eyes on the menu.

'Aren't you going to take a peak?' Cora asks.

Finn shrugs, 'No point. No one could compare to Nick.'

The group before him groan in frustration.

'We get it. You two love birds only have eyes for each other, no need to rub it in our face.' Ryder whines.

'I am not rubbing it in your face.'

'Honey, you're allowed to look at the menu without buying anything. I'm sure Nickolas turns his head once or twice.' Alex raises a hand to call over the waiter.

'If he does, never seen him do it.'

'For real?' Ryder sounds surprised.

'You guys know this is Nickolas he's talking about here.' Cora addresses the group. 'Recluse Nickolas, who lived at the centre and didn't even accept a booty call from Darren.'

'Wait, you know about that?' Finn quickly chimes in, though the looks on his friends' faces are all the answers he needs.

'Darren was like a dog in heat around Nickolas. But then you came along, and suddenly our favourite orderly wasn't so shut off from the world.' Cora smiles.

Finn can't help but smile along with Cora. After three years together, Finn still gets butterflies at the mention of Nickolas's love for him.

He and Nickolas played along with the lie of how they got together until the moment his friends left the centre, their treatment over, and his and Nickolas's relationship solid enough to prove it was more than some patient, orderly fling.

'Look, I'm not saying I'm jealous.' Ryder adds.

'You reek of jealousy' Alex cuts in.

'MY POINT IS,' Ryder tries to shut the remark down, 'We know you and Nickolas love each other and are one hundred percent devoted. But that doesn't mean if you look at some guy your friends are drooling over, you're suddenly flirting or claiming you love Nickolas any less.'

Finn knows they are right. But truth be told, the reason he doesn't look isn't because he feels like he's betraying Nickolas in some way, it's because he genuinely doesn't see the point. Nickolas is everything he's ever wanted, and no one could ever compare. Ocean blue eyes that Finn swears he has seen change like the ocean does during a storm. A cocky smirk when his boyfriend proves a point, and then a shy smile whenever words are difficult. Nickolas's actions then take over to help express those hard-to-communicate emotions. A part of Finn salivates at their slight height difference, and nothing warms his heart more than seeing Nickolas act tough and in charge when in public, but then lets go and becomes soft and caring in the privacy of their apartment.

And of course, Finn could wax poetic about that delicious ass. But he figures that's not something his friends need to know about, at least for Nickolas's sake. Even if they all know each other on a deeper level that some family and friends may never understand.

'Now that we've all come to agree that we're all lonely except for Finn, are you going to catch us up with things? Our group chat is very lacklustre without your presence.' Says Alex.

'I know. Every time I go to reply, something happens with work or my family messages, or—' he stops, aware none of the excuses is what his friends want to hear. 'Works going great, but I'm kind of over it.'

'Over it?' Cora repeats.

'It's the same thing every day, and I know routine is good for me, but routine in a schedule and acting like a robot are two very different things.'

'Robots are cool. Don't knock a robot.' Alex offers.

'Sex robots are cool,' Ryder clarifies, 'Finn's referring to those robots that work in a factory that put a lid on toothpaste for ten hours straight.'

'Ohhhh. Yeah, that's not cool. Don't be a robot.' Alex takes back the statement, which causes Finn to chuckle.

'I don't want to be a robot, that's what I'm saying. I want to go to work and *not* know what's going to happen that day. Have new discussions and be somewhat surprised.'

'So, look for something else.' Cora makes it sound so simple.

'Except what? Everything I consider has fine print regarding mental health and a box that needs to be ticked declaring we have never been committed.'

A chorus of mumbles breaks out amongst the group, everyone well aware of said box, which is interrupted when the waiter finally walks up to their table. Drinks are ordered, and then the discussion continues.

'I don't know. Nickolas says he will support me with whatever I choose, even if it means not bringing home a paycheck for a bit, but I don't think I could do that to him.'

'Don't find them like that anymore. You sure are lucky, Finn.' Ryder offers.

Finn knew he was lucky from the moment he woke up in the infirmary with Nickolas sitting by his side.

*

Thinking back to how he once viewed the trio he now calls his best friends, Finn is thankful that they opened their arms and gave him a chance, despite how rude he was when he was introduced to them at the treatment centre. He can admit that he was trying to shut himself off from any kind of relationship to protect himself during that time. But now, not only does he have a close group that understands him and supports him, he also gets to watch them thrive as they too grab their mental illness by the metaphorical balls, not allowing it to stop them from living.

His experience at the treatment centre where he met Nickolas and his now-friends was the complete opposite of the first clinic he was committed to. The one he was sent to for seventy-two hours, where he was informed of his diagnosis. He doesn't like to think of that time, nor does he talk about it often. And thankfully, there isn't much he remembers about the experience, except for the fact that everyone who worked there was a Brett.

He leaves the café with a promise to be more active in the group chat and a plan to catch up next month. Making his way towards the L, Finn's eyes catch the attention of a building under construction with a signboard outside of the building beside it. He thinks about what he saw the whole ride home and the few blocks he has to walk from the station to their apartment.

When he opens their door, Socks meows for his attention as he steps inside, and he can hear the shower running. Finn's mind doesn't even consider the thought of joining his wet and naked boyfriend, his thoughts still locked onto the building.

As they sit together to watch a movie, Finn's mind is elsewhere. He's so distracted that by the time the credits roll, he can't recall one single thing that happened. Wanting to settle his thoughts so he's able to get a good night's sleep, he word vomits what's been on his mind since leaving the café.

'Have you ever considered moving?' The second the words leave his mouth, Finn feels the tension in his boyfriend's body, as though the words are a personal attack.

'No...but I guess you have.' Nickolas spits back.

'I mean...It's not like the thought hasn't crossed my mind once or twice.' He wants it to seem as though this isn't a random, rash decision. That can be a sign of mania, and Finn knows he isn't manic. He has been taking his medication every morning and night, without hesitation, so this isn't sudden. He's been thinking about this for the past four hours, and that's all the time Finn needs to know he is level-headed.

'Once or twice? Wow, guess you've made your mind up then, no point asking me then, huh?' Nickolas pulls away from his hold and leans into the opposite end of the couch.

'Of course, I'm going to ask you. I just did, didn't I.' Finn knows to tread carefully.

'Sure, after you've made your mind up that you're tired of my shitty apartment.'

'No one is calling anything shitty, Nick. Don't go spinning this into something it's not.' He keeps his voice level.

'I knew this would happen.' Nickolas stands up, walking towards the kitchen and grabbing a beer from the fridge.

'Knew what would happen?'

'This. You'd start to see that there is more out there that you want for yourself and decide you don't want to live in...this anymore.' Nickolas moves a hand through the air, accentuating what 'this' is.

Socks leaps onto the couch, taking up residency on Finn's lap now that Nickolas has left it.

'Sometimes I wonder what goes through that thick head of yours.' He knows the words will instantly make matters worse, which is why Finn tries to say it without malice, but this is Nickolas he's talking to.

'Don't patronise me. I didn't grow up looking for riches. I grew up living in rags. This—' Once again, Nickolas points around the living room. 'A roof over my head, heat to keep me warm, and a safe place to sleep in are all the riches I need.'

Finn knows all this. He knows everything when it comes to his boyfriend. The multiple conversations they've shared – truths, fears, and dreams, spilling from them both after moments of passion or silence or anger. It's allowed Finn to read Nickolas better than he can read himself. There are tells: a gnawed bottom lip, difficulty making eye contact, cuticles that have been picked, and a short fuse causing everyone and everything to be an irritation.

He can understand Nickolas being somewhat defensive about moving; after all, this is the home he's made for himself, a safe haven, and after Finn made himself a fixture in the home, he's now asking Nickolas to up and move elsewhere.

He lifts Socks from his lap, their fur baby meowing in annoyance, but Finn's focus is on Nickolas, who has already finished a bottle of beer and is up to fetch a second.

'Nick, what's going on?' He asks calmly.

'Nothing, besides my boyfriend wanting to move me to the fucking West Side.'

'I never said where I wanted to move to.'

'So, visiting your friends in some bougie café has nothing to do with this sudden revelation of yours?'

'...no. Not exactly.'

'See, West Side.'

'And what's wrong with that?' Again, no fight is in his tone of voice. 'We aren't kids in the South anymore. Haven't been for a while.' Finn waits. 'A new postcode doesn't change who you are or where you came from, Nick.'

When Nickolas exhales a deep, trembling breath, Finn knows he's gotten through.

'Found out Dot's retiring and Lydia's leaving; was offered a job at a bigger facility. Now I come home to find out that my boyfriend wants to change this part of my life too.'

As Finn suspected, change is the reason for Nickolas's outburst.

He approaches his boyfriend the way one would walk up to a stray animal, takes Nickolas's hand, and leads them back towards the couch, where they take a seat on either end, knowing that space is a necessity when Nickolas is stuck in his head.

Starting with the easier question, he asks about Lydia. 'What facility?'

'Some hospital up North. She followed the money, I guess.'

'Nick...' Finn exhales, knowing that in a few days, Nickolas will understand that Lydia's decision to move isn't personal but simply a career choice, one that is no doubt beneficial for Lydia in the long run and not necessarily because their friend is, as Nickolas put it, chasing the money.

'I'm fucking annoyed, okay? I trained her, I encouraged her, and supported her when she needed the extra time to study and now, now she's leavin', and, I don't know, it doesn't seem right.'

'You're allowed to be annoyed, Nick.'

'I know I'm allowed...but I know I shouldn't be. It's her life.'

'But...' Finn prompts him.

With a groan, Nickolas continues. 'But...still feels like I'm getting replaced for something better.'

Finn crawls towards Nickolas and straddles his boyfriend's lap. He always finds it amusing that Nickolas is the bottom in their relationship, but loves it when Finn sits on those deliciously thick thighs, his weight bearing down on Nickolas like a heavy blanket.

'You're *my* something better, Nick. We could live under the L tracks if that's what we had to do.' Nickolas huffs at his comment. 'What I'm trying to say is, you're not being replaced. You're not being traded in for a shiny new toy, and the new apartments that have been built are cheaper than the rent we are paying here.' That gets him a look of 'bullshit' from Nickolas. 'It's true.' Finn confirms. 'They want to fill all the apartments with tenants to entice more people to the complex being built next door.'

Nickolas gives his hips a firm, comforting squeeze. 'You know I can't say no to you. Kinda what got us into this mess in the first place.'

'I know.' Finn grins. 'But I still want you to be on board with the idea.' They both chuckle. 'Besides, love is messy. It's why the good outweighs the tough.'

'You using another inspirational quote on me?'

'Dr Warnock loves a good quote' They both laugh, soaking up the endorphins, before Finn broaches the next subject.

'When is Dot's last day?' Nickolas's hands slide from Finn's waist, down to his thighs and rub up and down his legs.

'She said she'll stay on for the next three months, make sure they find a suitable replacement. All that shit.'

'Okay. So, for the next three months, you're going to enjoy every day you have working alongside, Dot. You're not going to mope or avoid her, and when the time comes, you're going to make plans to catch up at least once a week, even if it's for something as simple as getting a coffee.'

'You make it sound easy.'

'It is easy. It's what our minds do that makes things hard. Sometimes we have to shut out the noise and listen to who is actually speaking to us so we know what we have to do.'

There is a moment before they simultaneously say, 'Dr Warnock.' Chuckling at themselves, a welcome break from the seriousness of the conversation.

It's only a month later than Finn and Nickolas are signing a new lease agreement on their West Side apartment, a decision that Nickolas quickly came to realise was the right choice a few weeks after settling in.

*

'I'm over it. I can't work another day in that bookstore.' Finn confides in Dr Warnock. His bimonthly appointments are not only to keep a check on his medication, but also so he has someone to talk to who isn't biased, like Nickolas or his family can sometimes be.

'I've always wanted to do more, be more, make something of myself.' He explains.

'You still can.' Dr Warnock offered.

'Can I? Everywhere I go the application form asks about mental health. Wants to know if I've been committed.' He repeats what he told his friends over a year ago, but regardless of what he writes on application forms, he's being turned away left, right, and centre.

'There are certain fields of work that have high-stress situations, and at times these areas can involve making a decision that a sound mind would need to make.' Dr Warnock cuts him off before he can reply. 'I'm not saying that you are not of sound mind, Finn. But your medication can cause slips.'

'There's got to be other options. A way around the system.'

Dr Warnock reaches for a pamphlet in the drawer within the side table. Finn takes it, wondering what an LGBTQIA+ community centre has to do with his existential crisis.

'You could work here. They recently opened up, not far from where you live, and they are always looking for volunteers and paid staff.'

'You want me to be a counsellor?' Finn is surprised.

'Not necessarily. Some of the people who work there are in charge of finding housing options for these kids who have nowhere safe to sleep. They have a nurse to offer advice and help with matters such as safe sex, mental health checks, or even bandaging a wound after a fight or accident. There are kitchen hands to help with small light meals, and of course, staff that are on the phone constantly looking for more support and funding.'

In other words, Finn has options. Helping kids who were like him and Nickolas – scared and hiding, with nowhere to go and no one to offer help and support. This is that 'something meaningful' he's been looking for.

With a spring in his step, Finn leaves his session and walks straight to the community centre in the hopes of speaking to whoever is in charge.

*

'I did it.' Finn announces as he walks through the door. Nickolas is getting dressed to start a night shift at the centre.

'Got to be more specific there.' Nickolas leans in to plant a kiss on his lips before continuing to pack.

'I got a new job.' That seems to stop Nickolas.

'I didn't know you were looking. I mean, I knew you were over the bookstore, but...what job?'

'Down at the community centre. The one for LGBTQIA+ youths.'

Nickolas groans. 'I swear to God, Finn, if you start bringing kids here because you feel sorry for 'em I'll go live with your sister.'

'What's that supposed to mean?' He is genuinely hurt by Nickolas's comment.

'Oh, don't act so surprised.'

Finn holds his ground.

'Every time you see a stray animal on the street, you ask if we can bring it home, claiming Socks needs a companion.'

Nickolas points out. 'You have a kind heart, nothing wrong with that, but these kids are going to have sob stories, Finn, and they know how to manipulate to get what they want. I know 'cos I used to do the same, and so did you.'

'I did not.'

'No? You never used the 'my parents abandoned me' story to get extra food or a way to get an extension on homework?'

His mouth opens to argue his case, only for it to close when he realises Nickolas isn't wrong.

'Exactly. Most of 'em are going to be tough little assholes, hating on the system and life, wanting to get whatever they can for free. The rest will no doubt be scared shitless, and those are the ones you'll take pity on. You gotta learn to separate the two, and I don't know if you can.'

'Wow. Thanks for saying how you really feel.'

'Have I ever lied to you in the last five years we've been together? Hmm. Why start now?'

'Because now I want the support, since this is something I want to do, and I feel like I'd be good at it.'

'Of course, you'd be good at it, but what you're about to do isn't much different to me. You're goin' to see and hear things that make you hate the world more than you already do.'

'Let me guess, and you're worried it's going to affect my bipolar.'

'Damn straight I'm worried.' Nickolas drops the backpack and steps towards him.

'I'm always fucking worried, but we promised not to baby one another. Not to treat this relationship like a doctor and patient situation, so instead I have to sit back and support the guy I love while casually reminding him to be careful. Is that okay with you, tough guy?'

Finn grabs Nickolas by the collar of his shirt, their lips crashing together fiercely. Time is against them, so the kitchen table will have to do. He spins Nickolas around, catching a glimpse into those royal blue eyes, seeing how desperately he wants this, as much as Finn does. Pants get pulled down to mid-thigh, so his boyfriend's ass is on display, waiting to be taken.

What can he say, Nickolas caring for his wellbeing gets him hot.

*

Finn had finally found a job that made him feel worthy, all thanks to the persistence and suggestions from Dr Warnock. From the second he stepped inside, he loved everything about the centre and the people he was working with. But it was around the three-month mark that Finn had his first slip.

At first, he took the no-sleeping as a sign that he was nervous. A new job, a new role, new responsibilities. Who wouldn't be nervous? He was a twenty-four-year-old gay male with bipolar disorder. Finally, it felt as though life was giving him a break, his options no longer limited to busboy or janitor.

Of course, that's when the no-sleeping became something more. He'd walk into the kitchen, thirsty, seeking out a drink, only to open the top cupboard three times, each time knowing that wasn't where he wanted to look, but would go back and check it again to be sure.

He didn't feel manic, though that was the point. It's not until he'd do something reckless that he'd click and realise it was due to the mania. It's why it was Nickolas who noticed first. When Finn had come home from a five-mile run, he found Nickolas standing in the middle of a sea of papers, scattered across their living room floor with his scribbled ideas on how to improve the centre, a deep look of concern on his boyfriend's face. Finn instantly knew that his behaviour could no longer be considered new job jitters.

He fights the accusation. He argues that he's excited that, for the first time in his life, he has a purpose that doesn't revolve around his body. Nickolas doesn't push. After years of working at the centre, Nickolas knows the right way to approach the situation. It's why it only takes an hour for Finn to break down, realising that fighting Nickolas is only making it worse and that there is no shame in admitting he is slipping into a manic episode.

'Hey, it's okay. You knew this was part of it, and we caught it quick enough before anything could happen.' Nickolas places a tender hand on his back.

The underlying message is; before anything bad happened and people got hurt, before *he* got hurt.

'When your meds feel like they could be out of balance, what do you do?' Nickolas asks him calmly, without venom or judgment. Nickolas frames it so that Finn is still in control, that Nickolas is asking instead of telling.

'Up my downers, sleep it off, and call Dr Warnock immediately.'

'So that's what we're going to do.'

'We?' Finn looks up from where he's curled in the corner of their bedroom, not entirely sure how he ended up there.

'I'm not leaving you like this, Finn. Not because I don't trust you, but because I want you to remember you're not alone in this.' Nickolas reaches out and takes his hand, their fingers intertwining.

It's a couple of weeks before Finn feels balanced enough to return to work. No one looks at him with judgmental eyes or hides the knives when he walks into the break room. He's welcomed with open arms, warm smiles, and kids voicing how they had missed him.

Dr Warnock reminds Finn that his strength and drive to stay on top of his mental health are what helped him fight and not succumb to the mania, a feeling that is so free and liberating. He knows this to be true to some extent. After all, Finn's desire to not follow the path of his mother while remembering the things that happened after running away is a sure-fire way to stay medicated. But Nickolas is also a big reason. Nickolas is his strength when he has none. Nickolas is the voice in his head that is louder than the one telling Finn to enjoy the high and forget about the medications.

Nickolas didn't run when Finn screamed to be left alone, nor did he get angry after the adjustment to his medication left him unable to perform sexually. At night, Nickolas held Finn as he trembled and rubbed the ache from his muscles. Not once did Finn feel as though he was yet again a patient. No, this time he felt like a partner being cared for while ill. Similar to if he had the flu.

The cocktail the treatment centre started him on lasted five years before he had his first slip. Finn hopes the next one is just as long, if not more.

*

With the sun beating down, Finn is thankful for the autumn air taking away the heat. Running is his therapy, at least one of them. Dr Warnock is now a half-yearly occurrence, a small part of him worries about breaking that part of his routine.

Finn rounds the corner, not paying any attention to the road he is running on, but his mind is fully aware of the direction he needs to go. It reminds him of the way people can drive to a destination, but if asked to give directions, they'd have no idea how to explain the route to get there. As his chest begins to ache and his legs start to burn, he knows it's a sign that he's close to his destination. Even with the music pumping through his ears, it's not enough to drown out his thoughts, which today, are louder than ever before.

Finn stops running at a set of lights. He jogs on the spot, waiting for the little red man to turn green so he can cross. He steps inside the restaurant Jessica manages and takes a seat at the counter, his body sweating and his stomach hungry.

'You can wipe the seat clean when you leave. It's cruel that you expect my staff to clean up your odour that's soaking into the leather.' Jessica pours him a cup of coffee.

'And good morning to you too, sis.' He accepts the kiss on the cheek from his sister.

'What are you doing here, anyway? Don't you have a million things to do?' Jessica hands over a breakfast muffin while he's being berated.

'Couldn't sleep, so I went for a run.' He instantly notices the worry on his sister's face. 'Not like that. I'm fine, promise. I'm just...excited you know. Big day. I didn't think I'd get this chance after being diagnosed. And you know I can't sleep when Nick isn't home.'

'Oh, sweet face.' After all this time, the old nickname no longer has him feeling like a child, but rather a comforting nostalgia. 'Out of all of us, you were the one that wanted normality. Wanted to be more than what the streets thought of us Cunninghams, and you didn't let anything stop you from proving them all wrong.'

'Who'da thought I'd find it without having to leave town or join the army or some shit.' They both laugh as a waitress stops by to deliver a plate of eggs, toast, bacon, and sausage. Finn looks up at his sister, the answer clear as day.

'Eat up. Go home. Shower and get dressed. You don't want to be late.'

No. No, he didn't

*

Their apartment always feels empty when either of them is away. Finn walks through the door and sees Socks perched on the scratching post by the window, age starting to show on their fur baby. Nickolas's absence is evident from the silence, but Finn still sees him in the little details around their apartment, which is a perfect mix of them both. Throw blankets and pillows on the bed and couch; Finn. Cookbooks, the best pots and pans money can buy; Nickolas. Family photos line the walls, some of Nickolas with his mother and sister, others with him and Finn's family during random occasions and holidays. They have photos from the small trips they have taken together over the years. The one with Nickolas standing beside Mickey Mouse because Finn's niece wanted to go to Disneyworld one year for a birthday trip is always the photo that makes him smile.

Finn knows he'll meet up with Nickolas later, but after eight years together, the absence of his partner is noticeable. The time on their kitchen clock kicks Finn into gear. Shower. Shave. Get dressed and then get a move on. Finn has two hours; he finishes in one.

*

When he arrives at the Chicago Botanical Gardens, Jessica is waiting in the parking lot, looking as gorgeous as ever, and in no way would it look as though his sister had come from the opening shift at the most popular diner in Chicago.

'How did you get here before me? I was killing time with Socks because of how early I was.' Finn leans in to hug his sister, making sure neither of their outfits gets creased.

'Couldn't be late now; otherwise, you'd have no one to walk you down the aisle on your wedding day.'

A smile beams across Finn's face. His. Wedding. Day. He still can't believe it.

When Finn had planned a romantic dinner for Nickolas's thirtieth birthday at a high-class steak restaurant that stocked the best bourbons and had taken Finn a couple of months to save up for, he never expected to come back from the bathroom to find his napkin refolded by the waiter, sitting on the table, and hidden behind it, a white gold ring with an inlay of black mesh carbon fibre.

'You know I never saw myself getting married.' Nickolas began. 'Fuck, I never thought anyone would want to tie themselves to me unless my father had a gun held to their head as I said, 'I do.' Point is, there are a lot of things I never saw for myself until I met you. We always joke about being ghetto married, and I know everyone probably thought we were crazy to move in with each other after three months, but when you know, you know. Right?' Nickolas thumbed his lip, a telltale sign of nerves. 'I didn't care what anyone else said or thought because, at the end of the day, the only person who matters in this world is you.' Adjusting in the chair, Nickolas looked to see if any eyes were on them before continuing.

'I had this idea to go back to the beach tonight, the one we sat on the day you moved in, but then your ginger ass had to go and plan all this for me and the damn ring was burning a hole in my pocket, so...'

Finn finally looked up from the ring itself. A couple of stray tears fell from his eyes, but a smile was plastered across his face.

'From the first time I saw you, my mind and body knew that I couldn't let you go. The time we shared, well, I began to heal just from being in your presence. We belong to each other, Finn, but, I guess what I'm trying to say is, I want the world to know we belong together too.'

Finn waited, but it never came.

'You have to ask me, Nick. Otherwise, how can I give my answer?'

With a roll of majestic blue eyes, Nickolas bit his bottom lip and took one final sweep of the room before asking; 'Finn Cunningham, will you marry me?'

Unsure how it was possible, Finn's smile grew further. 'Course I'll marry you.'

Nickolas's hand had reached over the table, extracting the ring from its box so it could be placed on Finn's finger. The cool metal slipped on with ease; the fit was perfect, as was the man before him. Finn placed the palm of his hand on Nickolas's cheek; the cool metal warmed under the touch.

'Was wondering when the hell you were going to ask.' When they kissed, the restaurant erupted in applause. It was the reminder of the audience that kept their declaration of love PG, but by that point, they were both ready to get home, where they could celebrate privately.

The nerves begin to kick in as he and Jessica walk through the gardens. From his sister's olive-green silk strap dress and his tailored-fitted maroon suit, it's clear to onlookers that they are on their way to a wedding, though none of them know it is his.

The English-walled garden is in sight. European columns form a pergola with vines growing over the wood, shading their family and friends, as well as Nickolas.

Finn stops walking. The sight of his fiancé waiting near the wall in a handsome navy-blue suit takes his breath away. It doesn't feel real.

'Finn, you okay?' Jessica asks.

'Tell me this is actually happening. Tell me this isn't a dream, and I'm about to wake up in the treatment centre, the last eight years of my life being some hallucination to help me cope with being committed.' He runs his fingers through his hair, pleased that his straight, sleek back style isn't going to be ruined by his frantic energy.

'Finn,' Jessica's voice is stern, reminding him of the years when his sister told him off as though she was his mother and not the oldest of six siblings. A comforting hand grips his shoulder, the panic slowly rising inside of him settling long enough to look into his sister's eyes.

'This is real, Finn. The man waiting up there loves you with a love I've never seen before. It's real and pure, and honestly, I'm a little jealous you found it before the rest of us.'

Finn chuckles.

'You're healthy – mentally and psychically. Over the years, you have made something of yourself despite what the world, the system, and dare I admit, what I have said about you.'

The panic seeps away.

'Nickolas loves every version of you, Finn. Past you, present you, and whatever comes in the future, he will be there, loving and supporting you till the end.'

They say that when you die, a montage of your life flashes before your eyes. For Finn, a montage of his time with Nickolas plays before him, and he doesn't have to die to look back at the memories of his favourite moments spent with Nickolas that always erase any doubt over what they've built together.

Lazy Sundays before Nickolas goes to the centre to assist with visiting hours. Cuddling on the couch with Socks while watching rubbish television. Coming home to Nickolas cooking dinner, seeing a smile of pride on his fiancé's face as Finn moans at the burst of flavours. Date nights once a month where they promise each other to try something new; bowling, mini golf, dance classes, which only lasted one time because Nickolas went South Side on the instructor. Sex in public – that too only happened once after Finn was horny as fuck after seeing Nickolas go all South Side on their dance instructor. Endless moments of laughter, stupid fights, mind-blowing sex, passionate lovemaking, and reassurance when either one of them wakes from a nightmare. Moments throughout their years as a couple, all while Finn grew into the person he is today.

This is real. This is happening. This is his life. There is no denying that Nickolas loves him. Finn never doubted that. But he will, from time to time, doubt his mind, doubt what's real because what he has seems too good to be true for the gay South Side redhead who sold his body for money, slept with older men, and was diagnosed at seventeen with bipolar. When that doubt kicks in though, the support system he has built up – Nickolas, his family, Dr Warnock, Lydia, Dorothy, Ryder, Cora and Alex – those are the ones he can lean on.

'I'm ready.' Finn looks over, catching a glimpse of Nickolas, who seems nervous, though it could be because his small freakout now has them running behind schedule. He links arms with Jessica, and together they walk into view of the very small group they invited to witness. However, none of them matter, not when Nickolas is standing before him, hands clasped in front, blue eyes piercing into his soul as he walks closer towards his future.

Jessica pushes up on tippy toes to lay a kiss on his cheek before her attention turns towards Nickolas.

'He's officially yours. You hurt him. We kill you.' Everyone laughs for the sake of the celebrant, but Finn knows his sister is somewhat serious, and Nickolas has seen a dark side to Jessica after being wronged by a boyfriend.

They take each other's hand, neither of them commenting on their sweaty palms, too wrapped up in the significance of the moment. The celebrant begins to address their family and friends, most of whom are Finn's family, except for Dorothy, Lydia, and a few patients that both he and Nickolas kept in contact with. Whatever is being said, to Finn, it's white noise. He's lost in the hairstyle Nickolas has chosen, the smell of cologne making him feel nostalgic, and the shy blush that Finn falls head over heels for whenever his fiancé smiles as his eyes are cast to the floor. Nickolas is all he can focus on.

'Thought you might 'ave run off, seeing how you're never late for anything.' Nickolas whispers so only he can hear.

'Nothing could stop me from missing this.' Finn goes to lean in for a kiss, only for a very stern clearing of the throat coming from their celebrant to stop him in his path.

'Save it for the big finale.' Nickolas winks.

When the time comes, they each say their vows, keeping it simple, knowing all the words in the world wouldn't be enough to describe how they feel about one another.

'I, Nykolai Markova, take you, Finn Cunningham, to be my husband. To have and to hold from this day forward, for richer or poorer, in sickness and in health, to love and to cherish you, til death do us part.'

Tears glisten in his eyes. *In sickness and in health.* Finn has lived through this scenario multiple times with Nickolas by his side. Through unmedicated behaviour, self-harming, medication changes, and even the common flu that Finn was sure he was dying from. Nickolas stuck by his side for all of it. If this man before Finn can love him at his worst, then he knows Nickolas will always love him at his best.

Finn sniffs back the tears. 'I, Finn Cunningham, take you, Nickolas Markova, to be my husband.' A smirk appears on his fiancé's face as Finn uses the name he first knew Nickolas by. 'To have and to hold from this day forward, for richer or poorer, in sickness and in health,' he squeezes Nickolas's hand. 'To love and to cherish you, til death do us part.'

'You're not allowed to die before me, Cunningham.'

'You can't get rid of me. We're going together, in our sleep, holding one another close.'

A few witnesses can be heard sniffing.

'Now that Nykolai and Finn have given themselves to each other with these vows and the giving and receiving of rings, I now pronounce you husband and husband.'

In the movies, there is always an announcement that the couple can kiss, but Finn waits for no announcement. He leans forward, unable to hold back another second, his hands letting go of Nickolas's so they can hold his husband's face firmly while he seals their marriage with a kiss.

The cheers sound louder than Wrigley Field when the Cubs win, and the smile on Nickolas's face interrupts their kiss.

None of it matters though, because they are bound by law, union, and love, finally.

'What do you say we get out of here and consummate our marriage?' A wiggle of Nickolas's eyebrows and a bite of his lower lip already have Finn raging to go.

'After you, Mr Cunningham-Markova.'

As they walk hand in hand past the people who have loved and supported them through their darkest of times, he knows none will ever compare to Nickolas, his saving grace. It took the kindness of a stranger for Finn to believe he is more than his mental health. To believe that there is a light at the end of the darkness. Finn never thought he had the strength in him, but it was the voice of a person who knew nothing of him that pierced through the negative thoughts and reminded him to keep fighting and not let the darkness win.

Together, they will keep fighting. Mental health doesn't have a quick fix, and it also doesn't make him weak. If anything, it makes him stronger, knowing that he's survived the hurdles that have been placed in front of him.

Nickolas pulls Finn's hand up towards his gentle pink lips and lays a kiss upon his knuckles. Whatever the future holds, they're going to tackle it together.

Printed in the USA
CPSIA information can be obtained
at www.ICGtesting.com
LVHW050237010624
781580LV00001B/3

9 780975 669402